P9-DCS-316

"Simply put, the finest crime suspense series I've come across in the last twenty years . . . your basic can't-put-'em-down thrill rides."
—Stephen King

China Lake

"[An] exciting mix. Great stuff." —*Independent on Sunday*

"Meg Gardiner makes it all work . . . amazingly entertaining." —Stephen King

"With a colorful cast of richly delineated characters, a protagonist with whom the readers will easily identify—all big hearted, quick tongued, and hair-trigger tempered . . . a fast-paced ride through some of the more dubious nooks and crannies of the American dream." —*The Guardian* (UK)

"Fast and hard-edged. Buy it, read it." —*Hull Daily Mail*

"A cracker, with memorable characters, memorable lines, and a plot that races along to an explosive ending. A great summer read." —*Huddersfield Daily Examiner*

"Very well written, racy, and witty." —Tangled Web

Kill Chain

"Evan Delaney is a paragon for our times: tough, funny, clever, brave, tireless, and compassionate. The pace and inventiveness never flag, and the climax . . . is both nail-biting and moving. But the brilliant writing is what puts this thriller way ahead of the competition. Intelligent escapism at its best." —*The Guardian* (UK)

"I loved every minute of it. A breathtaking thriller, gripping and relentless."
—Caroline Carver, CWA Dagger–winning author of *Blood Junction*

"A rattling good read." —*News of the World*

"Brilliant." —*Evening Telegraph* (Peterborough, UK)

"The action is high octane from the first page. Once you pick it up, it's a very hard book to put down." —*My Weekly*

"Fast and furious." —*The Literary Review*

continued . . .

Also by Meg Gardiner

Mission Canyon
Jericho Point
Crosscut
Kill Chain

The Dirty Secrets Club

CHINA LAKE

AN EVAN DELANEY NOVEL

Meg Gardiner

AN OBSIDIAN MYSTERY

OBSIDIAN
Published by New American Library, a division of
Penguin Group (USA) Inc., 375 Hudson Street,
New York, New York 10014, USA
Penguin Group (Canada), 90 Eglinton Avenue East, Suite 700, Toronto,
Ontario M4P 2Y3, Canada (a division of Pearson Penguin Canada Inc.)
Penguin Books Ltd., 80 Strand, London WC2R 0RL, England
Penguin Ireland, 25 St. Stephen's Green, Dublin 2,
Ireland (a division of Penguin Books Ltd.)
Penguin Group (Australia), 250 Camberwell Road, Camberwell, Victoria 3124,
Australia (a division of Pearson Australia Group Pty. Ltd.)
Penguin Books India Pvt. Ltd., 11 Community Centre, Panchsheel Park,
New Delhi - 110 017, India
Penguin Group (NZ), 67 Apollo Drive, Rosedale, North Shore 0632,
New Zealand (a division of Pearson New Zealand Ltd.)
Penguin Books (South Africa) (Pty.) Ltd., 24 Sturdee Avenue,
Rosebank, Johannesburg 2196, South Africa

Penguin Books Ltd., Registered Offices:
80 Strand, London WC2R 0RL, England

Published by Obsidian, an imprint of New American Library, a division of
Penguin Group (USA) Inc. This is an authorized reprint of an edition pub-
lished by Hodder & Stoughton. For information address: Hodder & Stoughton
Ltd, 338 Euston Road, London NW1 3BH

First Obsidian Printing, June 2008
10 9 8 7 6 5 4 3 2 1

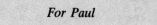

For Paul

ACKNOWLEDGMENTS

For invaluable help with this novel, I thank Ann Aubrey Hanson; Carolina Shreve; Sally Gardiner; Sara Gardiner, MD; Marilyn Moreno, attorney at law; Nancy Fraser; Adrienne Dines; Irena Kowal; Milena Banks; Melinda Roughton; Bonni Connell; Jane Warren; Mary Albanese; and Frank Gardiner, who gave me everything that counted. For their encouragement and advice, I also thank my agent, Giles Gordon, and my editor, Sue Fletcher.

1

Peter Wyoming didn't shake hands with people; he hit them with his presence like a rock fired from a slingshot. He was a human nail, lean and straight with brush-cut hair, and when I first saw him he was carrying a picket sign and enough rage to scorch the ground. The sign read, GOD HATES SLUTS, and he held it erect in his fist, aimed so mourners read it as we stepped from the church into the autumn sunshine. Behind him, his followers hoisted other placards. AIDS CURES WHORES. SEX ED = AIDS = DAMNATION. Ahead, the dead woman's daughter walked behind the casket, gripping her husband's hand for support.

When Wyoming saw her, he began chanting, "Hey, hey, what do you say? Claudine burns in hell today!"

That was when I made my first mistake. I took him for a grandstander, a bigot, a man who, from the looks of his sign, had trouble with women. And I underestimated him.

Wyoming was the pastor of a church called the Remnant, which proclaimed itself the last swatch of godliness in a pustulating world. They thought Santa Barbara, this postcard city of acrylic blue skies and red tile roofs, of coffee bars and beaches and Mexican-American warmth, was a sluice gate on the sewer pipe to hell. They liked to drive home the point by jeering at AIDS funerals.

We ignored them. The dead woman's daughter, Nikki Vincent, had known they were coming and told us to treat them as if they were invisible. Treat them like roaches underfoot.

Now Nikki laid a coffee brown hand on the coffin. Saying, *Don't worry, Mom, I'll take care of you.* Or maybe drawing strength from her mother one last time. Claudine Girard had never backed down from anything. A small woman with a Haitian French accent, she was an AIDS activist even before the disease raked into her. She had also been my university professor, who salted her literature classes with commands to stand straight and belly up to life. Her death seemed impossible.

She had been well-known in Santa Barbara, and reporters were clustering outside the Spanish-style church, under palm trees stirring in the breeze. They looked eager for action. Wyoming, anxious to supply it, tightened his bolo tie and stared at Nikki—seven months pregnant, holding on to her husband's arm and Claudine's coffin, ready to run the gauntlet.

He raised his sign. "Ding-dong, the witch is dead! Which old witch?"

The Remnant shouted, "The voodoo witch!"

It was twenty yards to the hearse waiting at the curb: a long way. The funeral director, usually all smooth, inconspicuous moves and black-suited calm, clasped his hands in dismay. Confrontational funerals were poor advertising for the Elysian Glen Mortuary. He urged the pallbearers forward. Nikki lifted her chin and followed, her face like varnished wood, sunglasses hiding her swollen eyes.

A snub-nosed woman jutted forward from the crowd. "Slut lovers! Queer lovers! Take your mumbo jumbo back to Haiti!"

Mourners deliberately looked past the protesters. We were a mixed bag—academics rumpled in grief,

Claudine's Caribbean family, and friends like me, with my Celtic looks, middle-class manners, and bitten-back shock. My own religion was a subterranean Catholicism that welled up for deaths and holidays. God-as-stink-bomb was a novelty to me. I felt myself fraying, but for Nikki's sake I kept walking, looking into the distance where the October air shimmered over the Santa Ynez mountains.

Peeved that we weren't responding to them, a crew-cut young man with acne pointed at Nikki. "We're talking to you, witch girl."

That blew it. Nikki's husband, Carl, who had the heart and temper of an accountant, turned toward him. "How dare you?" His hand was raised, index finger pointing. "How dare you speak that way to my wife?"

Peter Wyoming said, "Wife? You mean your ho?"

His followers laughed. They laughed and cheered and shook their picket signs.

Carl's owlish glasses were askew on his face. "Bastards! You call yourselves Christians? Shame on you."

Wyoming blinked with lizard quickness. His eyes were pale blue and looking at Nikki. "The Lord says, 'Your shame will be seen. I have seen your abominations, your adulteries and neighings, your lewd harlotries.'"

Carl's muscles bunched beneath his pinstripes. Nikki said, "Don't," but he stepped toward Wyoming. She glanced at me. "Evan—"

We grabbed his arms. He was two feet from Wyoming, cocking his elbow to throw a punch I knew I couldn't stop.

Then I heard Nikki's voice, close to his ear, speaking coolly and loud enough for Wyoming to hear. "He's an inbred, low-wattage, mouth-breathing redneck. He's not worth it."

The impertinent dignity of her outrage held Carl

back. His arm dropped and he turned to her. So he didn't see the smirk on Wyoming's face, the disdain that meant: No real man lets two women restrain him.

Wyoming said loudly, "You think Claudine was great, always promoting 'compassion' and 'cure' and 'education.' Those are just fancy excuses for whoring."

Ahead, the pallbearers slid the casket into the gaping embrace of the hearse. Nikki watched, her fingers clenched. I nudged Carl forward, tipping my head toward the reporters and saying, "All they'd notice is that you threw the first punch."

" 'Be wretched and mourn and weep,' " Wyoming intoned. " 'Humble yourselves before the Lord and he will exalt you.' "

The words struck and bruised: scripture as covering fire. Forget it. I was through holding back. "I just figured out your problem. You confuse humility with humiliation."

Crew-cut said, "Big words don't trick us. You'll burn in hell."

Nikki was biting her lip, walking at a heavy, pregnant pace, fighting not to cry in front of these people. Carl held his arm tight around her.

"Slut!" Crew-cut shouted as an afterthought, or maybe just punctuation.

I turned to face him. "Why is it that people with tiny brains always come out with that same, tired insult? Can't your skulls fit in even a slender second thought?"

His acne flamed. Before he could answer I spun around. Carl was holding the door of their car for Nikki, waiting for her to lumber in before slamming it. As he walked around to the driver's side, I saw the look on her face. It was brittle, and rupturing.

She was staring at the windshield, where a flyer had been stuck under the wipers. I hurriedly pulled it out. In lurid red print it said, YOUR NEXT. Beneath the words was a comic strip titled, "AIDS: God's Roach

Ho-tel." The cartoons showed Hollywood street tarts scratching at open sores, with the tagline, *Ho's check in—but they don't check out!* The drawings were gruesome and irritatingly professional. At the bottom of the page was a cheery note from the Remnant: *Visit us on the World Wide Web!*

Carl started his engine. Other mourners were yanking the flyers off their windshields, shaking their heads, crumpling them. Behind me, reporters were calling to Wyoming, clamoring for his attention. The hearse pulled away and Carl followed, heading up a somber procession, accompanying Claudine on her last journey.

Wyoming's dry, deep voice rose above the background noise. He was speaking to a television reporter, leaning into the microphone, sounding aggrieved. To let him have the last word here seemed intolerable. I began walking toward him.

I heard him say he didn't hate sick people—God did, and the Remnant was just stating that fact. The reporter leaned forward assertively, cocking his head to demonstrate attentive skepticism, asking Wyoming if he thought he had converted the people who attended the funeral.

"No, and I don't care one bit. 'Let the filthy still be filthy, and the righteous still do right.' "

"Excuse me," I said.

Wyoming, his followers, and the reporter looked at me. I said, " 'Blessed are they who mourn, for they shall be comforted.' " It was the first Bible quote I could think of, Gospel of Matthew, and fortunately it was apt.

Wyoming looked amused. His expression said, *Come on, swap chapter and verse with me; you'll end up as my chew toy.* The reporter pushed his sunglasses up his nose and twitched his mustache, not sure whether this interruption would make good airplay.

" 'Blessed are the merciful, for they shall be shown

mercy,' " I said. "I just wanted you to remember that,
Mr. Wyoming."

He surveyed me with a stare that started at my feet,
rode up my legs, and seemed to slide under my skirt
and blouse. He appeared unimpressed by what folks
called my tomboy figure—the sprinter's legs, spartan
chest, short, mussy hair the color of toffee. Still, by
the time his eyes reached my face I felt flushed.

The reporter said, "You seem upset about Pastor
Wyoming's presence, Miss . . ."

"Delaney. Evan Delaney."

The cameraman swiveled to spot me in the lens of
his minicam, but Wyoming jumped in. "Miss Delaney
thinks I'm cruel, but Claudine Girard sent people to
hell. Giving her a Christian funeral like a clean, decent
woman is obscene."

The reporter turned to me. "How do you feel
about that?"

I gestured at Wyoming and his people. "I think
we're looking at the dictionary definition of 'obscene,'
right here."

"Will you listen to that?" Wyoming said. "She up
and claims she's an expert on obscenity. Like that's
something to be proud of."

They each had a script: *Snappy Fundamentalist
Sound Bites* and *Lights, Camera, Emotion!* I was irrelevant. Wearily I held up the flyer and said, "Tell your
cartoonist that 'millennium' is spelled with two Ns."

Sometimes I am too clever for my own good. The
hip-shot quip can ricochet. As I walked away, Wyoming said, "Delaney, you said your name was? Tell
the cartoonist yourself. You're related to her."

I couldn't help it—I stopped dead and stared at the
flyer. The grim and flashy cartoons suddenly looked
familiar. It was the style, a cross between *Spider-Man*
and *Xena, Warrior Princess*. I flipped to the back page,
the final drawing, where she would sign it.

Damn. In tiny letters, *Tabitha Delaney*. My brother's wife.

Blessed are the meek, for they keep their mouths shut in front of TV crews.

At the graveside service Nikki stood as still as an icon, holding us, motionless and moved, straight through "Amen." But inside I was guttering with anger. Tabitha Delaney. The name flared before me like a lighted match. I left the cemetery hastily, with few words to the other mourners.

I headed to the Santa Barbara County Courthouse. Not because I needed a lawyer—I was a lawyer myself, though I had quit practicing to become a legal researcher and journalist, a pen for hire. I had also published a couple of novels, even had my new one, *Lithium Sunset*, in local bookstores. Tabitha's actions, however, had led me to put my fiction writing into suspended animation. I headed to the courthouse because I needed to talk, and not to Nikki.

I walked along the tiled hallway, scanning the judges' names painted in calligraphy script on the wall outside each courtroom. The building abounds with such calculated quaintness. I half expected to see horses tied to a hitching post on the lush lawn, and Spanish dons strolling the grounds in silver-spurred boots.

When I slipped into Judge Rodriguez's courtroom, trial was in session. A young woman sat on the witness stand, glaring at the attorney who was cross-examining her. The court reporter's typewriter clicked softly. At the defense table, Jesse Blackburn asked the next question.

"You entered the premises that night without permission, didn't you?"

"Nobody told me I couldn't." Beneath the high ceiling the witness appeared puny, her clothes and face beige and grim. Almost as grim as the Remnant protesters.

I slouched in my seat, hearing the flyer rustle in my pocket. It sounded like the noise of approaching disruption. If Tabitha was drawing artwork for the Remnant, she was nearby. She was *back*.

How was I going to tell my brother? How was I going to tell his little boy?

Jesse said, "Let me rephrase. Nobody gave you permission to duplicate a key and use it to enter the bookstore after closing, did they?"

"No," the woman admitted. "But I was taking my own initiative."

"Initiative isn't all you took, is it, Miss Gaul?"

Jesse leaned forward, his cannonball shoulders shifting beneath his jacket. He was the one I came to see, and he looked grave and handsome, with the afternoon light burnishing his dark hair and glinting off the earring he wore, even to court.

"While you worked at the bookstore you took numerous items without paying for them, didn't you?" he said. "I don't mean Beowulf's bookmarks, or sugar packets from the coffee bar. You gave yourself a five-finger discount on the *New York Times* Best Seller List."

The plaintiff's attorney stood up. "Objection. Assuming facts not in evidence."

Judge Sophia Rodriguez peered over her half-glasses at him. "Overruled."

Jesse took his time. Caution came unnaturally to him, but this was a big trial and he wanted to pitch a perfect game—no runs, no hits, no errors. And no easy feat. Priscilla Gaul's long-term thievery had ended disastrously on the night that the owner of Beowulf's Books decided to defend the store. Gaul had suffered what her attorney called "heinous and injurious bodily harm." That was why she was suing the bookstore for damages, and that was why Jesse's co-

counsel wanted him to cross-examine her, though
Jesse was a courtroom greenhorn, only twenty-seven
years old. Fight hard luck with hard luck, and let him
be the one to throw fastballs at her, low and inside.

Counting items on his fingers, he said, "An espresso
maker, a thousand dollars in cash, and the collected
works of Jackie Collins . . . do you deny that on the
night of the incident you had those items in hand?"

Bad choice of words. Her face bunched. "You're
doing it on purpose, talking about it like this. I
know it."

"Yes, I am. After all, it's the reason you're suing
my client."

He was always more canny than I expected, always
a surprise, which was why he could both entrance and
infuriate me. Shove the witness off balance, toss the
issues into the open, armed and ticking. That was
Jesse.

Gaul said, "I had my flashlight. I took it to the
bookstore that night to check that there hadn't been
another burglary. That's all I had 'in hand,' nothing
else."

In fact, she had been holding several ounces of hamburger. Ground sirloin, according to the pathology report. But he let her assertion pass, because Gaul
began rubbing her left arm to remind the jury what
she meant by *nothing*: that she no longer had a left
hand. She had been mauled by attack animals when
she reached behind a counter to unplug the espresso
maker. That was the reason she was suing Beowulf's
Books for nine million dollars.

He said, "And you fled the bookstore because . . . ?"

"Those *things* were going to rip my throat out. They
were wild; I thought they were a pack on the loose,
prowling around town—"

"Drinking espresso?"

Up popped her attorney. His name was Skip Hinkel,
and he wore a suit as blond and tightly cut as his hair.

He said, "Objection," but Judge Rodriguez gestured him down, telling Jesse, "Skip the commentary, Mr. Blackburn."

Jesse said, "And after you fled Beowulf's, did you contact the police?"

"No."

"Did you contact Animal Control?"

"No."

"Did you contact the owner of Beowulf's, to inform her that animals were loose in the bookstore?"

"No."

"Did you do anything besides hide in your apartment, buying jewelry from QVC until the infection to your hand got out of control?"

"I hid because I was traumatized! I had just been mauled by ferrets!"

And that, in a nutshell, was Jesse's problem—because California law restricted the possession of ferrets. Gaul's attackers, the beloved pets of the eccentric woman who owned Beowulf's, had been brought into the state illegally. They were contraband. And, worse for the defense, they were fugitives. To prevent their seizure the owner had spirited them into hiding. They were on the lam from the Department of Fish and Game, outlaw vigilantes of the genus *Mustela*.

"I have nightmares about it." Gaul said. "I see their little eyes and icky paws, scratching and flailing . . ." Her fingers made tiny, frenzied clawing motions.

Jesse merely watched her. "Is that why you put Valium in the hamburger? To calm them down?"

"Objection!" Hinkel's hands were in the air—outrage in action, a drama school pose. "He's harassing the witness."

Rodriguez gave him a gaze like lemon juice. "Asking relevant questions is not harassment. Sit down."

Hinkel sat, but would be up again. He had two chances to win the case—vermin and hysterics. I knew, because I had done the legal research for him, and had told him so. He had taken my derision for strategic advice and run straight to the courthouse.

Taking an irritated breath, Rodriguez said, "It's near the end of the day. We'll adjourn until tomorrow morning, when I want everyone calmed down." She clacked her gavel and stood up, gathering her black robe in her hands.

The bailiff said, "All rise," and everyone in the courtroom rose to their feet, except Jesse. He sat in his wheelchair as Rodriguez left the courtroom.

Conversation clattered and echoed as the room began emptying. While I waited near the door, Gaul and Hinkel walked past. Skip nodded but didn't greet me, knowing I wasn't in his rooting section. Jesse remained at the defense table while his cocounsel, Bill Brandt, critiqued his performance.

It had been two years since a hit-and-run driver smashed into Jesse's mountain bike, leaving him near death at the roadside, his spine shattered. He considered himself lucky. His best friend, riding next to him, had been killed. It took him a year of rehab and physical therapy to regain partial use of his legs. He could walk with crutches, but much of the time used a wheelchair, a lightweight model.

Setting his briefcase on his lap, he spun the chair and with two strokes propelled himself down the aisle. Spotting me, he told Brandt to go ahead without him. The older attorney eyed me quickly, with that knife flick of curiosity—*Are he and she . . . ?*—and slapped Jesse on the shoulder before pushing through the door.

Jesse said, "Another day defending truth, justice, and militant rodents. God, I love the law."

"And a grateful nation salutes you for it," I said. "What did Brandt think?"

"He wants me to rein in my mouth. No sassing the

maimed. Other than that he's thrilled. He's got one crip ripping up the other, so the defense inflicts all the damage and he feels none of the liberal guilt."

I didn't comment. I was used to his bluntness. "And what did you think?"

"Me, I'm riddled with guilt."

"You were born missing the guilt gene."

"Yeah, you got it instead. What are you blaming yourself for today?"

Leaving the courtroom, I started to smile. "Third World debt."

Eyeing my black suit, he asked how the funeral was. I said, "An incitement to riot." I handed him the Remnant's flyer. He looked at it with disgust. When I pointed out the artist's signature, he did the same double take as I had and said, "No way."

"That church is local, Jesse. I'm afraid this means Tabitha's in Santa Barbara."

He pointed at one of the drawings. "It means your brother should watch out."

Blatant as it was, I hadn't noticed it. Orange tongues of fire licked the hills. Black cracks rent the earth, swallowing the Hollywood sign, the U.S. Capitol, and a naval officer in dress blues.

"Reconciliation is definitely not on her agenda," he said. "What are you going to do?"

"Warn Brian, then track her down and find out what's going on. Maybe she isn't involved with the church. Maybe she drew the comic strip on commission."

"You don't believe that. Not with her background."

Right again, Blackburn. I looked away, trying not to think about her real agenda. But he touched my wrist and said, "What if she's come back for Luke?"

Luke, Brian and Tabitha's son, was six. For eight months he had been living with me—ever since Tabitha walked out and Brian was deployed overseas.

Jesse held up the flyer. "Evan, this is nasty stuff. I don't mean fun nasty; I mean raving, psycho nasty."

"You'd say that about church bingo."

"Listen. If Tabitha has started believing this garbage—"

"I know, Luke." I sighed. "I'll find her."

The guilt gene had caused a throbbing in my chest when my brother's marriage collapsed, a dull pain that insisted, *It's my fault, my fault.* Because I had introduced Brian to Tabitha.

Tabitha Roebuck was twenty years old when I met her, a waitress at a café I frequented. Perky and enthusiastic, she was blessed with a curvy figure, auburn curls that fell languorously from her loose hair clip, and a ringing voice that always edged on loudness. At the time, I was practicing law and looking for a way to jump the fence. At the café I would hunch over a legal pad, scribbling fiction with an aspiration akin to craving. One night Tabitha lingered at my table. Hesitantly, as if telling me something shocking, she said, "I understand how you feel about writing. Really, because I'm an artist."

She sat down. She told me she liked science fiction, since that was what I wrote, but she loved fantasy— tales featuring wizards, swordsmen, and beleaguered princesses. Leaning forward, she said, "Do your stories have dragons in them? Dragons are awesome."

But if her fascination seemed childlike, it was because she was test-driving her imagination. She had grown up in a home where creativity and even whimsy had been suppressed by an anxious, astringent fundamentalism. No secular music had been permitted. No secular boyfriends. And no secular literature containing pagan mythological beasts. That equated to dabbling in the occult. To Tabitha's mother, reading *Le Morte d'Arthur* was one step removed from conducting Black Masses around the kitchen table.

My story had no dragons, but the next time I came into the café Tabitha rushed toward me, eyes shiny, hands clutching illustrations she had drawn for the piece. The pictures were wild and romantic—the hero standing defiant against a heavy wind. I loved them. I was taken with her. When my older brother came to visit, I introduced them.

Everything about Brian stunned her: the raven hair and hot-coffee eyes, the cool-under-fire voice, and the confident, offhand manner. He was a fighter pilot and looked it, even out of uniform. She didn't hesitate, not for a second.

A new strand of her personality uncoiled itself: the minx Tabitha. In Brian's presence she became pert, impudent, flirtatious. She emanated a wholesome sexiness, as if her plaid Gap skirt covered a leopard-skin garter belt. Brian termed her "vivacious." But she also saddened easily, and hungered for clarity, security, and purpose. He decided to play the rescuer, imagining that at his side she would grow strong—and grateful to him. Her white knight.

They married within six months, and they doted and clung to each other with a passion that was both pure and excruciatingly cute. Then Luke came along, a child like a jewel, the proof and seal of their fusion. It was perfect.

And it all fell apart.

Tabitha hated life as a navy wife. She hated the transient postings—San Diego, Pensacola, Lemoore, California: too big, too hot, too isolated. She hated the mediocre housing and elaborate protocol, hated Brian's going to sea for months at a time. She must have been painfully lonely, but to my regret I did not sympathize. I was the daughter of a navy man, had grown up living the navy life, and had been a good little soldier. Brian had, too, and he expected his wife to be one. She wasn't.

She was going crazy, she said. She couldn't stand it, taking care of everything by herself, sleeping alone, being cooped up with a demanding child while he was away. *Quit the navy*, she said. And that, in the Delaney family, was the Wrong Thing to Say. That was asking him to cut out his own heart. After that he didn't see her as innocent and sensitive, but as immature and needy. So when his squadron was assigned to a Pacific cruise, her whines and threats all misfired.

It's not fair. I'm not going to be a single parent, not again—you try it and see how you like it. Why can't you work for United Airlines? He just looked at her as if she were nuts. Why in hell would he want to drive 737s? He was going to fly an F/A-18 out to the USS *Constellation*. He had the best damned job on planet Earth.

A week before Brian went to sea, she walked out. He called me, in tears, asking me to take his son for him.

Heading home from the courthouse, I stopped to see how Nikki was holding up after the funeral. Her house and mine share a property near Santa Barbara's Old Mission. She and Carl live in the Victorian home that fronts the street, while I have the smaller guesthouse at the rear of the deep garden. I arrived as the postfuneral gathering was winding down. Kids in dress-up clothes were playing basketball on the driveway, and reggae music was sauntering through the front door. Empty casserole trays sat on the dining room table. In the kitchen, cousins were washing dishes. Nikki was sitting on a black leather sofa in the living room, with her shoes off and her swollen feet propped on a coffee table. I gestured for her not to get up.

She patted the sofa. When I sat down she rested her hand on mine and said, "Heard you went back for a second round with the Holy Rollers. Mom would have liked your spirit."

I squeezed her hand, wanting to thank her but feeling vaguely embarrassed because Tabitha's drawings had added to her grief.

"You did the right thing," she said. "I was wrong about ignoring those people. We have to stand up to groups like that, keep right in their face, or they'll roll over us."

She laid her head back against the couch. Though pregnancy had generally given her a voluptuous glow, she looked drawn, and I asked if she was okay.

"I will be. Claudine didn't raise me to wilt."

A few minutes later I headed across the lawn to my house, an adobe cottage shaded by live oaks and surrounded with hibiscus and star jasmine. I moved Luke's bike from where it lay on the flagstone path, and opened the French doors. A cartoon sound track rolled over me. On television, Wile E. Coyote was chasing the Road Runner across a painted desert. From the far side of the sofa a small head popped up to see who was home.

"Hi, Aunt Evan."

I kicked off my heels. "Hey, tiger. Can you turn down the TV?"

Holding the remote two-fisted, like a ray gun, Luke lowered the volume and hopped to his feet. The babysitter, a college sophomore who moved with tropical lassitude, began tidying up juice boxes and popcorn detritus. My bachelorette pad had been turned into an adventure playground: The Navajo rugs, Ansel Adams prints, and Scandinavian furniture had been overlaid with home decor by Mattel and entertainment by Chuck Jones. Child rearing had fallen on me unexpectedly, but I knew enough to insist that my nephew watch classic television.

As the sitter was leaving, Luke said, "Guess who called on the phone?"

Anxiety nicked me. Please, not Tabitha.

"Dad!" The word infused him with energy. He followed me into the kitchen, bouncing on pogo-stick legs, black hair ruffling up and down. "He's going to our new house today and he'll get my room all ready for me."

My brother had just transferred to a new posting, the Naval Air Warfare Center at China Lake, California. He needed a few days before I brought Luke to him.

I said, "He can't wait for you to get there, bud."

He smiled. He had dimples and a missing bottom tooth, a Tom Sawyer smile that just knocked me out. His hands pressed against the sleeves of my white blouse. His fingers were grubby, slivers of playground dirt under the nails. I knew I'd have to wash the blouse, but those hands—the fidgety fingers, the light touch—so enchanted me that I said nothing to him.

He said, "I packed my bag."

"Already?"

"I could have packed yours too, but I didn't know where to put your special stuff, like sunglasses and vitamins. And, the custody papers."

His knowing about that gave me an electric ache. I told him he was right to let me take care of it. He asked if he could pack a cooler for the drive. "Next week," I said.

I took a soda from the refrigerator. Stuck to the door with magnets were a dozen snapshots of Brian—in his flight suit, next to his F/A-18 Hornet, with Luke perched on his shoulders. Jesse called it the Shrine. I had put them up so Luke would see his dad's face every day. So he wouldn't forget him.

In the display were photos I had taken a week earlier in San Diego, when the *Constellation* returned to port. The carrier's homecoming had been magnificent: sailors lining the edge of the deck, flags snapping in the wind, and families waiting on shore, thousands of people ready to burst. I looked at the photo I had taken as my brother reached us: Brian wrapping Luke in his arms, his face buried in his son's neck. The moment was glorious. It always is.

Luke squeezed my arms. His dark eyes were wide and shiny. They were Tabitha's eyes. He said, "How many hours is it until we go to my new house? I mean, *exactly*."

"*Exactly?* I currently estimate one hundred eighty-two."

Would he forget me?

Eight months earlier, Brian had flown out with his squadron. I cannot imagine his hand wavering on the stick as he swung into the wind for the carrier landing. But divorce is a buzz saw. It slices and mutilates, and I know that despite his cool mien he felt shredded. His commanding officer knew it too, telling him to suck it up, not to let a woman give him a case of the snivels. Understandably, the CO disliked the idea of Brian Delaney dropping a fifty-million-dollar fighter jet onto the deck while wondering where the hell his wife had gone.

Tabitha had disappeared. She emptied the checking account, withdrew the maximum advance on their credit cards, and took off. Traveling on cash, leaving no paper trail. We couldn't find her.

A month later the letters started coming. Addressed to Luke and mailed to my house, they bore neither return address nor apology. *Mommy wishes she could be with you, but she felt too sad and had to go away*, she wrote. *Maybe if Daddy would come home and take care of us, things could be okay.*

They were messages from Self-pity Land, that theme park beyond the reality horizon where mirrors magnify all complaints and "Who's Sorry Now" plays on an endless loop. They kept me awake at night. Did she think the letters made things better? That Luke would understand her? Intervene on her behalf with Brian, for God's sake? The kid was having night terrors, fighting at school, and hiding in his closet for hours on end. I had shelved the book I was writing so that I could take care of him. His face crumpled when he read, *Mommy loves you*.

Eventually, when he saw her handwriting on an envelope, he would turn his back and go outside to smash up his LEGO astronauts with a hammer. The tiny figures sprang apart violently, littering my flower beds with minuscule body parts. When they were all destroyed, he peed on the wreckage.

In July, to my relief, the letters had stopped. But now I had received a new message, from Peter Wyoming. *Tell the cartoonist yourself. You're related to her.* How did he know? Tabitha must have told him. And why would she tell him? Because she wanted Luke.

The spectral buzz saw revved.

One hundred eighty-two hours, just over a week, until I delivered Luke to Brian at his new posting. I did not like the timing.

"Luke," I said, "why don't you go play basketball with the kids at Nikki's house."

When he had run out the door I played a hunch. I phoned Directory Assistance and asked whether they had a listing for Tabitha Delaney. I had done this before, certain that she would eventually slide back to Santa Barbara. But the phone company had never had a listing for her.

Until now. The operator gave me a phone number, along with an address on West Camino Cielo. I felt cold. It was the house Tabitha had inherited when her mother died, a shambling home in the chaparral high up the mountains behind Santa Barbara. It was the place where SueJudi Roebuck used to interrupt dinner to speak in tongues and had egged Tabitha's school friends to undergo baptism in the hot tub. It was the house nobody visited a second time, the place Tabitha fled when she jettisoned her mother's fundamentalism. She had left it sitting empty for years.

I caught the babysitter halfway down the block and asked her to come back. I changed into jeans, boots, and a green corduroy shirt of Jesse's, and I grabbed my car keys.

The sun was flaring red in the west when I drove my white Explorer up a gully toward Tabitha's house, past sandstone boulders and gray-green brush. The air smelled thick with mustard and eucalyptus. The view of the city, two thousand feet below, was spectacular. Santa Barbara lay like a velvet sash between the mountains and the Pacific, smooth and glimmering.

The house itself looked neglected. Faded gray paint curled from the wood siding, and weeds spread across the lawn, humped and matted, like an overgrown beard. When no one answered my knock, I looked in the front window. The living room held some thrift-shop chairs and a worktable covered with pens, pencils, and drawings. In the dingy kitchen, shopping bags bulged with cans of creamed corn and SPAM. Was that what she had cooked for Brian? No wonder he had requested sea duty.

Stuck to the fridge was a drawing, held up by crown-of-thorns magnets. The Shrine, take two. It was a picture of Peter Wyoming. I leaned my head against the window. Tabitha had apparently come home in more ways than one.

I returned to my car and reread the Remnant's flyer. As I suspected, the hate rally at Claudine's funeral hadn't sated Peter Wyoming. He invited all right-thinking Christians to a "Postprotest Testimony" that evening. I checked my watch. Wyoming should be just warming up. I put the car in gear. And I started down the long road, the one to hell.

2

Peter Wyoming's church sat close to traffic on a downtown street, beneath a slice of moon in a sky gone indigo. The building had originally housed a furniture store, and through showroom windows I saw a hundred people seated on folding chairs, packed into a bare commercial space under fluorescent lighting. Music pulsed through the glass, a heavy beat pounded out on piano and electric bass, ripe with unsettling energy.

When I pushed open the door, sound and heat enveloped me. The room was thick with sweat and fervor. Perspiration sheened on thick male necks, and women fanned themselves with colorful Bible tracts. On a makeshift stage, the choir stood erect and fierce in scarlet robes, shouting about power in the blood of the lamb. Before them danced a trio of baton twirlers, teenage girls in sequined silver leotards who leaped and spun with martial-arts intensity.

Picking up a photocopied service sheet from a table, I stood near the door, looking for Tabitha, but saw only people cut from templates—women in skirts, with moussed pyramids of hair, men wearing jeans, boots, crew cuts. And there I was, Miss Sore Thumb, in my jeans, boots, and man's shirt. I crept back against the windows, trying to look inconspicuous.

As I scanned the room, a woman stepped forward to sing a solo. She was stout, with pebbly gray eyes and a clay-colored braid that hung down her back like a rope, and had an alto voice that brayed about the armies of God cutting down the wicked.

" 'Mow 'em down," she sang, " 'those sluts and queers!' "

" 'Mow 'em down,' " the congregation echoed, " 'too late for tears!' "

" 'Hey, feminists and liberals, this time we're getting biblical, takin' back the streets for a thousand years!' "

Whoops rose from the crowd. Batons spun like sparkling nunchakus. The soloist shouted, "That's it, people! Put your hands together, and let's get biblical with Pastor Pete!" The congregation applauded, the twirlers dropped into the splits, and Peter Wyoming stepped onto the stage.

He was crackling with energy, his ruddy face flushing, his sandpaper brown crew cut bristling. He put a microphone to his lips. "Getting biblical! Yes! Getting biblical here in Santa Barbara, USA," he said. "Telling those AIDS mourners exactly where they stand with God."

The foot stomping and catcalls increased. He gave them a conspirator's smile. "And wasn't it fun?"

They went wild, laughing and shouting. This was a victory dance.

"Nothing wrong with enjoying a church outing in the fresh air and sunshine. Doin' a little slut busting."

He let the thigh-slapping go on for a minute before raising a hand.

"And now it's back to work. 'Cause AIDS is just the tip of the iceberg, poking out of the sewer." He closed his eyes and shook his head. "And this tidal wave of depravity is a sign—a sign that we are approaching the last days of time."

Schmaltz and brimstone. I tried not to listen, knowing Wyoming would anger me, and continued looking for Tabitha. Still, I heard his undertones and heavy beats. Staccato references to hell. A list of Satan's current projects, from the teaching of evolution to the celebration of Halloween. A schedule of upcoming events: calamity, anarchy, damnation for all who didn't buy into the Remnant's brand of panic. And pounding beneath, the insistent, ostinato bass: *We are nearing the last days.* The end: It was the Big Bad Wolf of sermons, and had been since Caligula ruled Rome.

"Let's review." He snapped his fingers at the stout choir soloist, who handed him a dog-eared Bible. He opened it and read: " 'There will be earthquakes in various places, there will be famines; this is but the beginning of the sufferings.' "

Congregants bent forward, fingers flipping through Bibles to find the passage, filling the room with the desiccated crinkle of onionskin paper. He said, "This isn't news. Y'all are tracking quakes and hunger on your wall charts at home, right?"

A woman with pink eyeglasses held up a newspaper clipping, waving it like a winning raffle ticket. " 'Thousands Starve in Bangladesh!' "

He said, "Good," and continued with an eschatological checklist: wars, false prophets arising, and widespread delusion—a great deception. Dramatic pause. *"Deception."*

He tapped a finger against his temple. "Stay sharp. This is the age of the big lie, folks, so don't believe what you hear out there."

And *out there* was where his sermon promptly headed. The court system was a lie, he said, falsely legalizing queer sex and gun control. Science was a lie, an atheist plot to discredit the Bible with the big bang theory and the claim that AIDS came from African monkeys—monkeys!—when he *knew* God turned it loose at the Centers for Disease Control in Atlanta.

His voice began rising. The Catholic Church was a lie, nothing but witchcraft. Latin was a lie. Yup, Latin, a pagan tongue, supposed to be a dead language—but it wasn't dead; it's been kept alive as . . . what? As the language of law, and science, and the Mass, and *sorcery*. He chanted, *"Dominus Nabisco Shredded Wheat,"* and said, "How many of you seen a Mexican ballplayer trying to cross himself into a home run?" *Mexican* came out *meskin*. "Am I right? It's not coincidence. Can't you see, people, how they're all connected?"

I felt the hair rising on the back of my neck. I turned, saw a young woman in the back row looking at me, a teenager whose Kewpie-doll mouth punctuated her moon-round face. She was staring as if she had recognized me from a wanted poster. When I met her gaze her mouth narrowed to a slit.

"And then there's Satan's biggest lie—that the last days are a myth. He's slick at getting people to believe this."

The slit-mouthed teen whispered to a companion, and they both stared at me.

"The Black Death, H-bombs, comets flying at the earth, even Y2K—every time, folks start thinking this is *it*. And when it's not, people say, 'look at them idiots; what kind of morons would believe the Apocalypse was coming?' " He paused. "And Satan sits back and smiles. 'Cause he's gotten more people to ignore the Bible's warnings."

He gripped the mike with both hands. He had huge hands, miner's hands, rough and reddened. "But the end-times are not a myth." His voice spiraled down to a whisper. "The storm is coming, people."

His sudden quietude spread a chill across my skin, a deepening sense of unease. I had expected his preening righteousness, but not for his homily to loft into the eerie winds of biblical prophecy. I stood transfixed, even though the slit-mouthed teenager and her friend were muttering and giving me darting, nasty looks.

"Look around at the signs," he said. "The president of the United States now swears the oath of office facing the Washington Monument—a Masonic obelisk, a symbol of the occult. That is a message to the devil, saying the government is ready to serve him. American soldiers are getting anthrax inoculations. That is a sign they're preparing for the end-time plagues."

Wyoming wiped his brow. With his reddened cheeks, sore pink hands, and the scarlet choir behind him, he looked like a living alarm. "Satan is preparing for war. And who will fight him? The UN?"

"Foreign faggots!" a man cried. "They're in on it!"

"Who, then? Who will fight back?"

"Nobody—they're all gonna die!"

"Yes. Because nobody is going to fight Satan. Nobody . . ." Wyoming paused. "Except the Remnant. The few, the pure, the clean sons and daughters of the Lord."

Voices called out, "Amen!" and, "Right on!" Wyoming said, "Lucky for us, we have intercepted Satan's battle plans." He raised the Bible above his head. "It's all in here. We know what's coming."

Amid intense concentration, more nods, a woman said, "Tell us, Pastor Pete!"

"Tribulation is what's coming. Horrible, horrible tribulation."

The congregation held still, waiting to hear how horrible. They looked like roller-coaster passengers preparing for the first heart-stopping drop down the rails. Wyoming flipped to a new scripture passage.

" 'Behold, a pale horse, and its rider's name was Death . . . they were given power over a fourth of the earth, to kill with sword and with famine and with pestilence and by wild beasts of the earth.' "

Here we went. He had taken his time getting to the last book of the Bible, but he had to save the biggie for the end: Revelation, the zealot's favorite thrill ride.

"A fourth of the earth. That's one billion, five hundred million people, dead. Picture bodies stacked like cordwood in the streets of London and Paris. Imagine the beaches of Santa Barbara awash with bloated corpses."

Their pinched faces pictured it. Some shook their heads; others nodded with a serves-them-right eagerness. Though I felt cold, sweat pinpricked my forehead.

"And when bulldozers cart stinking bodies down Main Street, what will people do? They'll cry, 'Save me' "—he fluttered his wrists—"but they won't turn to the Lord for help; they'll turn to the strongman who claims he'll rescue them. The Antichrist."

He clenched the mike. "They'll turn to the beast; oh, yes, they will, the filthy people of the world will run right to him. And *soon*." He pointed to the showroom windows. "The beast is out there. Now, *right now*, working his way to power. That is the stone-cold ugly truth, people."

A fidget spread through the congregation, like the wave in a stadium.

"Now don't get twitchy on me. Scripture tells us to have endurance. That means hanging tough, digging in, fighting the enemy. 'Cause if Satan expects some meek, peacenik Jesus, he's in for a rude awakening. Jesus is no sissy. He will smite the nations, and he will rule them with a rod of iron."

He clenched his fist again. *"A rod of iron."*

The baton twirlers sprinted back onto the stage, carrying a large scroll. They unfurled it with a flourish. It was a six-foot-by-four-foot cartoon, reworking *The Last Supper* as a scene from *Platoon*. It showed Christ and the Apostles in combat fatigues, with camouflage paint striping their faces, weapons at the ready. Beneath the drawing ran the tagline: *He's back . . . and this time, it's scriptural.*

I gaped at it, appalled. Not because it depicted Jesus juiced on steroids and brandishing an M16. No. I stood horrified because it forced me to see the truth. Peter Wyoming did not speak in metaphors.

He slapped the poster. "We, the Remnant, are that rod of iron."

His face gleamed, grimacing. "We will suffer, and some of us will die. But get a load of what we win if we take this fight to the streets: We will reign with Christ a thousand years." He raised the Bible high. "We have it in writing. We win this thing and we'll be running the show for a thousand years! The millennium of the Lord!"

They cheered, they yelled, they jumped to their feet. The piano began banging. Wyoming stood with his chin raised, like *Il Duce*, and the choir started to sing.

" 'He holds me in his arms, my Lord Jesus Christ. He cocks me and aims me, held tight to his side. He squeezes the trigger, and bullets go flying—' "

My eyes were stinging, my ears ringing as the music swelled into the refrain:

" 'Lock and load! I am the weapon of the Lord. Lock and load! my savior cries—' "

He spread his arms. "Say it, people. What do you want?"

"Victory!" " Their shout shook the room.

My mouth had gone dry. The thought that Tabitha subscribed to this vision, and might want to subject Luke to it, nauseated me. The heat and noise and atavism pressed in, and I closed my eyes.

When I opened them again, the slit-mouthed teenager was standing up, pointing at me. Her lips were moving but her words were smothered by the music and the frenzy.

I felt my hands clenching at my sides. In my mind I heard Nikki's words: about standing up to them, keeping it right in their face. I held motionless, watching the girl's face stretch with anger as she realized no one had heard her. She jumped up on a chair.

"Unbeliever!"

*   *   *

She was five feet tall, weighed ninety pounds, and wore a ponytail tied back with a cascade of pastel ribbons. But she had a voice like a factory whistle and it cut through the roaring of the choir. Heads in the back of the room turned to look at me.

The girl said, "She's from the funeral, the one who heckled Pastor Pete. She's one of the AIDS people."

A bubble of empty space dilated around me, congregants shuffling away uneasily. The girl climbed off the chair and stepped forward. "What do you think you're doing, like, coming in here? We don't want your AIDS and voodoo."

Remembering the invitation on the Remnant's flyer, I said, "Being here is my postprotest testimony."

Her mouth pursed. "As if. You're not saved, I can tell."

"You can?" I inspected my sleeves and boots. "It shows? Where?"

Flippancy with proselytizers is ingrained in me. The smallest irritant will set me off, because I grew up in a household that did not suffer faith peddlers. The Delaneys did not buy vacuum cleaners from door-to-door salesmen, my mother always said, and we sure as hell were not buying God from them. When the Jehovah's Witnesses rang our bell my father would answer the door wearing boxer shorts, or whistle to the dog, calling, "Here, Lucifer!"

And after everything I had heard that day, this young woman, with her gerbil-colored ponytail and eyes like greenish copper, was not a small irritant. She was a thumb jammed in my eye.

She said, "You're polluting our sanctuary. You'll have to leave."

"But the kids' show hasn't started yet." I pointed at the service sheet. "Look, 'Small Fry Squad, explaining the Whore of Babylon through hand puppets.' "

She stared at me as if I were a gargoyle. "The Bible

warns us about people like you. 'Their throat is an open grave; they use their tongues to deceive. The venom of asps is under their lips.' "

I crossed my arms. "Smite me."

Her Kewpie-doll lips parted. I didn't move, though my heart was pounding.

A male voice spoke from behind me, low and sharp. "What's going on here?"

The girl smirked. *The joke's on you.* "Unbeliever, Mr. Paxton."

He was in his mid-forties, lean, tall, with the de rigueur crew cut, dressed in a plaid flannel shirt and jeans. He stood relaxed but his eyes were stony. He said, "This meeting is for glorifying the Lord, not heaping abuse on Him."

"No abuse heaped," I said. He was strongly built, quite imposing.

"Ain't no other reason you could be upsetting Shiloh," he said, "except by spreading lies and—"

"I know, the venom of asps is under my lips." His eyes flared briefly—a muzzle flash—before withdrawing into a squint. I said, "I'm looking for a family member."

Wrong answer. This was apparently the tip-off that a cult deprogrammer had infiltrated the service. Paxton grabbed my collar and said, "You're trespassing on private property. Come on. Out."

I resisted his grip, but a second man appeared and caught my arm. He was the crew-cut, acned protester who had called Nikki Vincent "witch girl."

Paxton said, "How many more a' you are outside?"

"Let go."

His grip tightened. "How many?"

"Nine. They're an all-nun softball team and they're carrying baseball bats."

Crew-cut jerked my arm. "Don't get cute with us."

His rough shove, his bully's sense of presumption, signaled the crowd that tonight we were playing full-contact denunciation. The bubble around me collapsed and people pressed forward, Shiloh foremost. Fingers poked me and I heard, "people like you" and "make me sick." A palm popped the back of my head. Crewcut's mouth slid open in an unflattering smile of gappy yellow teeth.

My anger went spinning over the top. Partly at myself, because damn if I hadn't asked for a smiting. I twisted toward the stage and called, "Pastor Pete!"

Up front, people were clapping in unison and the choir was singing a rompin', stompin' tune about stain and sacrifice. I called out again and Wyoming's eyes panned the crowd, his gaze lighting on the commotion, and on me.

I said, "I'm doing what you asked."

I knew that when he said, *Tell the cartoonist,* he didn't mean for me to seek out Tabitha at his service. But my words worked: They confused the crowd around me into stopping their jibes.

Wyoming put the microphone to his lips. "My, my."

He gestured the choir to hush. Slowly the crowd backed off, although Paxton kept his hand on the back of my collar, and Shiloh gave me a valedictory poke in the side with her car keys. Wyoming waited, letting people quiet down, and letting me appreciate the muscle surrounding me, and his authority over it.

He smiled. "I believe, Miss Delaney, you were saying something to me earlier about mercy."

Quiet smothered the church. I said, "About being merciful, not putting people at your mercy. But I get your point."

The crowd didn't like my lack of servility, taking it for backtalk. Wyoming's expression went as flat as a board.

He said, "Shiloh, Isaiah,"—apparently meaning Paxton—"thank you for your vigilance. You are the kind of high-caliber bullets the Lord needs in his ammunition clip." He pointed to Crew-cut. "You, Curt

Smollek. You gonna show this same fighting spirit when it comes time to confront the beast?"

"Yessir, Pastor Pete. Point me at him and pull the trigger." Smollek's hands mimed a pump-action shotgun. "He's going down!"

"Excellent." New expression: a patronizing smile. "Miss Delaney. You didn't need to cause a ruckus." He gestured to the front row. "Tabitha, come up here."

She rose and followed his beckoning hand.

Had she changed? Her white dress was longer, looser, hiding the high, pert butt that always attracted attention, but that may have been because she had lost weight. She was pale, almost fragile-looking, except for her face. With her wild auburn curls drawn back by a hair tie, her face shone. Her eyes were luminous. And they were only for Peter Wyoming.

As she stepped onto the stage he took her hand. "Someone's here to see you, lamb. But it's someone who *doesn't* see, and like all sightless things she's clumsy and destructive and causing a mess. Can you straighten her out?" Laying a hand on the back of her neck, he turned her to face me. "Tell Miss Delaney how you came to the Remnant."

For a second, then two, she stayed silent, staring at me, and I looked desperately for some acknowledgment that we were family, had been friends. *Don't,* I willed her. *Don't say anything.* But she had lightning in her eyes, a brilliant and pitiless force.

Her boisterous voice carried straight to me. "Jesus tore me from Satan's grip."

Wyoming said, "How did he do that?"

"He rescued me from an unholy marriage."

A discernible "Oh, no" rose from the crowd. Wyoming held up a hand. "Don't judge. It's easy for naive young people to get lured by 'friends' into liaisons with the unsaved. Isn't it, Tabitha?"

"So easy it's scary. They make the unsaved life look

exciting, and they're always eager for you to join it. And she seemed so honestly sincere." Talking about me, now. "Encouraging what she called creativity, but she meant secular art and fiction, just godless chatter. And I fell for it, and she ended up leading me to a dark, a very dark and powerful place. To life with him."

"Your husband." She nodded. "Tell them how dangerous he was."

"He . . ." She looked at her feet. "He's an officer in the navy. He had us get married by a Roman Catholic priest."

Silence. She might have been bragging that she bit the heads off kittens for sport. Paxton's grip tightened on my collar, and his breath blew across my neck.

When Tabitha looked up her expression mixed humiliation and defiance. "I confess, I was wayward. But the Lord found me; He showed me I was hanging over a pit, and right before I fell in"—she balled a fist—"He yanked me up and brought me to you."

Wyoming prompted, "And what did Jesus show you in that pit?"

"The truth about my husband. That he believed a false religion and fought for Satan's puppet government."

The line was scripted, and she recited it woodenly, but heads in the crowd nodded like toy dogs on car dashboards. My stomach was cramping. I wanted to scream at her, to correct her theology, to clarify her Mr. Magoo vision, to shout, *Tell them the rest; tell them you abandoned your kid.* But when I tensed to speak, Paxton's hand began twisting my collar, so I stood, silently fuming.

"I also saw the fruits of Satan's end-times hoaxes." Abruptly her voice took on conviction. "I've seen Christians driven to despair by these lies—it's horrible. But until you told me, I didn't know it was a demonic plot."

Boom, like a plank hitting me across the forehead, it made sense. Tabitha was talking about her mother.

Wyoming was nodding sympathetically. "Thank you for your honesty. But I don't think it's made a lick of difference."

He raised his chin again and looked down at me. A hundred heads swiveled to do the same. I stayed resolutely silent.

"Nope. Just like I thought." He sighed. "Tabitha, this mess is getting stinky. Take care of it."

He lowered the microphone and walked over to the choir soloist, leaving Tabitha center stage. The soloist took a handkerchief and dabbed the sweat from Pastor Pete's glistening forehead. Tabitha looked out at a hundred expectant faces.

She flicked her head at Isaiah Paxton. "Go on, then."

He propelled me toward the door. Off balance, I clawed for his hands, dragged my heels. Curt Smollek grabbed me and pulled me sliding along the floor. He leaned close and said, "Who has the tiny brain now, Miss Smarty-pants?"

I felt like biting him, but with the door looming I twisted my head toward the stage. Tabitha stood there like marble, white-clad and rigid.

"You may have bought into this circus," I called to her, "but remember—caveat emptor."

People actually audibly gasped. *Latin* . . . Paxton yanked on my collar. Smollek said, "Witch!"

I had defiled their sanctuary. Good. Maybe they'd have to sandblast the church, or raze it and pour salt on the ground. They hauled me to the door, bunching their muscles to heave me outside. Paxton said, "On three," reaching for the doorknob.

Before he touched it the door flew open. Outside stood a gaunt man, his face in shadow. Smollek jerked up short in surprise.

"Move!" The man shooed us aside and tottered forward into the light.

Smollek dropped my arm. He gasped, "Lord almighty," and flattened himself back against the doorway. The intruder lurched toward Paxton and me.

Paxton stared at the intruder, jerked me in front of him, and said, "Hold it right there."

Yeah, don't move or the heathen girl gets it. The intruder grabbed my shirt with clammy hands. His sour breath panted over me. "Out of my way!"

A small *eeiuu* crawled from my throat. His face was sweat limned and skeletal, his eyes alight with fervor or alcohol or fever, jittering around the room. He tried to toss me aside, couldn't. He tried again, looked confused, and finally just barreled into me and Paxton. Pinned between them, I smelled his reeking body odor. Paxton reached around me and grabbed his arms, saying, "Smollek, get his feet."

The intruder pointed a jerky hand toward the stage. "Her!" he shouted. "She knows. She knows!"

I tried to squirm free. The man was screaming, spittle arcing from his mouth. "You bitches and sons of bitches!" He blinked. "Oh, Jesus, look at that." His hand waved at the red-robed choir. "They're on fire. Ohh. Burning . . ."

With a groan, Curt Smollek found his courage. He lunged and clasped the man around the thighs, hoisting him off his feet. The intruder shrieked and bucked, arching his back. I pulled free and stumbled backward.

"I'll tell!" the man screamed. "Fuck everybody here! I'll tell!"

The congregation was on its feet. Onstage the baton twirlers were huddling together. Wyoming was snapping his fingers at the choir, telling them to strike up a hymn. They were ignoring him.

The intruder was thrashing, wrenching the scuffle toward me. I backed up, bumped into chairs, and the man raked the air with his hands, snagging my shirt, digging his fingers in, pulling me with him as Paxton and Smollek carried him toward the door. He kicked furiously and his knee caught Smollek in the chin. Smollek's head snapped back, the intruder twisted hard, and in a tangle we staggered toward the showroom window.

I saw it coming and shouted, "No!" But momentum had us. I tucked my head beneath my arms. We crashed through the window and out onto the sidewalk.

Glass spanked the concrete. I fell, still in my tuck, landing on Curt Smollek, feeling bones and flesh and bits of glass striking me. After a stunned moment I heard wails and scuffling feet. I rolled carefully to one side and saw people inside the church rushing to the broken window. Around me shards glittered on the sidewalk. Smollek was kneeling on all fours, his white T-shirt speckled with blood. The intruder was wobbling across the street, trailing a moan behind him. Chunks of glass protruded from his back and arms, but he seemed heedless. Paxton was on his feet. He grabbed Smollek's sleeve and dragged him up.

A dozen small cuts stung my hands and scalp. But I had been last through the glass, wearing long sleeves, and that had protected me. Delicately I stood up, careful not to touch the ground, feeling dazed and lucky.

The intruder's scream rose again, a long, foul curse. Suddenly headlights illuminated him. Brakes screeched and a heavy truck hit him, swept him under its wheels. His screaming stopped.

The truck skewed to a halt, tires smoking, farm produce spilling from its bed. I ran into the street. The truck driver jumped down from the cab. He dropped to the asphalt and stared under the front axle, crying, "Oh, God! Oh, God!"

I ran to his side. "Can you back the truck off of him?"

His jowly face was desperate. "He's caught. . . ."

Crouching next to him, I called 911 on my cell phone. The driver said, "He ran right out in front of me." I laid a hand on his back, told him the paramedics and a fire crew were on the way. He was shuddering.

I said, "We have to see if we can help him."

"Yeah," he said, but didn't move. "Christ, right out in front of me. I couldn't stop."

I looked around. The congregation was spilling out the church door. Smollek was sitting on the curb, head in his hands. Paxton, apparently untouched by shattered glass, was squatting on his haunches in front of the truck, peering underneath it.

I said, "Can you reach him?"

He looked at me. The white light from the headlights cast him in sharp relief. Without speaking he stood, brushed off his hands, and sauntered toward the crowd. His pace said, *Not my problem anymore.*

Dread wadded in my stomach, but I lay down and shimmied forward until my head was under the chassis. I smelled exhaust and grease, felt the heat of the engine, looked at the dark curve of the wheel. The man's legs, broken and limp, protruded from the wheel well, and his arm dangled, a Rolex shining on his motionless wrist. I couldn't see the rest of him.

I said, "Can you hear me?"

No response. Queasily I inched ahead. Stretching my arm, I clasped his fingers. "If you can hear me, squeeze my hand." Nothing. I said, "Help's coming," and, knowing I could do nothing more, pushed myself out from under the truck.

The driver was glassy-eyed on the ground, staring at that dangling arm. The air stank of burned rubber. I climbed into the cab and switched off the engine, grabbed reflective red hazard triangles from behind the driver's seat, and hopped out, jogging up the street to set them out. The Remnant milled near the church. Not one of them had stepped forward to help. A pasty

finger pointed at me, and I heard, "Her fault."
Louder: "She brought this on."

They were standing on the sidewalk, crowding up
to the curb but not stepping off, as if it were the edge
of a cliff. They were saying the accident was a sign . . .
a punishment or a warning. My foot hit something
slick—a broken pumpkin. That was what had spilled
from the truck, and that was what was holding them
back. Their shoulders were hunching away from the
orange gourds as though they were severed heads.

Then Peter Wyoming's voice rang out. "It's a taunt.
We're being mocked. Well, I got an answer to that!"

He stepped off the curb and jammed a cowboy boot
down on a pumpkin, squashing it. A second later the
choir soloist hoisted her red robe and did the same.
Then the twirlers, who ran into the street and laid into
a pumpkin with their batons like hunters clubbing a
harp seal. Then everyone.

Oh, no. I jogged back to the truck. The driver was
kneeling by the wheels, saying, "Hang on, buddy, help's
coming, hang on," a rosary of slender hope, chanted in
fear and guilt. From behind me came scuffling, grunts,
the wet crack of produce splitting open. A pumpkin flew
and smashed against the wooden slats of the truck. I
tugged on the driver's arm, urging him up. He stood, saw
the Remnant smashing his cargo, mouthed, *What . . . ?*
Someone pointed at the truck and called, "Look—
more!" A dozen people charged the vehicle, climbing
into the bed and flinging pumpkins overboard.

"Get in the cab." I pushed him toward the door.
He stared at the front axle, and I said, "I'll stay
with him."

He gripped the door handle, felt the truck rocking,
and stopped. Peter Wyoming was standing in the middle of the road, arms akimbo, face alight, looking at
the anarchy as if it were beauty revealed.

He tilted his head back and bellowed, "Getting
biblical!"

The driver said, "No, we'll both stay."

"Thank you."

From the distance, at last, came a siren. The blue and red lights of a fire engine strobed the night, flashing off buildings, asphalt, faces. Headlights backlit the Remnant into flat black silhouettes. I waved my arms, but the engine halted, motor growling, the crew doubtless confused by the scene.

For an awful moment I thought the Remnant was going to mob the fire truck. But Peter Wyoming spread his arms, in the classic gesture of the Good Shepherd welcoming his flock, and said, "Come on, people." They followed him back to the sidewalk, hopping down from the produce truck and clearing the road unhurriedly, slapping high-fives and pumping fists in the air.

The fire engine drove forward and the crew jumped out, wary and full of questions. The truck driver directed them toward the trapped man, and then we backed off as they set to work. The Remnant again massed on the curb, singing, "Takin' back the streets for a thousand years . . ."

Except for one figure, dressed in white, who stood staring at me. Tabitha. The lights of the fire truck spun across her. Red, blue, red, a shocking spin of color. I walked toward her.

"What's going on here?" I said. "What in the name of God is this all about?"

The strobing lights painted her face into a kaleidoscope of fear and ferocity. "You haven't been listening."

I jerked my thumb toward the produce truck. "That man may be dead. So you tell me, what happened inside this church?" She merely stared at me. I approached, breathing hard. "Why did you run away?"

"You don't get it," she said.

"Try me. Nothing you say right now could possibly surprise me."

Her voice, emanating from that voluptuous mouth,

sounded flat and disembodied. "Turn away from the deceiver and open your eyes, Evan. Something's coming that you can't stop."

Behind me radios were squawking, the fire crew shouting for equipment. Churchgoers were pushing past me, declaiming about blood and iniquity. Tabitha's lips parted. She was hanging on a decision whether to say something else. A scarlet choir robe swirled in front of her, lurid under the flashing lights.

She said, "You can't keep him. He's not yours."

Then the crowd swallowed her, took her from my sight.

3

When I arrived home I sat in the car, trying to shake loose from the evening's ugliness. I didn't want Luke to see me upset. But I kept hearing the crack of shattering glass, kept seeing Tabitha's high-voltage eyes, kept feeling the injured man's hand when I clasped it. It felt like gristle. I climbed out of the Explorer, slammed the door, and started walking up the street.

The fire crew had disentangled the man from the truck's undercarriage and lifted him onto a stretcher. Delicately, like a smashed chandelier they were trying to salvage. I didn't know whether he had survived the trip to the hospital.

I had no clue who he was, why he had invaded the service, whom he had been screaming at. I gave a statement to the Santa Barbara police at the scene, telling them what I had seen and that I thought the man was sick, physically ill. I also told them that I thought the Remnant was sick, infected with a pathogenic faith. They looked at the broken window and pumpkin-slick street, and shrugged, unsure how to log my comment. Cops wanted facts, not creepy metaphysics.

I pushed through the gate and followed the path under the live oaks back to my cottage. Before going inside I held my hands out, checking that they were steady, and urged a pleasant expression onto my face.

The living room was empty. The house was quiet except for the television, the local news on with the volume low, talking about a gray whale that had beached itself and died. I didn't hear Luke or the babysitter. I called her name, noticing that I didn't see her backpack or books anywhere. Calling again, getting no reply, I headed to the dark doorway of Luke's bedroom. When I nudged the door fully open, light fell on a man next to Luke's bed.

"Almighty Christ," I said.

"Quiet, you'll wake him."

"Jesse, don't scare me like that."

He turned and gave me a strange look, not expecting his presence in my house to scare me. He said, "I paid the sitter and sent her home. What's wrong?"

"What are you doing?"

"Just checking on him."

Luke lay with his pajama top bunched under his chin and his arms stretched over his head. I wrangled his quilt up to his chest and propped his teddy bear beside him. It had Brian's squadron patch sewn on its chest. Strike Fighter Squadron 151, the Vigilantes.

Jesse followed me out of the bedroom, closing the door noiselessly before saying, "Tell me."

I was on tiptoe in the kitchen, reaching for a bottle of Jack Daniel's, the whiskey I saved for intense occasions. "You were right. Tabitha wants Luke."

He was looking at the green corduroy shirt I had on, now grimy with road dirt, and at my hands, freckled with cuts. Wanting me to explain the rest. I poured two fingers. Drank, felt the JD hit my throat, leaned my elbows on the kitchen counter and rested my forehead against the glass in my hands.

"She's jumped on the bus. It's on fire, tires blown out, heading for a cliff, and she's honking the horn, thinking she's saved." I straightened. "I had the Remnant all wrong. They aren't ordinary fundamentalists; they're fanatical end-timers."

I started to tell him about it. He wheeled into the kitchen, turned on the faucet, and got me to set down the whiskey and wash out the cuts. While I talked, he found antiseptic and Band-Aids and stuck them on my hands with brisk male nonchalance.

He said, "Do you want to talk to a family law attorney? We have a guy at the firm who's a pit bull on custody issues."

"No point. Brian has custody stitched up; she can't just come and take him. Until she hits us with a summons, I don't need a lawyer."

"What are you going to do?"

"Hold tight and get Luke up to Brian's next week, like I planned."

He looked at the photos of Brian on the fridge. "Yeah, I'm sure Captain America will deal with it."

His voice had an edge, but I let the remark go because we were both worn out. He had worked late, I knew—he was still in his court clothes, with his cuffs rolled up, red tie loosened at his neck. When he spoke again his smoky voice sounded old.

"Tell me Wyoming's a scam artist, Ev. That he doesn't believe the bullshit he says, he just wants their money."

"No. I don't think so." I finished my whiskey.

"You think it's more than hyperbole, this First Church of the Assault Rifle stuff?"

"He's pumping them up to take on the Antichrist. Priming them for public violence. He's the one who goaded them to attack the farm truck."

Again I smelled burned rubber and saw the injured man's limp arm. . . . Why had he burst screaming into the church? What, I couldn't help thinking, had the Remnant done to him? I said, "I have a bad feeling that Pastor Pete has big plans."

Dead air hung between us until he asked, "Is this a Heaven's Gate scenario?"

Mass suicide. I exhaled. "They don't talk about

going to another realm—they talk about a Green
Beret Messiah storming to earth and leading them
into battle."

"Waco."

"Don't even say that word."

He held my gaze. Not offering platitudes, not saying, *It'll be okay.* I poured another drink.

He said, "How are you going to tell Luke?"

I hadn't foreseen that he would become so attached
to my nephew. But that was Jesse, the blindsider—he
was a shaman of cynicism with adults, but had a sure
touch with kids. Direct and encouraging, he put them
at ease, listened to them, got them to listen to him.
He had taught Luke to swim, taught him to love the
water as he did himself, having been a world-class
swimmer. I looked at him, at those blue eyes, at the
long hair and earring that proclaimed his pirate streak.
He was uncommonly handsome, and five years my
junior, but his face did not look young. His eyes were
as clear as ice and free from illusion.

I brushed a lock of hair off his forehead. He
squeezed my fingers, stroked his palm up my arm.

"Ouch," he said. Both of us started, and he looked
at the heel of his hand, where a drop of blood was
rising. Glass fragments from my sleeve. I said, "I'd
better shower."

Ten minutes later I was in my bedroom, buttoning
a clean blouse, when he called out, "You're on the
news." When I came back around the corner he was
sitting on the sofa, stretching to reach the TV remote.
He turned up the volume and I heard my voice scold-
ing Peter Wyoming with Bible quotations. It was a
report about Claudine's funeral. After the evening's
melee, that run-in seemed petty.

He said, "Way to go, Delaney."

He reached up, found my hand, and pulled me
down to him. Vining his arms around me, he kissed
me. Again, and again. I closed my eyes and leaned

against him. This was in the top ten, the best about him—this passion for me when he knew I was doing right. It went beyond seduction, beyond romance, to the bedrock. I clung to him, nourishing myself with the moment.

When I first met him, before his accident, I had presumed him one of those all-Americans who would soar through life on good looks, brains, and athletic prowess, blessed and untouchable. I didn't really know him. It took disaster for me to learn about his grit, and relentlessness, and his ungodly ability to touch me in exactly the right way. I kissed him again, letting my hands slide up his arms and around his back. He had a swimmer's physique, shoulders and arms like carved oak, strong from doing double duty these past few years. They were a shelter, and I curled against him.

He said, "Wish I could stay."

"I know."

He wouldn't spend the night. He had an early court date the next morning; he didn't live nearby, didn't have fresh clothes or the pain medication he needed. His broken back meant that things took time. The package didn't include spontaneity. Nevertheless he snaked his fingers into my hair, tilted my head back, and kissed me at the base of the throat. I felt his breath whisker my chest where my shirt gapped in the front. Then his teeth, teasing loose the top button, and his lips, brushing my skin.

And behind me, a small voice. "I'm thirsty."

I jumped, and Jesse's head snapped up. Luke was standing in the doorway, eyes fighting the light.

I lingered, but knew he wouldn't return to bed empty-handed, and got up to pour him a glass of milk. When I returned with it, he was tucked next to Jesse on the sofa. He drank the milk sleepily. After he finished it I took his hand and said, "Back to bed," but he pushed his face against Jesse's chest, ignoring me.

Jesse said, "Come on, I'll give you a ride." Levering

onto the wheelchair, he patted his knee. "Hop on, little dude." Luke clambered onto his lap.

Not long after tucking Luke in, he headed home. I walked him out to his car, which had a big engine and hand controls, bent to kiss him good night, and watched him maneuver in. A coolness had descended on the night, and as he drove away I stood by myself on the sidewalk, sore hands rubbing my arms. A chill breeze whispered across my shoulders.

Autumn: I was too tired to resist the imagery. Change was about to hit me, and I feared that it would strip off my facade, leaving the bare branches of my life exposed. Things had been going well—I had cash in the bank, and a novel that was going to be featured in the city's upcoming book festival. I even had a man who loved me. Yet once Luke left, I knew what I would see: the cobbled-together, freelance quality of my existence. I had a job scrabbling for legal piece-work. I had a lover who drove away at night. I had a room in the house that would soon be empty.

I walked back through the gate. Near the house I stopped to pick up toys Luke had left outside. *Star Wars* action figures—Qui-Gon Jinn, Darth Maul, names I knew better than those of the Apostles—they were part of the arcana of childhood I had recently learned about. Like knowing that, of the objects a little boy will stick up his nose, chopsticks look worse than M&M's but are easier to extract.

I tilted my head back. The stars were a wet blur in the sky. It was a kid's trick: Let the tears run back into the tear ducts. *I'm not crying, no, ma'am. Just looking for airplanes, Aunt Evvie.*

"Damn," I said, and walked back inside with my eyes streaming.

In the morning I said nothing to Luke about Tabitha, not wanting to unsettle him before school. He roused slowly, sparking up only when he saw his hair

in the mirror. I heard, "Oh, man, it's all scribbled."
It was a semiregular crisis. Brushing failed, and I had
to dunk his head under the tap. Out the door late, we
were still a block from school when the bell rang. He
broke into a sprint, mouth set, backpack bouncing,
and ran through the gate.

I spent the morning researching cases for an appel-
late brief I had been hired to write, chasing precedents
until the Westlaw search engine told me I had cornered the big ones. Several times I tried to reach my
brother, without success. I also phoned Cottage Hospital to ask about the church intruder's condition. They
gave me no information, not even the man's name.
That made me think his chances were poor.

Feeling itchy, I drove downtown to the Santa Barbara Public Library. I wanted to reconnoiter the Remnant, to scout Tabitha's new . . . What were they, soul
mates? Puppeteers? When she came at me, I wanted
to know whom I was facing.

The library was an airy Spanish-style building across
the street from the courthouse. Outside it, a banner
advertised the Santa Barbara Book Festival, a thought
that cheered me. But, scrolling through *News-Press*
back issues on microfiche, I found little cheery information about the Remnant.

The church, I learned, was just five years old. Before
then Peter Wyoming had run a carpet-cleaning business. Hearing the call to the ministry, he sold Spruce
Steam-Clean, started booing nonfundamentalist views
in public, and attracted followers—including a wife.
A weddings notice announced, *Peter Wyoming Weds
Chenille Krystall.* It was quite a name, and, from the
photo, she was quite a bride, stout and triumphant in
a virgin-white Stetson. It was the choir soloist, she of
the cool dabbing cloth and the shit-kicker cowboy
boots. Other recent stories covered Remnant protests
at the funerals of a Hindu coed who had been thrown
from a horse, and a gay man murdered during the

summer. The list of their protests read like a litany: *Resent, the End Is Near*. It wasn't much for me to go on.

Leaving the library, I crossed the street to look in on *Gaul v. Beowulf's Books* at the courthouse. Skip Hinkel, Priscilla Gaul's attorney, was pacing the courtroom, questioning a man from the California Department of Fish and Game. Asking, "What microbes does a ferret's mouth harbor?" "What's the PSI its jaws can administer?" Saying, "The ferrets involved in this case came from a Vancouver animal shelter—are Canadian ferrets especially ferocious?" Jesse was leaning his forehead on his hands, looking as if he'd had a long day already.

On the way home I spun the radio dial, hoping for the Dixie Chicks, but all I heard were reports about the beached gray whale. One station was mourning the beast's death, another discussing the logistics of removing it from the pricy shoreline property where it was decaying. They had a deejay at the beach. He sounded as if he were covering the *Hindenburg* explosion.

"It's an incredible sight," he reported. "Have you seen it, Corky?"

"No, Adam, but I'm planning to come down right after I go off the air."

Santa Barbara sometimes thought it was Monaco, but at times like this I knew I lived in the sticks.

At home I ate a tuna sandwich and tried another stream of inquiry, logging on to the Remnant's Web site. Its home page was eye shrapnel: spinning crosses, throbbing flames, multiple exclamation points. *Beast-Watch!!! Ho of the Month!!!* October's honoree was a U.S. senator.

One topic snagged my eye: *Big Brother is watching!!!*

Government computers, it warned, were recording all e-mail and phone conversations. Satellites were monitoring people's movements via anticounterfeiting strips in twenty-dollar bills. The purpose: to identify Christians, and, eventually, to track and capture them. The Remnant faithful should avoid phones, instant messaging, and the mail. Talking face-to-face was safest, and discretion was vital. Federal agents were adept at penetration. Confide only in a few other trusted church members. That way, even if part of the Remnant was compromised, it would not destroy the whole. No one could wipe them out.

I rubbed my forehead. This smelled like leaderless resistance, the paramilitary strategy fashioned by rightist Christian Patriots and antigovernment militias. The theory held that "resistance groups" shouldn't train a combat force, but should create tactical cells, small groups that planned and acted in isolation, on their own initiative. There was to be no chain of command, and thus no way to kill the Hydra by cutting off one head. Terror would be the gift that kept on giving.

My suspicions deepened when I checked out the Web site's "Links" section. I skimmed through *The Christian Guide to Small Arms*, patriot manifestos, and conspiracy babblings, crossing onto the turf of the loners, the outsiders, the digital screamers, a territory of inchoate rage and belief in the rectifying power of kerosene mixed with ammonium nitrate fertilizer. It made sickening reading.

The Remnant was planning something. But what, and when? I wondered if the church really advocated leaderless resistance. The strategy was not solely defensive. It granted cells the freedom to attack at will.

I logged off. Sat for a minute, my anxieties twisting and tautening. Thought, Screw it; this isn't helping anything.

I headed across the lawn and knocked on Nikki's kitchen door. She was home, having shut her art gallery for the week. She was sitting at the butcher block table, answering sympathy cards, looking wan in a bright, oversize Big Dog T-shirt that stretched across her belly. Bare of the elaborate silver jewelry she loved to wear, she seemed silent. I missed the *ting* of her bracelets.

I said, "How about taking a walk on the beach?"

At Arroyo Burro we walked barefoot on the wet sand, below a tall cliff. The waves ran cold across our ankles. A lone surfer sculpted turns on a glittering curl of water. The day looked polished, pure blue, and for a long while we were silent.

My worries about the Remnant refocused, from the elusive *what* to the confounding *why*. Why had they developed a hysterical cosmology? Was it grievance or gullibility? Were their lives so dull that they couldn't get their kicks from line dancing or whitewater rafting, but had to declare themselves the focal point of destiny?

Nikki said, "Mom hated the beach; did you know? She grew up on a tropical island, lived here twenty-five years, and could not abide the very idea of sand."

She smiled as she said it. We began reminiscing about Claudine, remembering her quirks and wit, her lack of bitterness after contracting AIDS, during a late-life relationship with an old flame from Haiti. Eventually Nikki began replaying the funeral, in detail. I knew she needed to hold on to it. But when she began talking about the protesters I fell quiet. She looked at me.

"You're awfully far away. Something going on?"

I started to shake my head, but she pointed at my hands—the cuts—and raised an eyebrow. "Dish it. I could use the distraction."

She listened with amazement and consternation. "Does Tabitha have spiders loose in her head? Male bashing during a divorce I could see, but joining a sect that says her man is Satan's toady—that's extreme."

The Remnant's antimilitary slant, I said, was one
thing that must have drawn her to the group. Another
was Pastor Pete's theory about end-time hoaxes.

Tabitha's mother, SueJudi Roebuck, had belonged
to a church that expected the Rapture to occur on
Pentecost 2000. When it didn't, her ecstasy shattered
into despair. Feeling betrayed and spiritually un-
moored, she spiraled into a depression from which she
never escaped. To Tabitha, a diabolical plot must have
seemed a compelling explanation for her mother's
despondency.

"But Peter Wyoming has inverted reality," I said.
"The fact that the world hasn't ended means that it's
about to. Complete normality proves the existence of
a demonic conspiracy."

"They're paranoid, Ev. That's how paranoids think."

"Absence of evidence equals proof. The silence
howls at them."

"Silence doesn't always mean inaction, though. Ever
hear the term 'cover-up'? And don't be so quick to
dismiss conspiracy theorists. They question authority,
and that's good. You want people doubting government spinmeisters and slick corporate mouthpieces."

"The voice crying in the wilderness."

"You got it. Peter Wyoming may sound whack, saying anthrax inoculations are part of the devil's end-
game, but don't take the Pentagon at face value. You
really think troops are just being protected against tomorrow's holy man with a missile launcher and a vial
of spores? In the fifties the CIA experimented on GIs
with LSD. And the army sprayed bacteria into the
air over San Francisco, they said to see how effective
biological warfare would be. Right. Warfare by whom,
against whom? It was American citizens who got
sick." She pursed her lips. "Pastor Pete didn't invent
Black Ops."

She got this streak from her late father, a Marxist
professor of politics. No matter how distracted or be-

reaved she was, I could always count on Nikki to back-
hand the conventional wisdom. It was one of her most
endearing traits.

"Besides, paranoia gets the blood flowing and lets
little people feel larger than life," she said. "Imagine
how important Tabitha must feel—expecting a global
cataclysm to detonate, with her new tribe at ground
zero."

"Armageddon's a real confidence booster. I never
looked at it that way."

"The Apocalypse. When you think about it, it's a
thrilling thought."

Taken aback, I stopped walking.

She said, " 'The present sky and earth are destined
for fire, and are only being reserved until Judgment
Day so that all sinners may be destroyed.' "

"Honey, sit down and put your head between
your knees."

"Therefore . . . 'What we are waiting for is what he
promised: the new heavens and new earth, the place
where righteousness will be at home.' " Sly look. "My
pop wrote a book on concepts of utopia. *Destined for
Fire*. Atheist perspective, but he got the title from
the Bible."

She turned and walked back toward me. "Evan, the
end of days doesn't mean the demolition of Earth—it
means the overthrow of the world order. The New
Jerusalem, that's a synonym for Up the Revolution,
baby. We're talking about the dawning of an age
where justice rules, and where there's no poverty, no
suffering, no death. And that, you'd better believe, is
one powerful idea."

I waited a beat. "Presuming you're a true believer."

"When it's your apocalypse, you're always the true
believer. That's the point. And everybody you hate is
gone, toasted in the cleansing fire."

Water licked her ankles and retreated. "But the
Apocalypse isn't about payback; it's about hope. It says

no matter how rotten things get, God's gonna win in the end. Good is stronger than evil." She paused, holding her hands out. "So, what are you afraid of?"

She had me. But to drive home the point she set hands on hips and said with comic exaggeration, "Don't you love Jesus, girl?"

Her brown eyes pinned me. She expected a serious answer. All my snappy comebacks wilted unsaid, and I looked down at the sand.

After a few seconds she waved a hand dismissively and started walking again. "Aw, you just can't see the bright side because you spent so much time creating catastrophes for your book."

My novel *Lithium Sunset* was set in a bleak future after a world war. A totalitarian army had conquered the heroine's people. Survivors on both sides had suffered flash burns and genetic damage in the thermonuclear exchange. Mutation and ritual suicide were commonplace.

"Mass destruction without purpose—that's a pop culture apocalypse, Ev."

"Oh, cut me to the bone."

"Your radioactive prairie has survivors, though. Your novel isn't about annihilation; it's about tenacity. Yeah, the characters are screwed up, they drink too much and listen to goddamned Patsy Cline music, but they hang in and keep on fighting. You like to write about people who have their back up against it. Nine hundred megatons of bomb craters across the landscape, that's just backstory."

I smiled. It was good to hear spirit in her voice.

"Face it, woman—sci-fi lets you imagine whole new worlds, and that's the buzz. 'In the beginning, God thought—*Hot shit! What'll I cook up today*?' Quite a kick, huh? You love possibility and creation. You're just too dark-minded to realize it."

"So, I'm the Gloomy Gus here, and the Remnant are the real optimists?"

"Ironic, isn't it."

I put an arm around her shoulders.

She said, "Of course, Pop's favorite quote was from Pascal—'Men never do evil so completely and cheerfully as when they do it from religious conviction.' Watch out for the event that convinces the Remnant it's *now*. They'll be joyful when they pull the trigger."

And, like that, she took a juddering breath and started crying. After a minute she said, "Mom should be here, tossing in some choice comments." She rubbed her eyes roughly with the back of her hand. "God sure lets the dog turds fly against the fan sometimes."

We rounded a point. To our stupefaction, ahead on the sand, surrounded by beachcombers, civil engineers, and a television news crew, was the whale. It dominated the beach, rising like a cartilaginous gray pudding, ringed by kelp and barking dogs.

A moment later the wind shifted. The stench hit, pungent and greasy, and the next thing I knew Nikki was bent over, throwing up. When she straightened again she said, "The Apocalypse is upon Santa Barbara. Live at five, on CNN."

At three I walked Luke home from school. Back home we sat on the lawn eating a snack, with sunlight speckling our shoulders through the greenery, and I broke the news.

"I have to tell you something important. Your mom has moved back to Santa Barbara."

He stopped sipping from his juice box and looked at me, brown eyes huge.

"She's living at your grandma's old house, up in the mountains."

He sat as still as glass, his colt's legs sticking out from his baggy shorts, looking as if he had heard something growling in the bushes. "Is Dad going to live there too?"

"No, he's still moving to China Lake. They aren't getting back together, bud."

Seeing a thousand-yard stare on a six-year-old is deeply disconcerting. I rubbed his shoulder, trying to bring him back. Slowly his lips parted and he said, "But she won't let me bring Teddy. I can't go there."

"What?"

The juice box dropped from his hands and dribbled onto the grass. He began kneading his fingers together. "She doesn't like my bear because he has Dad's patch sewed on him. The skull makes her mad."

It was true; Tabitha hated Brian's squadron patch, a death's-head with red eyes and a dagger clenched in its teeth. But I didn't understand what Luke was saying. His neck and shoulders were rigid, his fingers working painfully. His mind was grinding at an idea I couldn't reach.

"She won't let Teddy come, and I can't leave him here by himself. Don't make me stay at her house."

"No, Luke—oh, sweetheart, no." I pulled him into my arms. "You aren't going to her house. You're staying with me until I take you to your dad's."

Evan, you dumb ass. I held him, feeling his fingers continue to writhe, wanting to kick myself.

He said, "Promise?"

"Cross my heart."

But he had trouble believing it. He made me repeat the promise, insisting that I add "hope to die" and "stick a needle in my eye." And a while later, when I looked out the kitchen window, I saw him heading for the flower beds, carrying a handful of LEGO astronauts and a croquet mallet.

I phoned my brother again, this time reaching him at the base airfield. He answered the phone smartly. "Delaney."

"Hi, bro."

"Ev! Is my little man ready to move to China Lake?"

He started describing his new house, Luke's room, the school, and telling me how the town had grown.

We had lived in China Lake as teenagers, when our father was stationed at the naval base doing weapons research.

"It's cosmopolitan," he said. "It has traffic lights. Bet you can't wait to get back."

"Don't need to; I relive high school every time I open the oven."

I would rather have pounded tacks into my tongue than tell him. But some things I do straight: drink, sex, bad news.

"Brian—Tabitha's in Santa Barbara. I've seen her, and she as much as said she wants Luke."

Flat quiet on the line. "Not gonna happen. Next." Another pause. "What else? You're tweaked—I can hear it. Something's squirrelly."

"She's got religion, and I mean in the worst way."

Five seconds of silence. "Fuck me."

I could hear men's voices in the background, and the scratch of aircraft engines. "I'll have to talk about this later. I have a briefing," he said. "Listen. She doesn't see him, she doesn't speak to him, she doesn't touch him. Understand?"

"Absolutely."

"And, Evan . . ."

"Yeah?"

Loud talk behind him, as a jet took off. "How does she look?"

What could I expect? He had loved her a long time. I said, "She looks reborn."

4

The book festival kicked off that Wednesday, under harlequin-bright banners fluttering on lampposts along State Street. The city cooed about it with restrained zest. Enthusiasm would have seemed crass to Santa Barbarans, who cultivate casualness as exactingly as the Japanese cultivate bonsai trees. Still, I expected the festival to be an antidote to my anxieties, a glass of emotional champagne. I was scheduled to read and sign copies of my novel at Beowulf's Books, and let me tell you, applause makes me feel like a goddess. A mini Festival of Evan—bring it on.

Beowulf's lacked chain-store slickness. The staff favored berets and clogs, and the front counter was plastered with flyers promoting candlelight marches to save various outcast groups. "Liberate California's Ferrets," notably. The front window contained a crop of science-fiction titles, with a sign saying, MEET AUTHORS HERE.

Inside the door, a table displayed copies of my book, *Lithium Sunset*. I stood admiring it. The cover showed the heroine's strong face, a shattered landscape, and my name. I breathed in and felt famous.

At the back of the store I saw Beowulf's coffee bar, scene of the showdown between the ferrets and Priscilla Gaul. Observing me, an elderly woman approached. It was Anita Krebs, the owner.

"The security firm wanted to install TV cameras to catch the thief. Orwellians. Completely unnecessary— Pip and Oliver caught that sneak red-handed. So to speak," she said. "How are you, dear girl?"

Anita had a reputation as a peppery iconoclast. A leathery woman with a skullcap of white hair, she wore pendulous turquoise jewelry and an extravagance of fuchsia lipstick. She took my arm and led me toward some chairs set up for the reading.

"I delved into your novel again last night. It really is marvelous. Your concept so intrigues me, that tyranny forces its opponents toward both tactical ingenuity and aesthetic rigidity."

That sounded ostentatious, but I was pleased that she had looked beyond the plot, about the girl warrior who fights bug-eyed mutants.

"And the male character's eroticism—well! I quite fancied him." She gestured to the chairs. "Good luck. Sell a lot of books."

I was pumped, ready to go, and after she introduced me I read the scene where heroine meets hero. They're in a seedy tavern; she's a disillusioned guerrilla, he's a member of the resistance. She rebuffs him. He suffers brutal injury saving her life. The scene had heat, in the form of sexual tension and homicide, and I gave it all I had.

The audience liked it. Bookworms, fans of the genre, and my neighbors, they clustered afterward at a table where I sat to sign their copies. I acted charming and witty, and as other purchasers came along I floated through the afternoon in an expanding bubble of self-regard. When Nikki walked in, I thought it was the exclamation point on the day. She had on chartreuse maternity overalls, bright camouflage for her grief, yet she raised a camera and started snapping flash photos, saying, "Lord, oh, Lord, it's really you. Evan Delaney. I want to have your baby. After this one, I mean—this one belongs to Stephen King."

I felt *cool*.

It was just after she left, however, that the line formed. A young woman wearing fatigue shorts, a tank top, and a daisy in her hair—Lara Croft meets Joan Baez—came forward clutching *Lithium Sunset* to her breast.

She said, "I don't know how you did it. It's like Rowan"—the heroine—"is me. It's like you know my heart and my entire life."

This far exceeded the praise I'd been getting. I hoped she meant the heroine's can-do spirit, not her psychokinetic powers or her training in explosives. "Thanks."

She said, "I mean, I'm freaking. I totally, totally love this book. You're writing a sequel, right? Because Rowan rescues her lover, I know it. She *has* to."

The woman behind her, wearing shorts and a rude sunburn, said, "I want to know what planet the story takes place on."

"Kansas," I said.

Daisy-hair turned to the woman. "What *planet*? Do you even know what the novel is about?"

"The back cover says, right here," Sunburn said. " 'For Rowan Larkin, surrender couldn't end the war.' "

"No, it's *about* the ways society punishes people who don't conform. Why do you think Rowan gets banished for refusing to become a collaborator?"

A man in a Dodgers cap said, "Hey. Some of us haven't read the book yet."

"Come on, let me sign that for you." I agreed with her comments but wanted her to quiet down. "What's your name?"

"It's Glory." To the sunburned woman she said, "I mean, why else do you think Rowan kills the rebel commander?"

The man threw up his hands and walked away. "That's it. I want a refund."

I said, "No!" He kept walking.

A new voice said, "It's about staying true to your cause in the face of temptation. Right?"

Her cowboy hat was baby blue. Her small gray eyes were expressionless. Her analysis was off-kilter, and I knew, staring at the clay-colored braid hanging down her back, that she wasn't going to shut up about it. It was Chenille Wyoming.

To the crowd in general I said, "I'm glad you all liked the novel. But if you give away the ending I won't sign your books."

"I ain't giving nothing away. I'm letting everyone know you all got it wrong."

I had signed Glory's copy, and Chenille put her hand on the book to keep me from handing it to the girl. She told her, "Truck's out back. Go on." Without a word, Glory walked away. Others followed, Remnant members who had quietly positioned themselves around the bookstore. Chenille remained in front of me. Above the hanging moon of her double chin, her expression was placid. Her eyes were the lusterless gray of slate, small and stony.

My anger rose more quickly than my guard, and I took the bait. "Wrong. How's that?"

"Well." She whipped open a little spiral-bound notebook. "Let's start with that book on the best-seller table, *Cyber-Fables*. It's about hacker warlocks with magic only works over the Internet. Ha. Like Satan ain't been wireless since day one."

She pointed to the front window. "This book up there, it has people that change sex, shape-shifters. Now, you tell me where in scripture that's at. Another one has aliens from a place where they don't *die*. That is purely ridiculous. Death, that's the Lord's choosing time—else why do they say, 'Kill 'em all and let God sort 'em out?'"

My head was pounding. I said, "I can't remember, is that from Ecclesiastes, or *Full Metal Jacket*?" She colored. I handed her my book. "Thanks for stopping by. It's been a treat."

She shook it at me. "I ain't even started on you, missy. Look here—page one, nuclear holocaust. How stupid is that? Whole idea's obsolete. We know things ain't gonna happen that way. Then there's your time line. It's a far future—what, five, six thousand years? That's so optimistic it's just plain silly."

Anita Krebs approached the table, smiling thinly. "Madam, would you mind—"

"Lady, I ain't talking to you."

I said, "The jig's up, Anita. Scripture Cop's got us."

Chenille slapped the book cover with the back of her hand. "This story, it's fake. You just made it up. There's only one book tells us the truth, and that's the Bible. This"—she held up my book—"this ain't nothing but a lie."

I put down my pen. "Did you know that you have your head on inside out?"

"Don't mock me."

"Tell me the truth—how pessimistic am I supposed to be? Do I have time to order a pizza before the plane leaves the gate?"

"It don't matter. You ain't coming."

"But I already requested a window seat."

She stared at me. "Luke should not be in your presence."

I knocked the chair over backward banging to my feet. "Get out."

She turned on the heels of her baby-blue boots and started walking, an imperious stare on her face. I barged behind, trailing her outside.

Without looking at me she said, "He is a special little angel, far more precious than you can ever understand. Do you think we will let the dragon devour him?"

"*We?* There's no *we* here. You have nothing to do with my family."

She looked my way at last, appraising me as though

I were pathetic and dim-witted beyond belief. She began humming "The Battle Hymn of the Republic," and walked away.

I stood for a moment on the broad sidewalk, with shoppers and tourists rustling past me. Furious, I strode back inside. When I passed the display of my books I swung at it, smacking the whole thing down.

Anita walked up, fists on hips. "Later, you can explain why you did that. But right now will you finish signing for the people who waited through that show?"

I looked around. Everyone was staring at me.

The woman with the sunburn said, "Honey, I'm hooked. Give me two copies."

"Forget writing," said the man behind her. "Start videotaping your life. This beats the dead whale, hands down."

By the time I apologized and made nice and tried to snuff my instant reputation for being a stick of human dynamite, I was late picking up Luke from school. I parked across the street from the campus and trotted up the sidewalk, hearing the musical buzz of children's voices. Slowing at a crosswalk, I tried to spot Luke through the chain-link fence. He knew to wait on the playground until I arrived. Seeing kids swinging on the monkey bars resurrected sensations of calloused palms and skinned knees, the exhilaration of being six. I tried harder not to look rattled and angry.

I couldn't decide whether Chenille had come to Beowulf's to catalog books for burning, or simply to harass me. I heard her voice, her peculiar ungrammatical formality—King James English filtered through the trailer park—talking about Luke in terms both pointed and oblique. My head began pounding again. *I ain't even started on you, missy.*

A truck stopped to let me cross, a green Dodge pickup with oversize tires. Though it had a shiny urban-redneck look, four people and a dog sat in the back, pure *Grapes of Wrath*. As I passed, it accelerated with a muscular grunt.

In the truck bed sat a moonfaced teenager with a ponytail and a miniature-rose mouth. She was looking at the playground. I froze. It was Shiloh, the Remnant's designated denouncer, and she wasn't the only one watching the playground. All the Joads were.

The truck was cruising slowly along the fence. I started running after it.

For a few seconds I gained on it, before its engine blatted and it pulled away sharply. I stood blinking, stumbling to clarify what I'd seen in the cab: coils of auburn hair and a woman's slender arm. The fragmented image assembled itself into Tabitha. I tried to swear, but my throat was too dry.

"Scare tactics," Jesse said.

"Diversionary tactics." I flipped the car's sun visor down as I curved west and accelerated uphill on West Camino Cielo. "Chenille Wyoming was trying to keep me at Beowulf's by causing a scene. She wanted me to get to the school late."

Chenille—and Tabitha—didn't know that Luke had been told to remain on school grounds until I arrived, no matter what. Perhaps they had expected him to walk home alone, or to stand outside, looking around forlornly, until someone called his name and waved to him, beckoning him toward the smiling faces in the pickup truck. . . . Fear trickled cold down my back.

We raced up the road, past blue-gray chaparral and sandstone boulders. Jesse's hair whipped in the cool breeze flowing through the windows. He had on a black Pendleton shirt and khaki jeans over the long brace he wore on his right leg when he walked. It was early Wednesday evening.

"Something else bothers me," he said. "Chenille didn't have to read *Lithium Sunset* to cause a scene. She's taking a close interest in you."

But I didn't have time to think about it. We turned up Tabitha's driveway, bounced along the rutted dirt path, and pulled up to the house, noticing that the lawn had been mowed, weeds pulled, potted begonias set by the door.

I said, "Set phasers on be-a-bastard."

When I rang the bell, the door opened with a creak. Tabitha stood in the doorway, eyes sprung wide, pressing an artist's pencil to her lips. Looking elegant for a night home alone with the sketch pad, in a rose cardigan and long floral skirt that draped her figure.

"We need to talk about Luke," I said. Her eyes flicked beyond me, to the Explorer, and I added, "I didn't bring him. You aren't going to see him. You blew it today."

The pencil tapped against her lips. "What's Jesse doing here?"

"He's with me."

He was swinging toward us on his aluminum crutches. She stared at him. *Tap, tap, tap.* The pencil, and now her bare, painted toes.

"Tabitha," I said, astonished that I couldn't hold her attention. "If you or anybody from the Remnant gets within sight of Luke's school again, the principal will call the police. If you follow him, or try to speak to him, I will file a restraining order against you. Do you understand?"

She blinked, and tapped, stippling the pencil with claret-colored lipstick. Finally, as if just now hearing me, she said, "You can't stop a mother from seeing her own child."

"In this circumstance? You bet I can."

The pencil stopped. "I didn't think you could be so vengeful."

"Excuse me?"

"All I wanted was one glimpse of him, just to see with my own eyes that he's okay. One tiny glimpse, but even that's too much for you to stand."

Blood was pounding in my ears. "Can the act. You

walked out on Luke. Brian has sole custody, and from here on, you need a judge's permission to see him. And of course he's okay. Now."

She crossed her arms. "How would you know that, for sure? You're not his mother. You didn't carry him or nurse him. You're . . . day care."

Why didn't she just stab me between the eyes with that pencil? I stood there, hurt and speechless. Wishing Jesse would come and back me up—but he was standing by the garage, gazing in.

A shadow appeared behind her in the doorway, a man. It was Peter Wyoming.

"Miss Delaney," he said. "Tabitha? Invite her in."

My eyes widened, but hers jumped. She was nervous, I realized, to the point of twitching. Stiffly she said, "Won't you join us?"

I held back, looking toward Jesse, but he shook his head. Something outside had caught his attention. I heard music in the backyard, and women's voices. More people were here than I had imagined.

"Come see what Tabitha's working on. It's magnificent." Wyoming motioned me toward the living room, smoothly changing the subject. I wondered if the unexpected civility was a ploy, or simply his offstage persona. His craggy face wore a mild look. His blue and green plaid shirt gave off a *Father Knows Best* aura.

I walked in and stopped short. The walls were covered with drawings: black and white, a stark fantasia of biblical retribution that overpowered the room.

He gestured to a comic strip on the drawing table. "Edifying, isn't it?"

Hardly. Titled "HELL-o-ween," its illustrations juxtaposed satanists strapping a virgin down on an altar, and Caucasian tots dressing up for trick-or-treating.

He waved a rough hand at the drawings. "Look at the power in her work. It comes from the purity of her hand. Her line here, it's so clean."

He touched a drawing of a little girl, hands filled

with candy bars, carelessly dashing in front of a speeding car. The sparkles on her fairy princess gown
couldn't save her. The final sketch showed her huddled in a rocky corner of hell, costume in rags, flames
strafing her limbs.

Clean? The cartoons were grisly, the parallel with
the pumpkin-truck accident heartless. And Wyoming's
enthusiasm for the death and darkness in the drawings
seemed vaguely . . . pornographic.

He said, "You look shocked. She looks shocked,
Tabitha."

Though still jittery, she was pie-eyed, lapping up
his praise.

He wrapped an arm around her shoulder. "Bull's-
eye! You turned this around and rammed it right back
down the devil's throat, little lady."

As she flushed and bit her lip, it came to me: Her
cartoon was the Remnant's riposte to the pumpkin
onslaught outside their church.

"You believe the devil assaulted you the other night
with holiday decorations?"

"Pagans hold that jack-o'-lanterns are the repositor-
ies of damned souls," he said. "You don't think we'll
take that lying down."

"My God, what do you do when confronted with a
pumpkin pie? Drive a stake through it?"

"Halloween is a doorway to evil, an aperture
through which Satan attacks the physical world."

Tabitha said, "It gives him a fingerhold on children's
souls. We try to stop it."

"You're going to hand this out to kids?" I pointed
to the comic strip. "Do you think this will somehow
make you look like a caring parent?"

Wyoming said, "You're upset about her absence
from Luke's life. But that's all ending now."

With diminishing patience, I turned to him. "Will
you excuse us for a few minutes? I need to speak to
Tabitha alone."

Apparently people didn't ask Pastor Pete to leave a room. He raised his eyebrows at Tabitha, holding my uppityness against her. Her pale cheeks rouged.

Tilting his head toward the kitchen, he said, "Tell you what. Be a lamb and fix us up a plate of nibbles. There's a good girl."

Nodding, she fled.

In the backyard the music intensified. I glanced out a sliding glass door and saw the baton twirlers rehearsing. Barking commands at them was Shiloh, wearing a huge pink bow in her hair and a coach's whistle around her neck.

Wyoming stepped toward me. "I know you don't believe a lick of what I'm saying. But I'd like a favor. Put a stopper in the wisecracks long enough for me to ask you a question." His voice radiated a quiet heat. He said, "Have you ever confronted evil? I mean truly, personally, felt its touch?"

I backed up.

"Ah. You know what I'm talking about; I can see it on your face. Someone once harmed you physically, I'd wager."

He nodded, seeing that he had guessed right. It disconcerted and angered me.

I said, "What do you know about evil? Does it confront you regularly?"

"Yes." He sounded surprised that I would even raise the question. "Every time I speak out against depravity. It tries to stop me. When I protest at funerals I can sense it—a force, a blackness, a"—he sought for the word—"a malignancy. Of course I confront evil. I can feel it in the *air*. Spreading, coiling around me, touching me . . ."

Behind his pale eyes, emotion cracked open. For a moment I saw a bottomless, heartbreaking terror.

"*Every time*. It lurks, trying to slip past my defenses. . . ."

He swallowed, seeming pained, and shook his head.

Spreading. Did he actually fear getting AIDS? Then his lizard eyes recovered, constricting to cool focus.

"Evil's an intimate thing, isn't it?" he said. "More intimate than love, so much more intimate than sex. It's the entrapment. Remember how cornered you felt when you realized, *This is really happening to me.* The thick throat, the quaking in your bowels . . ."

The setting sun cast orange light onto the living room walls, giving a sense of vicious animation to the drawings tacked up all around me.

"Hold on to that feeling. *Know* it. Because the evil that harmed you hasn't gone away. It's out there, waiting. And it's hungry. It lusts to consume your body and your soul. So that when you're dead, it will possess you. Forever." His voice quieted to a hiss. "Now, Miss Delaney—now can you start to see the true force of the storm that's coming?"

A deep, inarticulate fear seeped through me. I looked away from him, out the back window, and saw Jesse standing at the corner of the lawn. He looked toward the house with an odd expression on his face.

Breaking the spell, Wyoming said, "Who's that?"

"My boyfriend."

"He has to leave." Abruptly, he started toward the sliding glass door.

Perplexed, shaken, I said, "Never mind, we'll both leave," and strode outside, desperate for fresh air, gooseflesh on my arms. The twirlers were acting flighty, like corraled horses before a lightning storm. Getting closer, I saw that they looked identical: blond, fit, with the artfulness that develops in girls who vie for teen trophies—a blue ribbon, prom queen, the quarterback. They were triplets. Shiloh blew the whistle and shouted, "Drop and give me thirty!" As they went down into push-ups, she marched toward Jesse.

"The girls are having a closed practice." Her tone was peremptory.

"For what?" he said. "NATO maneuvers?"

Wyoming walked up behind us. "She's trying to be polite here. But you're disturbing these young ladies."

Jesse said, "I thought disturbances were your department, Reverend Wyoming."

He looked at the crutches. "The sight of feebleness is always disturbing."

Jesse didn't move an inch, but I flinched.

"These young women shine with a strength that glorifies the Lord. It's a sign of their virtue and purity," Wyoming said. "But weaklings are a sign of decay, of sinfulness punished in our midst."

Jesse shifted his weight. He was taller than Wyoming, six foot one, and looked down at him. "I guess when you're used to picking on the dead at funerals, a live target must look scary."

"If you sow corruption of the heart, you will reap corruption of the flesh. The rot will erupt." He pointed at Jesse. "Whatever it is you have done, you should think hard about repenting it. Unless you truly want to go to hell."

"Been there, done that, got the wheelchair."

With the tinkle of ice cubes, Tabitha came outside, carrying a tray that held tall glasses of iced tea and Ritz crackers decorated with squirt-cheese crosses.

"Here we are," she said in her anxious-to-please voice. "Pastor Pete?"

He turned and saw her proffering the tray. "What's this?"

She lifted it toward him. He grimaced and twisted his head. "Take it away!"

He shoved it and the tray flipped. Glasses and crackers flew, splashing Tabitha and raining on the grass. Everyone stood motionless with shock and embarrassment, with music from Shiloh's boom box rattling the mountain air.

Wyoming said, "Get rid of it!"

Chest heaving, cheeks blotchy, Tabitha dropped to

her knees and began gathering up the debris. I said, "Jesse, let's get out of here."

A voice called from the house: "Peter! Peter Wyoming!"

A baby-blue cowboy hat appeared at the sliding glass door. Wyoming wiped his forehead with the back of his hand, jaw muscles popping. Chenille called him again. Nostrils wide, mouth white, he stalked toward the house, muttering, "Rot. The rot will erupt. . . ." Spinning back around, he shouted at Jesse, "Rot! You want proof? Look at Stephen Hawking. Scientist, and he paid for it!"

Jesse pivoted and headed across the lawn. When I murmured good-bye to Tabitha, she didn't look up.

Rounding the side of the house, we saw a blue pickup truck, baby blue, parked next to my car. Through the front window of the house we saw the Wyomings, Chenille circling Pete, talking and gesturing. On the front step stood Curt Smollek, the Remnant's crew-cut, pock-faced bully, arms crossed like a bouncer. I climbed into the Explorer. Soon Jesse pulled himself in beside me. He slammed the door and stared straight ahead.

I said, "He's seriously disturbed."

"No shit."

He was quiet for a moment. Absorbing, I feared, Wyoming's bigotry. But he said, "Know what's in the garage? Stockpiles of food in crates stacked to the roof."

I hesitated, key in the ignition. "Creamed corn and SPAM?"

"And beef jerky, three hundred boxes of Tampax, and a glass-topped freezer full of Tater Tots and Reddiwip. Plus something called the Revelation checklist. A hundred items you tick off whenever biblical prophecy comes true," he said. "It's a countdown."

"And?"

"Ninety-five were checked off."

Unexpectedly, someone tapped on his window—one more surprise, cherry on the weirdness sundae. Huddled outside was Glory, my fan from the book signing.

Her voice was hushed. "What I said at Beowulf's, I want you to know, I really meant it. I love your book. Totally, and that's the truth."

"Right. Gotcha."

"You have to believe me." She grabbed the window frame. "Please, Evan—"

"What's going on?" I said, nodding toward the house. "Why's everybody so excited?"

"Haven't you heard? He died."

Jesse said, "Who?"

She glanced around, fearful. "The crazy man, the one who broke into church and tried to attack Pastor Pete. He died this afternoon."

Jesse knocked on the door at seven the next morning. He always knocked before coming in, though he had a key. It was talismanic, a ritual. Sharp light was painting the grass and yellow hibiscus to a polychrome shine. The sky was smooth with promise, the air soft. I was still in my pj's, pouring my first cup of coffee, and Luke was sound asleep. Jesse was dressed for court in a black suit, white dress shirt, and royal blue tie. He rolled in and tossed the *News-Press* on the dining table.

"Local section, page one. They identify the guy." His tone said this was going to surprise me.

I found it below the fold: "Doctor's Injuries Fatal."

A Santa Barbara physician died yesterday of injuries sustained when he was hit by a truck while crossing Ortega Street. Neil Jorgensen, 51, succumbed to massive head injuries. . . .

"Jorgensen." I looked up, startled. "The plastic surgeon?"

"Seems like yesterday he was threatening to rip off your kneecaps."

Neil Jorgensen was a cosmetic sculptor to the posh and aging. A busy and expensive surgeon, he was also arrogant and incompetent—a terrible combination to let loose on your face with a scalpel. I had once served him with a summons for malpractice. He had taken it badly.

I rubbed my forehead. "I didn't recognize him. Not for a second."

"You said the man looked sick."

"Yeah, but Jorgensen . . . That time I served him, he called me the full spectrum of obscenities, up into the ultraviolet. How could I go through a plate-glass window with him and not have a clue?"

I recalled the feverish glow in his eyes, thinking about illnesses that could devastate a person's appearance. Cancer, or AIDS . . .

I said, "Something's screwy here."

"He probably agrees, being dead and all."

I gave him a look.

"Sorry, Ev. I know you tried to help him."

His remorse was for me, I knew, not for the late doctor. Jesse had an extremely pragmatic attitude toward sudden accidental death: Shit happens. Still, I wondered at the casual sharpness of his remark.

"Jorgensen's behavior makes no sense," I said. He had cared about only one thing: money. He ran patients through the operating theater like steaks through a meat saw to keep himself in Porsches. I had never heard about his being remotely religious or political. "What was he doing breaking into the Remnant's service?"

"I don't know."

Neither did the reporter who had written the story. The article did no more than quote hospital and police department statements. Suspecting that the Remnant's Web site might comment on Jorgensen's death, I flipped on my computer. I poured Jesse a cup of coffee and sat down at my desk. The Web site loaded.

UPDATE! FAGGOT DIES FOLLOWING DESECRATION ATTEMPT

A queer who tried to destroy the Remnant's sanctuary died yesterday. The rampage was stopped by courageous churchgoers, the queer ran away after his attack failed. Fleeing from horrified Christians, he collided head-on with a truck.

WHAT DID HE EXPECT?

"Surely, because you have defiled my sanctuary with all your detestable things and with all your abominations, therefore I will cut you down."

Jesse said, "Surprise, they trash the victim."

"Yeah, standard operating procedure." We looked at each other. "It doesn't scan, does it?"

The Remnant seemed delighted that Jorgensen had met his end. So why had Chenille and Pete been worked up about his death? The news had vexed them—and they had brought their pique into Tabitha's house. In fact, they had apparently taken over Tabitha's house.

The strangeness of it ate at me for most of the day. I worked downtown at the law library, distracted by everything: coins clanging into the photocopier, angst wafting from other lawyers in the room. Eventually I left and headed to the *News-Press* building in De la Guerra Plaza. I asked for Sally Shimada, the reporter who had filed the story on Jorgensen's death. Craving information, I hoped to get it from her, or to convince her to go after it.

Shimada came into the lobby with an athlete's long stride. She was young, with sorority-girl enthusiasm, trying to look sleek in her white turtleneck and paisley miniskirt. She had a glossy fall of black hair and angular features that were striking rather than pretty. Her handshake was firm.

I said, "I have some news that might interest you, about Neil Jorgensen's accident."

"You mean the Remnant's claiming he was gay?"

"No, another angle. An eyewitness account."

"Whose?"

"Mine."

Her face lit with an eager Miss California smile. This kid should never play poker. She said, "Come on back."

I went on the record. Sitting at Shimada's desk in the cluttered newsroom, I described the Remnant's church service, trying to impart the eeriness and alarm I had experienced, leading her to the moment Isaiah Paxton and Curt Smollek hauled me to the door, the moment when Jorgensen burst in. She was leaning toward me across the desk, eyes acute and unblinking. I paused, a long pause. "That's when Jorgensen started yelling."

Shimada spread her hands. "Yelling what?"

I waited, expecting that, like most reporters, she would fill the silence.

"Did he say anything specific?" she said. "Did he mention any names?"

"Like whose?"

"Mel Kalajian."

When I couldn't place it, she said, "Mel Kalajian, MD. He was murdered last summer. A gay man. The Remnant picketed his funeral."

Now I remembered reading about it. "Jorgensen didn't mention him. Why would he?"

"He was Jorgensen's medical partner. He was killed during a robbery at their offices in July, apparently when he caught some guy stealing drugs," she said. "He was also Jorgensen's lover."

I betrayed my surprise.

"It wasn't a secret," she said. "They weren't closeted, just sort of Republican about it. They wore Ralph Lauren and bought real estate together."

I considered it. "You think Jorgensen's grief overwhelmed him?"

"That's my take on it. He died because he finally found the strength to stand up to the Remnant. It's tragic."

She had already written the lead for her follow-up, I bet. She would play it for all the pathos and political correctness the story could offer. I dealt another card.

"How long did Jorgensen have? I mean, if he hadn't been hit by that truck."

Yes, playing poker would be a disaster for her. She leaned back, lips parting.

I said, "The hospital didn't tell you that he was ill?"

She blinked, looking as if she'd been caught with her skirt stuck in the waistband of her panty hose. I guessed that she hadn't spoken to anyone who had actually treated Jorgensen, but had written her story straight from a hospital press release.

"What about the paramedics?" I said. "Or his office? Nobody mentioned it?"

Her embarrassment was becoming palpable. She said, "What did he have?"

"I don't know."

"Then how can you say he was terminal?"

"You've never been around anyone who's seriously ill, have you?"

That was gratuitously rough, but I figured she needed a kick in the pants.

She picked up a pencil and started doodling on a notepad. Regaining her composure, she said, "You know, it's not every witness who shows up here asking to be interviewed. Exactly what are you after?"

"Off the record," I said, "I want to know what the Remnant is up to, so I can keep my nephew out of their path." She nodded, accepting it. "Listen, Sally. More is going on here than meets the eye. The Wyomings were really bent out of shape by the news of Jorgensen's death."

She stopped doodling. "Now, how do you know that?"

I stood up. "Check out what I've told you. If you think it's worth pursuing, call me. I'm in the book."

I saw myself out, gambling that I'd hear from her.

That evening Jesse and I took Luke out for tamales at Playa Azul and ice cream in Paseo Nuevo. Luke was gregarious, talking about school, and I ached at the thought of saying good-bye to this—to his classroom play-by-play, to the notes from his teacher that got squashed in the bottom of his backpack, to twenty other six-year-olds whose names I had never truly deciphered. Jesse listened, but seemed distant. When Luke was running up State Street ahead of us, rainbow sherbet dripping down his wrist, I asked what was bugging him.

He shrugged. "Work, tooth decay, the dumbing down of America."

"Pastor Pete?"

"Yeah, he's a piece of work. Mr. Virtue and Purity, protecting his über-twirlers from me. He's the kind who would have stoked the ovens at Buchenwald."

"Sorry I convinced you to go up there with me."

"Guilt—I knew it; you're having an episode. Quick, go bang your head against that wall."

I punched him on the arm. He said, "It could have been worse. He could have tried to heal me."

I touched his shoulder, stopping him. He wasn't an angry person, but with all the crap he had to contend with, the blues sometimes dogged him. Pastor Pete's taunts had, I thought, been one knock too many. People ribboned around us on the sidewalk. Gold light spilled from a nearby café, and Latin music pulsed through the air, cocky and sinuous. I took his face in my hands and kissed him.

"That's better," he said. "Don't worry about me. Feel culpable for something else. Ozone depletion."

When we returned to my house, he helped Luke pack his backpack for school the next day. Asking him, "Is that everything? Homework?" "Yep." Lunch? Yep. Dog biscuits? "We don't have a dog at school." "Right. Teacher biscuits?"

Luke laughed and pushed against Jesse's chest. Then his eyes rounded. "Wait. I have to show you my invention." He ran to his room. As he broke contact Jesse's energy seemed to dim, and I saw how tired he looked. He said, "I hope Brian realizes how completely goddamned lucky he is."

Just a moment later Sally Shimada phoned. "All right, I want to hear the rest of your story."

I perked up. "You found out what was wrong with Dr. Jorgensen."

"No, I found out that no one knows what was wrong with him. They're waiting for autopsy results. The coroner hasn't determined the cause of death yet."

"Your story said he died from massive head injuries."

"I may have drawn that conclusion prematurely," she admitted gamely. "Apparently the medical examiner thinks otherwise. It wasn't his injuries that killed him; it was something else. Something mysterious."

She sounded as if she had wandered into a Disney movie about a girl and her puppy solving the riddle of Spooky Gulch.

She said, "Want to hear the Remnant's comment on your eyewitness account?"

"The venom of asps is under my lips."

"Right! And I'm a media harlot, whelping false knowledge to the unsaved," she said. "I'm thinking about putting it on my letterhead."

I decided that I was starting to like Sally.

"Hey," she said, "a little bird told me that you and Jesse Blackburn are an item. Think you can get him to comment on today's story about the trial?"

"What story?"

I hadn't read anything in the paper except the article about Jorgensen. I found the local section, and there it was, top of page one. "Ferret Mauling Trial: Defense Attorney Has 'Secret Agenda.'"

"I'll call you back, Sally."

I hung up and looked at Jesse. Sardonic smile, weary eyes.

The attorney for the woman whose hand was bitten off by ferrets at Beowulf's Bookstore claimed yesterday that defense lawyer Jesse Blackburn is "biased" against his client. Skip Hinkel says that Blackburn humiliated Priscilla Gaul on the witness stand because he has "a secret agenda to promote possession of ferrets."

"Damn," I said.

Insists Hinkel, "I'm not saying the ferret lobby has paid him off, but I can't think of another reason for him, of all people, to be so rough on a handicapped woman."

"What a jerk." I tossed the paper down, thinking that Hinkel had proved more resourceful than me; he had come up with three ways to try the case: vermin, hysterics, and now defamation. "Judge Rodriguez should sanction him. She should fine his ass from here to Tuesday."

Jesse rubbed his eyes. "To Tuesday. Right. I'll draft a motion requesting it."

Luke ran back into the room holding aloft an elaborate construction of string, LEGOs, and duct tape. "This is so radical. It's a dispension."

Jesse held out his hands. "Sweet. What does it do?"

"It can be a sub or a jet. See, this part is the control panel."

"Jesse—" I said, but his slashing glance shut me up. He began discussing the invention with Luke, treating it seriously, asking questions. I turned back to the paper. This was what had been eating at him all day.

He said to Luke, "What's this?"

"I don't know. It was on my bed."

"Did one of your friends leave it here?" Any lightheartedness had left his voice.

I turned around. Luke was holding a small crown of thorns, the size of a bracelet, sculpted from shiny barbed wire. A metallic chill passed through me. I crossed the room and took it from him.

He said, "It's sharp. Don't let it poke you."

Hanging from it was a tag on which was written, *Let the children come unto me, and do not hinder them, for to such belongs the kingdom of heaven.*

Jesse and I exchanged a look. Carrying the crown, I walked to Luke's room. It looked orderly. No, it looked impeccable—compulsively tidy, almost sanitized. My breathing quickened. Luke hadn't done this. Someone had been in here. Then I noticed his bear, the teddy with the skull-and-dagger patch. It had a note pinned to its chest. Pinned like a voodoo doll, point stabbing inward. I picked it up. *For all they that take the sword shall perish with the sword.*

I backed out of the room. Jesse was still talking to Luke about the dispension, keeping his voice even, trying not to betray alarm. I headed to my bedroom, flipped on the light, and nearly screamed. A humanoid form lay on my bed. I grabbed the doorpost and closed my eyes. After a few seconds I could hear Jesse calling my name.

Turning around, I said, "We're spending the night at your place."

Luke popped up from the sofa and came toward me. "What's the matter?"

I grabbed him, spun him around, started pushing him toward the front door, too sternly. His face was a knot of worry. "Aunt Evvie, what's wrong?"

"You two go on. Right now."

Jesse asked no questions. "Come on, little dude. Don't forget your backpack."

But Luke wouldn't need his homework. I didn't plan to send him to school the next day. I didn't plan to bring him back to my house, or to stay in Santa Barbara once the sun came up. I had to get him away, up to China Lake. I led him out the door.

On my bed, atop my patchwork quilt, lay a life-size inflatable plastic doll. It was naked except for a witch's hat and a rubber mask shaped like a dog's face. In its left hand were pages torn from my book. They had been used as toilet paper. Between its legs were discarded condoms and smeared, stinking dog shit.

Written in excrement between its anatomically correct breasts was *SPY*.

On the nightstand next to the bed, placed carefully, was the wooden crucifix my grandmother had given to me. The figure of Christ had been pried off with a hammer and pounded into the wall, nailing a note above my headboard.

> *But as for dogs and sorcerers, fornicators, idolaters, and all liars, their lot shall be in the lake that burns with fire and brimstone, which is the second death.*

I picked up the phone and called the police.

5

When I finally crawled into Jesse's bed it was late.
The cops had come to my house, two uniformed officers who took down my story. Afterward, Nikki and
Carl helped me clean up the mess and pack Luke's
belongings into the back of my Explorer. Carl, raised
a Baptist, told me why the Christ figure had been
ripped off the crucifix.

"They think it's a graven image. They're calling you
an idolater."

The rest of the message I could decode myself.

I got to Jesse's place near eleven. He lived on Butterfly Beach in Montecito, with the mountains hard
behind and the surf at his doorstep. The house was
glass and pale wood, with tall ceilings, hard floors,
wide doorways, and no steps. A cloak of Monterey
pines shielded it from the road. When I walked in he
was working at the kitchen table, amber light reflecting his image off all the windows. The stereo was
playing something old and acid, Steppenwolf. He
stopped typing when I told him I was getting Luke
out of town. The hardness around his eyes looked
indelible. We stared past each other, too wound up
to touch.

I checked on Luke, who was far beyond the wall of
sleep, and went to bed. But I lay awake in the dark,
listening to breakers crash outside, watching shadows

stroke the ceiling. The pines shrugged and hissed in the wind.

SPY. The Remnant wanted to scare me away from talking to the press. I didn't doubt that. Yet they usually welcomed media attention, good or bad. It had to be Jorgensen, I thought. They didn't want people looking at his connection to them. At the Remnant's service, he had shouted, *I'll tell.* But he hadn't. Whatever it was, he hadn't had the chance. And I recalled Isaiah Paxton strolling away from the accident scene looking like a man whose problems had just been solved.

An hour later Jesse finally came in. He undressed, slid exhausted into bed, and lay on his back, running his fingers through his hair. I rested my hand on his chest.

He said, "Chaos theory must explain times like this. How one moment you're fine; the next, bang, you get hit by a rogue wave."

"Chaos, that's your name for God?"

In the dark, a bitter laugh. "Random Causation, Lord of the Chance."

A feeling gnawed at me, growing stronger. "I don't think the Remnant is randomly causing problems for us. I think it's designing them."

He stilled. "You don't think it's coincidence that Tabitha showed up right now?"

"No. Whatever they're planning, I think she's part of it. And so is Luke." I propped myself up on an elbow. "Chenille said something at the book signing— that he's special, more precious than I could understand. Jesse, she's never even met him. But she talked like the Remnant has a claim to him."

Outside the ocean rolled, an erosive drumbeat.

He said, "Hit the road early."

For a moment I felt hollow. Then his arms coiled around me and he was pulling me on top of him, framing my face with his calloused hands, guiding me

down to kiss him. I shut my eyes, feeling the heat of
his skin, needing the taste of him. I kissed him hard,
and then etched my lips along his jawline, down his
neck, across his chest, teasing him with my mouth,
feeling the warmth and smoothness of his flesh under
my lips. With my fingers I chased along his ribs and
down his arms. Lifting his hand, I kissed his wrist and
took his fingertips one at a time into my mouth. I
heard his sudden intake of breath. His hand pressed
against my back in rough caress.

This was a dance we had choreographed through trial
and error, in the face of irremediable facts. He had a
spinal cord injury; he had limited movement and little
feeling in his legs; he needed plenty of stimulation to
get hard enough for sex. We'd had to abandon old ex-
pectations, look past damage and loss, and find something new. To my joy he was a fearless and unabashed
lover, and I found his body to be just fine, lithe and
lean, tan from swimming outdoors. He was the place
where I could forget everything, and right then that was
what I felt desperate to do. He lifted me up above him,
slid my silk camisole over my head, and kissed my
breasts and belly. Feeling the brush of his beard, I
moaned. He grabbed my legs and swung me into place
above him. The sheets tangled. I tossed them aside.

We made love with silent urgency. Afterward we
lay wordless, entwined. It was my last night in harbor.

The morning began in red sunshine, with the Pacific
soothing the horizon and Luke thrilled to hear we
were going to China Lake. Energized, he was like a
bee in a jar, zigzagging everywhere. I had to roust him
out of the bathroom, where Jesse was shaving, and
from my car, where he was trying to stuff his "dispension" into a duffel bag. But I couldn't complain. He
was lofting his happiness like handfuls of confetti,
showering us with spirit and tenderness.

He jumped up from the table when Jesse came to

breakfast, rushing toward him. "Did you know I was going to Dad's house? This is the best surprise!"

"You're a lucky kid," Jesse said. "Your dad is going to be so happy to see you."

"Will you come visit me? If my house has steps I'll tell you so you can bring your crutches."

"Good thinking."

"And you can teach me to swim the butterfly."

"Absolutely."

Jesse raised his palm for a high five. After they slapped, he pulled Luke in for a hug. "I'm going to miss you, but you're going to be great," he said. "You're going to be just great."

China Lake is two hundred miles and a world away from Santa Barbara, in a high desert valley on the eastern slope of the Sierra Nevadas. Luke and I got going just after nine. About eleven thirty we crested a range of hills and entered the tawny expanse of the desert. Soon after, we passed Edwards Air Force Base, where Chuck Yeager broke the sound barrier and where the space shuttle first landed. I began to relax.

An hour later we stopped for gas and snacks in Mojave, a town that consists, as far as I can tell, of a railroad freightyard and a vast tarmac covered with mothballed airliners. Luke had dozed off but woke when I killed the engine. He stirred, sweaty and disoriented, and said, "Are we there?"

He sat in the car with unfocused eyes and his damp hair stuck to his head. As I filled the Explorer's tank a black Jeep swung into the gas station, stereo blasting. Two men about my age hopped out. They were a type I recognized—close-cropped hair, polo shirts hanging over Bermuda shorts, swagger tucked into an easy stride. While I stood inside the minimart waiting to pay, my arms laden with sodas and cinnamon candy, one of them got in line behind me carrying a six-pack of beer.

When I stepped up to the counter he looked at the candy and said, "Red Hots?"

To play or not to play the game? I opened my wallet while the clerk rang up my total. "They're good for highway driving. Hot stuff keeps you awake."

"Don't tell me a gal like you relies on candy for an explosion of sensation."

I gave him a sidelong glance. He had a square jaw and a slight smirk, and his eyes were hidden behind Oakley sunglasses. He said, "Hi, I'm Garrett." He was that sure of himself.

"Explosion," I said. "The usual metaphor is fireworks, but I guess a slam-bang missile shot is what I'd expect from a fighter jock."

He snorted a laugh. "But it's a heat seeker."

The teenage clerk was looking flummoxed, and the next line would be about going down, so I grabbed my purchases and headed for the door.

He said, "One direct hit and you'll be begging to—"

"No way, flyboy. And especially not in flames." I pushed through the door.

His friend was running a squeegee across the Jeep's windshield. A California Highway Patrol car was parked behind my Explorer, and the CHP officer was sauntering toward the minimart, counting out change for a cup of coffee. I was anticipating the next nugget of innuendo, not watching traffic on the highway. Maybe that was how the green Dodge pickup got by me.

I heard, "Too bad you don't want to experience air cover."

"Oh, you're offering protection?"

"One hundred percent."

"An officer *and* a gentleman," I said. "Guess I had you figured wrong. Maybe you guys aren't fighter pukes. Maybe you're cargo haulers."

He slapped a hand to his chest, pantomiming heartbreak at the insult. I climbed in the car, saying, "Keep your hand on the stick. You'll stay happier that way."

He opened his mouth to respond, but stopped when he saw Luke. A kid—that confused the rules of engagement. I drove away feeling one up.

The last fifty miles of the journey cut across the rugged landscape you see in Marlboro ads. The autumn sun was slung low when I accelerated out of Red Rock Canyon onto a rising plain. Ahead, a ridge of hills began rising—the tail of the Sierras, California's spine. Homestretch. I nudged the Explorer up to seventy-five mph.

Luke, reviving, looked out the window. "Where's China Lake?"

"There." I pointed to the right.

In the distance, the city tumbled across the vast bed of a dry lake. It had the lonely, tenuous appearance of so many desert towns, the look of gravel spilled on a grand and merciless landscape. The navy built the base during World War II, as a site for testing air-launched rockets, precisely because the place is so remote. The Naval Air Warfare Center stretches north to the Panamint mountains across seventeen hundred square miles of test ranges and restricted airspace. Beyond that is Death Valley, and, farther east in Nevada, more closed military skies: Fallon, Nellis, and Groom Lake, popularly known as Area 51. This was the closest place I had to a hometown, a city that stops dead at the razor wire bordering the base, birthplace of the Sidewinder missile.

Luke said, "Dad said if we get there early enough, he'll take me to the airfield."

"You may be in luck, tiger. We should hit town in twenty minutes."

Traffic was light. One car headed south toward me. In the rearview mirror I could see a single vehicle, small and distant. It was black—maybe the flyboys' Jeep.

The car heading south was a big American sedan, which made me lift my foot from the accelerator, because big American sedans can turn out to be police cars. I was decelerating toward the sixty-five-mph limit when it sped past—a Kern County Sheriff's cruiser. I glanced at the speedometer and the wing mirror.

Is there anything worse than seeing a cop hang a U-turn toward your car?

He flipped on his lights. I muttered, "Shit," and Luke's head popped around. "Forget you heard that," I said, pulling over on the shoulder.

Deep breath. I knew I was busted, even as I flash-fried excuses to serve up to the deputy. Luke squirmed around to watch him approach along the passenger's side. He said in astonishment, "Are you getting a ticket?"

"Afraid so." I put down the window on his side. "Afternoon, Officer."

He looked seasoned, a bulky man with a boxer's flattened nose. "License and registration please, ma'am."

I handed them to him. "Sorry, Officer. Guess I was in too much of a hurry to get this boy home to his dad." Shameless, but I thought it had potential.

"Your license lists a Santa Barbara address. That's the other direction." His voice was as dry as the air.

"Luke's my nephew, I'm taking him home to China Lake—"

The vehicle that had been behind me streaked past. It was indeed the pilots' black Jeep. The flyers honked, hooted, and laughed as they drove by. I felt sunk.

"Wait here," the deputy said. He walked to his cruiser, talked on the radio, and returned, this time to my side of the car. "Step out of the vehicle, please."

This was wrong. He should have been writing up the ticket, not ordering me around. I opened the door and got out.

"Place your hands on the roof of the vehicle."

Apprehension rose in me like cold water. He was going to frisk me. I leaned forward and rested my palms on the car. Felt his hands patting me down. He found my house keys and cell phone in the pocket of my jacket, left them. Luke was shrunken in his seat, as inert as a mannequin. The deputy took my arm and swung it behind my back. Warm metal flipped around my wrist. He cuffed the other arm and led me to the cruiser.

Shocked, I sputtered the obvious. "Am I under arrest?"

"Get in the car."

He pushed my head down, forcing me into the back-seat behind the steel-mesh screen. Shutting me in, he walked back to the Explorer, opened the passenger door, and crouched down to speak to Luke. After a minute he returned to the cruiser. The car rocked as he sat down in the driver's seat.

"What's going on?" I said. "Why are you holding me?"

He grabbed his radio and called the dispatcher. "Verifying I do have Luke Delaney with me at present. Shall I bring the child into the China Lake station?"

The reply crawled with static. "Negative. China Lake police are rolling to your location with Mrs. Delaney, ETA twenty minutes."

Holy God. I leaned toward the screen. "Listen to me. Luke's mother does not have custody of him. Repeat, she does not."

He started writing on a clipboard. "The boy told me he hasn't seen his mom since January. Says his dad brought him to your house one night and left him there."

His voice was like a slap. The accusation was clear: He thought Brian had stolen Luke and stashed him with me. Luke had simply told him the truth, but his six-year-old's phrasing had convinced the deputy he was an abducted child.

"No. His mother's lying. You cannot let her have Luke."

He got out of the car. "This time you aren't giving her the slip."

"I have proof of custody." He was walking away. "The papers are in my car. Green backpack on the backseat." He slowed. "They're in a manila envelope. Check it out!"

He looked at me, and at the Explorer, and at Luke, considering. I said, "Please!" Finally, he opened the back door and reached in for the backpack. *Yes.* My heart was hammering. He set the pack on the cruiser's hood and unzipped it. *Yes.*

He pulled out Luke's dispension.

I felt the blood drain from my face. He tipped the pack upside down and shook it. Out fell my camera, lipstick, chewing gum. No manila envelope. He shot me a look that said, *Gotcha, stupid.* With horror, I remembered Luke scrounging in the car at Jesse's. When I wasn't looking he must have removed the envelope from my pack to make room for his invention.

I shouted, "Luke put it somewhere. Ask him; he'll know where it is!"

"Save it."

I blinked. Then I yelled, "Luke!" The deputy scowled. "Luke, the custody papers. Get the papers and show the policeman!"

"Hey!" The deputy pointed at me. "Shut that mouth or I'll stick a gag in it."

I yelled, I begged him to search my car, to rip it apart. He ignored me. Luke didn't move a muscle, even when the deputy squatted down to chat with him. I lay down on the seat, slipped my hands under my butt so that they were in front of me, and yanked on the door handle. Locked.

Twenty minutes, the radio dispatcher had said. Less now.

I wriggled my jacket around until I could pluck my

cell phone from the pocket. Thinking, Call Brian, he'll come, find Brian. I stared at the phone. I didn't have his new number. *Dammit!* I phoned information, losing time. I bent low in the seat, out of sight, and got the number for the naval base. Another minute gone. Two. I finally reached the airfield. I told them to find Brian, told them it was an emergency, get him *now*.

The phone stayed quiet. Overhead, thunder rolled across blue sky. I looked out the window, saw Hornets, F/A-18s, carving arcs through the air. If that was Brian flying, I was hosed.

Then his voice came on the line. "Evan, what's wrong?"

"Tabitha's trying to grab Luke. Get out to Highway Fourteen with the custody papers." I told him he had fifteen minutes, max, calculating that the airfield was about twelve miles away, and the papers who knew where.

He said, "Stop her. Do anything it takes to keep Luke with you until I get there."

"Did I mention I'm handcuffed in the back of a sheriff's car?"

"Anything, Ev. I'm on my way."

He broke the connection and I stared at the phone, hands shaking. *Anything.*

I called the police. A woman's voice answered, "Nine-one-one emergency," and I said, "I want to report a child abduction in progress."

"A child is being abducted, ma'am?"

"He's going to be, in a few minutes."

"Where is the child now?"

"In my car, on Highway Fourteen south of the Walker Pass turnoff."

The deputy stood up from his crouch and looked toward the cruiser. I hid the phone on my lap. His attention stuck, then loosened again; he looked away.

The dispatcher was saying urgently, "Ma'am, are you being pursued?"

Briefly my legal training turned me stupid, as I thought, Am I? *Pursue: to chase; follow* . . . before a smarter part of my brain screamed, *Lie!*

"Yes! I don't know if I can keep ahead of her much longer. Please send the police; she has men with her; I won't be able to fight them off—"

The back door of the cruiser popped open, the deputy's mass filling the space. He grabbed the phone. I slumped against the seat, feeling time tick away.

A China Lake police car arrived ten minutes later, pulling off the road in a cloud of blowing sand. Behind it came the green Dodge pickup I had seen outside Luke's school. Brian, I thought, please hurry.

The China Lake officer, a rangy woman with big legs, walked around to open the police car's passenger door. Tabitha got out tentatively and stood facing my Explorer, her auburn curls and soft white dress swirling in the breeze. From the green pickup emerged Chenille Wyoming in a lavender Stetson, and Isaiah Paxton, looking as hard as a length of pipe. They hung back, watching Tabitha.

She ran to the Explorer. At the open door she stopped. Her fingertips went to her lips, a movement of delicate anguish. She threw out her arms and burst into tears.

I shook the mesh screen, yelling, "No!"

Her loud voice carried clearly. "Luke, it's Mommy. Come on, sweet pea." She tilted her head in sweet cajolery and gestured, *Come here*, with her hands.

And, for the first time since the deputy had pulled me over, Luke moved. He scurried away from her to huddle on the driver's seat. Tabitha flicked a nervous glance at Chenille, who said, "What are you waiting for? Get him."

No, I thought, I can't let her. I can't.

I lay down on the seat and kicked both feet against the window. Nothing happened. I kicked again,

screaming this time, and heard a dull crack. Once
more, hard as a mule, and the window collapsed into
beads of safety glass.

The door behind my head flew open. The deputy
loomed above me, shouting, "Stop!" I kept kicking
and yelling, smelling his leather gun belt and British
Sterling cologne. He yanked me out by the collar. I
dropped back, hit the sand, felt the breath clap out
of me. The China Lake cop appeared and helped
him flip me facedown. I felt a knee in my back and
grit on my cheek, heard the cop say, "She's high.
It's PCP."

The deputy flattened his nightstick against my neck.
"Don't move. I mean do not even breathe."

I had to squeeze out the words. "That man has
a gun."

"Jesus H. Christ." The deputy exhaled harshly.
"That's what gun racks are for. You think he should
hang potted flowers from it?"

"You're *not* going to let her put Luke in a truck
that has a rifle within reach. You're *not*." They pulled
me to my feet and marched me toward the China
Lake police car. I said, "And how are they going to
belt Luke in? That truck has three seat belts and I
count four people. That's illegal."

"So's resisting arrest. Now shut up before I jam this
stick down your throat."

They shoved me in. But, slamming the door, the
China Lake cop said, "She actually has a point."

"Make Tabitha go back to China Lake and rent a
car!" I said. "And I'm not high—I'm trying to stop
you from making a terrible mistake!"

Outside the window Paxton appeared, his face in
shadow. He said, "What a way for the boy to remember you."

Chenille barked, "Tabitha! Enough of this. Get
your son."

Anxiety had stretched Tabitha's thin face like a bal-

loon. Cops were watching, and her Remnant over-
lords, and her sweet talk had driven Luke onto the
floor of my car. She reached for him. He leaped up
and scrambled over the gearshift into the backseat.
She grabbed after him but he opened the back door,
jumped down, and broke for open desert. I yelled
"Run!" and he did, beautifully, with a high kick in the
back, such a little kid to have an Olympian's stride,
as I shouted, "Go faster"—faster, away from all this,
forever.

Paxton caught him. He grabbed him by the shirt
and brought him back thrashing and screeching.
Please, Jesus, I begged. Let this be a witness to the
cops. Let this *testify.* I cried, "Look at him!"

But Chenille was showing the deputy some pa-
perwork. Paxton, his face like cracked ice, handed
Luke to Tabitha. Luke arched his back and pushed
against her with his arms, head back, howling at the
sky.

She didn't flinch. She cinched her arms around him,
securing her grip, speaking quietly to him. Paxton
and Chenille grabbed his kicking legs, pressed him
against Tabitha's chest, and led her toward the pickup truck.

Luke shot a hand out, sobbing. "Aunt Evvie!"

My heart broke.

Tabitha turned him away. Chenille shook her index
finger at his nose. Her face was a hot rock. I read her
lips: *Naughty boy.*

Luke folded. His limbs went limp, his face blank.
When Tabitha set him in the truck he looked like a
broken doll, arms floppy, eyes empty.

The China Lake cop said, "Be sure he's belted in,
now."

That was when we heard the horn, urgent and
angry. A red Mustang was barreling down the highway toward us. Tears sprang from my eyes. It was
Brian.

He skidded to a stop and leaped out, lace-up boots hitting the ground, green Nomex flight suit snapping in the wind. He sharked toward the pickup truck. His black hair was sweaty, his mouth a slash, his voice a razor.

"Take Luke out of the truck, Tabitha. He's coming with me."

The cops started toward him. Tabitha shriveled back, covering Luke with her body. Paxton stepped forward and said, "The child is with his mother now."

"Move aside."

"I don't snap to when you give orders, Commander."

"Let me make this simple. My son is coming with me right now. I'm not going to say 'pretty please,' or kiss the ass of that Bubba Gump preacher you worship. I don't have to." He held up a sheaf of papers. "I have a court order."

The female cop took them. Brian peered into the truck. "Luke," he said, "everything's going to be okay." The answering silence was like a wound. The cop flipped through the custody documents. Brian looked into the police car, locking eyes with me. He was at full throttle, running white-hot.

He said, "What the hell are you doing cuffing my sister in there? She's the one Luke's supposed to be with, not these clowns."

The deputy said, "Take it off the burner, pal."

Paxton spit on the ground. "Delaney, don't you get sore dragging such big brass gonads in the dirt all day long?"

The cop shifted her broad hips. "We have a problem here. These papers seem to be in order, but so were the documents your mother-in-law showed me."

"Who?"

She pointed to Chenille.

"Calamity Jane?" Brian looked Chenille up and down disdainfully. Her face curdled into a sour pudding. He said, "She's not Tabitha's mother. Tabitha's mother killed herself two years ago."

The wind dropped; the air seemed to hang. The deputy said, "That's it. I'm taking every last one of you in to the station."

6

At the China Lake police station I waited alone in an interview room, sitting under fluorescent lights so bright that they buzzed, staring at cigarette burns in the Formica table. I could hear voices raised down the hall. Brian was turning the station into a verbal free-fire zone. The door opened and a detective walked in, a redheaded man in his fifties who was built like a side of beef. His plastic glasses were scratched and his breath whistled through his nose. He held a file folder in fingers as thick as cigars. He sat down across the table from me.

"I'm Detective McCracken." His voice, clashing with his physique, was melodious. Mirandizing me, he sounded like a poet. He said, "I'd like to get a statement from you."

"Fine."

He slid a pen and a blank sheet of paper at me. "I'd like you to write down what occurred this afternoon, if you don't mind."

I didn't know police procedure, but this didn't sound standard. Still, I started writing. I got through half a page and he stopped me.

"That'll do. If you'll sign it we can chat."

I added my signature and pushed it back at him. "You could have just asked me for a handwriting sample."

He took a letter from the file folder and compared it with what I'd written. He said, "I'm no expert, but I'd say they match."

He handed the letter to me. Signed with my name, it began, *Dear Tabitha, You bitch*. It tossed around threats in the copious, haphazard way that a child shakes sprinkles onto sugar cookies, ending with, *Show your face again, and I* will *get you. You aren't seeing Luke; you can forget it!! I'll never tell you where he is at. Evan.*

My face was burning. "So they have fourth graders writing their forgeries."

"The signature's actually quite good. However . . ." He picked up the statement I'd written. " 'Continually escalating harassment . . . inadvertently misplaced the custody papers . . .' Well. Sounds a bit different."

His nose whistled. He took more papers from the file folder—legal-looking documents, and an orange flyer. It was the "HELL-o-ween" comic. On the back, mocked up to look like the stolen-children pleas you see on TV, was the headline "MISSING." And there, photocopied, was last year's Christmas-card snapshot of Luke, heartrending in his little elf's cap. Next to it was a drawing, with the caption "Age progression— artist's conception." She really was a damned fine illustrator. She had him, down to the lost bottom tooth.

McCracken then held up my set of custody papers. "We found them in your car."

I waited.

He said, "You aren't going to be charged with child abduction. But you'll have to deal with the sheriff's department regarding the damage to their cruiser."

"I'll pay for the broken window."

"Under the circumstances, I'll recommend that they release you on your own recognizance, or at low bail."

"Under the circumstances," I said. "Wow. How magnanimous of you."

McCracken pondered me through his scratched eye-glasses. "If you don't mind a suggestion, I think it would be a good idea for you and your brother to take an anger-management course."

Hitting him on the head with the chair, I decided, would be a bad idea. I counted to ten. I said, "I want to file a complaint against Tabitha and her friends for false arrest, malicious prosecution, and stalking."

"Sounds like you've been talking to a lawyer."

"I am a lawyer."

His eyes refocused behind his scuffed lenses, maybe seeing a new explanation for my apparent belligerence. He said, "The sheriff is waiting to process you. Come on."

I was booked, photographed, fingerprinted, and stuck in a holding cell. But McCracken, true to his word, convinced the sheriffs to release me on OR, and an hour later I walked out, free. The lobby of the police station was empty except for a uniformed cop behind the front desk. I didn't see Brian. I pushed through the front doors into the fresh air, and the sun hit me. I took a breath, tilting my face to the sky. It was a bottomless blue, with an immensity I'd forgotten, dwarfing the sawtooth mountains that rimmed the horizon. Dry air, wind, rock, it was coming back, physical memories, the elemental feel of this place.

Behind me came a hawking sound. I looked around. Isaiah Paxton was leaning against the building, cleaning under his fingernails with a pocketknife.

"So you think my rifle is a danger to your nephew. How many guns you think his daddy carries aboard his warplane?"

Walk away, I thought. Let it go. But I couldn't. "Not one single gun that could end up aimed at Luke."

"Bringing the boy here, you're dropping him into a death zone. Out there"—his eyes jinked toward the naval base—"they cook up every warhead you can load on a missile, from plutonium to anthrax. Up against that, my rifle is man's best friend."

"What a lonely life it must be. Just you and your illusions."

"I forgot, you're a navy brat. Got a tailhook lodged in your brain." He wiped his knife clean on his jeans. "You think your brother flies around testing this stuff blowing up sheep, or breeze-block buildings? Wake up. They test it on Bible-believing Christians."

The knife hung in his hand. I inched back, anxious to get away from his bizarre convictions and cool, burnished rage. But when I turned toward the door he blocked my way.

"You don't believe me? Military has a million acres here, and you step foot on it, they shoot to kill. That ain't to protect little desert wildflowers; it's so we can't spot the prison camp."

I said, "Please move."

"We call it the great deception," he said, "ignoring what's right in front a' your nose, but I think you're just plain finger-licking stupid. The army used to set off A-bombs and march soldiers across ground zero, right under the mushroom cloud. Guinea pigs—that's all they was to the brass. I watched my daddy die of lung cancer because of that, just being a young private didn't know any better but to follow orders." He snapped the knife shut. "Course, nowadays they're saving their forces for the invasion, so they test their stuff on civilians. But they can't loose it on protected minority groups, queers and kikes, niggers and gooks, or—"

"Stop." I turned away.

He grabbed my arm. "Woman, you don't never walk away when a man is talking."

"Let. Go."

His eyes were sheer blue, pale like blisters. His

Western shirt smelled of sweat and dust. "And you don't never tell the law to take away my rifle."

From the corner of my eye I saw the lobby door swing open and a swatch of lavender emerge. "Isaiah."

"This is my business, Chenille."

More sharply she said, "Ice." It took me a moment to figure out that she was still addressing him, *Ice* a nickname. He gave me a crushing look and said, "Never." Shoving me aside, he headed for the parking lot.

Catching my breath, I turned to go back inside, but Chenille stood in front of the door, arms crossed, having taken the handoff in the Harangue Relay.

She said, "You done turned that little boy into an animal. It's unbelievable."

Beneath eyebrows plucked razor-thin, her eyes were a harsh and ageless gray. Dry flesh puffed around them. She could have been anywhere from her mid-thirties to her mid-forties, and I saw how she had passed herself off as Tabitha's mother.

I said, "I have never been as proud of Luke as I was this afternoon."

"Proud? The boy don't need pride; he needs discipline."

"Don't ever scold him again. Don't you dare open your lips or raise that nagging index finger to him." I pulled the door open. "I'm pressing charges against you."

Her face turned pinker than her sweater. "Luke needs correction. What's he had from you? Single woman who drinks and fornicates with a cripple."

Her eyes enlivened, savoring the hit. Pleased with herself, she walked away.

A few minutes later I was pacing the lobby, rocked by Chenille's insult more than anything else. Hurt, angry, I nursed my shock, formulating too-late comebacks, wondering, Is that what people really think when they see me with Jesse? Bald prejudice hadn't hit me before. It was a fresh cut. The cop behind the counter glanced at me disinterestedly.

From the back of the station Tabitha walked into the lobby, her white dress hanging tiredly on her. She was alone, and she looked reduced, as if something had evaporated. My pulse jumped.

Her eyes arced. "Don't celebrate. This is nothing to rejoice about." She started past me. "And it's not over, either."

"Oh, yes, it is. You crossed the border today from outrageousness into total stupidity. You'll never get Luke back now."

She stopped. Angry tears rose in her eyes. "It'll never be over. And you know why? Because down deep, beneath that clean-cut front he puts on, Brian has a heart of death."

Even in the circumstances, this statement truly shocked me. I said, "Do you honestly feel the need to hate him so much?"

She stared, confounded. "This isn't about hatred; it's about salvation. How do I get that through to you? Getting saved—when it happens, you *know* what you have to do, because it's like this flash and roar; the bottom drops out and your whole life—"

"Honey, get yourself a new song and dance. This is a police station. They've heard that jailhouse conversion sung in every key on the scale."

Her chest rose and fell. "You know what? This is like that Mad Max movie you love so much, *The Road Warrior*. Mel Gibson has to keep driving full speed no matter what. If he stops or swerves he dies. Well, if I swerve from God's path I'll die an eternal death in hell. Me and my son. So don't tell me to stop, ever."

Pressing her lips white, she ran outside. The sunlight caught her, white dress flaring like a star shell.

"Ev."

I turned. Brian was walking toward me, carrying Luke. Beside them lumbered Detective McCracken, his mouth thin. With reserve he said, "Again, my apologies, Commander." He ruffled Luke's hair. "Be good for your dad, pardner."

Luke sank his head into Brian's shoulder. Brian's face had as much expression as a totem pole. But as soon as McCracken walked away, he loped across the lobby and bear-hugged me. His green flight suit felt rough and smelled of the cockpit: of plastics, close air, and exertion. He gave me a huge, amazed smile.

"My sis, the tough chick. Kicking windows out of cop cars." He kissed the top of my head. "Thank you."

"Are things straightened out?"

He made a disgusted sound. "We're dealing with cops who were snowed by a Christmas-card photo. Yeah, everything's dandy. Handing Luke over to the Lost Tribe of Insanity, that's a goof any rube could make."

I raised an eyebrow, urging him to watch his words. Both Luke and the uniformed officer behind the counter were listening, the cop pursing his lips.

Brian looked out the door. "Is she gone?"

"Yeah."

His gaze lengthened. "They've turned her mind into a toxic waste dump. The lies she was telling . . ." An injured look fled across his face. "Let's get out of here."

Outside, Luke squeezed his eyes shut against the sun. Brian said, "And don't worry about offending these cops. They're the same hicks who busted you for possession fifteen years ago, and all they demonstrated today is gross incompetence."

I faltered, taken aback. However, I said nothing, because just then I saw the two trucks parked next to Brian's Mustang—Chenille's baby-blue job, and the green Dodge. A dozen people sat in the back of them. I spotted Curt Smollek, and Shiloh, and Glory, my erstwhile fan. Isaiah Paxton leaned against the Dodge's bumper. A creepy feeling threaded across my skin, like a crawling blue worm of electricity.

A spotted dog thrust its head out the window of Chenille's truck and started barking, a sharp, repeating-rifle sound. *Rak-rak-rak.*

Beyond the truck stood Tabitha, and next to her Peter Wyoming. He had an arm around her shoulder and was speaking in a low voice, with his head dipped toward her. I recognized the look she was giving him. *The Minx returns.* I drew in a breath, hoping Brian hadn't noticed, but of course he had. That was the point.

I murmured, "Just get in the car, Bri."

Paxton said, "You think this is settled, you got another think coming."

This was intended to be a piece of street theater. I put my hand on Brian's back, trying to keep him moving, but he couldn't let it go any more than I could. His face had gone scarlet. He set Luke down, telling me to hang on to him.

He walked toward Wyoming. "You. Elmer Gantry."

Wyoming didn't move. He stood consoling Tabitha, looking like an ad out of a western-wear catalog, bolo tie over a white dress shirt, brown jeans with fancy stitching, tan cowboy boots.

Brian said, louder, "Hey. It's time for you to hit the road, go back to snake handling down in Appalachia. Are you listening?"

Wyoming's complete indifference to Brian convinced me that he was. And I grasped that this was the apex of the man's gifts: not bringing people to Christ, but bringing his adversaries to hysteria.

Paxton started toward Brian. "Why don't y'all show some manners and shut up, instead of interrupting the Lord's work?"

"My apologies to the Big Man," Brian said, "but why don't you go fuck yourself?"

Brian shoved past him and grabbed Wyoming's arm. "You leave me and my family the hell alone. Got that? Or I swear that you and Tabitha and all your followers, down to your butt-faced dog, will regret it. I will put you down permanently, so far under that you'll have to crawl up a sewer to see the sky."

Wyoming had a strange look on his face, an extraordinary look. He was staring at Brian's hand as though its touch were liquefying his flesh. He swallowed hard, almost gagging, and wrenched loose.

He bared his teeth at Brian. "What *are* you?" He rubbed his arm. His face looked as if it had fissured. "You lay hands on me but you're not even *here*. . . ."

Tabitha stood bone-still, her hand over her mouth. Shiloh got up in the back of the truck, the quote queen ever ready with scripture, and pointed at Brian. " 'We wrestle not against flesh and blood, but against' "—her voice quavered—" 'against the rulers of the darkness of this world. . . .' "

Then Chenille swept toward her husband. "We don't have to take this. Peter, get in the truck."

He moved robotically. Chenille jerked her head at Paxton, got him to help her shuffle Wyoming into the pickup. She slammed the door, hurried around to the driver's side, and fired up the engine.

Wyoming slapped his hand against the window, fingers spread. His eyes were kinked with alarm. "What are you trying to do to me?"

We retrieved my Explorer from the highway and picked up McDonald's for Luke. Happy Meal: misnomer of the day. We drove to Brian's place, a beige stucco tract home with a neon green lawn the size of a Ping-Pong table. Packing boxes and cheap modern furniture filled the house. Using a box as a table, Brian set Luke a place to eat in the living room and turned on Nickelodeon. Luke looked glazed. Brian kept up a stream of chatter, trying to coax Luke into engaging, without much luck. Do you want ketchup on your hamburger? Want me to take the pickle off? How about the TV, shall we find Scooby-Doo? You don't watch that anymore? Oh. Awkwardness for everyone. And would you like fries with that?

When Luke finally started eating, Brian and I went into the kitchen. He unzipped the top of his flight suit, revealing a white T-shirt and his dog tags. Opening two bottles of Corona, he handed me one and stood by the sink drinking the beer from the bottle. Through the kitchen window the sun, falling toward twilight, cast jaundiced light across his angular face.

He said, "Wyoming's a head case. Is he on drugs?"

"I'm starting to wonder."

"Well, he's seriously into the freak zone. They could be dosing Tabitha too. Maybe that's how they're controlling her. They lace her Kool-Aid, crank her up until she thinks she sees Pastor Pete with a halo and me with a rotting devil's head."

"It's possible," I said. "But her conversion isn't a pharmaceutical reaction, Bri."

He leaned back against the kitchen counter and ran a hand across his bristling hair. "That woman, Chenille. Pretending to be Tabitha's mother—what a mind job."

He was right. Chenille's masquerade had implications beyond scamming the police. After Tabitha left home, and her mother's church, SueJudi had barely spoken to her. The rift never mended. One winter morning SueJudi dressed in her finest clothes and drove north to the wild beaches near Vandenburg Air Force Base, where the U.S. Air Force Space Command tests its ICBMs. She smoked a pack of Camels, took off her jewelry, and walked into the pounding gray surf. They found her body downrange from the ballistic missile launchpad, as though she were a rocket that had fallen back to earth, having failed to achieve the stars.

Tabitha never cried, Brian told me, never in front of him. But deep in the night he would hear her in the bathroom, sobbing. When he tried to comfort her she would turn away, stony. Their marriage had already been corroding. Asking how she was doing always elicited "fine" and then silence. Eventually he stopped asking.

Enter Chenille Wyoming.

"Talk about laying on a guilt trip," he said. "Every time she sees Chenille, Tabitha's going to feel like she should be making up to SueJudi."

"And this time she'd better do what Mommy wants."

"Mommy." He scoffed. "Her husband sure isn't playing Daddy, though." He tilted his head back, draining the beer bottle. "Shit. And they want to add Luke to their nuclear nightmare family."

I said, "Tomorrow morning we'll get to work on a restraining order."

"A piece of paper saying, 'Keep away.' That will solve exactly nothing." He took a new beer from the fridge. "Do you carry a weapon?"

"No. And don't think it, Brian. That would create a world of problems."

"Bingo. That's exactly what I want—to create an immediate problem for anybody who tries to touch Luke."

"Forget it. It won't help for both of us to carry."

I didn't have to ask whether he had a sidearm. I knew he kept it on a shelf in his closet, the same place our dad had always stored his service automatic.

He said, "You've been a lawyer too long. After-the-fact maneuvers won't help. We have to deter further attack, and we do that by projecting force. Tomorrow we're buying you a gun."

"No."

He started to say more, but I stopped him. "It's a moot point. California has a ten-day waiting period for handgun purchases."

"That can be dealt with."

"The subject is closed."

"No. Kathleen Evan . . ."

I turned and stared out the window. The mountains had darkened to black, and crimson twilight striped the horizon. After a moment Brian put down his beer. "I need a shower." He left, his boots heavy, his dog tags ringing. I massaged my temples. Rocky homecomings: China Lake had supplied them to my family in abundance. I didn't care for this vivid, second-generation replay.

After a minute I went into the living room. Luke's dinner was congealing on his plate. I sat down next to him. "How are you doing, champ?"

"I'm cold."

I snuggled him next to me on the sofa. He wriggled and sighed and stared across the room with a bright heat behind his eyes.

I turned off the television. "Let's talk about it."

Tension was strumming through him. I kissed the top of his head. "It's okay."

His voice sounded very small. "I put the custody papers in the seat pocket behind you." Mouselike: "I'm sorry."

"It's okay. I'm not mad at you. But from now on you have to leave my things where I put them, all right?"

A tiny nod, but no relaxation. I held him close. "What else?"

"That lady with my mom said I was naughty. Is that why the police arrested you?"

"No." Jesus in heaven. "Absolutely not. You did nothing wrong. You were a really brave boy today. Your mom lied, and so did that woman with her. She's the one who was wrong."

"Tell her." Fat tears pooled in his eyes and fell onto the blanket. "Tell that lady I'm not bad."

I felt a squeezing in my chest. I clutched him. "I already did."

He looked up. "For real?"

"Yes." I wiped away his tears with my thumb. "Listen to me. Sometimes grown-ups can be mean. They say things that are hurtful. When that happens, you have to remember that the people who love you know, totally and positively, that you are a great kid."

"Is Mommy mean?"

Just then Brian walked into the room, dressed in a white polo shirt and jeans, hair wet and spiky. Luke's words pinned him in place.

He said, "Mommy isn't mean. Mommy is"—a wince—"mixed-up."

He sat down next to us. "What happened today was unfair. But the world can be a tough place. So you have to know who's on your side, who to count on. You count on me and Aunt Evan. We're here to take care of you. And you count on yourself. You stand up for yourself and you trust yourself to know what's right and what's wrong."

Luke sat very still.

"It's like when I'm flying. The carrier counts on me and my squadron to protect it from the enemy. I count on my wingman to tell me when trouble's coming. And I count on myself to take action, because I'm the one flying the plane."

Luke pondered it for a while. "Is Jesse on my side?"

I said, "Of course."

"Nikki and Carl?" I nodded. "And my teacher?"

"All the way."

"I thought so." He tilted his head toward Brian. "Can I see your F/A-eighteen tomorrow?"

"You bet." Relief threaded his voice. "Come here—hop on your dad's lap."

But Luke burrowed against my side. Brian's eyes,

20/10 vision, trained to spot a MiG at fifty miles, didn't see it coming. They turned sooty with rejection. Give it time, I didn't say. Ease off, understand that he just needs the familiarity of me, and by the way, petulance ill becomes a grown man. I said none of that, not with Luke there. Instead we listened to the wind surge outside, until Luke's eyes closed and his breathing deepened. Brian scooped him into his arms and carried him to bed.

When he returned, I said, "How did you know about my dope bust back in high school?"

"Dad."

Fifteen years later I felt myself heat up. "He promised not to tell you."

He shrugged. "He was so angry—"

"Don't remind me. He went off like a grenade."

Driving home one night, four of us girls had been stopped by the cops. It was Abbie Johnson's pot, a baggie in her pocket that I didn't know about. But it was my car. We got probation. Folks treated me as if I were destined to be a crack whore or, worse, a communist. My parents made me clean toilets with a toothbrush.

Brian said, "No. Dad was angry at the cops and the judge."

I gaped at him. "What?"

"He thought they did you an injustice. He couldn't stop harping on how unfairly they treated you."

My whole body seemed to be ringing. Add a new revelation to the canon. Revise the texts.

I said, "This is why I don't come back to China Lake. My life is lying in wait for me, and it's not even the life I knew."

I slept on the sofa that night. About midnight I woke with a start, understanding how Tabitha had gotten my signature on the forged threat letter: she had traced it from the copy of *Lithium Sunset* I had signed for Glory at Beowulf's Books. Annoyed, I punched the pillow. I felt soft flesh near my shoulder. Luke's hand was peeking over the edge of the sofa cushion, just touching me. He was lying on the floor beneath.

Across town, about the time that I was sinking back to sleep, Sammy Diaz was closing out the cash register at the Pump 'n' Go. Sammy was barely seventeen, just growing wispy sideburns, but it was his dad's service station, so he took care of shutting down for the night. He noticed the two pickups at the pumps, crammed full of people—Anglos in their Sunday best, except for the big lady in the lavender broncobuster outfit who was squeegeeing the windshield of the Chevy. They were at the pumps a long time, pouring a quart of oil into the green Dodge, the lavender woman stopping into the minimart, asking him where they kept the Reddi-Wip. He pointed her to the refrigerator in the back of the store.

Things started getting weird when another customer came in and said, "Some guy's locked himself in the men's room and won't come out." Sammy hated messing with the men's room. Cars he loved, and handling the cash register was fine, but the men's room . . . man, he had no plans to become a janitor. Still, you helped a customer, so he took the men's room key off the hook behind the counter, went around back, and knocked on the door.

A voice said, "It's occupied."

Sammy could hear water gushing in the sink. Matter of fact, he could see a dark trickle curling out from under the door, rolling toward his feet. He knocked again, saying, "Sir, are you all right in there?"

"Just fine, washing up, just washing my hands."

The customer, an old white guy wearing a John Deere cap, said, "I can't wait all night." He said, "Open it; I gotta take a leak."

Sammy jammed the key in the lock and turned.

Steam billowed out, thick with an ammonia funk,

rising from the hot water faucet. Inside, pressed back against the wall, stood Peter Wyoming. His arms were frothy with liquid soap from the dispenser. He was staring at the overflowing sink.

He swung his head toward Sammy. "I said I was washing up. Do you comprehend what it means to be clean? 'Cleanse your hands, you sinners.' "

The John Deere cap pushed past Sammy, unzipping his pants and heading for the urinal. A moment later he groaned with relief.

Behind Sammy came the sound of squeaky boots. The lavender woman appeared at his shoulder and said, "Peter. We're ready to go."

John Deere said, "Judas Priest, lady. Close the damn door!"

Wyoming said, "Give me a minute. I'll wash them off. I will." But he looked at his arms as if they were strangers, maybe his Whore of Babylon hand puppets doing a raunchy skit at the ends of his elbows. He didn't move.

She clapped her hands. "Peter Wyoming!"

He pointed a soapy arm at her. "This is on your head. Today's performance was poorly managed, and look at the result."

"It was your idea."

"Chenille! Jeremiah two!"

She got mad, Sammy was sure. She squeezed her mouth into a tight line and said, " 'Though you wash yourself with lye and use much soap, the stain of your guilt is still before me.' "

John Deere shook himself dry. "Christ on a pony. From now on I'm pissing in the bushes."

Wyoming turned on him. "Don't bother with modesty. Can't you see what she is? 'A wild ass, in her heat sniffing the wind!' " He raised high his soapy hands. "Who can restrain her lust? None who seek her need weary themselves!"

A new man pushed Sammy aside and went in, a tall

dude, slim and strong, with a dark face. He said, "Pastor, it's getting late."

The sight of Paxton seemed to calm Wyoming. He let his hands drop and took the paper towels Paxton handed him, using them to carefully, carefully dry his hands. Done, he let them flutter to the wet floor. That was when he noticed Sammy standing fretfully in the doorway.

Wyoming leaned forward, chin first. "Are you saved?"

Oh, crap, Sammy thought. Then Chenille tried to take Wyoming's arm. He pulled away and walked off, shaking his head.

Sammy watched them go out of the corner of his eye. Why did the nutcases always turn up when he was by himself? Holding his breath against the stink, he turned off the faucets and waited to see if the sink would drain.

Outside the men's room, Paxton and Chenille were lagging behind Wyoming. Paxton said, "I told you this stunt with the cops was a bad idea. It's way past time for showboating. It's time to get down to it."

Later, Sammy told this to the police. But just then he didn't look up. The sink was clogged and the floor was slippery. Damn, this tore it. He was definitely going to study harder for his SATs, get into a good college, and get the hell away from gas station customers forever.

But first he had to ring up the sale for the two pickups. When he got around to the pumps, though, they were pulling out without paying. He ran after them, yelling, knowing he wouldn't catch them. The people in the back of the green Dodge just stared at him. He glanced down to get the license number. The truck had no plates.

7

Brian headed to the airfield at six the next morning. On his way out he shook my shoulder and murmured for us to come over to the base about noon; he'd gotten a visitor's pass for me. I squinted up at him. Though woozy with sleep, I had the feeling that he'd been standing over me for some time, wondering why Luke had crawled onto the floor next to me, and probably feeling second-best. When he left, the heels of his old cowboy boots clicked on the tiles in the front hall.

After breakfast Luke and I unpacked boxes and then took a bike ride to his new school. It was hot, but China Lake sprawls across a flat valley floor and it was easy riding. The streets were wider than the Champs-Élysées and sported the names of first ladies: Mamie, Jackie, Lady Bird. The dry air and beaming sun did nothing to lessen my tension headache. Luke was subdued, and I felt uneasy, wondering where Tabitha and the Remnant had gone, and what lay out there in the shining desert day.

At the school Luke seemed excited to spot the first-grade classroom, with its purposeful clutter and Halloween decorations. On the playground he climbed a jungle gym, and hopped down complaining that the metal was hot. The day was mild compared to what the Mojave can throw at you, but we weren't used to it. We came home sweating and thirsty.

Around noon we drove to the base. I showed my pass at the gate, where a sign reminded drivers to arrange a police escort if they were delivering explosives. Things looked familiar. The Phantom jet still posed on a pedestal inside the gates. The office buildings and laboratory complexes remained lemon yellow, flat-roofed, and nondescript. The cottonwood trees had grown taller. Traffic was lackadaisical.

At the airfield we parked near the control tower and walked toward the tarmac. Fighter jets and attack helicopters sat gleaming in the sun. The smell of jet fuel wafted to me. A Harrier roared off the runway, engine exhausts glowing orange. Inside one of the hangars a squadron emblem was painted on the wall: *VX-9 Vampires*. And what, I thought, would Tabitha make of *that*? Luke bent his head down, away from the blistering white sunlight, pressing the heels of his hands against his eyes.

"Here." I took off my sunglasses and set them on him. They looked huge, turned him into a miniature Blues Brother. "Better?"

An F/A-18 howled down behind us. Luke clapped his hands over his ears. Soon a second Hornet came in, tires screeching as they hit the runway.

I said, "There's your dad."

They taxied past, and I glimpsed the first pilot's brown face beneath his helmet. Brian was following behind him. Brian parked and spooled down the engines, and an enlisted man brought a ladder so he could climb down from the cockpit. When he hopped to the ground, I set my hands on Luke's shoulders. This was how I wanted him to see his father: next to a fighter jet, with parachute straps and survival gear hanging from his shoulders, his helmet tucked under one arm. As warrior, protector, defender of the free world. I felt my throat closing up, and didn't care if it was syrupy, blubbery sentimentality. This moment showed Luke something worthy, something pure.

It was this way whenever I went to an airfield. It had been this way when I was little and our dad took us to see the Blue Angels. As they swept overhead, all turbine roar and gleaming metal and aerobatic beauty, Brian squeezed my arm and whispered, *Someday that'll be me.* And it had been this way the first time I watched him fly in, and he sauntered toward me smiling that world-eating smile.

Captain America, Jesse called him. Damn right. Why shouldn't I adore him?

He and the black pilot walked toward us, chatting. When he saw Luke, Brian waved, calling, "Hey, there, little man. Come meet Commander Marcus Dupree."

Dupree exuded calm power. He had a strong handshake, a direct gaze, and a creamy bass voice that crooned, "So, this is the famous Luke Delaney." A minute later he was putting his helmet on Luke's head, and Luke was trying to talk and look around, his head wobbling when he turned it.

Brian was smiling, though it stretched his features tight, telling Luke that Dupree's call sign was "Dupes." Handing back the helmet and saying, "Come on; I'll show you the Hornet," he took Luke's hand and walked toward the jet, talking about the wings, the control surfaces, swinging Luke up onto his shoulders and pointing out the twin tails.

Luke said, "What's your call sign?"

Brian touched his name tag, BRIAN DELANEY, LCDR USN, "SLIDER." He said, "Can you read that?"

Luke said, "It's you."

Dupree and I hung back. He said, "I heard what happened yesterday. Hell of a homecoming."

"You're not kidding."

"They both look wasted. Are you going to stick around for a while?"

"A few days."

"Is there any way you could extend that?"

"Why?"

His voice sounded as soothing as a late-night jazz deejay's, but his words jarred. "I've known your brother a long time. And I have to tell you, right now he's riding right out on the edge."

"He's had a rough time," I said, too strongly. "I mean, I know divorce isn't combat, but it's still a bitter thing."

"Life deals rough times to all of us. But it's dangerous for a man to develop a taste for bitter things."

I turned to face him. "What are you saying, Commander?"

"It's Marc. I'm saying that Brian is soaking his head in acid. You need to help him take a deep breath and calm down before he has a helmet fire." He paused, and clarified: "Before his brain gets so scrambled that he does something stupid, in the air or on the ground."

"How come you didn't have the missiles loaded on your jet?" In the backseat of Brian's Mustang, Luke was excited and talkative. "It would be so cool to see them."

Brian was driving us around the base, a nostalgic tour, taking us through its small-town center, past the community swimming pool, baseball fields, a church, a McDonald's. I was quiet. Marc Dupree's words had stuck to me like gum.

"How do they sound when you shoot them? Like *shhhook*, or more like *crishshsh*? That would rock."

Half the houses on the base had been torn down. Whole neighborhoods, my puberty, safe streets where we lived with cheap, tidy houses and well-ordered expectation, were gone. Even the roads had been ripped up. Military downsizing. I said, "Ronald Reagan isn't in the White House anymore, Toto."

"Ding-dong, the Cold War's dead."

When our family was stationed here, this place had a buzz. The Soviet threat had imbued people with purpose. More PhDs lived here, per capita, than any-place in the country, and they were scientists and engineers, like my dad, who took it as their personal mission to develop technology that would save the lives of American pilots. Of course, I had seen the view from the high school—sports, liquor, sex, fast cars, kids ejecting to more populated and temperate places the instant they got their diplomas, which is why Santa Barbara has a high percentage of China Lake alums. But teenage boredom didn't make China Lake a death zone. The town was nowhere close to Isaiah Paxton's dark vision of spook heaven, Anti-christ central, a secret, deadly city.

Brian was pointing at a vacant lot, saying, "Remember when?"

Luke said, "Can't I see what a missile looks like? Please?"

Brian looked at him in the rearview mirror, half-amused, half-exasperated. "Fine." Swinging the Mustang into a hard U-turn, he headed off base.

We found what Luke was looking for at the China Lake Museum, a small cinder-block building that housed great themes—life versus death, predator versus prey. A wildlife diorama showed stuffed rattle-snakes and coyotes pouncing on small mammals, with the victims posed in the moment preceding death. A poignant tableau, lunch. But Luke didn't care about that. He headed straight for the Sidewinder missile.

It was a lean weapon, a slender metal arrow about ten feet long, positioned on the downward arc of flight. Luke looked at it, goggle-eyed, and then touched its guidance fins, and stood in front of it with arms flung outward, as if it were about to impale him. He asked how many of them Brian could load on his jet, and how far they could fly to blow up a target. Brian pointed out a photo of an F/A-18 firing a Sidewinder, explaining how the missile attached beneath the plane's wing, and how he fired it off, calling, *Fox two.*

"That means heat seeker," he said. "Fox one means it's a Sparrow missile."

From across the room a woman said, "Oh, my hell. Evan Delaney."

I turned, surprised and oddly wary. She was six feet tall with shaggy blond hair and round-rimmed glasses, wearing a museum badge.

"Abbie Johnson."

"Give the girl a cigar. And it's Hankins now." She had a bright alto voice and a big smile. "My God. Last time I saw you I was bent over barfing after running the four hundred."

Actually, the last time she had seen me was in court, the day we were sentenced for the pot bust. But I knew what she meant. On the track team I used to take the baton from her in the 4x400-meter relay. She had been whip-crack fast and threw up after every race. We called her the Vomit Comet.

"Not doing much running these days, though." She lifted up her billowy skirt to show me, above her white Reeboks and gym socks, a fat surgical scar. "Dirt bike wreck, back in college. And I know you won't believe it, but I said adios to the partying, married a dentist, and started having babies. The fastest little buggers on the street. I'm Mrs. Civic Duty, rah-rah China Lake, and get your jaw up off the floor."

It was coming back to me now—that I could never stay mad at her. Though the years had dramatized her physique, expanding it to Wagnerian proportions, I said, "Abbie, you haven't changed a bit."

She laughed. "Dammit, gal, you either. What's your life story? Married? Kids? This your family?"

Brian had wandered away, but when I introduced him he turned and gave a pro forma smile. Abbie said, "I remember you!" Looking at Luke, she said, "He's gorgeous. Your wife must be a knockout."

Brian's smile went starchy. "We're getting divorced."

"Oh, sorry."

"Yeah, well." He looked as if he'd been turned into cardboard. Put him into the wildlife display, he'd have fit right in with the rabbits.

Fortunately the phone rang at the front desk. Abbie went to answer it, and Brian said through his teeth, "Let's go." He took Luke's hand and headed for the door, ignoring Luke's, "But, Dad . . ." I followed, waving to Abbie on my way out.

She cupped her hand over the phone receiver. "Tonight. There's a bar on China Lake Boulevard, the Lobo. It's Friday. Come on down."

Nodding vaguely, I chased Brian outside. Luke was saying, "Why did we have to leave?" and Brian was telling him to get in the car. Luke turned on the whine. "But I wanted to stay."

Brian shook his head. "In the car. Now." He redlined the Mustang pulling out of the parking lot.

"Well," he said. "That was certainly fun."

He turned and smiled, and my heart sank. I knew that smile. It was ghastly, all teeth and vinegary eyes, the smile that told you how truly pissed off and resentful he felt. He really was running ragged, with all the sharp bits grinding just under the surface.

Driving back to the airfield to pick up my Explorer, we passed an elementary school on base. Fire trucks were parked on the playground, cordoned off behind yellow police tape. Near them stood two dozen people swathed head to toe in green protective gear with air tanks on their backs.

Startled, I said, "What's that—the hot zone?"

"Hazmat training."

"At a school? What in God's name does the cafeteria serve for lunch?"

"This is a weapons testing facility. How many hazardous materials do you think I carry every time I lift off the runway?" He snorted. "I mean, air warfare is purposely lethal."

I was remembering what Isaiah Paxton said to me

about testing plutonium and anthrax, his assertion that the navy threw Christians to the isotopes and microbes.

"Have you been vaccinated against anthrax?"

"Six shots over eighteen months. You shouldn't look so shocked. The world is a nasty place. Grow up and smell the coffee, sis."

I gave him a slow, cold look. We cruised along the schoolyard fence. One of the people in protective gear watched us pass, face hidden behind a plastic faceplate.

I said, "Why don't we back up and unkink whichever string is tangled so tight?"

"After experiencing the past twenty-four hours, you think I'm the one who's tangled up?"

"Brian—"

"It's simple, Evan." He chopped his hand against the dashboard. "Here, good guys. There, bad guys. It's my job to see that it's them, not me, who ends up in a smoking hole."

Famous last words.

8

I don't hate guns. Like most military brats, I grew up around firearms. My father kept his .45 at home, and his friends occasionally returned from overseas with souvenir weapons dubiously acquired in foreign alleyways or from opposing forces. They'd let us shoot them at the firing range. I know how to sight a target down the barrel of a rifle, and how to steady my hands against the recoil of a semiautomatic pistol. The kick you get when you pull the trigger is literal. But it's a rush I didn't want lying dormant in my house. I didn't own a gun and didn't care to.

The argument flared up after dinner that night, starting with a quarrel about Jesse. Brian and I were doing the dishes, getting ready to take Luke to see the new Disney movie, when he phoned. I told him about all that had happened, and talked to him about seeking a restraining order, and mainly tethered myself to the sound of his voice. He said he'd gotten a line on something interesting, a family who had quit the Remnant and might talk about the church. After a while I put Luke on the line and went to help Brian load the dishwasher. We could hear Luke's end of the conversation, *yeps* and *uh-huhs*, Jesse doing most of the talking. Brian had his back to me, scrubbing a skillet.

He said, "I don't want Jesse applying for any restraining order."

"Please don't dismiss the idea. It protects you and gives you leverage in court."

"I mean I don't want him doing the work. I don't need a lawyer in Santa Barbara. I'll get someone here."

"I just thought—"

"It's my responsibility. I'll handle it."

"Jesse's a good lawyer."

"Jesse isn't Luke's father. I am."

I stood there with soapy water dripping from my hands. "Brian, I have never for a moment forgotten that."

In the living room, Luke giggled over the phone. "That's *so* gross!"

Brian made a wry face. I felt a gnawing sensation in my stomach.

Brian and Jesse rubbed each other wrong, had from the start. Wires had crossed the minute they shook hands. Brian and Tabitha were visiting, and we met Jesse for dinner at the Palace Grill, where you shouldn't possibly have a bad time. There's Cajun food, a voluble crowd, and Louis Armstrong on the stereo. Tabitha was in a winning mood, feeding Brian bites of her crawfish étouffée, saying, "Baby, you'll love this." The sign on the wall said, LAISSEZ LES BON TEMPS ROULER.

But the good times hadn't rolled. Jesse had, and that was the problem. As soon as he said hello, Brian's self-assurance withered into awkward diffidence, with typical symptoms—staring, fumbling for words, patronizing Jesse with praise. *So, you're a lawyer? Quite an accomplishment. You have a house, your own place? That's great.* And Jesse responded, shall we say, sharply. He wielded the sarcasm like a cannon.

Brian, looking at the wine list, quietly asked me, "Does Jesse drink?"

Jesse said, "Not tonight, he's driving. But he talks." He picked up his fork. "He even feeds himself."

And later, caught staring at the wheelchair, Brian said, "That looks real, uh, sporty. You must play a lot of basketball."

"Not a day in my life."

I jumped in. "Jesse's a swimmer. He was NCAA champion in the two hundred butterfly his senior year."

Tabitha said, "Wow, awesome." Brian looked at him, perplexed, and Jesse knew he was trying to work out the timing, wondering, *Before or after the accident?*

Jesse said, "Yeah, you have to watch it or the chair drags you to the bottom." He waited a beat, ensuring that Brian was disconcerted. "And you would not believe how rough things get in the wheelchair diving competition."

There was a stuffed alligator on the wall. I wanted to stick my head inside its jaws and tell the waiter to snap them shut.

Afterward, Brian was riled with me for being riled with him. "It was a legitimate assumption."

"It was stereotyping. Jesus, wheelchair basketball? Get a clue."

"The guy has a chip on his shoulder the size of Nebraska."

"Maybe you just bring out the worst in him."

"Right. Leaving the restaurant he says, 'Stick with me; you'll get the best parking spots.'" I stifled a laugh. He said, "He's a riot. Human napalm. Just watch that he doesn't start turning his grudges on you."

Now Brian stood at the sink, scrubbing a pan that was already clean, hot water turning his hands pink.

I said, "Brian, nobody is trying to take your place in Luke's life. Nobody ever could."

The skin on his face was tight. "I know you mean

it. But you have no idea how hard it is, no idea at all, what it's been like to spend this year ten time zones away from my little boy." He dried his hands, threw the towel on the counter. "No idea."

Luke hung up the phone and bounced into the kitchen. "You know the dead whale? Jesse told me they pulled it off the beach with a boat, only these two guys on Jet Skis wanted to see it up close, and crashed into it." His eyes were popping. "Blubber all over them."

Clearly it was the funniest thing he'd ever heard. Brian said, "That's great." He shooed Luke out, telling him to go get ready for the movie.

He said, "Ev, I can never repay you for taking care of him this year. If it hadn't been for you, I would have been totally lost. But I'm here now, and I have to deal with this situation. So we're going to do things my way."

He checked that Luke was out of sight, and went out to the Mustang. He came back with a brown paper package in his hand. "This is for you."

He unwrapped it. It was a pistol.

"Where'd you get that?"

"Go on, take it."

"Forget it. That thing's not legal."

He pushed it toward me. "You want protection? This is it."

I raised my hands to ward it off, shook my head, and turned on my heel. He said, "Evan, don't be stupid," and that did it. I headed for the door.

"Forget the movie. I'm not going." I went out, slamming the door behind me. He yanked it open and followed me outside.

"No, Brian. I'm not taking it."

"Evan!"

That was when I felt my car keys in my pocket. Without another word to him I hopped in the Explorer and gunned backward out of the driveway.

I can only wonder what would have happened if I had stayed.

I headed for the boulevard, radio blaring, head pounding. *Don't be stupid.* I accelerated. Above me arched the night sky, gravid with stars. They were numberless, shockingly bright, with that diamond clarity you can see only in the desert. How dared he? How dared Brian try to bend my life to suit his views? His own life was swirling around the rim of the toilet.

Before I knew it I found myself outside the Lobo, the bar Abbie Hankins had told me about. The gravel parking lot was filled with pickup trucks. The marquee promised, GOOD STEAKS LIVE MUSIC. Sharply amplified rock 'n' roll boomed through the door. I had twenty bucks in my back pocket. I parked and headed in.

The place was packed, the dance floor hopping. The room smelled like eau de Budweiser. The color scheme was neon beer sign and cigarette smoke, the dress code Harley-Davidson T-shirts or Western wear, with silver belt buckles the size of land mines. In the back, cue balls cracked at the pool tables. The band was hammering through "Brown Sugar" with rough, seductive energy.

The "good steaks" claim was false advertising. What the Lobo offered was that Friday night small-town thrill: ninety-nine-cent pitchers and an insistent backbeat.

Just what I needed.

From the pool tables came a call. "Hey, woman!"

Through the smoke I saw Abbie, vivid in a hot-pink T-shirt, waving a pool cue in the air like a battle standard. I worked my way toward her. Bent over the table next to her was a big man with chestnut hair and thick glasses. He fired off a shot, banging a ball into a side pocket.

Over the music Abbie shouted, "My husband, Wally."

He shook my hand. He had a kindly face, with proportions that reminded me of a Saint Bernard, and I could picture him in his dentist's office, soothing anxious kids, revving his drill.

Abbie said, "Let me finish this game." Pushing her glasses up her nose, she strode around analyzing the configuration of balls in front of her, chalked her cue, and proceeded to run the table. When she stretched across the green felt to slam home her final shot, Wally said, "Shit!" and walked away.

She threw back her head and laughed. "He's always the same, a total two-year-old unless he wins." She waved me toward a table. "But he's a maniac in bed, and I get free dental."

Back in school she had been wild, willing to try anything, usually when she was slick with chemical lubrication. This was how she had settled down.

Dropping onto a chair, she said, "So, what's your story? What did you do after I got you into trouble senior year? You a drag racer, or hairstylist, a nun, what?"

The music thumped through the bar, the band now into "Sweet Child o' Mine." I said, "I'm a writer."

She slapped the table. "How cool is that! Anything famous?"

Wally came over holding three beers. "Good game, killer."

"Honeybear, Evan's a writer."

"No kidding," he said. "Have I heard of you?"

This question is inevitably a prelude to my embarrassment. Still, when he asked what I'd written I told him *Lithium Sunset*.

"No. Really?" I nodded. He leaned back and called to a man at the bar, "Chet! This is the gal who wrote *Lithium Sunset*."

Chet was a chemical engineer in a Grateful Dead T-shirt, and he had friends, rocket scientists. They crowded around the table. They had questions.

"The mutants. When they hunt underground, do they use echolocation?"

"Why doesn't the rebel girl use her psychokinesis to blow up the armory?"

"The girl, Rowan?" said Chet. "She's hot."

Well, what do you know? I had a following in high-desert cowboy bars. I drank my beer and started feeling better.

Wally said, "Where'd you come up with the title?"

"It's a reference to nuclear detonation."

"Right," Chet said. "From the fuel used to ignite the thermonuclear burn."

"Ah." "Of course." The rocket men nodded to one another.

I said, "It's a metaphor for endings, and—"

"But your description's inaccurate. Modern fusion devices don't use pure lithium in the secondary."

Rocket One pointed at me with the neck of his beer bottle. "And the explosion isn't a sunset, more a big puking dawn, spewing thermal radiation and gamma rays."

"To be precise," said Chet, "you should call it *Lithium-deuteride Sunrise*."

"Oh, right."

"Definitely."

"You writing any more stories where Rowan gets it on with a guy?"

"Boys!" Abbie said. "Scram!"

They left two beers later. By then I had taken turns dancing with them, and with Wally, and with Abbie, jostling around the dance floor while the band raged through "Livin' La Vida Loca." By the time I left the bar Abbie's cheeks were bright from alcohol and laughter. She gave me a hard hug, telling me good-bye with a wistful look, as though we'd left something unfinished.

Halfway across the parking lot I heard her calling my name. She was trotting toward me, running stiffly on her battered knee. The marquee lights illuminated her blond hair. She screwed up her face.

"Shoot, I didn't say this earlier because I'm too ornery to admit my mistakes. I want to apologize for getting you arrested that time. I shouldn't have made light of it."

"Accepted. Thanks, Abbie."

She hugged me. "Don't wait fifteen years to visit China Lake again."

So, nostalgia can not only be exhumed, but exorcised. I watched her head back toward the bar, glad that I had come tonight. Two women stumbled out the door, laughing wildly. They waylaid her with effusive greetings. Turning, I walked toward my car, flicking off the alarm with the remote control.

I stopped. The Explorer was scrawled bumper-to-bumper with spray paint. Runny red letters, two feet tall. *Bitch. Whore. Liar. Snitch.*

Bile rose up my throat. A rear door screamed, *Blow job*. The tailgate said, *Doggy sty—* That one trailed off with a smear, suggesting that the vandal had been interrupted before spraying *-le*. Either that, or we were talking about an obscure insult that I didn't understand.

In the darkness, muffled beneath the music, I heard an engine start. I turned and kicked a spray can. Across the road a vehicle pulled away fast, its taillights receding to hot red pinpricks. I picked up the can. It reeked of paint fumes, and I put it inside the back of the car. Evidence, as if the police would care. I looked around the parking lot, hoping someone had seen what happened. The only other people out here were Abbie and the two women, walking back to the bar along the far side of a row of trucks, deep in giddy conversation.

Abruptly they stopped. I heard, "Oh, my hell."

"Abbie, hold still. Don't move."

"Look at it; something's wrong with it."

I heard growling.

"Abbie, it can sense fear. Hold still."

After that it happened quickly. Abbie turned, ran, and flew off her feet, struck from behind. She fell from sight and started screaming.

I ran toward her, through the row of vehicles, and pulled up with a gasp. She was down, balled up with her hands over her face, and a coyote was tearing at the sleeve of her shirt.

One of the women screamed, "It's killing her!"

And I had left the damned gun at Brian's house.

I yelled, "Run into the bar. Get help."

I picked up a rock and threw it. Missed. The coyote sawed its head back and forth on Abbie's arm. She kept on screaming. I found another rock, took aim this time, and hit the coyote in the face. It flinched and released Abbie's arm. It looked up at me, its head low and tilted to one side, its eyes psychedelic gold in the light of the marquee. I thought I was going to wet my pants. Its muzzle was lathered with foam.

Abbie tried to inch away, but it crouched and snarled at her. She froze.

Dry-mouthed, I willed my arms to wave at the animal. "That's it, look at me. Look over here. This way." I glanced toward the bar. The band was blaring "Hollywood Nights." Where the hell was help? I said, "That's right, you stupid dog. Look at me."

It did. It raised its head and started padding toward me. I took a step back.

"No. Stay. *Stay.*"

The sound of gunfire cracked the night air, and I jumped. The coyote dropped to the ground. A man walked past me toward it, pointing a pistol at it. People began rushing out of the bar. Abbie stood up, holding her arm, grimacing.

Wally broke through the crowd. "Oh, Abs . . ."

Blood seeped from between her fingers. She looked

at me in shock, and then Wally led her inside, saying, "Watch out. She's hurt."

People crowded around the fallen coyote. The shooter stepped back, and I recognized him—the square jaw and supreme self-possession. It was the pilot who had flirted with me at the gas station in Mojave, Garrett.

I said, "Is it dead?"

He nodded distractedly. "That's no regular coyote." He looked at me. "I saw the way you drew it off of her. That was righteous."

"It was rabid," I said.

Men were meddling with the carcass, muttering comments. "Look at the size of that thing." "What is it, part wolf?" They rolled the animal over to see where the shot had landed, grabbing paws and turning.

I said, "Don't touch it."

Laughter. One man said, "Honey, dogs don't bite once they're dead." To prove it, he lifted the head by the scruff. When he saw the lather around the mouth he dropped the coyote and jumped back, wiping his hands on his jeans. They all did.

9

When I returned to Brian's house the wind was rattling through the trees, and shadows jousted on his lawn under the sickly yellow glow of a sodium streetlight. Wally had taken Abbie to the emergency room. I had come straight home, deciding to report the vandalism to my Explorer in the morning, when sunlight would dispel the fear that was greasing the recesses of my mind.

The lights in the house were off. Brian and Luke must have gone for ice cream after the movie. I exhaled, knowing I needed to declare a truce with Brian, cool things down.

The front door was wide open. I stopped in the center of the lawn. "Hello?"

No response. The interior of the house was an inky void. I got out my cell phone, about to call the police, but I didn't want to put out a false alarm. My pulse was pinging in my ears.

From the depths of the ink, light flickered. Flashlights? I dialed 911.

"I have a prowler." What was that light? Not flashlights—their beams would have been white and directional, and this flickered yellow.

"It's a fire." I started toward the door. "Send a truck, the house is on fire." I broke into a run. "Brian! Luke!"

At the darkened doorway I stopped. Gut check. Every self-defense lecture I'd ever heard said Do Not Enter. I held my breath and reached inside, groping for the light switch.

"Is anybody in here?" My hand hit the switch. The hallway and living room lit up, the walls seeming to leap at me. They were covered with red spray paint. The living room had been devastated. Everything was flipped, strewn, trashed. Words on the walls picked up the themes scrawled on my car. *Faggot. Fascist. Devil.* And something new: scriptural references. *Mt. 4:8–9. Rev. 13:1, 4. Rev. 13:18.*

My breath came harshly. My muscles felt rigid. An orange reflection jittered across the back wall. I kicked the door hard to check that no one was hiding behind it. It cracked against the wall. I ran inside.

"Brian!"

I ran down the hall, into the kitchen, and hit the lights. Nobody there. No fire. The flames were outside, in the back. I grabbed the fire extinguisher, ran to the sliding glass door that opened onto the back patio, and fumbled with the lock. The flames flickered brighter. Damn, how did this stupid door unlock? Through the curtain sheers I could see orange light reflecting off the back fence, and now I could hear a crackling sound. The door, the door! With a hard jerk it opened and I rushed outside, fire extinguisher up and aimed.

The smoke hit me right away, and the heat. And the smell—garbage, plastics, old food. The trash can sat on the corner of the patio, flames jutting above its rim. The smoke roiled the darkness. Leaves spun and jerked into the air, yellow dimming to red. The trash can had been stuffed to overflowing with branches that stuck out above the top. The flames licked upward along two tree limbs, and for the life of me it looked like a burning bush. I sprayed it with the fire extinguisher. Powder shot out in a cold white cloud.

The flames fell back and the heat broke in groping waves. The smell worsened—hot leather, rancid meat. Holding my breath, I inched forward. The extinguisher shoved away the smoke and revealed the fuel for the fire. My mind did a backflip, telling me, Uh-uh, that's not what I'm seeing, not a chance in hell, bub.

What I had taken for branches were cowboy boots, protruding upside down from the trash can. Scorched and smoldering, they were attached to legs, and I knew why the overwhelming smell was beef barbecued in Levi's.

Dropping the extinguisher, I stumbled backward, my hand covering my mouth, feeling that if I didn't run, my skin and muscle would slough right off. I fled back through the house and crashed out the front door, knocking into the woman standing on the porch. She shouted, "Police!" but I couldn't stop, kept going, and fell into the bushes, vomiting until I thought I'd choke.

It was a long time before they brought out the black body bag on a stretcher. The police cars had turned off their flashing lights, and the drone from the fire department's pumper truck had died. Firefighters were reeling in the hose that ran from the truck through the front door and out to the patio. Even the neighbors had begun to wander back to their homes. Only small groups of them remained, huddled in their pajamas and jackets, watching and pointing and speculating, along the edges of the light.

I sat in the back of a China Lake police cruiser with a blanket wrapped around my shoulders. I felt cold, and very alone.

Brian and Luke had not returned home.

An officer approached, the woman I had careened into at the front door. It was the rangy China Lake cop with the big legs. Her name tag read, LAURA YEL-

TOW. With her was Detective McCracken. His massive torso filled my field of vision.

Yeltow said, "Do you know who the deceased is, Ms. Delaney?"

I felt as if something were ripping open inside, letting a cold wind blow through me. "No. I didn't look." I was too terrified to say that it might be my brother.

The paramedics rolled the stretcher down the driveway, toward an ambulance waiting at the curb. I said, "Wait. I have to see who it is."

I climbed out of the patrol car. Hesitated. "Is it . . . I mean, the fire . . ."

McCracken said, "The face will be identifiable. The flames didn't reach it."

Nodding, I went to the ambulance. McCracken told the paramedics, "Unzip the bag."

The zipper hummed. The smell flooded my sinuses, the night became bright and flat, and a buzzing began in my ears. I saw the face, and then I was sitting on the sidewalk with my feet splayed out in front of me. Yeltow's hand was around my shoulder, her face a throbbing yellow underneath the sodium streetlights.

Her voice broke through the hum in my head. "Can you identify the decedent?"

Maybe I nodded; maybe I didn't. "It's Peter Wyoming."

At one a.m., sitting in an interview room holding a cold cup of police station coffee, I was still answering questions for Detective McCracken.

I had gone out about seven, I told him. Brian was home, but planning to take Luke to the movie, the seven-thirty show. I didn't know if they actually saw it. I left the Lobo about ten thirty, after catching a different show, the live-animal act.

McCracken said, "Being at the Lobo at ten thirty is no alibi."

I clarified. I had been at the Lobo all evening. My companions were Abbie Hankins and her husband, Dr. Wally, plus Chet the engineer, two rocket geeks, and half of China Lake. And I didn't know why Peter Wyoming was at the house. I couldn't believe Brian would allow him on the property.

Across from me, McCracken rested his thick arms on the table. His red hair shone under the fluorescent lights. "Do you have any idea who might have done this?"

I looked at him as if he had a head the size of a tick. I said, "The Remnant."

"You think the church had something to do with the killing?"

"Of course."

"Wyoming's own flock. The folks who practically regarded him as God."

"You saw the house. The walls were covered with citations from the Bible."

He thumbed a piece of paper on the desk, creasing it with his nail. His breath trilled through his nose. "You're very observant. I mean, noticing that while you were rushing to grab the fire extinguisher."

Brian had been mistaken to consider this man dumb.

McCracken folded the paper again and creased it. "You know, you keep telling me how this church group is out to get your family. But it wasn't your brother dead at the house; it was their pastor." Fold, crease. Fold, crease. Like origami. "The day you came into town. Is it true your brother threatened Reverend Wyoming?"

"What? No."

"Right outside this station. He didn't say Wyoming would regret crossing him? Something about putting him down permanently?"

I heard a ghostly echo in my mind. *Smoking hole.*

I said, "No, it wasn't like that. Brian told him to leave us alone, or else . . ."

" 'Or else'? Really."

"No, that's not what I—"

"Where is your brother, Ms. Delaney?"

"I don't know."

"You have any idea where he might have gone?"

"Gone?" The import of the question hit me. "He hasn't gone anywhere, unless the Remnant has taken him. There's a difference."

"I understand the difference. And either way, believe me, we're looking for him. Don't worry, if he goes home he'll see the yellow tape and figure out that he should call us."

The tape was strung up to keep crime scenes from being violated. But at Brian's the scene had been violated when I ran through the house, when I sprayed the extinguisher around the patio, and especially when the firefighters trampled in, dragging hoses across the carpet and shooting a high-pressure spray at the fire, the body, and everything in a ten-foot radius around it.

I said, "How much forensic evidence will anyone be able to recover from the house? The fire crew wasn't looking to preserve the scene when they went in."

"Are you a criminal lawyer?"

"No."

"Then why are you preparing a defense?"

There was a knock, and a plainclothes officer leaned into the room, a man with prematurely white buzz-cut hair. McCracken excused himself to talk to him in the hallway. After a few minutes he came back in rubbing the red stubble on his chin.

"Ms. Delaney, about your vehicle."

"I can't get it repainted tonight. There's nothing I can do about it."

"Will you step out to the parking lot with us?"

Outside, the plainclothes asked me if I minded letting them look inside the Explorer. I hesitated. They waited. I knew they would find a way to get in, with or without a warrant, and given the direction of McCracken's questions I thought it wise to cooperate. I unlocked the doors. The plainclothes flipped up the tailgate. "There."

He pointed at the can of red spray paint. I had forgotten about it, and now, I knew, that meant I was screwed.

McCracken said, "Do you want to explain that?"

"I found it next to my car at the Lobo. I meant to give it to you. I just forgot."

The two cops looked at each other. Plainclothes said, "Mind if we take it now?"

"Go ahead."

"You don't suppose we'll find your fingerprints on it, do you?"

"Right thumb and index, near the top, where I picked it up."

Plainclothes put on latex gloves and dropped the can in a clear plastic bag labeled EVIDENCE. He said, "Heard that the sheriff had to replace the window in one of his cruisers. Looks like you're a quick study in car vandalism."

McCracken sent him away. I stood there with my face burning.

"I didn't do this," I said. "And I didn't deface the walls at Brian's house."

He looked up at the night sky, thoughtful for a moment. "Tell me, does your brother possess a firearm?"

He knew the answer to that. I said, "His service automatic."

"Do you know where the weapon is?"

"No. Why do you ask?"

"Peter Wyoming did not burn to death. A gunshot killed him."

He looked down again. "We've spoken to Reverend

Wyoming's wife. She says her husband scheduled a meeting with your brother tonight to mediate the custody dispute."

"That's absurd."

"He scheduled the meeting for ten o'clock at your brother's residence."

"She's lying."

He tilted his head and gave me a look both analytical and strangely concerned. "You have issues, don't you? About trust."

When I didn't reply, he said, "Why would Mrs. Wyoming lie about this?"

"Because Wyoming didn't want to solve the custody dispute; he wanted to kidnap Luke. Brian would not have let the man through the front door."

"So how do you explain Wyoming's presence at the house?"

"Maybe he was trying to break in. Brian wasn't home."

He rubbed his chin. "Well, see, here's the thing. About ten o'clock, that red Mustang your brother drives was seen parked in the drive. A few minutes later it went tearing down the street with the tires squealing."

My stomach dropped. "Seen by whom?"

He widened his stance, indicating he'd had enough of the verbal sparring. "You want forensic evidence? The bullet that killed Peter Wyoming is a nine-millimeter." He tilted his head to check that I was following.

I felt queasy. Beretta nine-millimeter pistols were standard-issue sidearms for NATO troops, including U.S. naval officers.

He said, "Even a bunch of hick China Lake cops can put this one together."

"You're wrong," I said. "Something's happened to my brother. You have to find him."

"Oh, don't worry about that," he said. "We will."

*   *   *

I slammed the car into gear. My brain was stalled, obstinate with denial.

It wasn't true. McCracken had everything assbackward. I screeched out of the police station and up China Lake Boulevard, fuming about McCracken's arrogance, his gullibility and small-town shortsightedness, his weakness for the obvious solution and refusal to see the situation in its awful complexity, its clarity, its complete simplicity that I and apparently I alone perceived. I had to confront the Remnant. I had to find Chenille Wyoming and force her to recant her lies. Who knew how, but I had to try. She had to be nearby if McCracken had seen her within the past few hours.

I had to find Brian and Luke.

I drove back to the house. It looked desperate, dark and scary. I found a piece of scratch paper, wrote a note, and left it under a rock on the driveway. *B— I'm OK. Call. E.*

I checked into a hotel, a place with worn maroon carpet and wall clocks showing the time in Rio and New Delhi. The doughy young desk clerk, distrusting a late-night guest who carried no luggage and stank of burned garbage, called the manager. He said without a hint of welcome, "May I help you?"

"I need a room. There was a fire at my house."

The clerk actually escorted me down the hall to my room. I said, "Do you have a laundry service?" She told me I could send my things out in the morning, and I decided not to dicker. I said, "I'll pay you twenty bucks to throw my clothes in a washing machine right now." When she had carried my clothing away I stood under a hot shower, scrubbing until my skin stung. Afterward I huddled naked under the bedcovers with the lights blazing and the television tuned to CNN.

My mind pinballed. Peter Wyoming had been shot,

then burned. What was the message in that? Did it relate to the messages spray-painted on the walls? The scripture citations, strangely, had stuck in my mind. In the nightstand I found a Gideon Bible.

Matthew 4: 8–9. The temptation of Christ—"The devil took him to a very high mountain, and showed him all the kingdoms of the world and the glory of them; and he said to him, 'All these I will give you, if you will fall down and worship me.' "

Revelation 13: 1, 4—"And I saw a beast rising out of the sea . . . and men worshiped the beast, saying, 'Who is like the beast, and who can fight against it?' "

Revelation 13:18—"Let him who has understanding reckon the number of the beast, for it is a human number, its number is six hundred and sixty-six."

The hairs on my arms stood up. Devil worship? What in hell? These passages had been chosen with care, by someone who had arrived at the house ready to spread the word, in cherry red spray paint, in blood, and in flame. I closed the book.

Where were Brian and Luke? If they were okay, Brian would have phoned me. He had my cell phone number. I took the mobile from my purse, as though holding it would make it ring.

The battery was dead.

I tossed it on the nightstand and slid down onto the pillow. It made no sense, none of it. It was all contradiction, chaos. From deep within I heard a dead voice. *The evil is out there, waiting. And it's hungry.*

I sat up, frightened. Pulling the hotel room phone onto my lap, I called Jesse.

His voice was thick with sleep. Without preamble I said, "Babe, things are bad. Pastor Pete's dead." I started telling him the rest. It didn't take long before he was wide-awake and thinking more clearly than I was. He stopped me.

"Brian's going to need a criminal lawyer."

I didn't respond.

"Someone who can swing a big bat," he said. "It's imperative. The cops are going to go for him like hyenas at a kill. He has to protect himself."

I stared at the ceiling. "Right."

He said, "Is Luke with you?"

"No." I let him glimpse the maw of the chaos. "I don't know where Luke is."

Stunned silence on his end, for long seconds. He said, "I'm coming up there."

The desk clerk returned my laundered clothes about four a.m. Despite everything I had dozed off, and I stumbled to the door wrapped in a sheet. I thanked her and tossed the clothes on a chair, falling immediately back into bed.

A noise at the door woke me sometime later. It was the sound of a key being slipped into the lock, and I became immediately, fully alert.

The key turned. A vertical strip of light slivered in the doorway. But I had put the chain on the door, and it caught with a crack. Someone emitted a soft sound of annoyance. I tossed off the covers and started pulling on my clothes as fast as I could.

A voice stage-whispered, "Evan, let us in."

I stopped. "Brian?"

"No, it's Elmer Fudd. Open the door."

I felt like punching him. But when I took the chain off the door, my animus ebbed as quickly as it had risen. He looked as if he'd aged ten years. Luke was asleep in his arms.

"Where have you been?" I said.

"Marc Dupree's place." He walked in. "I couldn't get through to your cell phone. I called every hotel in China Lake until I found you."

"How did you get the key?"

"You're Delaney; I'm Delaney. The desk clerk didn't question me."

He laid Luke on the bed. His black hair was tangled

and his white shirt was stained with chocolate ice cream. I covered him and turned out the light.

Brian said, "What's this about a fire at the house?"

I pulled him into the bathroom and shut the door. I could barely contain the volume of my voice. "Peter Wyoming is dead. Did you know that?"

But of course he did. It was all over his face.

"The police are looking for you," I said. "Did you know *that*?"

"Figures."

I tried to breathe slowly. "What happened?"

"Wyoming called me after you left the house. He wanted to see me."

"You're sure it was Wyoming?"

"I . . ." Puzzled look. "Yeah. That dry, cornpone voice. He said he had to talk to me, that it was extremely urgent."

"And you agreed?"

"I told him he could go to hell. So he said, 'I know I'm the last person you want to talk to, but it's an emergency.' Then he said, 'We're in great danger.' "

" 'We'?"

"That's the word he used. I don't know if he meant him and me, or he and his church, or whether it was a royal 'we.' And he said he had found out what was going on. I asked him what he meant and he said he couldn't tell me over the phone. Then he goes, 'You're the only one who can help now.' "

"You?" He nodded. "So you said yes?"

"You would have too, if you'd heard his voice, Ev. He sounded—"

"Psychotic?"

"No. The opposite. He . . ." He paused. "Have you ever heard a cockpit tape of a guy who knows he's about to buy the farm? His engine's flamed out or he's in an unrecoverable spin, and the canopy won't open or the seat won't eject, and he's talking in this level voice, maybe stressed from high Gs but not panicking, saying, 'I've done this, I've tried that, now I'm trying X,' looking for the way out of it. But sometimes he knows, this is it. His voice takes on this tone. Finality, maybe. Totally lucid, flat finality." He looked at me. "That's how Wyoming sounded."

He started pacing the tiny confines of the bathroom. "He wanted to come to the house, but I said no way. So we agreed to meet out in front of the Nazarene church downtown. He told me he could be there by ten. I took Luke to the movie, and afterward dropped him off at Marc's place. And I stopped back by the house on the way downtown, and—"

"Dammit." I stared at him. "You went back to get the gun."

"Yes. But that's not the point. The house was destroyed. The furniture was trashed and stuff was spray-painted all over the walls." He stopped pacing. "It was a setup. I tore out of there back to Marc's, thinking they were going after Luke again."

Under the bathroom's bright makeup lights, his face looked bleached. His eyes had a glossy sheen. My stomach was cramping.

"Everything, Brian. That's not all that happened."

He started to protest.

Hurt and anger suddenly weighed on me like a rock. "Don't lie to me. If that's all that you saw, you would have called the police right then."

Still he hesitated, breathing loudly.

"I found the body, Brian."

He drew up in shock. "Christ. Oh, Evan."

"Tell me the rest."

His shoulders slumped and he reached tentatively out to touch my arm. "God, I'm sorry. It never occurred to me . . ." He rubbed his forehead. "Yeah. When I went in the house I saw Wyoming lying there on the floor."

"What?"

"Evan, I apologize. I didn't figure on you coming

home and finding that. But Jesus, when I saw him, when I saw what they'd done to him, in *my house*, and God, after he'd told me we were in danger—I had to protect Luke. I thought they were going to grab him; that's all I could think about, so I—"

I held up my hands. "Wait. You saw Wyoming's body in the house?"

"Yes." Baffled look.

"Describe the scene."

More confusion. "He was lying on the living room floor. He was knocked back against the couch, with his head propped up and a big red stain in the middle of his chest."

"You're positive he was dead."

"Definitely mort."

I breathed. "I found his body stuffed in a trash can on the patio, on fire."

Our eyes met, both of us realizing that the killer had been in the house when Brian arrived, and had hidden, then finished his death scene after Brian left. Fear skittered down my spine. Brian's face blanched.

He said, "I put you in danger. You could have walked in on him after I left. . . ."

"You have to tell this to the police."

"They won't believe me."

"You have to try."

But anger and a feeling of futility were ballooning in me. Brian's behavior had probably hosed him. He had fled from a murder scene, which police and prosecutors capitalize on as consciousness of guilt.

I said, "Where's the gun, the one you tried to give me?"

"Nowhere."

I almost popped off the floor. "Brian, *no*. Tell me you didn't get rid of it."

"Hell, yes. I don't need a firearms charge against me, carrying a concealed, unregistered weapon. That could be seen as conduct unbecoming."

"They could have run ballistics tests on it, proved it wasn't the murder weapon."

He blinked. He hadn't thought of that.

I ran a hand through my hair. "Where's your service automatic?"

"Where it always is. The closet."

"You sure?"

His mouth hinged open, and I knew he wasn't.

I said, "You didn't get it when you went back to the house?" He shook his head. "You didn't even check?" He closed his eyes. Desperation began welling up, a dread that his nine-millimeter was gone, in the murderer's hands. I said, "You have to get to the police station right away and try to salvage this situation."

"Not yet."

"Yes, yet!" I held my hands out, aghast. "What the hell are you talking about? They'll think you're hiding out. With me." Which was exactly what he was doing. "Listen. This is critical. The police can do a gunpowder residue test on your hand. It'll prove that you haven't fired a weapon, but the test has to be done within a few hours of firing."

"How do you know?"

"Because I'm a frickin' lawyer, Brian! Because I watch cop shows!" I said, "What time is it?"

"Almost six."

It was too late now. I sat down on the edge of the bathtub. "You should have gone to the police last night."

A fierce light flashed in his eyes. "Do you understand why I didn't? Do you have the slightest clue? I was looking for *you*." His chest rose and fell. "Evan, think about it. Peter Wyoming was murdered at my house. The police are going to arrest me."

"Not necessarily." It sounded weak, even to me.

"Yeah, they are. Homer and Jethro down at the station will put two and two together and get seventeen. If I had called the cops from the house last night I would be in jail right now, and Luke would be prey for Tabitha. The instant I'm behind bars she'll make a play for custody." He raised his hands, pleading. "I couldn't possibly go the police until I was sure that he was safe with you. You're the only person I trust his life to."

Touched, I stood up and hugged him. But I felt undone by this whole sad, frightening conversation.

He said, "I'll go to the police. But first I want you to take Luke someplace safe."

I nodded, understanding. Going back to my house in Santa Barbara was not an option.

I stepped out of the hug. "Mom and Dad won't be home for ten more days."

Our parents, divorced twelve years, were taking their annual vacation together. They were on a cruise in Southeast Asia.

"Call them," he said. "Ship to shore. They'll fly home."

"I'm hiring you a criminal lawyer. Jesse's looking into it."

"You told Jesse?"

I held up a hand. "Don't. It's the wrong time to get huffy, bro." I gave him a stern look. "You need Jesse right now. You do."

He was fighting the thought that he needed anything, because he was heading where pilots dreaded to go: out of control. But the trajectory was out of his hands.

I tried to put a lighter tone in my voice. "Trust me; I'm a lawyer."

He eased down. "And a frickin' one, at that."

"We'll get through this." I set my hand on his shoulder.

"I'll call Detective McCracken."

Dimly we heard a knock on the motel room door. I stiffened. The knocking turned to pounding. A voice shouted, "Police. Open up."

They had a warrant for Brian's arrest. Murder one.

10

Brian asked the police for one small measure of grace. "Cuff me out in the hallway. Don't do it in front of my son."

They declined. Laura Yeltow was the one with the handcuffs, and she locked them on him there in the room, binding his hands tightly behind his back before leading him away. She said nothing to me, but gave me a look that said it all: *Accomplice.*

Momentarily I felt swamped, unable to move. Then I saw Luke huddled on the floor beyond the bed, knotting the edge of a blanket in his hands, his lower lip quivering. I picked him up. He wasn't heavy, just all skinny legs and elbows. He started crying, shuddering in my arms. I rocked him back and forth, telling him lies.

"It's going to be okay," I said.

The sun was just rising, stark gold in a sharp blue sky. When Luke calmed down I put him in the car and headed for the police station. The spray-painted vulgarities on the Explorer blared crimson in the dawn. We stopped at a bakery, where the owner stared silently through the front window at the car. At the station I sat Luke down on a chair in the lobby with a sweet roll and a carton of milk, and got absolutely nowhere with the police. McCracken wasn't on duty. No one had any information for me. Brian was still being booked, and I wouldn't be able to speak to him for hours.

Heading back to the hotel, I passed the corner of Brian's street. Inevitably I slowed and looked toward his house, about sixty yards up the road. Sitting on the sidewalk outside it were two people. Holding picket signs. I stopped.

Luke said, "What's going on?"

"Can't tell. Don't worry about it."

I idled there in the middle of the road, aware that I wasn't going to have to search. The Remnant wanted me to find them. They were waiting for me.

I was not about to confront the Remnant with Luke in tow. Back at the hotel I called Abbie Hankins and asked if he could go over to her house.

Abbie and Wally lived on Nancy Place, in a sand-toned Spanish-style tract home with projectile toys scattered across the lawn. Wally answered the door holding a cup of coffee in one hand and the *Los Angeles Times* tucked under his arm.

"Ah. The coyote tamer."

He had a soft and silly smile. Together with the gold-rimmed glasses it gave him a cuddly-bear look. He gave me a kiss on the cheek. Abbie came from the kitchen, drying her hands on a dish towel. She had a gauze bandage wrapped around her arm but otherwise looked chipper.

I gingerly touched the bandage. "How's it feel?"

"I'm like an old boot, too tough to chew up. Just needed stitches. I have to get the rabies vaccination series, which is a major *ick*. But it could have been a lot worse. I owe you, kid."

A toddler came running up to us, a girl wearing a bib with HAYLEY stitched on it. Her hair was an Edgar Winter blond, her hands and lips covered with powdered sugar. She wrapped herself around Abbie's sturdy calf and stared at Luke.

Abbie looked at Luke too. "Wally got doughnuts for breakfast. Want some?"

He just leaned against me. Abbie gave me a sober look.

Wally said, "Abs, show Evan what you found."

She brightened. "Oh, you'll get a kick out of this."

Hoisting the little girl onto her hip, she led me into the kitchen, which was wallpapered yellow-and-green plaid, far too bright for my state of mind. On the table sat a high school yearbook, with a set of dog's paws embossed on the cover and the title *Paw Prints*. She said, "Remember when we were Bassett High School Hounds?" It was the yearbook from our freshman year—pimples, algebra, menstrual cramps. Abbie flipped it open to a photo of a track meet. There we were, running the eight hundred meters, gasping as though we'd run out of oxygen high up Mount Everest.

"Brian's in here, too," she said, turning to the seniors' portraits. "Look, Luke—here's an old picture of your dad."

Seeing Brian's photo, I let out a breath. He positively gleamed. His face had the smoothness of someone who hasn't yet been planed by experience. I couldn't bear to look at it.

"Hey," Abbie said. "Hey, gal, what's wrong?"

I pressed a thumb and finger against the corners of my eyes, saying nothing. I heard Abbie murmur to Luke and Hayley, telling them to go watch television, to take the box of doughnuts with them. A second later I felt her hand on my shoulder.

I breathed. "A man was killed last night. The police think Brian did it."

She didn't flinch. She just held on to me while the dike burst. Wally poked his head in the kitchen and she shooed him away. She let me cry, and then let me tell her about it, and she didn't look horrified, or titillated, or offer her own verdict.

"Do what you have to," she said. "Luke can stay all day if you need him to."

Somehow I'd known she wouldn't drop the baton.

The picketers were Shiloh and Glory, the Remnant's human antonyms. Shiloh, the martinet Bible-quote champion, held a placard reading, MURDER; Glory, louche and chesty in her Lara Croft fatigues, carried MARTYRED. They made unlikely partners, but then, I had never seen anyone from the Remnant alone. This bunch did faith as a cluster suckle at the teat of Peter Wyoming. I wondered what would happen to them now.

I parked in front of Brian's house. When they saw me coming Glory tensed up. Shiloh pursed her Kewpie-doll mouth and planted her feet wide.

She said, "This sidewalk is public property. You can't silence us."

"Picket all you want. I'm looking for Chenille Wyoming."

"We're not afraid of you."

"Of course you're not. Don't be dramatic."

But her knuckles were white, gripping the picket sign. Her tiny nostrils were flaring when she breathed. Glory was biting her lip and blinking hummingbird-fast. They were, in fact, afraid of me. Their grief and bewilderment were very real, and I suddenly felt callous.

I said, "I'm sorry about Reverend Wyoming's death."

"As if." Shiloh raised her chin, but it was quivering. Glory's shoulders shook. Tears started spilling, jinking across a scar at the corner of her left eye.

I said, "I need to speak to Chenille Wyoming."

"She's at Angels' Landing," Shiloh said. When I cocked my head, she added, "Our church retreat, out in the backcountry."

"How do I get there?"

She stared at me for thirty whole seconds, fussing with her ponytail, maybe screwing up her courage, or maybe trying to discern whether I was flesh and blood, or a specter, hobgoblin, some sort of golem. Then she set her picket sign on the lawn. "Get back in your car. We'll take you."

We drove south out of town into open desert, eventually turning off the highway onto a dirt road. The land became increasingly hilly, until we crested a rise and drove down into a sandy clearing filled with pickup trucks, mobile homes, and a ramshackle cabin.

"This is it?" I said.

The place looked like a low-rent concentration camp. Jerry-rigged electric wires hung from poles around the clearing, and in a rickety barn old vehicles sat up on blocks, spattered with droppings. I could see dark forms in the rafters, nesting birds.

A hand rapped on my window. I started. Next to the car stood Isaiah Paxton, his flinty face in shadow.

He said, "Kill the engine and step out of the car."

When I got out a hot breeze blew across me and a tumbleweed, an actual tumbleweed, bounced past. Though the compound was nearly empty of people, I had an intense feeling of being watched. Outside the cabin door Curt Smollek was standing sentry, one hand holding a rifle, the other hand picking at a pus-filled zit. He eyed me from behind his probing fingers. Next to him a blue-eyed dog crept forward from the shadow of the building, its chain clinking. Panting, it watched me too.

Paxton said, "Miz Wyoming will see you in a minute."

He called Shiloh over and handed her a device that looked like a portable bar-code reader, the kind supermarkets use when checking stock on the shelves. She told me to hold out my arm.

"Why?"

Here, she didn't feel frightened of me. Her hall-monitor snottiness returned. "It's an Antichrist detector." Grabbing my wrist, she ran it along my arm. "It checks to see if you have the mark of the beast."

Holy cow. You really can buy anything off the Internet.

She pushed the hair off my forehead and waved the device over my temples. "It detects microchips and tiny tattoos."

It *was* a bar-code reader. Paxton watched tensely, looking ready to drop me if the device started beeping or horns erupted from my skull.

She lowered her hand. "You're clean."

"If that thing really works," I said, "you might think about using it *before* you hitch a ride with someone you distrust."

She, Paxton, Glory, Smollek, and the dog all glared at me. I felt my bravado flaking away. What the hell was I doing here?

The door to the cabin opened. I braced myself, expecting Chenille, but it was Tabitha who burst through the doorway. She raced at me, eyes bulging, hands out like claws, a moan rising from her throat, turning into a shout.

"Brian killed him! He killed Pastor Pete!"

Her hair was unkempt, her face pale, her lips so dry that they had cracked and bled. She grabbed my shirt.

"Did you know? Did you watch him do it? Oh, Lord!" She threw her head back and keened. "Why didn't you stop him?"

And as suddenly as it had ignited, her ferocity flamed out. Sobbing, she collapsed against me. Instinctively I put my arms around her to keep her from falling, and she wept into my shoulder, clinging to me. Paxton's face tightened into a hard knot, as if he'd caught us in a monstrous impropriety. He pried Tabitha loose and led her toward the cabin, his hand on the back of her neck. I took a step back, wondering what had just happened.

At the door he looked over his shoulder at me. "Come on."

Hesitantly I went in, with Shiloh and Glory following me. The air was stifling. The venetian blinds were drawn, and the living room sat in dim, sallow light. The wooden floor creaked under our feet. I drew in a breath. Chenille was sitting on a black Naugahyde sofa, with the three baton twirlers arrayed at her feet. She was dressed completely in white—cowboy boots, skirt, blouse, fingernail polish, lipstick, eyeshadow, Stetson, so gleamy that she seemed to suck in what light infiltrated the room. In front of the sofa, where you would expect a coffee table, sat an empty coffin.

Her eyes, dark marbles, rolled upward at me. "The law says we got to put Peter in that box. They won't let us transport a body without it being in a casket."

I said, "I'm sorry for your loss, Mrs. Wyoming."

"Mr. Law also says we got to put my Peter in a state-approved cemetery, with that casket set inside a cement vault down in the grave, so no body fluids or putridity can seep out. Like they think his sweet incorruptible flesh could damage the *dirt*."

I swallowed. Why on earth had I thought I could interrogate this woman about her husband's murder?

Her gaze cut away from me, toward the kitchen. Tabitha stood by the stove dabbing her eyes with a handkerchief, speaking quietly to Paxton. Chenille called to her. Sniffling, squeezing the hankie, Tabitha came into the room.

Chenille looked down at her hands resting on the frosted expanse of her lap. "You know I don't hold it against you, bringing Brian Delaney into our midst. You didn't know what he planned to do. You didn't intend to cause this catastrophe."

Tabitha's head dropped.

"But we're entering a time when we can't afford fatal errors anymore. Even though you're forgiven, we got to maintain discipline." She smoothed her buckskin skirt. "Half rations. One week."

Incredibly, Tabitha nodded. Her jaw tightened, and hot red patches rose on her cheeks, but she said nothing. Chenille twitched her Stetson and Tabitha fled to the kitchen, dismissed. Then the snowy hat clocked toward me.

"Now. I want you to hear what I got to say. Even though it soils me to be in the same room with you, I want you to witness, then go back and tell them they ain't winning."

I didn't dare interrupt to ask her who *they* were.

"They think this clears the way. They think with Peter gone, the beast has clear sailing to power. They're mistaken." Her eyes had a dark, hot-coal heat. "We ain't even started to fight. Ain't even cocked a fist yet."

She stood up. Slowly she reached down into her right boot and drew out a hunting knife. Looking straight at me, she said, "Shiloh."

The girl scurried forward.

Chenille said, "My hat."

Shiloh lifted it from Chenille's head delicately, as though removing a bride's veil, or carrying a bomb away for disposal. My pulse jumped in my neck. Chenille slid a hand across the length of her long clay-toned braid.

"Scripture tells us hair is a woman's pride. She wears it long to glorify her husband and his authority over her."

She looked at my short 'do. The purity of her loathing pierced me.

"But my man is gone. So today I'm telling you we forsake our bodily glory. We go forth shorn, ready for battle."

Smoothly, she swung the knife and sliced off the braid.

"Go tell Satan's lackeys we are combat-ready. Here, show 'em I ain't messing around."

Rattlesnake-quick, she threw the amputated braid at me. Reflexively I caught it. Its warmth and hefty smoothness took me by surprise, and I dropped it with a shudder.

Chenille pointed the knife at my midsection. "Get going."

No problem there. I forced myself not to run, just to maintain my self-respect.

Outside, Curt Smollek was lounging against the front fender of my Explorer. He gave me a slow yellow smile and pointed to the graffiti that said, *blow job*. "You advertising, or what?"

He had put the inflatable doll on my bed, I felt certain. I said, "Move."

Then I saw that he'd set his rifle down against the car, and had my vehicle registration in his hands, along with things I'd had in the glove compartment—a Mavericks CD and Michael Crichton's *Timeline*.

"Give me those, you pissant Gestapo wannabe."

He jerked back, playing keep-away, and knocked his rifle over onto the sand.

Behind me I heard Paxton coming, his voice glacial. "Pick that up."

Smollek quickly grabbed the weapon. "Sorry, Ice. But she's carrying contraband. Ungodly music and satanistic books."

I reached for the CD but Paxton stopped me. "This land is the sovereign property of the Remnant, and you made yourself subject to our jurisdiction when you come on it." He nodded to Smollek. "Confiscate the banned items."

Nothing raises the blood pressure like realizing you're in a losing battle. I grabbed the registration and got in the car. As I fired up the ignition, Paxton tapped on the window. I didn't roll it down.

He leaned close to the glass. "You know them signs

the government hangs on the fences out in the back ranges at the base?"

I knew. USE OF DEADLY FORCE AUTHORIZED BEYOND THIS POINT.

"From now on," he said, "them's the rules of engagement." His breath frosted the glass. "You been warned."

I spun the wheels accelerating away.

The Explorer flung up a rooster tail of dust as I sped back toward town. My hands gripped the wheel, chalk white. Pulling back onto the paved road I bounced hard onto the asphalt and kept going, ignoring the crunching, banging noises in the back end of the car. Pointless exercise, that was what I had just engaged in. Pointless and stupid. All I had done was fan the flames of antipathy, and maybe inflate the Remnant's lust for dominance. Sovereign land, my ass.

A question poked through the anger. Who owned Angels' Landing? The Remnant? Or did the church have followers in China Lake? I could check public records and find out. It seemed a small point, but I was grabbing at singularities. I blew past the city-limits sign.

Again I heard a strange sound. Buzzing. I looked in the rearview mirror and saw a brown and unruly swarm. The car was full of wasps.

Then they were all around me, frenetic, humming like a severed power line, battering against the windows, the dashboard, my hair. A sudden hot sensation stunned my arm, and I jerked it off the wheel, hit the brakes, felt a second sizzle and jab on the back of my neck. They were everywhere. I felt a tickle down my shirt and then a sting on my chest. The car slewed to a stop, jumping the curb into a vacant lot, smashing into a yucca plant. I flung open the door and leaped out.

I batted at my shirt, at my hair. I waved my arms,

spun, and finally dropped to the ground and rolled over and over, feeling something crawl down the waistband of my shorts toward my crotch. I yanked down the zipper, pulled off the shorts, and lay there slapping at my panties.

One of my eyes was beginning to close. All over, I felt as if I were alight. The wasps had stopped stinging, but still I shook my head and spit and flailed my arms. I felt hot exhaust on my shoulder, realized that the car's engine was running and I had rolled near the tailpipe. I looked up and saw *Doggy sty*——

I heard a car door slam. Vaguely I thought about my graying panties, recalled my mother warning me to throw away ratty underwear before I got caught in an accident with my skirt around my knees. I hate it when I ignore her and she ends up being right.

A man appeared above me, silhouetted in the wicked midday glare, and dropped to my side. "Don't move."

I stopped fighting, but my limbs kept shivering despite the sun and the heat of the sand. The man carefully picked dead wasps from the front of my blouse. His face was indiscernible, backlit into silhouette.

"You must have been stung a dozen times. Dammit. You allergic? Let's get you to the emergency room."

I squinted up at him. "Are you a doctor?"

"No, ma'am." He moved out of the sun, and I saw his face. Mr. Square-jawed Fighter Jock. "Garrett Holt, U.S. Navy, at your service."

11

Holt was waiting when I finished up at the urgent-care medical clinic, standing in the waiting area with his hands planted on his hips, concern on his face. I snugged the pink beach towel around my waist like a sarong. He had found it in my car and flung it around me before putting me into his black Jeep for the ride to the clinic.

He said, "What's the verdict?"

He was in uniform, khakis with lieutenant's bars on the collar, his shirt and trousers pressed as smooth as sheet metal. He wasn't a big man—about my height. He had a terrier's frame, with compact muscularity. He had wiry brown hair cut close to the scalp, and dark brows that balanced his big jawbone.

I waved the Benadryl tablets and ointment the doctor had given me to keep down the swelling and the itching. "I'm not in anaphylactic shock, or I'd already be dead. They didn't consider this so much an emergency as an annoyance."

I felt hot and crampy. Walking out into the sunlight, I flinched and squeezed my eyes shut for a moment.

He said, "Can I drop you somewhere? Home?"

"Just back to my car, Lieutenant."

"It's Garrett." He opened the door to his Jeep and held it for me. "You look shaky. Can I get you a cup of coffee first? Maybe a sandwich or a piece of pie?"

Single-malt scotch sounded about right. "Thanks, no. You're very kind, but I need to get home."

He painted my face with his eyes. "Do you have to pick up your little boy?"

"He's my nephew."

His shoulders relaxed, and eagerness ignited behind his eyes like afterburners. The kid wasn't mine. His gaze flicked to my left hand. No ring. I could practically hear him thinking that this sortie would be easier than he'd thought. No opposition was going to rise up over the horizon to challenge him. No husband, no kid, nothing.

I felt miserable. Why had I flirted with him at the gas station in Mojave? I might as well have tossed him a raw steak. Or lace panties. I felt embarrassed and chagrined. Just what I didn't need—a horny sailor with a king-sized ego, who'd gotten a good glimpse of my undies.

He put on his Oakley sunglasses and pulled out onto the road. "I have a confession. I spotted your car and was following you, hoping to maybe ask you out for a drink."

I leaned gingerly against the seat back. "I wondered about the coincidence."

"Guess this isn't a good time."

"The middle of a Russian missile attack would be better."

The Jeep had a raw ride, with a stiff tranny and rudimentary suspension. When we hit a dip in the road I bumped the seat, and my back started itching insanely. I scratched but my hand couldn't reach the epicenter, and I started squirming against the seat like a bear scraping against a tree. It didn't work.

He said, "Need some help? I can reach that spot."

Considering that I wanted to give him the brush-off, letting him touch me wasn't first on my list of solutions. I stretched my arm over my head. "I can get it."

"You sure about that?"

I couldn't reach it, not without a rake. My skin felt deranged. "God, yes. Please."

I leaned forward and he started scratching, hard. Tears of pure, base joy welled in my eyes, and I stifled a moan, not wanting him to know that this was better than sex. It was deliverance.

"I have to ask you," he said. "Why were you driving around with a bag of wasps in your car? Do you collect insects or something?"

I sat up straight. "What bag of wasps?"

A brief, quizzical look. "In the back of your Explorer. When I got the beach towel to wrap around you I found a Ziploc baggie open underneath it. Some dead wasps were stuck to the inside of the plastic, so I figured—"

"Son of a bitch."

No wonder Curt Smollek had been wearing that nasty smile when I left Angels' Landing. He had sabotaged me. We pulled up next to the Explorer at the vacant lot. I opened the tailgate and saw the Ziploc bag. Smollek must have put it there, loosely covered with the towel, rigged to let me drive awhile before the wasps escaped. Garrett stood close, almost close enough to set me itching again, and reached for it. I nudged his hand aside.

"Don't touch it. There might be fingerprints on it," I said. "Somebody put that baggie in here to mess me up, and I think I know who."

He squinted at me. "Just how bad a bad day are you having, exactly?"

I summed it up for him. "Things are FUBAR."

He laughed humorlessly and said, "I know where you're coming from." He knew the World War II expression, Fucked Up Beyond All Recognition. He decided he'd better go with me to the police station.

"You don't have to, really." I slid into the Explorer,

trying to sit without actually touching anything, including the air.

"If you walk in by yourself they'll laugh in your face. But they might listen if you bring along a witness, especially one in uniform."

But the police laughed in my face anyway. I spoke to the white-haired plainclothes officer, the man who had found the spray-paint can in my car. He ran a thumb back and forth over his lips, amusement playing in his eyes.

"Were these wasps infesting the neighborhood, or just your backseat?"

I handed him the baggie, which was resting on a piece of cardboard I'd found in the vacant lot. He tried to hide his smile. "Fingerprints. Whose, exactly?"

"The wasps'. Who else?" I bit off the *stupid*, but sarcasm crackled in my voice. "The people who put this in my car."

He took the baggie, but I knew he wasn't going to do anything. He said, "Now, had you had a run-in with these particular wasps before? Was there bad blood between you?"

Garrett pulled me away before I could retort. But he went back to talk to the detective, getting close to him—not challenging the man, but projecting his presence. He said, "You might have the courtesy to treat a citizen with respect." The detective's eyes flattened with resentment.

Outside the station, Garrett stared at the livid sawtooth mountains on the horizon. He said, "He's a smug bastard."

"He thinks the police have won themselves a big victory, arresting my brother."

He looked over his shoulder. "Ridicule—what a crap investigative technique. Is that how they gathered evidence against your brother? That's how they brought in an F/A-eighteen driver, a veteran?" He made a disgusted sound. "Anything I can do to help, let me know."

"I appreciate it." But I didn't need a sidekick. I needed to get Luke the hell out of town.

He said, "Rain check on that drink?"

I shrugged noncommittally, and he gave me a dry smile. He said, "I'll call you when the missiles launch."

Public Records was around the corner from the police station at the China Lake Civic Center. After Garrett left, I went and dug up information on the ownership of Angels' Landing. I didn't have a parcel number or street address for the property, but found a map covering that section of desert and pieced it together by tracing the dirt road I'd driven. The land belonged to a woman named Mildred Hopp Antley. The name meant nothing to me. I found a phone book, but no Antley was listed.

I drove back to the hotel to clean up. The stings throbbed. Everything agitated them—walking, blinking, even the ticking of the wall clocks at the front desk, telling me it was nighttime in New Delhi. Grimacing, I got halfway across the lobby before I saw Jesse sitting there, waiting for me.

"Hey, sugar." Arms wide.

He had on worn jeans and a yellow Gaucho Swimming T-shirt. His laptop computer was open on a table, the ferret trial being ever with him.

Anticipating his first question, I said, "Luke's okay."

"God." He exhaled. "I had a long drive waiting to hear that." He brushed my hair off my face with his fingertips. "Shit, what's wrong with your eye?"

The desk clerk was gawking. I said, "In my room." Down the hall, I closed the door, tossed him the antihistamine ointment, and started stripping off my clothes. "Rub it on me, all over."

"Hell." He stared. "You've been playing with the Remnant again."

"Every last inch, Jesse. Before I start gnawing on myself."

He squeezed the ointment onto his fingers and started rubbing.

I said, "Brian's been arrested."

His fingers stopped. His eyebrows rose. "On what evidence?"

"Bullshit evidence. He argued with Peter Wyoming. He left the crime scene because he thought Luke was in danger. He has a handgun. It's all speculation."

"But enough for a warrant?"

"Welcome to the high desert, where the brain cells are thinner."

He started rubbing again. "Brian is asserting his innocence?"

"Yes."

He backed off. "You all right?"

"No."

He stopped rubbing, with his hand on my hip, and looked at me with electric blue eyes. He swung over onto the bed and drew me down into his arms. I laid my head on his shoulder.

"Five minutes," I said. "Just give me five minutes. Don't say anything."

The jail adjoined the police station at the Civic Center complex. Jesse and I signed in before going to the visitors' room.

He said, "Why are the cops looking at me like that?"

"You're the newest exhibit in the Delaney Family Traveling Zoo. Ignore it."

The visitors' room was painted canned-tuna beige. This being a small-town jail, the Plexiglas divider between prisoners and visitors was only seven feet high, so people could talk without phones. Grime was accumulating along every surface, the smut of despair building up into a greasy layer that dulled the room. When the jailer ushered Brian in, my stomach cramped. His shoulders were slumped, his black eyes dull. In the bright orange jail coveralls, he looked diminished, an ember of himself.

He sat down. He tipped his head, said, "Jesse."

"Brian."

He asked about my eye, and I told him it was a wasp sting. He said, "You should be thinking of heading out."

"I wanted to see you first."

"How's Luke?"

Ineptly, I tried controlling my face. "He's worried about you."

"Is he someplace safe? Right now?"

"He's with Abbie and Wally Hankins."

"When are Mom and Dad flying back?"

"I haven't gotten through to them yet."

"Why not?"

"They're somewhere in the South China Sea. Give me time."

He ran his hands through his hair. "You can't stay in China Lake."

Jesse said, "They can stay at my place until your parents get back. The Remnant doesn't know where I live."

They looked at each other like dogs about to bark. Brian said, "Yeah. Okay."

I said, "I've retained a criminal lawyer. He'll be here later this afternoon."

"Somebody local?"

Jesse said, "From Bakersfield, a real pro, Jerry Sonnenfeld. He has fifteen years' experience trying capital cases."

Capital cases. Brian shifted uncomfortably in his seat.

"He knows his shit. Listen to what he says," Jesse said. "Have you given a statement to the police?" Brian shook his head. "Good. Don't."

"They wanted to know about my automatic," Brian said. "What I did with it. But I didn't do anything with it—it was on the shelf in my closet."

"Not anymore. You can lay money on it."

Brian's face was tightening. "They found the brass in the living room. A Winchester nine-millimeter cartridge, NATO spec. It's the ammunition I use. Someone's figured out how to hose me, royally, right up the ass."

His skin had gone pale. He took a long time getting the next words out. "Tabitha knows I always keep my weapon in the closet. If it's gone . . ."

I wanted to shake him. Despite everything she still had a grip on him. But I knew what he wanted to hear. "I can't believe she had anything to do with murdering Pastor Pete."

That soothed him, like putting a Band-Aid on a sucking chest wound. We talked for a while longer, about meeting with his lawyer, about arraignment on the murder charge, and about the fact that he wouldn't be granted bail. When he heard that, the light in his eyes withered like ashes at the burned end of a cigarette.

"This place is bad," he said. "I mean smeared-shit-on-the-walls, drunks-hallucinating, don't-bend-over-in-the-showers bad. And while I'm in here, the Remnant's out there, on the loose—" He broke off. "I have to get out of here, Evan."

"I'm working on it."

"I did not do this."

"I know you didn't."

He searched my countenance, looking for doubts. I did what Luke would do: I drew an X on my chest. Then I pressed my hand against the Plexiglas. After a second, he placed his hand on the other side, across from mine.

"I'll get you out," I said.

Cross my heart and hope to die.

12

It was three o'clock by the time we picked up Luke. Jesse was driving, as his car was not a billboard for obscenities. Clapton was on the stereo, *Crossroads*. I was staring out the window, downbeat. The relentless sunshine emphasized the bleached, hardscrabble isolation of this place. Jesse, however, waved at the horizon, saying, "This landscape is astonishing. My God, that's Mount Whitney, and it must be a hundred miles away. It's beautiful here. So unconstrained."

I grunted. He asked if I disagreed, and I said, "To get me back here they had to bring me in under arrest."

He changed the subject. "I started to tell you on the phone yesterday about this family who used to belong to the Remnant. A doctor at the rehab center knows them. Their daughter has cerebral palsy." He made a face. "Pastor Pete apparently expressed his disgust about 'weaklings' to others besides me. I spoke to the husband, and he said they'd be willing to talk about the church."

I thanked him.

"And that reporter called me looking for you. Sally Shimada." I groaned. I didn't want to speak to the press. He said, "She wanted to talk to you about Dr. Neil Jorgensen."

I hadn't been thinking about the plastic surgeon's

death, but my interest was immediately piqued again. "What did she say?"

"Just that she really wants you to call her." He imitated her peppy voice. "Really, really, *really*."

The Hankinses' front door was open to the fresh air, and when I knocked Wally boomed, "Enter!" Jesse popped a wheelie up the step. Inside we found Wally on the floor, kneeling over a Lionel train set. He looked at Jesse, surprised, but quickly smiled his Saint Bernard smile and came over to shake hands.

I hated this moment. The looks, the unspoken questions, the uneasiness able-bodied people often manifested around a wheelchair—it always balked me. Jesse usually rolled over it, like jumping curbs, but I worried about it wearing on him.

Wally, however, was affable, and Abbie could not have beaten around the bush if she'd had a map. She gave Jesse a frank look over her glasses. "Well. There are certainly a few things Evan didn't tell me about you. Was it a car wreck?"

"Hit and run."

"Bummer." She looked at me. "That'll teach me not to complain about my knee surgery anymore. And jeez, look at you; let's put a bag of frozen peas on that eye."

In the kitchen I said, "How's Luke?"

"He's been great. Quiet, but no probs. He's out back with Travis and Dulcie."

Through the kitchen window, the kids raced in and out of view. Luke was running behind a Little Tikes push-car, propelling it around the lawn. Dulcie sat at the wheel, steering erratically. Travis was spread-eagled on the car's roof, shrieking and sliding from side to side.

"They're fine," Abbie said. She handed me the peas. "But before they come in, what's going to happen with Luke's mother? Will she take him, since Brian's in jail?"

I shook my head. "Brian has sole custody, and he's made me Luke's guardian. Tabitha can't even visit him without going to court. And if she tries to get custody, she'll face the fight of her life."

"Good."

Jesse had found the high school yearbook on the table. Abruptly he snorted, held it up, and pointed to my class photo. Braces, bad hair, and a distressing attempt at eye makeup.

I said, "I'd like to see one of you, back when you were learning to shave."

Then I had a thought. I asked him to look up Antley, the name of the woman who owned Angels' Landing. He flipped through the index and shook his head.

I thought some more. "Try Hopp."

There it was, page one sixteen. I said, "Casey Hopp. Know the name?"

Abbie shook her head. The photo showed a group of students slouching against a chain-link fence, with the caption: *Detention Club.* Casey Hopp was at the edge of the group, wearing a grungy flannel shirt, a beanie pulled low, and a glare.

Abbie said, "Is that a girl or a boy?"

I couldn't tell. But I was going to find out.

The back door banged open and the kids came in, out of breath. Dulcie and Travis immediately gave Jesse the full stare. Luke came over to him, an inscrutable worldliness limning his little face, one hand raised in greeting like a movie-version Sioux.

Jesse said, "Hey, little dude. How's it going?"

"My dad's in jail."

"That sucks." Mr. Matter-of-fact.

Dulcie tugged on Abbie's shirt. "I thought you weren't allowed to say *suck*."

Abbie rubbed her shoulder. "Sometimes you just can't say it enough."

* * *

We stayed that night in China Lake, simply too tired to drive. In the morning I spoke to Brian. He sounded more dejected than before. The night in jail had sapped his spirit. It was sinking in: There wasn't going to be a quick fix.

Playing the good citizen, I informed Detective McCracken that I was leaving town. He was displeased, but didn't stop me. I asked him how long it would be before I could get access to Brian's house, and to my surprise, he said, "Anytime. The techs finished with it yesterday. We pulled down the tape."

Steeling myself, I decided to get in and out quickly, just retrieve my gear and pack a few things for Luke. But after standing outside for five minutes I couldn't bring myself to open the door. Thinking I might ease into the idea of going inside, I walked around to the backyard. The garbage can was gone, the patio a mess. I didn't approach the spot where the fire had been. Instead I peered through the sliding glass door at the dishevelment inside—the trashed furniture, scripture-scrawled walls, tracks of firefighters' boots. It looked debauched.

"Evan?"

I jumped.

Marc Dupree walked onto the patio. "I just came from seeing Brian. He told me I might find you here."

He was completely put together: voice creamy, aviators' wings shining on his shirt, trousers creased sharply enough to slice a cake. The khaki uniform complemented his brown skin. His sunglasses reflected the keen morning light.

"I wanted to make sure you know," he said, "everybody in the squadron is in Brian's corner one hundred percent. This is totally bogus."

"Glad to hear you say that." There was something else. I said, "What is it?"

"It's just . . . shoot. There's no delicate way to put this."

"Then speak frankly, Marc."

"Well . . ." He glanced off at the mountains. "You know that Brian thought Peter Wyoming was sleeping with Tabitha."

My head started pounding. "No, I didn't know that."

"All this time he's been wondering who it was, and when he finally gets a chance to confront him, the bastard gets shot in his house."

My heart sank. "You think he had a helmet fire."

He put up a hand. "I'm not saying Brian did the killing. I'm saying he melted down when he found the body, which is why he left the scene."

A love triangle. This was awful. This was motive. I pinched the bridge of my nose. "You didn't tell this to the police. Say you didn't."

"Of course not. I'm telling you so you'll understand why he acted out of character. He feels enormously guilty about leaving you to find the body."

With his eyes hidden behind the aviator shades, all I saw when I looked at him was my warped reflection. Something wasn't right here. His posture, his rectitude, didn't jibe with the way his wide mouth pinched after he spoke.

It hit me: He should have been Brian's alibi.

"Marc, you told the cops that Brian was at your house Friday evening, that he left for only a few minutes. Didn't you?"

The expression on his face didn't change. "I told them I had total confidence that he was innocent."

"That's not the same thing."

"Brian did not commit this murder. Period. I'm offering you my word on this."

"So you didn't alibi him." My head was really hammering. "Why in hell not?"

"I can't, at this moment in time."

Like a dust devil, suspicion began spinning in me, dragging up memories from China Lake—of the stone-faced lying that went with military secrecy, of the dispassionate smoothness with which a uniform could invest a liar.

I said, "You can't alibi him, or you won't?"

The wind lashed up. Though it made me wince, it didn't so much as cause a quiver on his sleek, pressed facade.

He said, "I'm telling you this much as his friend. But that is all I can say at this moment. I thought you would be pleased to hear it."

"Brian is up the creek without a paddle. It does him no good for you to hand me a bouquet."

He said, "Your brother is straight about this. You should be too."

Straight—that meant Brian knew Marc wouldn't speak up in his defense, and accepted it. All at once I wondered if Marc had in fact been home Friday night—or whether Brian had gone to Marc's house at all. I wondered if, instead, they'd been on the base.

What if Marc had been on duty, night-flying over the back ranges, performing a classified weapons test? If so, he wouldn't even have told his wife. And he wasn't going to tell me or the police. Briefly, for one fissile moment, I hated it all. The navy, my whole family tradition—all it meant was bigger booms, new and improved death, all to protect the edge, to ensure that the U.S. Navy swung a bigger dick than the other guy. The Big Ssssh was part of the strategy, and it was the reason crackpots believed there were aliens running around Area 51, and CIA satellites that watched you take a pee, and that government concentration camps lay beyond the horizon, awaiting prisoners of the beast. And the irony? In the end, the navy's new toys got written up in *Aviation Week* anyway.

But Marc Dupree was not going to violate regulations even to save Brian from a murder charge. Standing there, beyond the vault of reason, I felt my own head ignite.

"You have a different concept of friendship than I do. I'll see you, Marc."

I went inside and slammed the door behind me.

Dust motes rose and jigged around the hallway when I stepped inside. I was shaking with anger. The air smelled acrid. Fine black fingerprint powder covered numerous surfaces. On the living room floor a deep red stain spread in an irregular circle. A thin trail of blood ran across the carpet to the patio door. Queasiness grabbed at my stomach. Somehow I hadn't seen it the night of the murder, perhaps distracted by the vandalism—the brighter, bigger, redder things scrawled on the walls. I found myself surprised that the trail wasn't thicker. And I thought: Why had the killer dragged the body outside?

Conceivably he had set the body ablaze to destroy evidence. Fingerprints, fibers, evidence that he had scuffled with Wyoming, whatever. But if that was the goal, the killer could simply have burned the whole house down. No, a deeper motive underlay the method of destruction.

Stuffed in a trash can. If that wasn't symbolic, nothing was.

A banshee image hissed in my head: the killer hiding in the house while Brian stumbled on the scene . . . hiding, and waiting, and then arranging the macabre pyrotechnic exhibit for my interactive viewing horror. The hatred, the disdain, and the cool nerve it must have taken—it staggered me.

Outside, the wind licked the walls of the house. I hurried to gather up my things. I wanted someone to come in and rip out the carpet, wash the walls, and paint the whole damn place. But, turning the key in the lock, I doubted whether Brian would ever make this his home; whether he and Luke would ever, in fact, set foot in the house again.

*   *   *

A hot and capricious crosswind chased us all the
way to the coast. It was a Santa Ana, a wind that
strips the view to a bright and exposed base coat, a
wind that opens abrasions. The Pacific glared gold in
the sun, with whitecaps shearing off toward the west.

Luke was riding with me, and he was the one who
spotted the brown cloud seeping above the mountain-
tops. We were only twenty minutes from Jesse's house.
Here, the coastal range butts up against the shoreline.
Above the peaks, in the brilliant sky, rose a single
cloud.

"That's smoke," Luke said.

I hunched and peered out at it. "You think so?"

"I think there's a fire."

I thought he was right. I turned on the radio. The
station was playing its usual anxious-white-boy rock
'n' roll, so cataclysm hadn't yet descended. But it was
high fire season, that time of year when the world
saw news footage of movie stars wielding garden hoses
against a mile-wide flame front, trying to douse their
Malibu digs. Anything was possible, and could happen
in the snap of a finger.

Californians attack fire as mortal enemy, as tragedy,
as monster. But fire is integral, in fact vital to this
ecosystem. It's restorative, a form of purification.
Some local plants actually need the heat of the flames
to germinate. What has gradually become a tragedy is
fire suppression, a hundred years of snuffing out blazes
in their infancy. The foliage builds up and up, so that
when a fire inevitably starts, the resulting blaze is a
conflagration, huge and devastating. Still, if it's your
house, your town, you stand and fight.

A minute later we got a better view. In the mountains behind Carpinteria the cloud rose in a fat pillar,
spreading high into the sky. At its base, along the
chaparral-covered slopes, it was a thick and churning
column.

Luke pointed. "I see the fire!"

Briefly a flare of red spurted from the brown boil. I blinked, and it was gone.

Traffic began slowing. People were simply rubbernecking, but if the wind blew the fire this way, the CHP could close the freeway, and that would be a mess. The 101 Freeway is the main road into Santa Barbara, which lies like a bracelet between the mountains and the ocean. The city is vulnerable to road closures. Several years back a toxic chemical spill shut down the 101, virtually cutting off traffic to Los Angeles for weeks. I lurched to a stop in a hail of brakelights.

Luke said, "I bet they'll send the planes."

The U.S. Forest Service has an air-attack base at the Santa Barbara airport, and when a big wildfire hits, the planes soon lumber into the sky. We had seen them that summer, DC-7s and C-130s and P-3s, flying to fires in Montana and Arizona. Heavy at takeoff, they strained off the ground, piston engines roaring, skimming the roads and buildings beyond the runway. Old warriors, they looked heroic.

Luke squirmed for a better view at the smoke. "Look! It's number twenty-three!"

He pointed at a bright streak, white with an orange nose and tail, flying low, almost invisible against the mountains. It angled toward the fire and, just before it disappeared into the cloud, opened its bomb bay doors. Red slurry dumped from its belly, pluming down on the flames. A moment later the plane broke out of the smoke, climbing to escape the turbulent air near the fire. It banked toward the coast, heading straight for us, getting larger, louder, until it grumbled overhead only a few hundred feet off the ground, engines booming loud enough to shake human bone.

Luke said, "Wow!"

"Really."

It banked right over the ocean, heading for the airport to tank up.

"What happens if they fly through the fire?" he said.

"Those planes are tough. They'd be okay."

"They could paint the plane with the red stuff, so it wouldn't burn up." He watched it receding along the coastline. "Should we say a prayer for them?"

I looked at him, surprised. "If you want."

He closed his eyes, then opened them again. "Should we say a prayer for the other fire pilots, too?"

The sobriety on his face was devastating. I said, "Do you want to say a prayer for all pilots?"

He nodded and shut his eyes. I found myself unable to pray along, angry, knowing that the universe was cruel enough to trick a little boy, to let him send out his deepest longings without promise of an answer.

13

When we finally reached Butterfly Beach, Jesse took Luke bodysurfing. I skipped it, sitting outside on Jesse's deck with a cold Heineken in hand, watching the two of them make their way into the surf. Salt spray was luminous in the air. Luke was a sprite, wiry arms waving as he met the first breaker and it broke around his legs. He yelled, "It's cold!"

Jesse came behind him, sitting on the sand, sculling backward on his butt, pushing with his better leg, pulling with his arms. When he bought the house, with the sand and the rocks between him and the surf, I thought he was subjecting himself to a nasty joke, a constant, cosmic black eye. Instead he had spent weekends clearing a path to the water. Now, a minute behind Luke, he rolled into the breakers. He embraced a receding wave and became an aquatic creature, graceful and confident, gliding toward Luke, arms arcing in that easy, powerful freestyle he had, water shimmering on his shoulders in the sunlight.

I tilted my head back and drank deeply. An air-attack plane hunkered by, heading back to the airport.

When Luke and Jesse splashed back up onshore, I swaddled Luke in a thick yellow beach towel and ran him a shower in the guest room. The house had three bedrooms veering off the large open space comprising living room, dining area, and kitchen. Just as Jesse

came through the patio door, I was looking in his
refrigerator. I asked him what he wanted for dinner,
onions or baking soda. He coasted toward the far side
of the living room, rubbing a towel through his hair,
and said, "I haven't had time to shop." He put a CD
on the stereo. Hendrix, *Electric Ladyland*. Turning up
the volume, he went into his room, heading for the
shower.

I scrambled eggs, toasted a couple bagels, and called
it dinner. Jesse emerged after his shower, barefoot, in
a white T-shirt and jeans, and said, "Smells good."
He set the CD to play "All Along the Watchtower."
Hendrix's guitar hit me like wind shear, like a scythe.

There must be some kind of way out of here. . . .

Sundown was coming, and it was Martian red in the
smoke from the wildfire. The light angled through the
wall of plate-glass windows facing the beach, landing
bloody-bright on Jesse's handsome face, and tinting
his white T-shirt crimson. Coming into the kitchen, he
uncorked a bottle of pinot noir and poured two
glasses. Then he reached for a bottle of prescription
pills. Tipping two into his palm, he swallowed them
with the wine.

"Pain's bad?" I said.

He shifted himself in his seat. "I've had better
weeks." He drank, and changed the subject. "I didn't
tell you about the whale."

"Luke did. Some Jet Skiers got a blubber facial."

"City engineers had winched the thing to a fishing
trawler and were towing it out to sea. The jokers who
hit it were crawling drunk." He spun languidly to face
me. "The next day, when they woke up in the hospital,
these bozos called me. They wanted me to sue the
city for their injuries. Thanks to *Gaul v. Beowulf's
Books*, I'm suddenly an expert on wild-animal litiga-
tion." Caustic face. "I declined the case. Told them
to call Skip Hinkel."

"Speaking of whom . . . ," I said.

He snorted. "Judge Rodriguez scolded him for slagging me off to the press." Another swallow. "So Skip told the Department of Fish and Game that I was harboring the ferrets."

I was putting plates on the table. I stopped. "No."

"It was an anonymous tip, but nobody else would have done it. A Fish and Game inspector showed up at the office on Friday. It's hard to get much work done when an officious little man with a cage is scurrying around the firm."

"I can't believe Skip."

"Sure you can. He's a jackass. It's an FFL."

FFL, Fucking Fact of Life. His term for things you couldn't change.

I said, "No, it's not. It's your reputation."

"I'm tough. My rep will be fine."

After dinner, darkness came quickly. When I put Luke to bed, I came back to find Jesse on the sofa, watching an *X-Files* rerun. His mouth was pressed tight, his shoulders crooked. The pills weren't working. I stood behind the sofa and began kneading the base of his neck, feeling resistance, stiff muscles fighting me.

I tapped his shoulder. "Lie down on the floor."

He got on his back on the rug. I knelt down next to him and started stretching his legs, one at a time. I bent his knees, circled his ankles, and rotated his hips, working his hamstrings, calves, quads. I had no training in physical therapy but knew he needed to preserve his range of motion to keep from developing contractures, locked joints that could further disable a paraplegic. He lay there, looking tight. The lights were low, the TV flickering; Mulder confronting the Cigarette-Smoking Man. Mood lighting.

He said, "Why do you think the killer burned Pastor Pete's body?"

At once I found I had a throbbing headache, and the wasp stings were itching like crazy.

I said, "He could have been a psychopath, or trying to destroy evidence."

"He?"

"Or she, or they."

He worked himself up onto his elbows. "If the killer wanted to get rid of the evidence, why didn't he dump the body out in the desert? The Mafia does."

"Maybe he was worried that the neighbors would see him removing it. I don't know; maybe he came to the house on foot and had no way to carry it."

He said, "I think it's something else. The way the killer positioned the body in the trash can, it seems like ritual. Or rage."

For a minute we listened to the surf murmuring outside. Then Jesse held his hand out. I pulled him to a sitting position. Tucking his feet in, he sat cross-legged, leaning back against the couch.

He said, "Do you still think the Remnant has big plans?"

I rubbed my temples. "Yes."

"Do you think Pastor Pete's death derailed their scheme?"

"No. Chenille indicated the opposite, that now they're more determined than ever to battle the Antichrist." I paused. "It brought back something Nikki said to me. That we should be on guard against an event that convinces the Remnant that the end is *now*."

"Their leader getting turned into a Roman candle, that would do it."

"That's what scares me."

He took my hand, ran his fingers up the inside of my arm. Even with everything going on, his touch was electric.

I said, "But I can't fathom how framing Brian fits into their plans. If it does."

"You're damned loyal to Brian, know it?"

His eyes, cobalt in the dim light, had a coolness that

made his statement less than a compliment. Slowly he said, "Ev, have you thought about the fact that he doesn't have an alibi?"

I hadn't told him about Marc Dupree's refusal to provide that alibi. "I think one of his friends can."

"A naval officer?"

"Yes. Another pilot, a commander."

"Gosh, then he ought to be out in no time flat."

"What do you mean by that?"

He glanced at the TV. Mulder and Scully close, but not touching. "I mean that you canonize the U.S. Navy. You think the cops are a bunch of podunk hicks, and the navy can do no wrong. But I hate to tell you, law enforcement doesn't genuflect the way you do."

"That's a harsh assessment."

"But accurate. The China Lake police don't care that Brian is a fighter pilot. You don't see that because you worship him."

"You're being unfair."

"Face it, you do. You fall on your knees and don't look up or around or even consider the possibility that he isn't being straight with you, that he had threatened Peter Wyoming, and that he could have—"

"Don't." I stood up. "Don't say it. Do not even think it."

His eyes had turned hot. "This is called denial."

"No."

Humorless smile. "I rest my case."

"Jesse, shut up."

"If you're not even willing to consider the possibility, then you're not being a good attorney."

"I'm not an attorney in this situation; I'm Brian's sister, and I refuse to think that way. Don't you dare suggest it."

"Ev. You need to step back and look at the situation objectively."

"Bullshit. You're suggesting that Brian did it."

"I'm telling you that the police didn't behave like total idiots when they arrested him. He had motive, means, and opportunity. And face it, Peter Wyoming attacked Brian at the core of his life, by trying to take Luke. Isn't it possible that Brian snapped and took matters into his own hands?"

"No."

"You and I weren't there, so how can you be sure of that?"

Never had I felt so angry with him. "You just hit the nail on the head. You weren't there. So don't speculate. Just because Brian gets on your nerves, you think he's a murderer? You are full of shit, Blackburn."

A scuffling sound and a small frightened noise came from the front entryway. I looked around and saw Luke jerk his head back around the corner, out of sight.

"Oh, my God."

Luke's feet beat a tattoo back to his bedroom.

I spun on Jesse. "Dammit! He heard!"

Jesse started pulling himself up into the wheelchair. He looked devastated, but I was too incensed to care. I ran to the guest bedroom. The light was off.

"Luke?"

He was curled in a ball beneath the bed. When I reached under and touched his back, he jerked away. I lay down on my stomach and tried to slide under the bed.

"Luke, sweetheart. Come out."

"No." Tears in his voice.

"Please, tiger. Come here."

But he only curled tighter and lay crying quietly.

Jesse appeared in the doorway. "Luke? Hey, little dude, I—"

I waved him away.

It took me half an hour to talk Luke out from under

the bed. And though I got him tucked back beneath the covers, he wouldn't talk, didn't relax when I told him Jesse didn't mean it, that I was sorry he had heard us arguing . . . but why should he? My words sounded inept and insincere.

I found Jesse by the living room windows, staring out across the breakers. The wildfire's ruddy glow tinged the eastern sky.

He didn't look around. "I am so incredibly sorry."

"How much do you think a six-year-old can take before his spirit breaks, Jesse?"

He closed his eyes. His shoulders dropped. He said, "Evan . . ."

I heard remorse in his voice, but also contention. I said, "You really don't want to get into it with me right now. Take my word for it."

More seconds passed.

I said, "I need some air."

I went down to the beach. The night was hot, the sky piebald with moonlight and fireglow. The surf hissed and ran across my bare feet like a foamy tongue. My head pounded. I walked for only fifty yards before breaking into a run.

How could Jesse think that Brian had killed Peter Wyoming?

The waves splashed over me and I picked up speed, hearing my feet hit the sand, just going, wanting the beating of my own heart to drown out all other sounds, all other thoughts. I ran and ran for miles, until finally I knew I had to turn around, and I came back hard, with my lungs burning from the smoky air. When I stopped I set my hands on my hips and tilted my head back. My face felt as if it were glowing with heat. Beneath my sodden shirt strings of sweat ran down my back. The stings throbbed.

The waves, so cold when I started running, now invited. I looked around—not another person was in sight. I stripped down and splashed into the water. When the surf reached my thighs I dove through an incoming breaker.

The water cooled my skin and soothed the stinging. Stroking farther out, I rolled onto my back and stared at the Milky Way. Firelit, the stars were a ruby vein in the night. The waves lifted and rocked me, and the world felt primordial.

Eventually I rode the waves back to shore. Walking up the beach toward the house, I saw that the lights were on in Jesse's bedroom. It was an invitation. But I didn't know whether he was waiting to offer regret or further argument.

The warm air felt refreshing on my bare skin, drying me as I picked up my sweaty clothing and carried it onto the deck. I brushed the sand off my feet with the T-shirt, getting ready to go inside.

Without warning the beam of a flashlight hit me full-on.

A man said, "Don't move."

Too late. I jerked my clothes up in front of me, ludicrously trying to protect my modesty. I yelled, "Jesse!"

The man stepped onto the deck. Behind him came someone else, also holding a flashlight. I couldn't see their faces.

"Jesse! Set the dogs loose!"

Flashlight number one wavered. "Hold on! Freeze, and don't say another word. California Department of Fish and Game!"

14

The flashlights stepped onto the deck and bobbled toward me. Flashlight Number One said, "Identify yourself."

"For crying out loud, you want ID? I'm naked!"

"Well . . ."

My fright vanished. "Get the hell away from me. And turn off those lights."

"This is state business, lady."

I could see him now, a short man with a clipped goatee and a hairless head that gleamed in the moonlight. He was holding a wire animal carrier and staring at my chest.

"Shut off the flashlights and turn around, numskulls!"

They hesitated. I whistled loudly through my teeth, as if summoning Cujo.

Flashlight Two, needle voice and shaky hand, said, "I wouldn't do that if I were you."

The patio door opened. The flashlights swung around to spotlight Jesse in the doorway, looking infuriated.

Flashlight One repeated, "Fish and Game!"

"I know who you are, Ranger Rick. Now get out of here." He angled in front of me. I crouched down behind him and started dressing.

"We have a report that you're harboring contraband animals. We're here to check it out."

"Not without a warrant you aren't. Get off my property."

"We saw the lady—"

I popped up and peered at him over Jesse's shoulder. "You thought I was harboring ferrets? Hey, doofus, *where*?"

"I—"

Jesse said, "Hit the road. Go back to Jellystone Park."

After that, after Jesse slammed the door on them and called them grandstanding assholes, dickhead rat catchers, he stopped, looked at me, and burst out laughing. " 'Hey, doofus, *where*?' Talk about grace under fire." He cajoled me, against my deepest, grudge-loving impulses, to smile. And later in bed he held me to his side, sailing his fingertips up and down my thigh. And it was almost enough.

But in the morning a faint odor of discord lingered over us, in silences and awkward glances. Perhaps it's a law of physics—conservation of rancor. It never completely dissipates, just fades into background radiation. Heading out the door on his way to court he called to Luke. In the broad entryway he spoke softly to him.

"Last night I said things I shouldn't have. I have a big fat mouth and sometimes I hurt people's feelings. I'm really sorry about what I said about your dad."

Luke rocked back and forth, staring hard at Jesse's red tie.

"I know how much you love your dad. And I know that he loves you more than anything in the world. I'm going to do everything I can to help him out." He paused, watching Luke rock. "Okay?"

Luke offered a tiny nod.

"Okay. Be good for your aunt Evan. Wait till she's

out of the room before you eat the Halloween candy
I hid in the cupboard."

Luke perked up. "M&M's?"

"And Reese's peanut butter cups. Ssh. She's looking
at us."

Jesse caught my eye. I knew what he was thinking,
and had to agree: His apology was deftly done. But
he had said nothing about Brian's innocence.

I spent the morning on the phone, conferring with
Brian's criminal lawyer, talking to Luke's teacher
about why he might miss school for a couple of weeks,
trying to track down my parents in the Strait of Ma-
lacca, and rearranging my work schedule. I was falling
behind, and did need to earn a living. My royalties
from *Lithium Sunset* covered my monthly breath-mint
purchases, at best.

I also called the Eichners, the ex-Remnant family,
arranging to meet with them that afternoon. Kevin
Eichner cautioned that they'd never met Tabitha. I
told him that didn't matter and laid my own cards on
the table, explaining that Brian had been arrested. If
they were uncomfortable talking to me, I said, I'd
understand.

After a delay, he said, "No, we'll talk. We want to."

Nikki Vincent was going to watch Luke for me, so
after lunch we met her at the zoo. The palm trees
swayed and the sea lions barked. The place had an
artful matchbox atmosphere—tiny habitats, a prairie
dog village, a miniature train—but was hazed brown
beneath the smoky, *Blade Runner* sky. Nikki looked
regal, walking slowly, silver jewelry gleaming, her
great belly swelling beneath an orange sundress. I
hugged her and asked how she was feeling.

"I've never heard of a pregnant woman actually ex-
ploding, but I'm wondering if it's possible. I am
woman, hear me blow," she said. "How about you?"

I told her about my fight with Jesse, how he had
doubted Brian's innocence.

She said, "Want me to slap him around?" Then she shook her head. "You cannot spend your time being a mediator between your brother and your man. You have to tell these boys to put away their peashooters and get behind each other."

I sighed. "I have."

"Tell you what. I'll slap them both around, as soon as Brian is cleared."

I squeezed her hand. "Thanks for saying that."

Kevin and Alicia Eichner lived in Summerland, a seaside village of surf shops, organic restaurants, and hardy tans. Their tidy blue-and-white bungalow had an immaculate Ford F-250 pickup in the driveway, with a carpenter's silver tool chest in the bed. Plastic windmill flowers twirled in a flower box on the porch, and a plywood ramp, sanded and painted, ran up to the front step. Their daughter, the girl with cerebral palsy, must use a wheelchair, I knew.

Alicia Eichner was as trim as the house. She wore a crisp pink top and pressed jeans, sprayed her dark hair tall on top, and had a broad mouth and a bronze complexion that suggested Mexican heritage. Kevin Eichner stood six foot four, was sandy-haired, with a full mustache and a loose, gregarious smile. He wore shorts with Caterpillar boots, and had a pair of sports sunglasses hanging around his neck from a cord. He said yes, he was a carpenter.

Alicia poured soft drinks and we sat in the small living room. The two of them, side by side on the sofa, looked apprehensive.

She rubbed her hands together. "I just have to start by saying, when we joined the Remnant we didn't know it was"—her broad mouth crimped—"a cult. I mean, we would never join a *cult*. But the Remnant just seemed like a real great church, full of committed Christians."

Kevin said, "They was totally clear about where they

stood." He held his hand up like a meat cleaver. "They had a message that hit you right between the eyes. We thought we was headed in the right direction."

Alicia said, "And they cared about us. They were always *so* happy to see us at services. I mean, we'd been invited to join."

I said, "How's that?"

"A teacher's aide at Karina's school asked us. Karina, that's our daughter."

She retrieved a framed photo from a bookshelf. Karina was about thirteen, and had Alicia's brunette hair and broad mouth. She was smiling crookedly, with her thin face tilted toward the camera at a sharp angle.

Alicia said, "There was this teacher's aide; she told us the Remnant had great activities for kids, plus it was where we could find the answer. And Karina, she'd taken a shine to Shiloh."

"Shiloh," I said.

Kevin said, "Shiloh Keeler, yeah. She's a real little drill sergeant."

Alicia clasped her hands together. "The first few months we felt like we'd found a home, like we really belonged. Everybody had this great spirit, and the church was doing good things. Like Chenille Wyoming's outreach program for runaways."

I didn't know about that.

"She goes to homeless shelters and even out on the streets talking to these girls. And it *works*. She gets these street kids to come to church, offering hot food and a warm place to sleep, and promising not to contact the police—"

"Or their pimp," Kevin said.

"Or that. Ever. She lets these girls know they'll be safe. It's wonderful. Course, lots of them drift away, you know, not liking the discipline, but some stay. Like Glory Moffett."

"Chenille's pound puppy."

Alicia said, "Kev, that isn't nice."

I sat back, taking this in.

"But after a while," Alicia said, "things got weird."

They looked at each other, deciding where to start. After a moment Kevin said, "Pastor Pete had problems with dirt." Sour smile. "He thought the whole world was filthy."

"He had a germ phobia," Alicia said. "You ever notice his hands, how they were all red and sore? That's because he couldn't leave the house if he didn't wash them twelve times. And his sermons—it was always germs, germs, germs. They were the devil's handiwork, or else God's vengeance. That's why he made everybody protest at these AIDS funerals. He was obsessed."

Kevin said, "Tell her about the gifts."

"Oh. People in the church were expected to manifest a gift of the Holy Spirit. Parents were supposed to watch for it in their children."

"What sort of gifts?" I said.

Kevin crossed his arms. "Like singing, or marksmanship." I raised an eyebrow, and he said, "Yeah. Pastor Pete liked the showbiz gifts, but Chenille and Ice Paxton, they favored kids that showed a knack for survival skills." His loose smile was gone. "At church one week, this ten-year-old gets up and fieldstrips an M-sixteen. I'm thinking, 'Whoa, this ain't kosher.' "

Alicia's hands were turning white, clenching each other. "But Karina, you know, with her cerebral palsy, she . . ." She stopped, looking strained.

I said, "You found out how Pastor Pete felt about people with disabilities."

"No," Alicia said, "not then, or we would have gotten out right away. No, people were really being caring toward Karina. Like Curt Smollek used to joke around with her, and Chenille, she called Karina her 'little lamb.' "

Kevin said, "What happened, I got stupid and asked

Paxton about this kid showing off with the M-sixteen. I tell him I believe in self-defense, but where does the Bible talk about riflery skills being a gift of the Spirit? Oh, man. Did he ever give me what-for. He says, 'If you're having doubts it means Satan has invaded your mind.' "

He took out a pack of cigarettes, asking if it bothered me. I shook my head.

"Then Chenille comes by in her big red choir robe, looking like *Attack of the Killer Tomatoes*, and Paxton gets her in on the act. Kevin's having qualms, he says. And she says I better stop listening to the devil, and start watching for my own daughter's gift to manifest. And zoom, we're off to the Twilight Zone."

He lit up. "She tells me to watch close, 'cause Karina's gift won't be flashy. Well, big duh, flashy is the Brueghel triplets with their gift of baton twirling, and Karina drives a power wheelchair. So Chenille gives some examples, herself the biggie, gift of prophecy, but there's also Glory—she has the gift of submission, a humble gift but still very valuable. And Paxton says, 'Hold on, submission isn't a gift; it's a product of discipline.' He's talking *gifts*, and he's thinking Karina may be given the power of discerning spirits, or the interpretation of tongues; those would be useful to him as head of church security. Like she could spot demons in a crowd, or decipher secret codes."

He flicked ashes into his empty soda can. "They scared me into shutting up." Shaking his head, he said, "Head of security. I mean, come on, when did you ever hear of a church had a security department, outside of maybe the Vatican?"

He stared at his hands. "Plus, if he was head of security, where was he the night Pastor Pete got killed?"

It was a good question. I said, "What do you think?"

"Honestly? I think he got sloppy. I think he was

tired of Pastor Pete and his antics, and maybe let down his guard. He didn't like these protests the pastor planned, said publicity only drew the attention of the feds."

"He talked about that? Openly?"

"I overheard it doing some carpentry work at the church. I hear Paxton complaining to Chenille, saying, 'It's time to take the active hand and get down to business.'"

I heard a clock ticking. "What business?"

"Don't know."

"Do you have any ideas?"

"Chenille, I think she had it in her mind to change the way the church was run." He shrugged, indicating this was conjecture. "She told Paxton to cool his jets. Went, 'let Pete be the public face of the Remnant.' The way she said it, it sounded like other stuff was going on behind the scenes."

"What stuff?"

We sat, listening to the clock tick.

Kevin said, "Well, Pastor Pete and his missus wasn't getting along so hot."

His face was heating up, and Alicia's eyes were shimmering. I sensed that they felt a desperate urge to talk about the Remnant, even to a stranger. I let him roll.

"Chenille and Pete was having differences. Marital and theological. See, Pete, he was a fire-breather, but Chenille, she thinks she's a prophet."

Alicia said, "She has dreams. And visions."

Kevin crossed his legs. His foot started jittering. "What do you know about Chenille's background?"

"Nothing."

"Hold on to your butt," he said. "She was a hooker."

My lips parted in surprise.

"And a junkie."

I said, "This is for real?"

"Oh, yeah," he said. "She used to work out of this club downtown, supposedly being an exotic dancer, but you know. Guy from work remembered her; she had this act where she sprayed whipped cream on herself, like a bikini, and the customers would lick it off."

That, I knew, was an image I'd be seeing in my bad dreams.

Alicia said, "She never hid it. Pastor Pete mentioned it in his sermons—about Jesus bringing Chenille to the Remnant to be cleansed in the blood of the lamb."

"Except I don't think he believed it. I think he still thought she was *filthy*," Kevin said. "He and the wife would act chilly toward each other, and then, wham. Sex rules."

Alicia blushed.

"He'd go on a tear and order married couples to abstain from sex." He snorted. "Right. I hear that, I'm thinking '*hello*—we know you ain't gettin' any, buster.'" He turned to Alicia. "Tell her about the women's weekend."

"Oh. We had a retreat out at this place in the desert."

I said, "Angels' Landing."

"Yeah. A real dump. Chenille held this 'deep teaching' session one night around the campfire. And let me tell you, it was spooky stuff." She exhaled. "She talked about motherhood during the Tribulation, when the Antichrist ascends to power and believers are persecuted. She said Christians were going to have to go on the run, and we'd need to travel light 'cause we'd be carrying out hit-and-run raids. She was talking about the Remnant being a guerrilla army."

I said, "Lock and load."

"Exactly. She quoted from scripture, about the end—how when it starts you have to get out on the double, and how Jesus said, 'And alas for those who are with child and for those who give suck in those days!' And she said that's why her humiliation was really a blessing from God."

"Humiliation?"

"She can't have children. Back when she was unsaved she got chlamydia, and it made her sterile. She thought it was her punishment for being a prostitute."

She started fiddling with her wedding ring. "For a long time she prayed to be healed—she was desperate for a child—but finally she saw that being barren was a gift. Her shame was her strength. 'Alas for those who are with child.' But see, she would never be with child, so she could devote herself totally to the fight."

She looked at me. "Chenille said it was destiny. She was prophesied to lead the resistance against the Antichrist. That's when I saw that her ego was out of whack, when she thought the Bible was talking about her, personally."

I started to speak. Kevin said, "Wait, it gets better."

Alicia twirled her wedding ring. Her pupils were large. "By now I had goose bumps. We're around this fire, it's pitch-black, we can hear animals squeaking and slithering out there in the dark, and Chenille tells us the time is near, signs are everywhere, the storm's coming. She gets real intense and says it's up to us. Jesus can't do it alone; we have got to take the active hand."

Active hand. I felt itchy again, didn't speak, didn't want Alicia to say what she was going to say.

She leaned forward. "She was telling us we were going to kick it off."

I said, "The end."

She nodded. "She said the Lord was growing impatient. He was tired of waiting. We were going to have to get biblical, and soon."

Kevin said, "I'll tell you who's tired of waiting; it's Chenille, and Ice Paxton, all them people in the Remnant with their pitiful little lives, crazy to feel like somebody."

I said, "She actually told you that the Remnant is going to flip the switch on Doomsday?"

"She didn't use those words, but she laid a hand on my arm and said, 'Alicia, it's gonna be toughest for you, 'cause you know there is no way on God's green earth Karina will be able to go where you got to go, or do what you got to do.' I just sat there in shock. And she quotes scripture again—how the sun will be darkened and the stars will be falling from heaven. I'm thinking, 'So?' My God, did she think I'd walk away from my baby, go out and start blowing things up or whatever . . . ?"

She pressed her fingers to her eyes. "By the time we got home I had hives. I was a total wreck."

I said, "Is that when you quit the church?"

"No." She looked at the floor, and at Kevin, and finally at me. "I know it sounds crazy now. But Chenille had been so kind. She always prayed for Karina, and wanted to know if she was improving. She even asked if the doctors were up on the latest therapies, you know, saying some of these new drugs might help. . . . It warmed my heart. I thought she was truly compassionate. That with her past and all, she understood tough times."

She looked at me, desperate for empathy, clearly hoping I didn't regard her as a total fool.

She said, "I went to Pastor Pete. I thought he could counsel me, explain what Chenille had said in some . . . logical light."

Kevin got up, went to stare out the window at the smoke-burnished sky.

"But Pastor Pete confirmed everything Chenille had said, and more. He told me God had chosen me to make this sacrifice, to make up for my past sins."

"Sacrifice," Kevin said. "My little girl, he meant."

Alicia's face was tight with anger. "He said it was obvious I had some big repenting to do. He told me in my past I must have been dirty. That's the word he used, *dirty*. That's why Karina was born 'defective.'"

Kevin turned around. "And that, you better believe, is when we got the hell out of there."

The smoke from his cigarette languished in the air, almost as thick as their hurt and unease. I didn't know what to say. Then a small yellow school bus pulled up outside. Alicia's face cleared and she hopped up, saying, "Good, you'll get to meet Karina." I stood up, too, and said I'd taken enough of their time. I walked outside with them to the bus.

The driver was working an electric lift, lowering Karina's wheelchair to the curb. Karina wore jeans, Reeboks, and a bright pink knit top like her mother's. In her brunette hair she had a dozen tiny hair clips that looked like gently roosting butterflies. She waved jerkily when she saw her parents.

Kevin said, "Hey, silly puss," and Alicia kissed her, asking how school was. Karina rolled her head and worked her mouth to say, "Good." They introduced me as a friend who was visiting. Karina eyed me brightly. After a minute Alicia told me good-bye, saying, "I hope this has been helpful," and Kevin walked me to my car.

He watched them go inside. "Couple more things I wanted to tell you, out of Alicia's earshot. She don't need to get more upset than she already is. What she said about those people at the church who cared for Karina? By the end, I didn't buy a bit of it. That guy Curt Smollek, he creeped me out in a major way." He made a face. "You ever seen a kid who liked to pull the wings off bugs? That's what Smollek reminded me of."

I grimaced.

"Yeah, really. And Chenille Wyoming. Alicia liked her 'cause Chenille overcame so much, and always acted gentle with her. But let me tell you, Chenille was not so gentle with other people. I seen her smack the baton twirlers in the face for messing up their routine." He crossed his arms. "She's totally two-faced. That stuff about going on the run, traveling light—well, she's a junk-food junkie. Tell me how she's gonna conduct hit-and-run raids carting Cheetos and Reddi-Wip everywhere she goes. And"—he looked toward the house—"I think she's still on drugs."

"Seriously?"

"Just before we quit the church, she asked me to do her a favor. The next time I took Karina to the neurologist, could I get her some supplies."

"Narcotics?"

"Yeah. I shut her down, said absolutely no way. She kept wheedling me, saying it's not wrong if it's for the greater good, that she couldn't get them herself because she was being watched by the government. Total crap. Not only was she still doping, but she was fixing it so I'm the one who gets caught if anything goes wrong. Greater good—right. That whole church is a sick bunch of phonies."

"I'm sorry it turned out so badly for you."

"Live and learn." He smoothed his mustache. "So, if it wasn't your brother, who killed Pastor Pete?"

"I have no idea. How about you?"

"How many people hated his guts? I couldn't begin to count."

15

The CCTV camera bolted above the entrance to Strider, Baines & Moore, stockbrokers, captured the footage. It shows Jesse coming through the door at 12:32 p.m. on October twenty-first. The tape quality isn't great. Even with him walking slowly on crutches, the black-and-white video gives him a smudged, grainy look. He talks to his broker for about half an hour, and the camera records him leaving just before one o'clock. Less than a minute later, it catches a young woman walking up the street in the direction he had gone. She's in frame for only a few seconds, just enough to make out her round face and the big bow in her ponytail.

Jesse next stopped into his bank, which had better-quality cameras. On the tape the ceiling lights reflect from his wraparound sunglasses. A bank manager, a woman in a snug brown suit, greets him and ushers him to her desk. He talks to her for a good while, discussing a refinance on his mortgage, rates having dropped. She's attentive.

So is the round-faced girl with the ponytail, standing at a central counter filling in a deposit slip, and filling it in, endlessly. Two other young women soon join her, blondes with glazed lipstick and identical back-combed hair. They too begin filling in deposit slips intricately, watching him.

From their whispers and covert curiosity, they're apparently figuring out that Jesse had money, more than he'd earn on a junior associate's salary. What they didn't know was that he had clawed a settlement out of the driver who injured him. It had been a tough fight, because the driver was a software millionaire who didn't want the world to know he'd rammed his BMW into two people while enjoying a front-seat blow job. But Jesse had forced him to pay restitution, enough to fight off poverty for life.

The bank manager shook his hand before he stood to go. The girls at the counter waited until the door closed behind him, and then followed him out.

The day of Peter Wyoming's funeral started when my cell phone rang at three forty-five a.m. Stumbling out of Jesse's bedroom in the dark, I smashed into a coffee table and fell onto the sofa, cursing. My father was on the line, Philip James Delaney, Captain, USN, Retired, calling from Singapore.

"Evan, the cruise line says you phoned with an emergency. What's wrong?"

Hearing his deep voice, that tough, crisp tone, comforted me. I hated telling him the rotten news, destroying his time with my mother. My parents got along smashingly—for two weeks a year, in international waters.

He listened. "Did you just say Brian is in *jail*?"

I told him I needed them to come get Luke, and he jolted me wide-awake.

"We can't. Your mom's in the hospital. Dengue fever."

He went on, saying, "Don't worry, Sis, you know what a tough little bird she is." Trying to reassure me, calling me by a pet name from my childhood. "But I can't leave her alone ten thousand miles from home." I felt my plan blowing to pieces. Luke wasn't going anywhere. "I'll get there," he said, "but it'll be at least a week." *Buck up,* he said. *Keep the pressure on the police, without remorse. Damn that Tabitha.*

The sunrise was clearer that morning, still redshifted but not so pungent with smoke. The heat and wind had broken, letting the forest service contain the fire. After breakfast Luke and I took my car to the shop to get the obscenities painted over, picked up a rental car, and went to Jesse's office so I could speak to a family law attorney. His name was Solis, a man built like a crate and as bald as an egg. While Jesse watched Luke, I talked to him about getting a restraining order against Tabitha. He asked if I had thought about long-term custody issues.

"You mean, if Tabitha gets visitation rights?"

"Yes," he said, drawing out the word. "And if your brother isn't in a position to have Luke live with him."

I felt my face flushing. "You mean, if his case goes to trial—"

"And beyond. If he's convicted, things will become much more complicated for you."

I said, "They have the wrong man. Brian's going to be exonerated."

"That would be our best-case scenario, of course. However, I do know something of your brother's case, and—"

"You've been talking to Jesse."

"Yes, he briefed me on the situation."

He talked on after that, but my mind was wandering into weedy fields of anger. Jesse had told him Brian was guilty.

When I got back to his office, Jesse said, "You have lunch plans? I thought we could take Luke—"

"Yes. I do. Maybe you could take him."

"Sure." He looked puzzled. "Did everything go all right with Solis?"

"Yes."

He tilted his head, hoping I would explain my mood. I said, "I'm going to Peter Wyoming's funeral."

Surprise on his face. "Is that why you're all wound up?"

"I'm fine." I was ready to staple his face to the desk.

"Evan?"

If I had been Luke's age, solving this problem would have been straightforward. I would have jammed him in the face with a crayon. But I was past that now, into the era of the slow burn, the issues that clung to you unwanted, like toilet paper stuck to your shoe as you traipsed out of a public lavatory.

"It's nothing. I'll see you later."

The Remnant's furniture-showroom church was full when I arrived. Through the plate-glass windows I could see the choir on the stage, and the baton twirlers, wearing black sequined leotards and dark little veils over their faces. The big window that I had crashed through with Dr. Neil Jorgensen was boarded up. A poster adorned it, a drawing of Pastor Pete. Clearly it was Tabitha's, and it was one of her finest. He looked noble and besieged. *Wyoming Agonistes*. Beneath the poster someone had hand-painted a Bible quote. *Slain for the word of God and for the witness he had born*. The handwriting was neat, no drips, didn't match the obscenities on my Explorer. Shiloh had probably painted this. A cutesy little circle dotted the i in *slain*.

Hoping to avoid a fresh smiting, I was hiding in a long black dress, sunglasses, and a hat. Men were standing outside the door watching all who came in, so I hung back until the music struck up and they went inside. I followed.

The church was packed. I saw several journalists, including Sally Shimada and a TV crew. Black clothing smattered the crowd, but there was far more flannel, and camouflage gear, than I had ever seen at a funeral. The atmosphere was jagged. I had been to funerals for people who died unexpectedly, even violently, and so anticipated the sense of shock, suppressed hysteria, and unbearable heaviness that reverberated in the Remnant's chapel. But it was pitched so high here that the air almost jangled. And there was another feeling loose in the room, a feeling not just of outrage but of anticipation. The evidence was lying up front in an open coffin.

That was my first surprise: that the mortuary had been able to salvage enough for the corpse to go on display. The fire had not destroyed Peter Wyoming at all. He looked pale and peaceful in his casket, his bolo tie shining under the fluorescent lighting. You couldn't see the bullet hole or the burn marks for all the flowers surrounding him—lilies mounded on the casket, and huge arrangements on easels: a crown of thorns, a rod of iron, and the pièce de résistance, a mini handheld vacuum cleaner with the epitaph *Slut Buster*.

The choir's red robes swayed and randomly shimmied as members broke down in tears. They were singing about heaven cracking open with peals of thunder to destroy the destroyers of the earth. Flanking the stage were Curt Smollek and Isaiah Paxton. Smollek was affecting a Secret Service–agent, eyes-on-the-crowd look, but far too late to protect his pastor. Wyoming had known he was in danger on the night he was killed, and reached out not to his security detail, but to Brian. That was what convinced me that the church lay behind his death.

I still couldn't make sense of why Wyoming had called Brian. My brother insisted that Wyoming had been lucid that night, but I wondered if he had been acting under some pharmaceutical impulse. Having seen his bizarre behavior at Tabitha's house and outside the China Lake police station, I suspected that the drugs Chenille wanted Kevin Eichner to steal had been meant not for her, but for her husband.

I spotted Tabitha sitting on the aisle, and my stomach twanged. Her black dress clung to her—for dear life, it seemed. With her pale skin and sorrowful eyes she looked gothic, like a Faulkner belle driven mad by war and hunger. I wondered whether she was grieving Wyoming as her minister or as her lover. Or maybe her raggedness really was hunger, considering that Chenille had put her on half rations. A part of me wanted to grab her, drag her out of here, and stick her under a cold shower.

The hymn finished and the eulogies started, a man from the congregation taking the stage to recall the wonders of Pastor Pete. "Saved me from the bottle," he said. A second man came up, blowing his nose into a handkerchief. "Diagnosed my wife's cancer, Pastor Pete did. Also her cheating." Others followed. "He showed me the light." "Showed me how to get stubborn stains out from my carpet." "He purged me of my craving for tobacco." "For junk food." "For Thai strippers." The congregation nodded and sputtered. "Drove Satan out of my son; he don't cross-dress no more." "Taught me good hygiene." "Made the world make sense." When the last speaker stumbled sobbing from the stage the choir broke into a new number that sounded, so help me, like "Amazing Rage." The twirlers swung into a fresh routine, two batons apiece, flinging them toward the lights and catching them blind, veils hindering their view. A woman in pink plastic eyeglasses rushed the stage, shrieking, like a fan at a Tom Jones concert. Smollek grabbed her as she threw herself at the coffin. The hymn modulated up a step and the twirlers reached the climax, stopping dead, posing with their batons high and crossed, as though on Calvary.

Then, as the last notes faded away, Chenille stood up. The crowd hushed.

She looked like a new creation. Gone were the pastel flamboyancies. She had stripped down to the unvarnished wood. Her black outfit was severe, almost like a Mao suit. With her braid chopped and her face scrubbed of makeup, she looked androgynous.

She stared out across the crowd. "Not one a' you should be surprised. We knew this was coming." She turned to the coffin. "He knew it." She reached out and rested her hand against Pete's embalmed cheek. "Didn't you, baby?"

Around me the reporters squirmed, startled and excited by this unusual display.

Tenderly she said to the corpse, "Revelation eleven. It was you, honey. It all fell on you to take the weight of what it meant."

A reporter behind me whispered, "What's she talking about?"

"The Tribulation," a woman murmured. "Revelation says God will send two witnesses to prophesy. They'll be killed, but resurrected."

It was Sally Shimada. I was impressed.

Chenille said, "Death ain't the end, not by a long shot. For the Lord says if anyone harms his witnesses, thus he is doomed to be killed."

A woman in the congregation shouted, "Amen!" Another yelled, "Justice for Pastor Pete!" I shrank inwardly, knowing that they were talking about Brian.

Chenille said, "Justice? Oh, justice is coming. Scripture tells us. 'For the witnesses lay dead in the street, but then a breath of life from God entered them, and they stood up on their feet, and great fear fell on those who saw them.'"

Sally said, "She's quoting the passage out of context."

Chenille spread her arms. "So what are you all bawling about? Didn't you just hear me? 'They stood up' "—she pounded her shoe on the stage—"on their feet!' "

Turning again to the coffin, she leaned down, putting her face close to Pete's, and stared into his closed eyes. She said, "The tomb is not for you. Ain't no grave gonna hold your body down." She kissed him on the forehead. "No grave. Nohow." She kissed each of his eyelids. "We're ready and waiting, baby."

She kissed him on the lips.

The reporters collectively drew in a breath. So did I. I didn't know whether her marriage really had been discordant, or whether that even mattered now. Whatever the truth of her private life, this was a remarkable performance.

Chenille straightened. "Pete met his destiny and he met it like a man, going straight ahead. He didn't sit around, and we can't sit around neither. The Lord expects us to act. You want your part of the prize? It's time to get yourselves up on *your* feet."

She drew in a breath. "People, the storm is here."

The energy that surged through the room was palpable. Shiloh rose to her feet, raised her arms, and cried, "Let's get biblical!"

Pallbearers approached the stage. Paxton lowered the lid on the coffin, pausing to take a last look. For a second his face lost its focus, looked like hot grease jumping from a skillet. Then he shut the lid carefully, and with the other men hoisted the casket onto his shoulders. They carried it outside and slid it into the bed of his green pickup. Chenille climbed in next to it and Paxton pulled out, driving slowly up the street. The crowd followed en masse.

It got confusing after that.

A block from the Remnant's chapel was a skateboarding shop, a place that gave them spiritual eczema, called the Church of Skatan. As the green pickup crawled past, a rock flew from the crowd and bounced off the store's brickwork. Then came trash from the gutter, and a boot. A baton, which was quickly retrieved. Then eggs, which was when I knew that this was premeditated, and wouldn't be pretty. They splattered on the window. The storekeeper was shutting the door, asking people to calm down, but had to duck when a brick came tumbling at him. The window went in a great crystal cataract. The green pickup inched on. Men jumped through the window and started throwing merchandise around the store. Skateboards came shooting out the broken window. Inside the storekeeper begged them to stop. Then he came flying through the broken window too. Chenille stood meditatively in the bed of Paxton's truck, eyes front, like a statue of the Madonna being paraded through European streets.

I stuck near the reporters. The TV reporter and his cameraman were moving with the crowd, and Sally Shimada was jogging behind them, reciting a running commentary into a Dictaphone. The pickup pushed on, reaching State Street. Tourists and townsfolk slowed on the sidewalks as the Remnant streamed into the road. Traffic cascaded to a stop. Distantly I heard a siren.

Shiloh marshaled the baton twirlers into a phalanx pushing everyone out of their way, marching past stopped cars and confused pedestrians. The enormous black velvet bow in her ponytail bobbed up and down. She started chanting, like a drill sergeant leading boot camp recruits on a march.

" 'I don't know but I've been told—Satan's teats are mighty cold.' "

Ahead, a police car pulled into an intersection, lights flashing. I looked around. Tabitha was lagging behind the truck, looking burdened. I saw Glory. She was clapping along with the chanters, but her fist pumping looked lackluster.

Sally Shimada jogged past me, speaking breathlessly into her Dictaphone. "A patrol car has stopped at the corner of Canon Perdido Street, but the officers have not intervened with this impromptu funeral cortege."

I almost congratulated her on being able to run and say *cortege* at the same time. But she was off up the street, her glossy black hair swaying back and forth.

More eggs flew, hitting a New Age store called
Crystal Blue Persuasions. On up the street, and they
spattered a yoga center, a gallery called Prints of
Darkness, and, for unknown reasons, Starbucks. Glory,
I saw, was dropping back and edging toward the sidewalk. She was trying to slip away. Ahead, eggs, trash,
a skateboard went into a store window. I heard the
Remnant's favorite musical accompaniment, shattering
glass. And now a police siren, and a bullhorn ordering
people out of the street.

I slid up beside Glory and took her arm. Her lips
parted and she squinted at me. The scar at the corner
of her eye gave her a straggly look. "Evan?"

"Let's talk."

"No." She looked over her shoulder. "They'll notice
I'm gone."

The TV reporter and his cameraman scurried past
us, filming as they went. I pulled her inside the door
of a sushi bar.

I said, "Later, then. Tonight."

In her hand she held an egg. She had a homemade
tattoo on her hand, blue ink, with the angry look of
jailhouse skin art. She hesitated, finally saying, "I get
off work at nine, at the university. Meet me outside
the marine biology lab."

She turned and hurried up the street. A police car
drove past, lights going. The counterman from the
sushi bar came around and peered out the door, just
as a flickering object arced toward another storefront.

"Holy shit," the counterman said. "It's one of those
what-do-you-call-its, the bottle with a rag soaked in
gasoline."

"Molotov cocktail."

Crash, flash, smoke billowing from the storefront. I
stepped out onto the sidewalk. "Can you see which
store it is?"

"Yeah." Grim face. "It's Beowulf's."

16

"Gutted," Jesse said.

We were in my rental car, driving along the edge of the University of California campus, high on a cliff overlooking the black ocean. The car's headlights swung over eucalyptus trees, low cinder-block dormitories, and the Institute for Theoretical Physics, home to several recent Nobel Prize winners.

Jesse was leaning against the door. "Not just the bookstore, Anita too. You should have seen her standing there in the ruins. She was shaking, looking about two hundred years old, with her little hands balled into fists, muttering, 'Fascists.'"

The road descended to meet the jutting rocks and the beach at Campus Point. I swung into the parking lot outside the marine biology lab, and my headlights caught Glory sitting on the hood of a dented silver Toyota Celica. She was wearing a tie-dyed T-shirt and carpenter jeans, and a blue bandanna tied around her head.

Jesse said, "Let's see how she justifies their riot today."

"No." I turned off the engine. "Don't antagonize her."

"She just helped destroy Anita's entire life."

"I know. But I want to find out what she knows, so don't blow it."

Glory was walking toward my car with her hands jammed in her jeans pockets. Jesse eyed me hotly. I said, "Please," wondering whether it had been a good idea for him to come along. He was angry at the Remnant, and I was still piqued with him. Then he gave a small nod. I got out.

Behind Glory the surf crashed across the rocks. Moonlight reflected from tide pools, a milky shimmer. She said, "I can't believe I'm doing this."

"Things are getting out of hand, and you know it."

"Yeah. Protesting is one thing, but wrecking those stores . . . man, that's something else."

I said, "Today was just the start. What's next?"

She didn't answer. Jesse was still getting out of the car, and she was outright staring at him, watching him pull the wheelchair out of the backseat.

Finally she said, "Chenille . . . having her in charge has changed everything. And I don't mean she's going to bring a woman's touch to the church and soften things up. You have no idea what she's like."

Jesse rolled up. "Hooker with a heart of gold?"

I touched his shoulder, warning him to cool it.

"You shouldn't make fun of Chenille," Glory said. "She's very tough. Way more intense than Pastor Pete. And she's acting with total conviction. She has *seen* things. You know, visions."

"What has she seen?" I said.

"Martial law."

Jesse snorted.

"Yes. The people in Washington, they're the devil's pawns," she said. "The government is going to declare martial law and turn the country into a police state."

From Jesse's expression, I could tell that he thought she was talking the same talk as right-wing political pundits. He didn't yet grasp that she was speaking literally.

He said, "Who in Washington?"

"The whores and queers in Congress. The germ

doctors at CDC getting ready to poison us. The Pentagon, conspiring with the UN to enslave us."

"Gee," he said, "couldn't you be more precise?"

She caught the sarcasm. "You bet. Chenille says the Pentagon ordered Brian Delaney to kill Pastor Pete. It's part of the plot to bring the Antichrist to power."

"Glory," I said, "does that actually sound credible to you?"

She looked at me as though I were ignoring a meteor flaming toward my head. She said, "Revelation, chapter eleven, verse seven. It says the beast will kill the witnesses, and now Pastor Pete's dead. It *happened*."

Jesse mumbled, *"Post hoc, ergo propter hoc."*

She frowned at him. "What do you mean by that?"

I said, "Never mind. Glory, Brian didn't do it."

"I can see you're really struggling with this. That's because you're under the great deception. But so is your brother. The Pentagon probably lied to him, maybe brainwashed him, could have told him Pastor Pete was a security threat or a foreign agent. See what I'm saying?"

"I see." It was like arguing with a brick. "Tell us about this plot to impose martial law."

"The government is assembling its forces to subjugate humanity to the beast. This is *it*. Things are gonna get bad. And soon."

Jesse said, "How soon?"

"Real soon. The government's going to attack on the devil's night."

My stomach ached, but he was lost. "What's that?"

I said, "Halloween."

That was ten days from now. He leaned back, startled.

Glory explained, "Halloween is a doorway to evil. Every year satanists kill kids with poison in Halloween candy, and they slaughter pets and rape virgin girls."

HELL-o-ween. He said, "Those are urban legends. They're not true."

She said, "Listen to me. It's a night when the wall between worlds gets thin, and Satan can reach into the physical dimension with incredible power. That's why it's the night the government is going to attack."

Jesse didn't bother to hide his incredulity. I said, "What's the Remnant going to do?"

"This is the scary part. Inside the Remnant there are . . . different levels. Different groups, like. And there's one crew that's especially close to Chenille, really intense."

Jesse said, "Define 'intense.' "

She said, "Chenille has a group of totally dedicated people, really hard-core loyalists. This is what scares me. . . ."

She looked around the parking lot. There was nothing but the surf and the stars. Nevertheless she scrunched her shoulders, looking furtive.

"Man, this is hard for me."

I couldn't let her quit talking. I said, "It's okay. I'm scared, too."

Her head snapped around. "Don't say that. You're the one person I thought wouldn't be afraid."

"Why?"

"You're the only one I ever saw stand up to Chenille."

The statement took me aback. Feeling so big in her eyes discomfited me.

She pulled the bandanna off her head. "You've got to understand, the Remnant saved my life. No lie—if it wasn't for Chenille getting me out of a bad situation, I'd be dead by now. And she brought me to a place where things were clean, and true, and where I *mattered*. *Me*. In the Remnant, I *meant* something."

Sensing that she wanted me to pull her along, I said, "But things have changed."

She stared at the dark ocean. "Chenille said when I came to the Remnant that my life would be bound for glory. That's why she gave me this name. It's not my original one, you know. But then she sent me out here to get a job as a janitor."

"She insisted that you take a custodial job?"

"She said it would teach me humility. As if I didn't get enough humility before I was saved, spreading my legs in the back of strangers' cars in exchange for drugs."

She gave me a sidelong glance, trying to see if she had shocked me. I rested a hand on her shoulder.

Her voice gathered heat. "And you notice *she* didn't take a humiliating job. She appointed herself soloist in the choir. But no, she showed me the classified ad and told me to go apply for it. And you know what? I did a lot of down-and-dirty stuff before I was saved, but even when I was living on the street I didn't think, 'Wow, if I ever get out of this, I'm gonna get a real great *menial* job.' Like, I used to go to the library. That's how I got into science fiction. I read Orson Scott Card and Octavia Butler, totally amazing stuff. Oh, and Connie Willis . . ."

I said, "*Doomsday Book*."

"Yeah! I'd sit there wishing *I* could travel in time. . . ." She stopped. "But since then, I've found out that the future is more shocking than what you read in SF novels."

Jesse was tapping his fingers against his knee, letting me know that he was restraining himself from open derision.

She said, "I loved your book, Evan. But then I'd remember, This is unscriptural, and I'd feel so *dirty*. . . ."

Jesse said, "Knowledge. The love that dares not speak its name."

She said, "Lust for knowledge caused the Fall.

When Eve ate the apple from the Tree of Knowledge."

"And your church is working its ass off to eradicate what we've learned since then. You know, burning bookstores."

It had been a mistake for him to come. He was justly angry, but if he kept this up the meeting would be over in about ninety seconds. I said, "Jesse—"

Glory said, "Learning isn't the supreme good. Truth is, and faith."

"Yeah," he said, "ignorance is bliss."

"You know, if you believed in God, you'd be walking."

Shit. Point of no return.

He nodded, an exaggerated *aha!* nod. "I see. And what else?" She looked at him crooked, and he said, "What else would I get for believing in God? How about incredible sexual stamina, or—ooh, a private jet? Can I make a list?"

I put my hands up in a T and called, "Time-out."

They looked at me.

"I have a question," I said. "The Remnant isn't big on book learning, so why did Chenille tell Glory to take a job at a university?"

They stared at me, thinking about it. Finally Glory said, "She said the reasons would become apparent in time."

We listened to the surf ramming the rocks.

Jesse, calming down, said, "Sabotage."

"That's my guess," she said.

"Where do you work?"

"Biological Sciences."

An ideal target for Pastor Pete's hatreds—all those microorganisms, all that Latin terminology. But something about it bothered me, a niggling thought deep in my brain, one I couldn't quite reach. I walked toward the edge of the asphalt. The wet sand shone pale silver when the waves receded. In the far distance I could see the Goleta Pier, and the Beachside Restaurant bright against the shore, its lights ticking on the water.

I said, "These hard-core loyalists. Who are they?"

She said, "Ice Paxton, Shiloh, Curt Smollek, the Brueghel triplets . . . maybe ten or twelve people."

Jesse said, "You?"

"No. I'm not in the inner circle." Her voice stung with the rejection.

I said, "Tabitha?"

"No."

Relief brushed over me. I was surprised at how much I had been rooting for that answer, how much I hoped that Tabitha wasn't totally gone.

"Tabitha's star isn't rising anymore," she said. "She was more Pastor Pete's favorite than Chenille's, especially after she botched the mission to rescue her little boy."

Jesse said, "Rescue? That's what you think it was?"

"Whatever. Pastor Pete was sympathetic to Tabitha afterward, but Chenille thought it showed she lacked the guts for field operations. So now Chenille's freezing her out."

Lack of courage, I thought, had nothing to do with it. Jealousy did. Tabitha had whipped it up in big helpings—for Brian, Chenille, and who knew who else.

I walked back toward her. "Why does the hard-core group scare you so much?"

"Because they've stripped off the trappings of this world. They've sold their homes and possessions to prepare for the devil's-night assault."

A chill had crept over the air and clung to me. "Preparing. To counterattack?"

"They're going to stage a preemptive strike."

Jesse said, "Jesus."

"When?" I said. "Where?"

"I don't know."

"You have to."

"Operational details are need-to-know only. And janitors don't need to know."

Jesse said, "When they sold their things . . . what did they do with the money?"

The look on her face told him he should have known. "They bought weapons."

I closed my eyes.

She said, "They have a stockpile, enough to start a war."

His face was fierce. "You have to find out their plans."

"I can't do that."

He said, "I don't believe you."

Her voice took on vigor. "I've been shut out. Can't you see that? I'm destined for scut work. I'm going to be a foot soldier or worse. Cannon fodder, or an air tester. Seeing if I can breathe in an area without coming down with anthrax."

I took her arm. "Leave," I said. "Leave the church. Tonight."

"I can't."

"Sure you can."

"Go back on the outside? No way. I'd be damned."

"If you come with us, we can get you protection."

"You mean from the police? You're crazy. The police are part of the government network."

"We'll get you to a halfway house, or another church. . . ."

"The Remnant will find me. Can't you understand? There's no way out. I'm trapped."

She buried her face in her hands, sobbing. I put my arm around her shoulder, feeling bereft.

17

On the way home Jesse phoned the police, leaving a message for a detective he knew. Back at his house we paid the babysitter and sat wearily at the kitchen table, worried and at loose ends.

He said, "If Tabitha's on the outs with Chenille, the church could lose interest in Luke."

"Let's hope."

He could tell I didn't believe it. His face, drawn with fatigue, fell further. I realized he had been trying to reassure me, and felt a rush of tenderness for him. I put my hand on his.

"I'm sorry that Glory gave you the business."

"Nobody's as zealous as a reformed whore. Get yourself a crucifix lobotomy! Everything will look so simple afterward!" He laughed humorlessly. "Like it's made her life a bowl of cherries."

"You're made of pretty strong stuff, you know it?"

"It's my heathen heart. Solid stone."

I leaned over and kissed him.

I said, "But next time try not to argue with someone I'm pumping for information."

"Ever hear of Good Cop, Bad Cop?"

Cockiness, that little edge, was creeping back into his voice. I said, "Ever hear of fanning the flames? You just never met a bone you didn't want to pick."

I got up from the table. The surf had come up, big rollers heaving onto the beach, boiling white in the moonlight. I checked my phone messages. The *News-Press* reporter, Sally Shimada, had called again.

Though it was almost eleven on a worknight, when I phoned back her beauty-contestant voice sounded perky. "Evan—wow. I was wondering if I'd ever hear from you."

I could hear the television in the background. *Sabrina, the Teenage Witch*, or perhaps *Animaniacs*. I told my brain to shut up.

She said, "I want to talk about your brother's arrest." She sounded as if she were staring at a big hunk of prime rib, saying, *Is that for me? Can I have a sharp knife?*

"I'm off the record, Sally. Background only."

I told her about the Remnant attempting to abduct Luke outside China Lake, about Brian trying to protect his son, and about his innocence, his sterling character, his patriotism. I practically hummed "The Star-Spangled Banner." I kept my back to Jesse, not wanting to see his expression.

She said, "I have information that this was a crime of passion. That your brother's ex was in love with Peter Wyoming."

"Who told you that? Wait—you've been talking to Detective McCracken."

I deflated. Sally wasn't quite the naïf I had imagined, and I wished that I had told her my side of the story sooner. I started stalking around Jesse's living room. He sat at the kitchen table, watching me.

I changed the subject. "I saw you at Wyoming's funeral today. You impressed me, knowing that Chenille was quoting scripture out of context."

"You think a good Buddhist girl can't get her hands on a copy of the New Testament? Yeah, she was definitely twisting it to suit her message. Revelation eleven, go on and look it up. Delaney, that sounds Irish; you must have a Bible lying around somewhere."

At Jesse's house? Maybe to prop up an uneven table leg. But that was why I had brought the Gideon Bible from the China Lake hotel.

She said, "Revelation eleven talks about the tribulation, and says that a 'faithful remnant' of Christianity will be preserved from destruction. It also talks about two witnesses who testify to God's truth. Now, my concordance says these are symbolic witnesses, that they might represent Moses and Elijah, or the early Christian martyrs, or—"

"I get the picture. Chenille was taking it literally."

"And the witnesses' resurrection—"

"Represents the triumph of the church, but she was also taking it literally."

She said, "Maybe I should get a photographer to stake out the cemetery, huh? Catch Pastor Pete's revival. *That* would be a deadlock on a Pulitzer."

My eyes fell on chapter twelve. The Woman and the Dragon. Chenille had talked about a dragon when she confronted me at my book signing. She'd said she wouldn't let the dragon devour Luke. . . .

"Sally, look at chapter twelve."

"Hang on." I heard her flipping pages. "Revelation twelve. 'Now a great sign appeared in heaven: a woman, adorned with the sun . . . She was with child and wailed aloud in pain as she labored to give birth. Then a second sign appeared in the sky, a huge red dragon which had seven heads and ten horns. . . .' "

I said, "This would be the devil, would it not?"

"Yes." She continued reading. "'. . . the dragon stood before the woman who was about to bear a child, that he might devour her child when she brought it forth.' "

My head began pounding again. There was more,

and I read along with Sally: " 'She brought forth a male child, one who is to rule all the nations with a rod of iron.' "

A rod of iron. I saw Pastor Pete's gleaming eyes and clenched fist, remembered him proclaiming these words. My mind was spinning. What twisted mix of biblical literalism and dementia had led Chenille to connect this passage to Luke? Did she see him in a messianic role? Was he some sort of chosen one?

Sally said, "Does this mean something to you?"

"I don't know."

She said nothing, hoping I would fill the silence, but I kept quiet. After a moment she said, "All right. Do you want to hear about Dr. Neil Jorgensen, MD, deceased?"

"Oh. You bet."

"You're not going to believe what I found out."

"What?"

"What killed him."

"Sally—"

She told me. I blinked, and held the phone away from my ear, staring at it as though it had just bitten me. Jesse spread his hands and gestured, *What?* Eyes wide, I walked toward him.

I said, "Would you repeat that?"

Sally said, "Neil Jorgensen died of rabies."

Sally couldn't stop talking. She may have botched her initial report about Jorgensen's death, but now she had the bit in her teeth. She had interviewed the county coroner about Jorgensen's autopsy, and had spoken to the pathology lab that had come up with the diagnosis.

"Of course, the hospital didn't suspect rabies, because of all Jorgensen's other injuries. Rabies causes acute encephalitis, but Jorgensen's head trauma masked it. Plus the disease is rare in the U.S."

I listened, puzzling over how Jorgensen could have contracted the disease. "Don't you get rabies from an animal bite?"

"Usually. But it's possible for people to get it if infectious material gets into, say, their mouth or a wound."

"Infectious material. Such as . . ."

"Saliva."

"How about blood, animal droppings . . . ?"

"No. The virus gets into you through saliva and spreads along the nerves to the spinal cord and the brain. You can't get rabies from petting a rabid animal or from contact with its blood, urine, or feces."

"But if Jorgensen was bitten by a rabid animal, why didn't he seek treatment immediately? He was a doctor."

"I don't know," she said. "The coroner is stumped."

"Could he have come in contact with the virus in his medical practice?"

"Theoretically, I suppose . . ."

I heard the sound of paper flipping. Sally must have been reading from interview or research notes.

"Nonbite exposure would mean getting contaminated with live virus, or with infectious material such as brain tissue. But according to my data, that's a remote possibility except for laboratory workers. And Jorgensen was a plastic surgeon, not a pathologist."

I said, "What data is that?"

"From CDC—the Centers for Disease Control and Prevention, in Atlanta. That's where the coroner sent Jorgensen's tissue samples to be analyzed, to confirm the diagnosis."

Ah, those nasty germ doctors whom Chenille expected to poison us any day. Sally went on. "And a bunch of people who came in contact with him have to get PEP."

She was really getting into this. I said, "What's PEP?"

"Postexposure prophylaxis. The emergency room

doctors and nurses, lab technicians, firefighter-paramedics—everyone who was exposed to Jorgensen has to take the rabies vaccine."

My brain froze. "Sally, I was exposed to Jorgensen."

"What?"

"That night, before he got hit by the truck. I fell through the plate-glass window with him, and I got cut."

"You can't get rabies from that kind of casual contact."

I felt my throat constricting. "You don't understand. When he came into the church he grabbed me. He was crying and spitting, and you said that saliva—"

"Oh, my gosh."

Jesse came over to me, his face troubled, mouthing, *what*? I found a piece of scratch paper and wrote *CDC* on it, and pointed to his laptop computer.

Sally said, "Maybe you should get in touch with your doctor, Evan."

Rabies kills up to seventy thousand people worldwide every year. Dog bites cause most cases in the developing world, but American victims usually contract the disease when bitten by a wild animal. In one gruesome instance eight people died after receiving infected corneal transplants. Rabies affects all mammals, and the outcome is almost always fatal.

That was the CDC Web site, sugarcoating things.

The World Health Organization site was no better. Nor the Pasteur Institute's. They were all epidemiological fright wigs, scaring the piss out of me.

Rabies incubates in the central nervous system, generally for three to twelve weeks, and during that time the infected animal—or person—shows no sign of illness. Eventually, however, the virus reaches the brain and erupts into pain, paralysis, insanity, and death. Just six people are known to have survived the disease.

You get better odds with Ebola. I didn't sleep.

At dawn I called my doctor's office, telling her service, yes, page her, get her out of aerobics class or off the toilet and have her call me, and on second thought have her meet me at her office in half an hour. I was there in twenty minutes, waiting on the steps with the sun on my face, surrounded by orderly, bright flower beds, imagining how I'd look when I started foaming at the mouth.

Soon the doctor came up the walk carrying a coffee mug, with the *News-Press* tucked under her arm. She was a stylish woman in her fifties named Lourdes Abbott who had a no-nonsense manner and a perpetual furrow between her eyebrows.

"Come on in." Inside, she started flipping on lights. "I've already talked to the Public Health people about this. They'll be contacting you for an interview." She tossed the paper on her desk. The rabies story was prominent. She pointed me to a chair. "Talk."

I told her about Jorgensen screaming and spitting in the direction of my face. She drank from her mug.

She said, "Do you remember being hit with saliva?"

"I'm not sure. I didn't have to wipe it off, but . . . I don't know."

Her furrow deepened. "Show me where you were cut."

I held out my hands, where scabs were now faded, and parted my hair to indicate nicks on my scalp.

She said, "How did you take care of these cuts afterward?"

"My boyfriend washed them out at home about half an hour later."

"Soap and water?"

"Yes. Then antiseptic and Band-Aids. And I showered and washed my hair."

"Why do you keep scratching at your back and abdomen like that?"

She declined to comment on the wasp stings. She

just wrote everything down, and then stared at the page.

She said, "I think the risk to you is low. In fact, I question whether you've even been exposed. However, you had broken skin, and Dr. Jorgensen had confirmed rabies. It's a gray area, but call me risk averse. I'm going to recommend that you get vaccinated."

I nodded, oddly both frightened and relieved. She described the vaccine schedule, five doses administered over a twenty-eight-day period. A jab in the arm, not the stomach like in the old days. I kept nodding, saying, "Right, let's do it." She insisted this was precautionary, playing it safe. My head bounced up and down like a beach ball. I told her that Curt Smollek and Isaiah Paxton might have been exposed. Then I asked whether rabies was more common than I had known, and told her about the coyote attacking Abbie Hankins in China Lake.

She frowned. "You've come in close proximity to confirmed rabies twice within the space of seven days?"

"Yes. Two hundred miles apart."

Her furrow turned so deep that the bottom lay in shadow.

"Dr. Abbott?"

She tapped her pencil against the notepad. "I don't want to speculate."

Speculate your ass off, I almost shouted. "Please."

"There is a significant reservoir of the disease among wild animals in California. But this is highly unusual. Either it's a statistical anomaly, or we're seeing evidence of an emerging outbreak."

Dr. Abbott sent me to the emergency room at St. Francis Medical Center for the first injection. I felt numb. While I waited for my shot, edgy thoughts suggested themselves—about germs, and coincidence, or the lack of it. And it all went back to Dr. Neil Jorgensen.

Coming out of St. Francis with a Band-Aid on my arm, I decided to stop by the medical building down the hill on Micheltorena Street, where Jorgensen and Mel Kalajian, late MDs, lovers, and partners in plastic surgery, had kept their offices. In previous times, the parking lot had gleamed with expensive cars, especially Neil Jorgensen's latest Porsche in some blazing color. Now the lot was empty. But the office door opened when I turned the knob. Seeing no one, I called out, "Hello?"

From the back a voice answered, "Right there."

A moment later a chunky woman in a green suit, with tiny rimless glasses and her hair in a twist, came around the corner. She stopped when she saw me.

"Oh—I was expecting Dr. Marsden. Are you with his practice, Ms. . . ."

"Delaney. No, I'm not. I'm . . . I knew Dr. Jorgensen."

She set down the file folders she was carrying. "Because the office really isn't open." She glanced around at the waiting room, with its soothing gray carpet, Gorman prints of Navajo mothers, and coffee table covered with issues of *Fortune* magazine. On the counter were wilting flower arrangements with sympathy cards taped to them.

She forced a smile. "Sorry, it's just that I'm expecting another surgeon who's thinking of buying the practice." She put out her hand. "Esther Olson. I'm the office manager."

I didn't know how to work into the conversation I wanted to have, but Esther Olson sounded as if she wanted to talk. I said, "Any chance that the new doctor will keep the staff on board?"

"Who knows?" This time her smile failed, flat out.

"Had you been with Dr. Jorgensen a long time?"

"Thirteen years. Since before Dr. Kalajian joined the practice. Oh. Who would have believed, both of them . . ." She closed her eyes and rubbed her forehead. "When Dr. Kalajian passed away, we didn't think we could keep the practice going. Dr. Jorgensen was a wreck, and some patients didn't want to come to an office where a man had been . . . where someone had expired. But we pulled together and Dr. Jorgensen soldiered on. . . ."

I had forgotten that Mel Kalajian was murdered in this building. Now I recalled that he had interrupted a robber. Olson's gaze lengthened, giving the impression that she was seeing the office as it had been in happier, more profitable times, when Neil Jorgensen had snipped, peeled, and liposucked Santa Barbara's richest. On his best days Jorgensen could turn an eye lift into an excavation. On his worst . . . I shuddered to think of him operating when, as Olson described it, he was a wreck.

She brought herself back. "Did you know Dr. Kalajian too?"

"No," I said. "This must have been an awful year for you."

She took off her rimless glasses and cleaned them on a handkerchief. "Yes. Ever since that night in July . . . when I got that horrible phone call from Dr. Jorgensen, telling me that Dr. Kalajian had been . . . that he was gone."

"Dr. Jorgensen was the one who found his body?"

It was a question too far. She put her glasses back on and scrutinized me.

She said, "I'm sorry. How did you say you knew Dr. Jorgensen?"

"I knew him in a professional capacity."

"You're a doctor?"

"No."

I really must train myself to lie reflexively. Esther

Olson was no dummy—she may have idealized Neil Jorgensen, but she knew how often his patients looked in the mirror and decided to sue.

She said, "You're a lawyer?" Quickly she eyed my jeans and T-shirt. "A process server?" She took a step back, as if to prevent me from touching her with a summons and complaint I might have hidden in my bra.

"A lawyer," I said. "But I'm not here because of any court action, Ms. Olson."

"For God's sake, the man is dead. Can't you people leave him alone?"

"I called the ambulance for him the night he was hit by the truck."

"Oh . . ." She had been pointing toward the door, about to kick me out, but now her fingertips went to her lips. "You're the bystander. We've been wondering if we'd ever meet you." Her lips began trembling. Softly she touched my arm. "Thank you."

She gestured to a sofa. "Please, I'm sorry, sit down. I've so been wanting to talk to you. You're one of the last people to have spoken with the doctor. He never came out of his coma, you know, but you were there— maybe you can tell me what happened and help me understand what led him to that church. I need closure on this."

Her eyes were bloodhound sad. I didn't want to tell her that Jorgensen had ended his life screaming the F-word. Instead I explained how he had interrupted the service, saying, "He was quite upset."

"You were inside the church? I thought . . . the paramedics said . . ." She withdrew several inches. "Are you a member of the Remnant?"

"No. Not a chance in hell."

I told her a bit, and she drew closer again. She said, "They're vicious people, the Remnant. They picketed Dr. Kalajian's funeral."

"Ms. Olson, this will sound strange, but I'm going

to say it anyway. I think that somehow the Remnant was responsible for Dr. Jorgensen's death." She stared, and I said, "I know it sounds crazy."

"No, you're right. I can't put my finger on why, exactly, but you're right."

Leaning forward anxiously, she again asked me to describe Jorgensen's final minutes. I tried to convey his confusion and foul anger. She shook her head.

"That had to be the illness," she said. "He just wasn't like that."

Actually, in my experience he had been a virtuoso at conjugating the verb *fuck*, but Olson wouldn't have considered that a testimonial. I said, "Do you have any idea how he contracted rabies?"

"None. It's simply inconceivable." She exhaled sharply. "And now those people have to take the vaccine. . . . Watch, next thing they'll be filing lawsuits against his estate. You mark my words."

Not wanting to get my butt kicked through the door, I decided against telling her I was one of those people. Changing the subject, I said, "Dr. Kalajian's murderer. Was he ever captured?"

"No."

"I understand that Dr. Kalajian interrupted a robber who was after drugs."

"That's what the police think. But . . ." She scrunched up her mouth, clearly trying to decide whether she wanted to get into this. "It bothered Dr. Jorgensen, and now it's bothering me. The circumstances . . . just don't add up."

She told me the sequence of events leading up to Mel Kalajian's death. It was a weeknight in early July, and Kalajian had been visiting postsurgical patients at St. Francis. He left the hospital at seven thirty and walked back to the office, which was closed by then.

Kalajian, said Olson, was a tall, well-built man in his early forties. He took care of himself, working out five days a week at the gym.

"He lifted weights, you understand? He was strong."

He had gone into his office. Then—perhaps noticing lights that shouldn't have been on, or hearing a noise—he went to one of the treatment rooms, which was outfitted for minor surgery. It was his penultimate act in life.

From the disarray in the room it was clear that Kalajian had put up a fight. From the amount of blood pooled around his body it was clear that he had fallen on the spot where he was stabbed. He had been rammed through the chest with a liposuction cannula.

Olson said, "The police weren't forthcoming, except to say that they thought a drug addict had broken into the office. Dr. Jorgensen couldn't get any more information out of them no matter how strongly he insisted."

I pictured the stalemate at the police station: Jorgensen arrogant and grief-stricken, the police defensive, hackles up.

"Dr. Jorgensen thought a patient was involved." She looked to see if I was skeptical.

"Why?"

"When the police let us back in the office, Dr. Jorgensen found something. It was just a little thing, but he thought it was significant. He found a sheet of paper under the receptionist's desk, from a patient's file—the information sheet they fill out when they first come in. He went to stick it back in the file, but the file was missing. He was convinced that someone had taken it, someone who didn't want anyone to know they had been here. Which would be someone involved in the robbery and murder."

I guess I did look skeptical.

"I know that's a leap. But he tried checking out this patient. Her name was on the information sheet. It turns out the name, the address, everything was fake."

"Did he tell the police?"

"Yes. But they thought it was a dead end. Whoever's fingerprints were on the sheet, they had no police record. The police never came up with a real name. After that they lost interest."

"What was the name she gave?"

"I don't remember. It wasn't anything distinctive."

"Do you know anything? Age? Ethnicity? The reason she came in?"

"No, and I couldn't tell you even if I knew. That would violate doctor-patient confidentiality. Why?"

"Because I bet Dr. Jorgensen thought she belonged to the Remnant. When he burst into the church that night, he pointed and shouted, 'She knows.'"

Her neck stretched and tightened. "Oh, my God."

She glanced at the file cabinets and computer systems behind the front counter. "Do you think you could recognize her?"

"Possibly, if she's from the Remnant."

"Come here." She went behind the counter and flipped on a computer. "Our recent patient files are on the computer, and they include photographs. We have digital-imaging software that allows the surgeon to alter photos, to show the patient how they'll look after their procedure." The computer booted up. "I shouldn't be showing this to you. But if you think you can recognize this woman . . ."

"I won't spy on personal data, I promise." I sat down at the desk.

She said, "There are hundreds of files. All I know is that this woman was Dr. Kalajian's patient, and—"

Just as I set my fingers on the keyboard, there was a knock on the door.

Olson said, "There's the buyer. Listen, go on and search the database. But please don't say anything while I give him this tour."

An older man came in wearing a bespoke suit and

a look of polite curiosity. Olson starched on a smile and marched across the room, her hand extended like a saber.

I started by searching for names I knew. Tabitha Delaney. Nothing. Good. Chenille Wyoming, Shiloh Keeler, Glory Moffett. Nothing. I set search parameters to bring up Kalajian's female patients from the past year and began clicking through files, starting with A. Up flashed photo after photo of middle-aged skin, adipose tissue, marbled flesh and lumps and massed unhappiness, all within the normal range of human design. B, C, D. More faces looking for gratification via the knife. E, F, G. An occasional birth defect or disfigurement as the result of accident or disease.

H through N. Up popped a Technicolor shot of someone's ass. It was a stupendous ass, its immensity evident even in 2-D, but skillful lifting and repacking had molded it into rounded twin powerhouses—regal Clydesdale buttocks. Kalajian had been an artist.

My eyes fell on the patient's name. *Olson, Esther.* Just then she came back into the lobby, chatting with the new doctor. Quickly I clicked to the next file.

There she was. The longing, slightly nervous look in her eyes grabbed at me. The name on the file read, *Peters, Kelly*, with a big red notice attached: PAYMENT OVERDUE. Looking at the before photo, I now knew why she had that scar at the corner of her left eye. Kalajian had removed a blue-ink tattoo of a teardrop.

It was Glory.

My heart was thumping. This was what I had hoped to find—confirmation that the Remnant had been here. Yet to think that Glory might have killed Mel Kalajian made my eyes ache.

Olson walked the doctor outside. I began printing the file.

Glory. *It's not my original name, you know. . . .* And Kelly Peters wasn't her name either, I'd bet money.

Dammit. Had she broken into the office that July evening? Did Mel Kalajian find her with drug bottles in
her hands? Did she grab the cannula and . . . No.
Kalajian had been strongly built, and had engaged in
a hellacious fight with his attacker. Glory was a lightweight young woman. Those dots didn't connect.

The more I thought about it, the less sense that
scenario made. Why would Glory go to the trouble
having a tattoo removed if she simply planned to
break into the office after hours? Then it hit me.

Olson came back inside, alone.

I said, "How did the thief get into the office?"

She stopped. Her face rouged. "Why do you ask?"

Bingo. I swiveled on the chair to face her. "It wasn't
a break-in, was it."

"The drug cabinet was broken into."

"But the office wasn't."

She fussed with her loden green jacket, smoothing
it. I stared at her.

"No," she admitted. "They used a key. Dr. Kalajian
thought he had lost it, which is why we never rekeyed.
It would have cost money to rekey."

Her voice had gone up about half an octave. I saw:
She, the efficient office manager, had saved that
money, a fatal thriftiness.

I didn't want to spook her. I said, "I think I've
found your mystery patient."

Briskly she strode around to look at the computer
screen. "This is her?" She crossed her arms and tut-
ted. "She looks dishonest, doesn't she? You think
she's the one who . . ."

"I don't know."

A new thought was nettling me. Chenille had asked
Kevin Eichner to obtain drugs for her from a doctor's
office. What did she want from an MD that she
couldn't get on the street?

I said, "Esther, what drugs were stolen?"

She stared at the screen. "I couldn't say."

"Didn't you have an inventory?"

"Of course. They were controlled substances, and had to be strictly accounted for. The nurses gave an inventory to the police."

"Do you have a copy of it?"

"I don't know, and I don't see why you need to know." There was an edge to her voice—annoyance, or regret that she had revealed too much.

"Esther, this might help explain Dr. Kalajian's murder."

"I don't see how. You've found this"—she gestured to Glory's photo—"this creature. You should call the police. She looks like a drug addict."

"I'm going to call the police. But I don't think this was an instance of an addict killing someone who got in the way of a fix. I think the Remnant sent this woman here to steal particular drugs, and I think that Dr. Jorgensen realized it, too."

She pressed her lips tight. "Fine. All right." She grabbed a Post-it note and wrote down a name. "This is the nurse who handled the inventory. I hope I'm not making a mistake."

I stood to leave. "You aren't."

Three blocks down the street my cell phone rang. It was Jesse.

"What did the doctor say?"

"I've been a bad dog. I need shots."

Dead quiet on his end. "Evan, that's not funny."

"It's laugh or scream, babe."

"Jesus Christ, you really were exposed to rabies?" The vaccine was just a precaution, I told him, and he said, "I'll take the day off if you want. Trial's in recess. Are you okay?"

"I'm laughing, aren't I?" I told him to stay at work. His concern was heartening enough for me. "But there's something else. About Glory."

He listened, and whistled. "Call SBPD. Talk to

Chris Ramseur, the detective I know there. I spoke to him half an hour ago about the Remnant stockpiling weapons. This will really get him hopping."

"Right," I said. "Seeing Glory's photo on that computer was immensely depressing."

"Ev, snap out of it. Glory can't be your personal reclamation project."

"She isn't."

"Yes, she is. Tabitha has put up a wall, so you're trying to save Glory instead. Forget that she's your biggest fan, and a weeper; she's a class-A bigot and possibly a murderer."

Evan's pound puppy . . .

"Besides, she's already *saved*, right? She's fresh out of redemption coupons."

Luke was at Nikki's, and on the way to pick him up I swung over to Milpas Street and bought us all takeout from La Super-Rica. Standing under the orange roof of the taco stand watching the old lady hand-make the tortillas, smelling the cilantro and the luxuriant aroma of grease, boosted my mood. So did Nikki's overt concern when I walked into her kitchen, and her relief at hearing that my risk-averse doctor had sent me to get vaccinated. She smiled when I handed her the Super-Rica sacks, and said, "Oh, baby. Come to Mama."

We ate in the kitchen, with Luke sitting on my lap. Afterward I told Nikki to put her feet up and give me a list of chores. I was in the garage loading the washer when Carl's car pulled into the driveway. He often came home for lunch from the small software firm where he was an executive. He strolled up with his measured stride, exchanging his prescription sunglasses for his regular owlish specs. He had on a flawless charcoal suit and a royal blue silk tie, as much flair as his conservative tastes permitted.

I said, "There's La Super-Rica, but you'll have to wrestle Nikki for it."

"Never take on a pregnant woman when food is on the line."

I started the washing machine. "I'm not going to ask her to babysit Luke anymore."

"No, she wants to," he said. "It's a good distraction. He's a nice kid."

Faintly we could hear sounds from the school playground up the street. It reminded us both that Luke should have been there.

"No," I said. "I had been thinking of sending him back to school. But I've gotten information that the Remnant is stockpiling weapons, and were involved in a murder last summer."

I didn't have to say the rest: If something happened to Luke, or to any other child at that school, I would have to kill myself. And if something happened to Nikki . . .

Carl said, "The police?"

"They know."

He turned toward the house. Stopped. Raised a finger, to point or shake at me, then came over and hugged me hard. "Watch your back, girl."

18

With the brushfire extinguished, the sky freshened and the air sang clear. Hang gliders lazed above La Cumbre peak, and sailboats flecked the coastline. At lunchtime the next day Jesse headed to Los Baños pool, by the harbor. Two thousand meters freestyle soothed his aches, let him feel like a physical animal again. Swimming meant simplicity. There was no cross-examination, no screeching eschatology, no emotional subtext. There was only the rhythm of pull and recovery, and the water slipstreaming over him. After the freestyle, he felt pumped, knew his heart rate hadn't even hit one twenty, and decided to throw in a set of intervals. Ten times a hundred meters 'fly, on the three minutes. It was work, but not radical. His cadence wasn't what it used to be without the big dolphin kick anymore, but that was an FFL. He finished head down, lunging for the wall, and hung on the lane line, blowing hard. Nothing beat real exertion for improving your outlook on the world.

He was driving back to work when a woman ran into the street ahead of him. He yanked back on the brake, saying, "Shit," feeling the ABS judder as the car slowed. The woman was shouting, but not at him. She didn't even see him. She was barefoot, with hot rollers in her hair, and was toting a .22 BB rifle. She was aiming the gun at a skunk.

Traffic was approaching and cars were parked along the curb. He had nowhere to go to avoid her, and with one hand steering and the other pulling back on the brake, he couldn't pound on the horn.

The woman ran awkwardly. She had cotton wads stuffed between her toes, protecting the gleaming pink toenail polish she must have applied moments before grabbing her weapon. Still, she gained on the black-and-white animal waddling down the street. She sighted along the rifle barrel, as if she were Daniel Boone 'bout to kill herself a bear.

Jesse's car groaned to a stop. She fired. Missed. The skunk stopped and raised its tail. Just as it sprayed she fired again, and this time the skunk jerked, staggered, and fell over.

Jesse rolled down the window and stuck his head out. The skunk odor was appalling, but the woman seemed to notice neither the stench nor the fact that she had almost been hit by a two-thousand-pound vehicle.

He said, "Lady, what the hell are you doing?"

Warily approaching the little corpse, she nudged it in the belly with the barrel of the BB gun. It didn't move. She grabbed it by the tail, hoisted it up in the air, and stared it in the face.

She said, "Gotcha, fucker."

She held up the skunk like a trophy. Her hot rollers shone in the sun. "I seen it sitting in my bushes, looking at me funny. It was rabid, but I got it."

The panic had begun.

An investigator from the Public Health Department phoned me that afternoon, wanting details of my exposure to Neil Jorgensen. After answering his queries for fifteen minutes, I asked whether he knew how Jorgensen had contracted rabies.

"We aren't going to theorize for the general public, ma'am."

"I'm not the general public. He spit in my face."

He considered that, and gave me a crumb. "Well, in California, the significant reservoirs of the disease are in skunks and bats."

"How about coyotes?"

"That's possible, too."

After hanging up I phoned Sally Shimada. "Any more news on how Jorgensen became infected?"

I heard a pencil drumming against her desktop. "You know, I keep giving you the early edition. It would be nice to get something in return."

Uh-oh. I asked what.

"An interview with your brother."

"No, Sally."

"Come on, this is a big story. Especially with him being stationed at China Lake."

"What's that mean?"

"I hear how secretive that base is. They conduct top-secret research into who knows what. There's talk that they develop strange weaponry for the CIA. Stuff the public *never* learns about."

The Big Ssssh . . . here was the flip side of Marc Dupree's sworn-to-secrecy act. In an *X-Files* age, the American public believed the notion that the government was boiling up secret mayhem.

I said, "How does this connect to your story about Peter Wyoming's death?"

"It's a hook."

"It's preposterous, Sally. Trust me."

"Trust you? You grew up out there. You have to know the truth."

The truth? I pinched the bridge of my nose. The truth, from what I had experienced growing up *out there*, was that midrank naval officers could be ambitious, geeky, bureaucratic, and patriotic all at once. That, isolated in a hothouse desert laboratory with their families and neuroses, they knew how to keep their mouths shut, and they cared about beating back the reds,

and *really* cared about keeping young men alive up in
the sky, and that they did so by inventing things that
killed people. But, remembering barbecues where officers got weepy or combative from cheap, excessive
bourbon or cheap, excessive adultery; remembering
men with fine minds who went bankrupt or attempted
suicide or, if lucky, made it to AA, I thought the truth
was this: Left to their own devices, these guys couldn't
organize a secret carpool.

But Sally didn't want to hear that. She wanted in-
trigue, government-within-government, strange lights
in the night sky. And I felt a scratch in my belly,
telling me that I should pay attention to what she was
saying. Because it didn't matter if it was true; it mattered that people would act on the belief that it was.

I hedged. "I'll speak to Brian's lawyer. You find out
about the rabies."

For the rest of the day I made phone calls and ran
errands. I spoke to the SBPD detective, Chris Ramseur, about Glory, and kept trying to reach the nurse
from Neil Jorgensen's office who had inventoried the
stolen drugs. I ordered more flowers to be sent to my
mom in the Singapore hospital. I picked up my Explorer from the paint shop, and went grocery shopping
to stock Jesse's fridge. Then, checking with my ama-
teur's eye to make sure that the Remnant wasn't following me, I stopped by my house. I picked up my
mail and clean clothes and, on impulse, the necklace
my grandmother had given me for my first Holy Com-
munion, a small gold crucifix. It felt comforting around
my neck, reminding me of Grandma's touch.

In the morning I drove Luke to China Lake to see
Brian. The autumn sun was already low over the
mountains when we arrived, and under the blue arch
of the sky the town looked stark and bright. The drive

had bored Luke beyond words, but when we parked in front of the jail he sat up straight, eager, scared, and totally in the dark about what it would be like to see his father here.

"Okay, tiger, a few things first," I said. "When we see your dad the room will have a big window in the middle. We'll be on one side and he'll be on the other, so you can't hug him."

He listened, breathing in and out, looking at me with large, dark eyes.

"And he has to wear jail clothes."

He said, "Can I talk to him?"

"Yes. You bet. Come on, let's go in."

We waited in the visitors' room side by side, staring through the Plexiglas barrier. Luke's face was world-weary, almost middle-aged with anxiety. When the guard unlocked the door on the far side and Brian stepped in, Luke stilled. So did Brian, his face flash-freezing somewhere between joy and horror.

"Hi, Daddy."

"Hey, champ."

There is no such thing as a good jailhouse conversation. Brian strained at ludicrous small talk, sitting hunched forward, his shoulders rounded like a bull-dog's. Luke looked as if he had been launched into space, a place where there was no air, no up or down, nothing to hold him to the ground. I upset Brian with the news that our mom had dengue fever, and annoyed him with Sally Shimada's request for an interview. Absolutely not, he said. I asked what his lawyer was telling him.

"He thinks the cops have two competing theories about the . . ." His eyes flicked toward Luke. "About Peter Wyoming. It was either homicidal jealousy or a weapons sale gone bad."

I sat forward. "They think you were selling weapons to the Remnant?"

"Stuff must be missing from the base. The navy has inventory problems, I'm in the navy, ergo it has to be my fault. Two plus two equals seventeen."

But I wondered if the Remnant could be stocking its weapons cache with arms stolen from China Lake. They thought the base was the Super Death Weapons Emporium—they'd probably love to get some of its hardware for themselves. I kept the thought to myself, not wanting Luke to hear it. I said, "What's your lawyer doing?"

"He's planning strategies. I told him the only strategy that counts is to catch the fu— catch whoever did it."

"I'm working on it," I said. "Does the name Mildred Hopp Antley ring a bell with you? She owns the Remnant's retreat, and we went to high school with—"

"Casey Hopp." He started. "Christ."

"You know this person?"

"She was a hard case, a loser with a big red L on her forehead. She had a thing for me. Don't you remember?"

"I didn't even know that Casey was female."

"She and this gang of girls used to park up the street from our house, hoping for me to come out. Next morning we'd find beer cans and cigarette butts piled along the curb."

The vaguest recollection stirred in me. "That was Casey?"

"Oh, yeah. Is she involved with the Remnant?"

"I don't know."

He was sitting up taller. "You'll find out, right?"

"That's my plan."

The door behind him opened. A guard stepped in and said visiting hours were over. Brian didn't even turn around. "Fine."

I told him good-bye and stood to go, but Luke didn't move.

He said, "When are you coming home?"

Brian looked at me. I felt like barfing, wanted to shrivel up and die.

He said, "I don't know, bud. Soon, I hope."

For a six-year-old, hearing that from his father was like tumbling beyond the rim of the solar system into a vast empty nighttime where not even the sun could reach him. The silence stretched.

Brian said, "You be good for your aunt Evan."

Luke's shoulders rose and fell. I thought he was going to start bawling. But instead he anchored himself, found his own gravity. He stood on the chair, pressed his hands to the Plexiglas, and planted a kiss there for Brian.

"I love you, Daddy."

"I love you too."

I thought Brian couldn't say any more, and I took Luke's hand to go. But near the door my brother called to me. His eyes were narrow, fighting tears. I asked Luke to wait there, and walked back to the barrier.

Brian said, "Don't bring him back here." Then he turned and walked away.

Casey Hopp. The name couldn't be coincidence. This town was too small, this nightmare too heated, too tightly coiled around my family. Where was Casey Hopp today? *Who* was Casey Hopp today?

I headed for Abbie Hankins's house. Her toddler, Hayley, was riding a trike on the driveway, blond hair haloing around her head in the breeze. Abbie pushed open the screen door, giving a big wave, saying, "Hey, woman."

I said, "Remember the yearbook photo of Casey Hopp? Can I see it again?"

She pushed her glasses up her nose. "I've got something better."

She had found a yearbook from the subsequent

school year. "Senior portrait of Miss Hopp," she said. "And guess what? Casey wasn't her real name. It was a nickname for her initials, K.C."

I leaned over her shoulder, examining it.

Hopp was named Kristal, and in the photo she looked incensed, perhaps because the photographer had posed her wearing a fake fur stole that was a million miles from her Detention Club clothes. She had prominent cheekbones, long straight hair, deep-set eyes under thick eyebrows. Something seemed familiar about her, perhaps the way she held herself, the way the loathing poured off the page. I felt suspicion trickling through my mind.

"I'd like to take this to the police," I said. "Maybe they have an artist who can do an age progression."

"A police artist? In China Lake?"

Right. Probably the only person around who could draw an age progression was Tabitha. What I needed was the computer-imaging program from Neil Jorgensen's medical practice. I mentioned this to Abbie and she said, "Stop. Miss Thing, you are in luck. Wally uses that program to show parents how their kids will look after orthodontia."

Wally's office was in a strip mall near the center of town. We walked into that dreadful dentist's-office Muzak-and-crepe-sole hush, hearing the squeal of a drill in the back. A hygienist stood near the front desk with a green surgical mask hanging around her neck. "Emergency," Abbie said, coming through, "need to use the computer." The hygienist didn't blink at seeing her, me, Luke, and the three Hankins kids, and I wondered how often she rolled in here like this.

Abbie set Hayley on the counter and started scanning the yearbook photo into the computer. Over her shoulder she said, "By the way, our canine friend who tried to make a meal out of me?" She raised her arm, showing how well the bite was healing. "It wasn't a coyote."

"Say again?"

"It was a coydog. A coyote-mastiff cross. Some wild boy got in with Fifi and bred a litter of hybrids." She stared at the computer screen. "And"—she typed—"Animal Control says it was domesticated. Its last meal was Pedigree Chum. Somebody owned that thing, and they're going to be in a world of trouble if Animal Control finds out who. And I can't wait."

Wally finished his drilling and joined us, his huggy-bear face unnaturally serious. When Abbie brought the photo up on-screen, he said, "Let me."

A man who spent his days staring at people's mouths, he was adept at visualizing the changes that time causes in a face. He drew down the mouth, added the start of jowls, thinned the eyebrows, lengthened the nose. "It's not conjecture," he said. "It's based on the subject's underlying anatomy—bone structure, muscle attachments—and on what we know about the aging process." The image changed, and a hot prickle began inching up my spine.

I said, "Give her a rough life and some weight."

He added puffiness around the eyes. Sun damage. Alcohol damage. Widened the neck to accommodate rolls of flesh. Finally he said, "This?"

The simulacrum had an artificial quality, but was recognizable.

I said, "It's Chenille Wyoming."

Chenille knew Brian. She had known him for almost twenty years. She'd had a thing for him. I drove toward the police station, puzzling over it. The meaning of it eluded me. Kristal C. Hopp, K.C., Casey, had progressed beyond the Detention Club into drug abuse and sexual licentiousness. She had landed in Santa Barbara, ever-popular destination for high school grads bailing out of China Lake, such as I. Along the line she had become Chenille Krystall. I remembered the showy name from her wedding announcement. Finally she had emerged as Chenille Wyoming, insurgent wannabe with designs to become history's most famous reformed whore. She planned to outdo Mary Magdalene in the biblical byline—to be known not as disciple, but dominatrix.

I stared at the road. Waves of heat hovered above the asphalt.

Chenille Wyoming, would-be whip cracker of kingdom come, had once loitered up the street from my house, smoking and drinking and watching for Brian. All for nothing; all for his silent rejection. And then, this year, he had crept back into her life when Tabitha joined the Remnant. Tabitha, Brian's chosen and Pastor Pete's new darling, with her pure drawings and clean hand. How many flavors of envy could we cook up here?

As I'd told Jesse, I believed that the Remnant had deliberately incited Tabitha to ruck up my life, Luke's life, and Brian's life. Could a decrepit high school jealousy lie behind it? If so, Brian had not given Chenille reason to relent. When he had seen her, he hadn't even recognized her. He had treated her as *nothing*.

Now she believed that he had killed her husband, and she wanted retribution. She wanted it against the whole world. My palms felt sweaty on the steering wheel.

Detective McCracken, however, had a different reaction. Holding the age-progression picture in his cigar-stub fingers, with his breath whistling through his nose, he thought about it and said, "A high school crush. So what?"

"So . . ." *What?* "At the very least, it shows that she withheld information from you. That she knew Brian."

"You've forgotten what it's like in a town this size. Everybody knows everybody. I don't expect them to tell me about each romance they had back in high school."

"It wasn't a romance," I said.

"Oh, an *unrequited* crush. An even stronger connection."

I sagged. All I could think was to change the subject. "Have you found the murder weapon yet?"

He said, "Do I work for you?"

Driving back into Santa Barbara the next day, Luke and I heard the radio news report that a car had crashed into the HoneyBaked Ham store on State Street, apparently after running down a stray cat. "Let us remind you," the reporter said, "that a Previa minivan is not the appropriate tool for dealing with loose animals. If you suspect an animal is rabid, phone Animal Control."

Back at Jesse's I checked for phone messages, but had none. I tried again to reach Dr. Jorgensen's inventory nurse, but got no answer. My intuition was poking me like a sharp fingernail, telling me that the stolen drugs had something to do with the Remnant and with Jorgensen's death, so I called Kevin Eichner. I got him on his cell phone at a construction site, and told him my suspicions.

His voice was quiet. "She couldn't get me to steal for her, so she put the thumbscrews to Glory. Man, Glory's gift of submission really did come in handy."

I asked if Chenille had been specific about the drugs she wanted him to obtain.

"Morphine—she said we'd need to lay in a supply for treating casualties during the Tribulation. And any therapeutic drugs the neurologist had, in case we had to counteract nerve gas or chemical attack. I'm telling you, she's a few beers shy of a six-pack."

A short while later I drove to the doctor's office for my second vaccination. Dr. Abbott had ordered a supply of the vaccine. As she swabbed my arm I said, "What kinds of drugs would a neurologist keep in stock? Someone who treats cerebral palsy patients?"

She had been expecting a question about rabies. "Why do you ask?"

"It's for a case I'm working on."

"Well, antiseizure and anticonvulsant medications, mostly. Dilantin, Tegretol . . . as well as migraine meds, and drugs for Parkinson's."

"And how about a plastic surgeon?"

"Anesthetics, sedatives—Lidocaine, Vicodin . . ."

"Any that would overlap with therapeutic drugs used by a neurologist?"

Her forehead crenellated. "Maybe Botox."

I raised an eyebrow. "It's not just a beauty treatment?"

"You know how Botox works, don't you?"

I knew. "It paralyzes muscles so a person can't frown. That smoothes the skin, giving a younger appearance."

Voluntary paralysis for the sake of vanity: It was death-mask chic.

"Neurologists sometimes use Botox to treat CP," she said. "It can control severe spasticity when other drugs fail."

I thought about it. "This is the poison that causes botulism?"

"Botulinum toxin, yes. It's an extraordinarily lethal substance. That's why only physicians should administer it. Neurologists inject it in minute doses, intramuscularly."

I drove back to Jesse's, distracted. I knew what he thought of the concept that paralysis perfected the body—that you had to be brain-dead to believe it.

He phoned shortly afterward, and we talked about meeting when he finished work. I told him about the Botox. Then, starting to feel that I was closing in on something, I once again phoned the nurse from Neil Jorgensen's office who handled the drug inventory. This time I got her.

"The robbery?" she said. "They mostly took pain medications."

"What about Botox?"

"Huh." She paused. "Funny you should ask."

"Why?"

"Because we expected to read about dead addicts the next week. Anybody who injected that stuff would have turned up stone-cold within a few days. And you know what? It would have been poetic justice. But it never happened, so maybe the robbers actually read the label on the vial."

Or maybe, I thought, they were saving it for another purpose.

Disquieted, I turned to my usual angst supplier, the Internet. A search for Botox found hundreds of Web sites, 90 percent belonging to plastic surgeons and bearing good tidings of great joy. "Dramatic results! Just one injection can immobilize muscles for up to six months!" But farther down my list of search results, the tidings darkened.

Potential use of botulinum toxin for biological warfare.

This wasn't Doctor Rex's Beauty Page; it was the Department of Defense, and I didn't have to read very far before my mouth went dry. The site couldn't have been clearer: Next to anthrax, Botox tops every bioterrorist's Christmas list. It's not just a party favor for trophy wives. It's so deadly that inhaling mere nanograms will kill the subjects who receive it. For *subjects* read airline passengers, the UN General Assembly, and your grandmother.

Still staring at my computer screen, I phoned a weapons expert I knew, a graduate of the Naval War College: my father. He was just waking up at his Singapore hotel.

"Biological terrorism? The poor man's nuclear bomb," he said, "and I don't like hearing questions about this from my daughter. What's going on?"

I gave him a thumbnail sketch of what I'd just learned.

"Biological warfare agents are a weapon of mass destruction that can be gotten on the cheap," he said. "You don't need isotope separation plants, nuclear physicists, or even plain old gunpowder and cannons. Pathogens occur in nature, or you can mail-order them from pharmaceutical houses. You get a terrorist with a high school chemistry set and some stick-to-itiveness, he could brew enough germs to kill tens of thousands of people. Or," he said, "a perpetrator could take the easy route and steal the prepared toxin."

Sweat prickled on my forehead. Steal the toxin? Chenille Wyoming, come on down.

My dad said, "Tell me why you want to know this, Sis."

Chenille hadn't wanted Kevin Eichner to filch drugs for treating chemical warfare casualties. Quite the opposite. She wanted to kick-start Armageddon by loosing the plagues of the Apocalypse.

Holding the phone, trying to keep calm, I walked out onto the deck. I said, "It's going to sound crazy."

His voice crackled. "The people Tabitha's mixed up with, you think they're trying to obtain BW agents?"

The ocean was glassy blue, the tang of salt sharp in the air. Out beyond the surf line a pelican raced along above the sea's surface. The Remnant, I knew, did not see this scene. They saw an entirely different version of the world, one hidden from light, similar to what physicists call dark matter—a universe where unseen forces clash, creating and destroying, controlling our destinies. And Chenille wanted to seed the clouds, unleash the storm. She thought that if she did she'd end up running the show: high priestess of the aftermath.

I said, "Yes, that's what I think."

A long, transpacific quiet stretched across the phone line. Then he said, "Aum Shinrikyo carried out the sarin gas attack on the Tokyo subway. And the Rajneeshis up in Oregon sprayed salmonella over salad bars in restaurants, sickened over seven hundred and fifty people. What you're thinking isn't crazy, Evan."

"Thanks, Dad."

He said, "Is there someone at the police department you can trust to believe you?"

I exhaled. "No. Not on such thin evidence. They'd think it's speculation."

"Listen," he said. "From a perpetrator's viewpoint, there are several advantages to engaging in chemical and biological warfare. One is ease of delivery— planting bug bombs, crop dusting on a cool night, there's just a whole slew of do-it-yourself ways to wipe out a large population. Another is the potential for escape. Germs incubate for days, weeks, even months. Biowar's effects aren't as immediate as those of a bullet. A terrorist can be long gone before evidence of the attack starts appearing.

"In fact," he said, "biowar victims may not even know they've been attacked. One thing that makes this a nightmare scenario is that you can have a hell of a time determining whether you're under assault, or are being struck by a natural epidemic."

A tickle started again, deep in my brain, the one that I'd been feeling off and on for the past few days.

"Here's the thing," he said. "You tell me this church is planning some sort of attack to occur around Halloween. That's a week from now. If they intend to release biological agents, they may do it before then. They may already have done it."

I stood up straight, feeling as if I had been jabbed with an ice pick. It was right in front of me. Incubation periods. Disease vectors. Emerging outbreaks and epidemics.

I said aloud, "Rabies."

19

Could rabies have been inflicted on Neil Jorgensen intentionally? If so, it meant that the coydog attack in China Lake had also been deliberate—and that the animal had been meant to assault me, not Abbie. The fact that the coydog had been domesticated now seemed sinister. It had eaten commercial dog food not long before its death, implying that it had been under human control in a rabid state. Was it possible? Thinking back to that night outside the Lobo, I recalled walking to my car, finding the vandalism, and looking around, seeing another car race away. The vandal, I had thought. But perhaps the vandal had dropped off more than spray paint.

My dad was skeptical. The military worried about many CBW—chemical and biological warfare—agents, he said, ranging from bubonic plague and smallpox to wheat rust and foot-and-mouth disease. Rabies was not high on that list. It acted slowly and was not easily transmissible. "Also, to weaponize a biological warfare agent you need an effective delivery system, one that can efficiently aerosolize the agent." Drily, he added, "Coyotes don't fit that bill."

But rabies was one of those pathogens that were plentiful in nature, I said. The disease was endemic in California's wild animal population, which was why parents taught their kids not to touch raccoons or possums. Trapping a rabid animal would require only patience, not sophistication. Likewise creating a kennel of infected wildlife. "We're not talking about rogue states tipping missiles with the stuff. We're talking about people obsessed with germs, itchy to get rid of folks they consider unclean." People who hankered after SPAM, Cheetos, and Doomsday.

He wasn't convinced. "Okay," I said, "don't call it bioterrorism. Call it biohomicide." Rabies wasn't an efficient germ warfare agent. Just lethal.

He said, "You need more evidence."

After I hung up, I told Luke to get in the car. We had enough time before we were supposed to meet Jesse. We drove downtown to the *News-Press* building. The willows in the plaza outside undulated in the breeze. The sun spread warmly across the building's red tile roof and lay chalk white on its adobe walls. Sally Shimada came to the lobby looking polished in a coral twinset that accented her glossy black hair.

"You must be here to pay off the favor you owe me." She smiled down at Luke. "Hello, young man."

He leaned against me. "Hi."

She said, "Your brother has agreed to the interview?"

"No. But I have news that'll stand your hair on end. Depending on what you've found out about Neil Jorgensen's death."

She tried to look peeved, but couldn't hold back. "It's going to be page one." She looked at the receptionist, and took my arm. "Let's go outside."

We sat on a park bench while Luke kicked a soccer ball across the lawn of the plaza, the sun shining on his dark hair.

"Jorgensen contracted rabies from a bat," she said. "Analysis of his virus samples showed a strain that bats carry. And it gets more interesting. The spooky thing about bats is that they can bite you and you won't even know it. Honestly. They're quiet, and their bite barely leaves a mark. They can nip you while you're sleeping and you won't even wake up."

"That's—"

"Creepy. What typically happens is that Joe Blow comes into the ER hallucinating and unable to swallow. The doctors suspect rabies but his family says he hasn't been bitten by an animal. Then, finally, they remember seeing a bat flying around his bedroom a couple of months back. But it's too late. Joe's dead."

"I know we have bats around here, but—"

"Wait. Public Health found evidence of bats in the attic at Jorgensen's house. You know, guano. Spattered on the floor." She wrinkled her nose. "The bats had gotten in through a hole between the chimney and the roof. But the hole was sealed up with Brillo pads."

An image of Jorgensen's attic formed in my mind. Spattered white droppings, brown furry forms clustered darkly in the rafters. It was an image I had seen before, in life. I tried to focus, to see it. Couldn't.

I said, "Steel wool is about the only thing you can stick in a hole to keep animals out of your attic. It hurts their noses."

"You don't get it. The Brillo pads sealed the bats *inside* Jorgensen's attic. He shut the bats in the house with him. He signed his own death warrant."

She was bubbling. *Page one.* It was like cocaine to her. I stared through her, trying to recall where I'd seen the image. . . . I grabbed her arm.

She said, "What?"

Angels' Landing. In the barn. Droppings spattered on old vehicles, and above them nesting forms hanging from the rafters.

I said, "Jorgensen's death wasn't a home pest problem gone wrong."

Her eyes were shiny, pinned on me. My head was pounding.

I said, "Let's call Public Health."

*   *   *

I reached the Health Department investigator who had interviewed me earlier, letting him know that Sally was listening on an extension across her desk.

"I heard about the bats and the Brillo pads in Neil Jorgensen's attic," I said. Then I leaped. "The hole where the bats got in. Was it natural or artificial?"

Deep, uneasy silence. "Ma'am, I think you'd better explain that remark."

Direct hit. Across the desk, Sally's eyes lit up.

I said, "Someone drilled or chopped a hole into Dr. Jorgensen's attic, didn't they? I bet you found fresh chunks of drywall and stucco on the floor inside."

"I am not going to comment on that. Our investigation is ongoing. Now, would you please explain how you came up with such a theory?"

"Call it a hunch."

"You'll have to do better than that."

"No, I think you will." I hung up.

Sally said, "Oh, my *God*. How did you know? Where are you going?"

I was halfway out the door. "To the police. Before Public Health calls and tells them I put rabid bats in Jorgensen's attic. And Sally? We're even. I just paid off my favor."

The detective, Chris Ramseur, was a placid young man with a banker's soft hands. He sat behind his battered metal desk at the police station sipping coffee from a stained *Star Trek* mug, listening to me lay out my theories, occasionally glancing toward the lobby, where a female desk sergeant was entertaining Luke. He wore a knit tie and blue checkered shirt and looked like an English teacher, perhaps one at the end of a tough week. Except for the eyes—his were hard and calculating. Calculating me.

I laid it out for him. The Remnant was assembling an arsenal, and it included not just firearms, but biological agents. Kevin Eichner had refused to steal drugs for Chenille, but Glory had gotten hold of Botox, at the cost of Mel Kalajian's life.

He had Glory's photo out on his desk. "This woman hasn't been turning up for work. We can't locate her."

Meaning they could neither verify nor disprove her involvement.

I stepped it up to the next level. Public Health, I said, would tell him that rabid bats were put into Neil Jorgensen's attic through a hole that was deliberately drilled, and then filled with Brillo pads.

Ramseur steepled his fingers. "You think the Remnant did this?"

"Yes. I think Dr. Jorgensen figured out that the drug thieves belonged to the church, and perhaps that they were after Botox. They wanted to get rid of him. But murdering both him and his partner would have drawn attention back to the medical practice and the robbery. So they found a way to make it look like a tragic illness."

Ramseur nodded. He finished his *Star Trek* coffee. I waited.

"I understand you're an author. Science fiction," he said, and I thought, I'm cooked. "This is a fascinating theory you've developed."

He opened a file folder. Now he was no longer the friendly English teacher, but the vice principal, pulling out my permanent record.

"You've developed quite an entanglement with the Remnant."

In the folder I saw a police report and the word *fax*. It had to be from the China Lake police department.

He said, "Witness to Neil Jorgensen's accident. Report of intruders in your residence, allegedly belonging to the Remnant. Arrest in Kern County for damaging a sheriff's department cruiser. Plus frequent mentions of your name in the paper. Oh, and your brother's arrest for the murder of Peter Wyoming."

He drummed his fingers on the folder. "Why do I seem to hear 'Dueling Banjos' in the background?"

I spread my hands out flat on his desk. "This is not some hillbilly vendetta between my family and the church. You know the Remnant is dangerous. I'm trying to tell you exactly how dangerous. They're not going to wait around for Jesus to call them long-distance; they're going to light up the night. Soon."

"I understand your concerns, Ms. Delaney. Thank you for bringing this information to our attention."

My face felt hot and tight when I got up and went to get Luke.

The lobby had turned loud. A little girl stood at the desk crying, and a woman was holding up a ball-peen hammer, saying, "I want him arrested!" The desk sergeant was staring into a shoe box on the counter.

"What," the cop said, "is that?"

The little girl's face puckered and she let out a droning wail. "It's Tooter. My hamster."

The mother said, "It got loose, and next thing we hear the neighbors screaming, saying, 'Watch out for the teeth!' " She waved the hammer. "This is the weapon he used."

The little girl wailed. The cop backed away from the shoe box. "Tooter was rabid?"

I grabbed Luke and walked out.

The courthouse takes up a city block, its dense white walls rising like cliffs, flanked by palm trees, giving off an aura of Spanish heat. Late-afternoon sun was etching the mountain ridges gold. Across the street from the courthouse entrance, the green Dodge pickup was parked in front of a fire hydrant. People noticed the man behind the wheel, whittling at a pencil with a pocketknife, and the woman next to him, sucking on a chocolate milk shake.

Inside the courthouse, Jesse was walking along the

tiled hallway, talking to a paralegal. The day had been
rough, fighting motions filed by Skip Hinkel. The paralegal commented that this whole trial could have been
avoided if crusty, eccentric Anita Krebs had only prosecuted Priscilla Gaul for burglary. If she'd been convicted, Gaul couldn't have sued for her injuries. But
Anita thought she had suffered enough, losing her
hand, and hadn't pressed charges.

"Yeah," Jesse said, "rough justice can turn out
rougher than people expect." He put on his sunglasses, about to go outside.

The woman in the green pickup sucked up the last
drops of her chocolate shake and chucked the paper
cup out the window. Passersby scowled but she ignored them, staring at the courthouse entrance. Jesse
and the paralegal came through the archway. The man
behind the wheel flicked shut his pocketknife.

A meter maid's three-wheeled scooter revved up
beside the truck. Beneath her motorcycle helmet and
aviator shades, the meter maid's face was pinched. She
grabbed her citation book. The woman in the truck
started swatting the driver on the shoulder. He fired
up the engine and hauled away, leaving the meter
maid scrambling to get the tag number.

Jesse met us at Rocky Nook Park. The oaks were
thick, leaves dry green, sunlight dappling the ground.
Luke was climbing on boulders by a dry creekbed,
and I was sitting on a picnic table, throwing acorns at
a tree. They cracked against the bark like gunfire.
Jesse came toward me slowly, careful with the crutches
on uneven ground.

"You and Detective Ramseur didn't hit it off?"
he said.

"He's filing me under K for kook." I flung another
acorn. "I might as well have handed him an alien
probe and a map of UFO landing sites."

"The folks at China Lake wouldn't like that. You giving away their secrets."

I gave him a look.

"Sorry." He sat down on the table next to me. "Tell me what you've got."

I told him about the stolen Botox, and the discussion of biological warfare I'd had with my father. I explained about Jorgensen's attic and the reasons why people bitten by bats don't know they've been infected until it's too late. About needing more evidence to connect this rabies outbreak to the Remnant, and about the clacking sound I heard in my head, a big clock winding down to Halloween.

He stared up the dry creek. The breeze stirred the trees, and sunlight shivered gold across his white dress shirt.

"I've been thinking about something," he said. "Rabies used to be called hydrophobia. Correct?"

"Yes. Because victims have difficulty swallowing. They don't want liquids."

He picked up an acorn, tossed and caught it in his hand. "Victims also get anxiety, confusion, numbness, weakness."

"And death."

He tossed the acorn, caught it. A distant light was working in his eyes.

"You know who had all those symptoms?" he said. "Peter Wyoming."

I stared at him.

"Think about it. That day we went to Tabitha's house, he knocked away a tray of iced tea, practically gagging. And in China Lake, when Brian confronted him outside the police station, you said he freaked out because Brian grabbed his arm."

I remembered it—Wyoming wrenching free, staring at his flesh in horror.

I said, "He practically hissed at Brian. . . . He said,

'You lay hands on me but you're not even here.' Brian thought he was high."

"It sounds like paresthesia. He could see Brian's hand but couldn't feel it touching him. His arm was going numb." He added, "It's a subject I know a lot about."

I blinked. "My God."

"There's your connection between rabies and the Remnant."

We looked at each other. Alarm and excitement crawled along my skin.

I said, "You really think . . . ?"

He nodded.

He tossed and caught the acorn once more, then rifled it up into the trees. It spit through the leaves. Crows burst cawing from the treetop, flying black against the sky.

He said, "Who's the guy you talked to at Public Health? I'll call."

My brain snapped into overdrive. Rabies—had Wyoming's killer set his body afire to destroy evidence of the virus? Had the China Lake coroner saved tissue samples that could be tested? If not, could we convince the authorities to seek an exhumation order? Talk about a mess . . .

"What?" I looked at Jesse. He was working himself back onto his feet, had said something I didn't catch.

He said, "You really spoke to your dad about germ warfare?"

"Yes."

"Dinner at your house must have been a barrel of laughs. Talking cluster bombs and biological attacks and 'pass the peas.' "

I heard the brass in his voice, and wasn't in any mood for it, not about my family. I said, "And where are you eating dinner tonight?"

He quickly gave me a contrite-schoolboy face, knowing he'd blown it. "Maybe I'll just go back to the office now."

"Excellent idea. Or maybe you could take up insulting people full-time. Folks would pay you just to shut up."

As I drove past the Old Mission church, my brain was still popping, working over my annoyance with Jesse like a hard piece of gum, but mainly thinking about Peter Wyoming. If he had been infected with rabies, had he contracted it accidentally, through some experiment gone wrong? Considering his germ phobia, I couldn't imagine him working with the virus. What could have happened?

Luke slouched on the passenger seat, kneading his fingers together, staring at contrails streaking the sky.

He said, "I don't want you and Jesse to get broken up."

I turned to him, taken aback.

"Don't fight with him. I don't like it."

"Luke, Jesse and I aren't going to—"

"I mean it."

"I love Jesse, Luke. We . . ." I rubbed my fingers across my forehead.

As if flak had started bursting in the air ahead, all at once I saw it. Jesse had given me shelter, and I was being so testy that he didn't even want to come home. The guilt light pinged on, and I saw, like a heads-up display, my own stupidity.

I said, "Get my phone out of my purse and dial Jesse's cell."

But when he handed me the phone, Jesse's number just rang and rang.

Back at the house Luke kicked the soccer ball to me on the beach, and I berated myself. How could I make up to Jesse? Vintage wine, a month in Tahiti, lewd sexual acts? I was brushing the sand off Luke's feet when I heard a car pull up.

"There's Jesse," I said. Maybe an erotic circus routine—a high-wire, the splits. Or fantasy. Naughty nurse. Girl gladiator. "Let's see what he wants for dinner."

But it wasn't Jesse. Looking through the slender panes of glass that flanked the front door, I saw a rusting station wagon held together by faded bumper stickers. QUESTION AUTHORITY. GET OIL OUT. It was empty, no sign of a driver. A small ball of anxiety congealed in my gut. I called Luke in from the beach and locked the plate-glass doors behind him. I looked out the front windows again and saw a woman emerge from the garage. She was wearing a broad-brimmed straw hat above a denim skirt and Birkenstocks. It was Anita Krebs, the owner of Beowulf's.

I stepped outside. "Anita?"

She raised a hand and kept walking toward the ancient station wagon. "Sorry to bother you. I can see that Jesse isn't here. I'll be on my way."

"Did you need something from the garage?"

She waved dismissively. "It'll keep. I didn't mean to disturb you."

Something was going on. But I said, "What happened to Beowulf's was appalling. I'm so sorry."

She stopped. Beneath the white skullcap of hair, her aged face wore a hardpan look. "They're Brown Shirts. Taliban. They want God to be a sharp, hard rock in your shoe." She crossed her arms. "Well, they won't win."

"Amen."

She snorted. "You should free yourself from that kind of language." She took off her straw hat. "Priscilla Gaul's attorney has filed a lien on the insurance proceeds from the fire. So that I won't even be able to rebuild the bookstore."

"Jesse knows?"

"Yes. He says it's a strategy to force me to settle with Priscilla out of court."

"Kicking you while you're down."

"It does feel that way." Momentarily the feistiness faded from her eyes. "They're all I have left, Evan."

"Who?"

She glanced toward the garage. "Pip and Oliver. With Beowulf's gone, I—"

"Oh, no." I started toward the garage door.

"You must understand. I have nowhere else to take them."

"No. You cannot leave your ferrets here."

I strode into the garage and flipped on the light. A scuffling sound came from under a tarp in the far corner.

Anita followed me. "It's this rabies scare—people are skittish. Even though they've been vaccinated, nobody will give them refuge."

I flung off the tarp. There sat an animal carrier, and inside it two small faces staring out at me. They were weasel-shaped, colored like Siamese cats, pale bodies with dark paws and faces. Their ebony eyes were alert.

"Hello, boys," I said. "Having a tough day?"

"There's no alternative. My God, people are running over Chihuahuas with riding mowers. Out there, these two would be at the mercy of the mob." She made clucking sounds at the ferrets. Her tough visage warmed, her eyes crinkling. "This is a case of necessity. And necessity is a legal defense."

"That'll never fly."

"I'm afraid you have no choice." Briskly she turned and headed for her car.

"Anita, you can't do this to Jesse." I grabbed the carrier and ran after her. The ferrets slid and banged against the sides of the cage.

She got in the car and started the engine. "I left their litter box and food in the garage. Let them out to play—they're delightful scamps. But do watch out; they can open cabinet doors."

I said, "I'll turn them in."

"No, you won't."

She was backing up now, with me running alongside the car. The carrier bumped against my thigh. From within it came squeaks and clawing sounds.

"If you turn them in they'll be destroyed," she said, "and you won't let that happen."

Flooring the station wagon, she accelerated backward up the driveway, zigzagging out of sight. I set down the carrier and stood there, breathing hard.

Maybe when I'm seventy, I'll learn to be that ruthless.

Luke came running up the driveway. "Who was that?"

"A lady Jesse and I know."

He crouched down in front of the carrier. "Whoa."

"Don't touch them. Keep your fingers away from the bars."

He curled his hands against his chest. "What are they? Are they ours?"

I picked up the carrier. "They're trouble. And they're all ours."

20

Sunset was pink and soft that evening, the light giving the ocean a vast silver sheen. I didn't know how I was going to tell Jesse about his two new houseguests, eating kitten food in their carrier in the kitchen. I had decided I couldn't leave them in the garage, where it would get cold overnight. Feeding them had unnerved me—open the cage door, shove the food and water inside, yank my hand back before they gnaw it down to bloody bone—even though Pip and Oliver had squeaked and leaped happily inside the carrier. They looked Disney-cute, and I didn't trust them for a second.

About seven thirty Luke was on the living room floor playing with his LEGO men. On the driveway headlights flared, shining through the slim windows along the front door. But from the sound of the engine I could tell that it wasn't Jesse. The bell rang. Outside, a woman stood under the porch light. I saw a slender curve of pale arm, sleeveless white cotton shirt, and green cargo pants. Auburn coils of hair.

It was Tabitha. My heart started pounding.

Through the door she said, "I need to talk to you. Please. It's important."

What was she doing here? Was this a new attempt to grab Luke? I looked beyond her, to the edges of the darkness where the porch light faded, trying to see whether anybody else was out there. It was impossible to tell.

She squinted at me through the narrow windows along the door. She was shivering and looked drawn.

"I'm leaving the Remnant," she said.

I didn't move.

"I'm quitting the church. I need help."

A thousand thoughts were pinging through my brain, and most of them were telling me this was a trick.

"For the love of God, I'm desperate." She tilted her head back and shut her eyes. "Please."

Luke stopped making explosion sounds. "Is that my mom?"

"Yeah, tiger. I'm going to talk to her for a minute. Everything's okay."

He was crouching on the floor with his LEGO men in his hands, as still as crystal. I told him to keep playing and stepped out onto the porch, pulling the door shut.

I said, "How did you find me here?"

"You weren't at home. I figured you'd be with Jesse."

"He isn't listed in the phone book. Who told you where he lived?"

"I called all the Blackburns in the book until I got his parents. I said I was FedEx trying to make a delivery, and his mother told me."

I clenched and unclenched my hands. Jesse would have to speak to his mother, presuming he could catch her when she was sober.

She said, "Nobody else knows I'm here. Truly. Evan, *please*."

She was haggard. Her eyes had a black brilliance, but it was a gambler's gleam, the shine that comes from betting everything on one last spin of the wheel.

I said, "You have two minutes."

"The Remnant is a house of lies. I know that now," she

said. "I've been a fool. Everything that's happened . . . I'm sorry for it. Truly, totally sorry."

The door swung open behind me. Luke stood in the doorway, hand on the knob. "Mommy?"

"Hi, sweet pea."

My stomach gripped. I waited for the Mama Minx act, for her to offer him a saccharine smile and soft words. But to my astonishment she looked abject.

She said, "How are you doing, honey?"

He shrugged. "Okay." He walked out onto the porch. "How are you doing?"

"Not so hot."

The moment stretched. She looked anguished, but I didn't care. I put my arm around Luke's shoulder. He gave her a bold, unfathomable stare.

He said, "We have ferrets in the house."

"Really. How weird," she said. "Usually you get mice, or maybe possums."

"Their names are Pip and Oliver, but Aunt Evvie won't let me touch them."

She looked bewildered. "She's right. They're probably filthy."

His fingers gripped the tail of my shirt. "I'm staying with Aunt Evvie. I'm not going with you."

Her face paled, down to her voluptuous lips. Her expression was one I'd waited nine months to see: shame. She blinked, she looked at her feet, she kneaded her hands together. I didn't give her a breath of relief.

Then she drew herself up. "What happened the last time I saw you, when I tried to get you to come with me . . ." Swallowing, she crouched down and looked him levelly in the eye. "It was a mistake. It was wrong. I'm sorry."

Luke clung tightly to my side. He said nothing.

"I won't do it again."

She looked up at me. Her eyes asked, *Okay?* I held on to Luke, not answering.

She said, "Brian is innocent. I can prove it."
I told her she'd better come inside.

I said, "Tell me."

"Brian is a scapegoat. Somebody else murdered Pastor Pete, and the church leadership knows it."

"Who?"

She peered into the kitchen. "Can I have something to eat? I'm starved."

"You have cartons of canned food in your garage at home."

"I can't go to my house. They're watching it. I haven't eaten since yesterday."

She really was thin, and quite pale. Her collarbones were protruding. I steered her into the kitchen.

The sight of the animal carrier stopped her. "Oh. Are those—"

"Ferrets. Don't ask."

I fixed her a plate, and she ate ravenously: the dinner leftovers, sandwiches, and a carton of milk. Luke sat across the table, watching her with reserved curiosity.

"I snuck out of Angels' Landing this morning with nothing but the clothes on my back. My money and ID is all in their lockbox. But I kept a car key hidden in my shoe, so I got to my car on the sly and booked out of there."

Her hands shook as she shoveled bites into her mouth. "We'd been on war rations, anyway, ever since Pastor Pete died. Eating from Tribulation supplies only, to keep from getting any tainted food. In case the government contaminated the water supply or something, Chenille said. Nothing could affect our combat readiness."

Her plate empty, she moistened a finger, dabbed crumbs with it, and licked them off.

Luke said, "Is there going to be a war?"

"No," I said.

He looked at me. "Dad's in jail. What would the carrier do, and his squadron?"

I reached across the table and took his hand. "There's no war. The people we're talking about like to use those words, but they're being ridiculous."

Tabitha's cheeks had splotched red. "Sorry," she said. "Luke, would you let me put on a video for you, while I talk to Aunt Evan?"

"Okay."

He led her into the living room and showed her the VCR. They both looked painfully tentative. She started a movie and returned to the kitchen table.

I said, "How can you prove Brian's innocent?"

"Ice Paxton told me." She ran a hand through her curls. "I've got to tell you from the start. Okay?"

"I won't stop you."

She took a breath and leaned forward, a confidante's pose. "Chenille can't stand me. It's because she hates Brian. Totally, hysterically, absolutely hates him. And I'd been his wife." She smiled sourly. "Of course, she didn't act that way when I joined the church. She liked me because I'd left him." She tilted her head. "You know she's from China Lake, right? She knew Brian in high school."

"I know."

"It was almost the first thing she said, the day she and Shiloh knocked on my door. 'Your name's Delaney? I went to school with a guy named Delaney.' And when I said we were getting divorced, she told me he'd always been a jerk—like she could commiserate with me."

"Did you say she knocked on your door?"

"They were canvassing the neighborhood. Evangelizing."

Canvassing the mountain backroads? That sounded unlikely. Again I got the feeling that Chenille was orchestrating events, that she had been circling my family like a buzzard.

She said, "But with him arrested, now she hates me too."

Animosity toward Brian was only half of it. "Could she have been jealous of the attention Pastor Pete gave you?"

Her cheeks warmed, and she dropped her gaze.

I said, "Tabitha, were you having an affair with Peter Wyoming?"

"No." Her eyes snapped up. "Absolutely not. How could you think that? He was my *pastor*."

She was physically recoiling from me. Could she really have been that oblivious to the situation? I thought not. She was either lying or embarrassed that I had noticed the attraction between them. But if Wyoming had been infected with rabies, and if she had been intimate with him, she was in danger.

I said, "You have to tell me the truth."

"*No*. Is that what people think? Did Chenille think that?" She put her hand over her mouth and let out a long, slow groan. "That's why."

"What?"

"Last night." She ran her hands over her face, as though trying to scrub it. "She tried to give me away as a prize. She told Ice he could have me as a reward for vanquishing the Antichrist." She pressed her fingers against her eyes. "She goes, 'Do it right and she's all yours, Ice.' He looked me up and down with those cold eyes and said—" She stopped, composing herself, lowering her voice. "He said I had good 'birthing hips.' Pronounce that, piece of tail."

I sat back. The spunk and spite in her voice more than anything convinced me that she truly had separated herself from the church.

She said, "Chenille told him he couldn't sample the goods. She's issued this rule—no sex until the Tribulation is over. But she let him inspect me."

Her hands had started shaking. "He took me to his

trailer and stripped me and examined me, and I mean every last inch. He didn't care what Chenille said; he was going to do it to me. . . ." Her eyes welled. "I tried to stop him, but he got on top of me and was trying to get his fly open, so I told him we couldn't, because my divorce from Brian isn't final and it would be adultery."

Tears spilled down her cheeks. "He slapped me. Said an unholy marriage has no effect, that I was a backslider and a slut, that he was my master and I had to submit to his discipline. . . ."

I said, "Did he—"

"He couldn't." Her gothic, lost-belle face turned disdainful. Her eyes were acid. "I guess having a woman stand up to him just let all the air out of his tires. He called me a cock teaser, said if I ever defied him again I'd be punished. But he left me alone. So this morning I snuck out."

She wiped her eyes. "And now they'll think I'm a traitor. They'll think I've gone over to the enemy, that I'm going to fight for Satan."

I gave her a moment to settle down. "What's Chenille planning on Halloween?"

"I don't know. I wasn't on the operational side."

"I know they're buying weapons." She nodded. I said, "It's military stuff, isn't it?"

"Some, I think." She pushed her lank curls out of her face. "Curt Smollek talked about getting hold of bayonets, flamethrowers if they could."

Her equanimity was unnerving. Quietly I said, "How about biological weapons?"

"Maybe. Chenille talks about unleashing plagues upon the unsaved."

Luke popped up, heaving himself over the back of the sofa. "Aunt Evvie, can we make popcorn?"

"Sure thing." I got up to fix it, my motions robotic. Tabitha sat quietly, gazing at him. He said, "I'm going to the bathroom," and her eyes followed him as he scooted from the room. I stood by the microwave while the popcorn rattled and clunked.

I said, "Okay. What did Paxton tell you about Brian being innocent?"

She grabbed a napkin and blew her nose. "Last night he told me that if I didn't submit to him, I could find myself getting blamed for Pastor Pete's assassination. I said, 'But Brian's guilty.' He goes, 'Brian is guilty because the military is guilty. But if you defy me then you take the side of the enemy, and you become guilty too.' "

" 'Brian is guilty because the military is guilty.' "

"That's what he said."

"What did he mean?"

"That it didn't matter who actually pulled the trigger."

My pulse was racing. "Does he know who did?"

We heard the toilet flushing. She said, "Quick, before he comes back. There's something else. Chenille didn't have plans just for me. She has them for Luke, too."

"What plans?"

"I don't know, exactly. She has this . . . this fascination with him. It's spooky."

Luke appeared, pointing toward the front of the house. "I heard funny noises outside."

Tabitha said, "You're out in the boonies here. You always hear funny noises."

Six-year-olds know condescension. His mouth went tight and he kept pointing.

I said, "Let's take a look."

The microwave beeped. Tabitha said, "I'll get the popcorn."

He led me into the guest room. "Don't turn the light on. It might run away if you do. It was coming from the bushes out there."

"What did it sound like?"

"Like something in the bushes." *Duh*.

I listened, but heard nothing.

He said, "Just wait."

Together we sat on the bed, peering out the window into the dark. I heard the wind rustling the Monterey pines, and saw the bushes swaying. Mostly I sensed Luke's warmth and energy next to me. His hair gleamed under the moonlight falling through the window. He had that soft, ineffably sweet young-child smell.

He raised a finger. "There."

Within the swaying bushes slid a shapeless form, dark on dark. Weightless and smooth against a backdrop of moonlit leaves, for a moment it took human shape. Gleam of metal, aiming skyward.

My pulse exploded. It was a man with a gun.

For a second I felt blank with panic. Then I said, "Get off the bed. Down here."

The coldness in my voice took Luke aback. In the moonlight I saw his missing tooth and his wide eyes. I pulled him onto the floor, holding him tight.

"You're shaking, Aunt Evvie."

The Remnant was coming. They had stalked Tabitha and were coming to take her back or to kill her. My breath caught. Or they were coming for Luke. Tabitha may not have left the church at all, but conned me. Either way, I had let her inside, let down my guard. The idiocy of it smacked me like a two-by-four.

Think. I had to call the police. But the guest room had no phone. I could call from the kitchen, but if Tabitha was waiting to grab Luke that could be fatal. I'd have to call from Jesse's bedroom.

And I knew that the police couldn't get here quickly enough. An armed man was outside; Tabitha was inside. I had to get Luke out of the house. Had to get away.

Luke said in a tiny voice, "I'm scared."

"Hold my hand."

Tabitha's car was parked on the drive, blocking my Explorer. We'd have to go on foot, reach a neighbor's house, shelter there until the police arrived. The Rosenbergs lived eighty yards away, through the trees. We just had to get there. And there was the rub: Jesse's house was largely glass, designed for three-hundred-and-sixty-degree views, and I hadn't closed the blinds. They were open in the bedrooms, in the living room, in the kitchen, and along the thin decorative panes next to the front door. Once Luke and I left the darkened guest room, we'd be on display like targets in a shooting gallery.

We couldn't bolt. We had to play it cool.

"Luke, listen to me carefully. I need you to do exactly as I tell you."

He watched me, his chest rising and falling sharply.

"We're going to go to Jesse's bedroom. Don't say anything. If your mom talks to us, I'll answer," I said. "You go into the bathroom, climb up on the counter, and open the window. And don't turn on the light. That's important. We're going to climb out the window and go to the Rosenbergs' house."

His hand squeezed mine. "The bad people are here, aren't they?"

I willed strength into my voice. "Yes. So we're going to be brave."

"Okay."

"Come on."

I stood up and led him into the hall and across the living room toward Jesse's bedroom. I heard the microwave droning again, more popcorn popping. Trying to seem offhand, I turned my head toward the kitchen.

Tabitha was leaning against the counter, watching the microwave. When she saw me she said, "I finished the first bag. Hope you don't mind. I found some more."

"No problem."

Luke stared at her and then at me. His face was fraught.

She said, "Everything okay?"

I kept heading toward Jesse's door. "Just checking all the rooms for noises."

She turned back to the microwave. Could she act so casual if she were about to attack us? Should I warn her? I had to decide, and I couldn't afford to be wrong.

Jesse's bedroom was dark, but light from the living room spilled in. I didn't want to close the door. Didn't want to look suspicious.

I whispered to Luke, "Be really quiet opening the window."

He let go of my hand and went into the bathroom. I picked up the phone from the nightstand and dialed 911. I said, "There's a prowler outside my house. He has a gun." Without hanging up, I dropped the phone on the bed.

Inside the bathroom Luke shuffled and huffed, pulling himself up onto the counter. The window slid open with a soft scritch. He stage-whispered, "Aunt Evvie, it's open."

"I'm coming." I hurried toward the bathroom door.

And heard Tabitha's voice. "What's going on?"

I spun around, heart thundering. She was silhouetted in the bedroom doorway, and she was reaching for the light switch. I hurtled across the room, scrambling over the bed, and slapped her hand down. Her mouth opened in shock. She tried backing away but I grabbed her by the shirt and pushed her up against the wall.

She said, "What is wrong with you?"

Her voice, always boisterous, rang loudly in the bedroom. I clapped my hand across her mouth so roughly that her head banged back against the wall.

"Make a sound and I'll knock you unconscious. I swear it, Tabitha."

Her hands clawed at my arm.

"Who is it outside?" I said. "Paxton?"

Sharp breath. Her eyes went round.

"Did you lead him here? Did you sell us out?"

Her eyes jerked back and forth around the windows. She started shaking, and I heard the unmistakable sound of liquid running onto the hardwood floor. I looked down. The crotch and one leg of her cargo pants were darkening with urine.

I took my hand off her mouth.

"They'll kill me," she said.

I didn't have time to apologize. "We're going out the bathroom window and heading for the neighbors'. Come on."

She pressed herself against the wall. Fear jangled in her eyes.

I grabbed her shoulders. "We have to protect Luke. We're all he has." She blinked. "You want to make up for the last eight months? This is it. Now *come on*."

For a second longer she held there. Then, steps hesitant, she came with me into the bathroom. The window, high up on the wall, gaped open. Luke was crouched on the counter, shivering. His eyes went to Tabitha.

"Your mom's on our side," I said. "Hop down for a sec."

I climbed onto the counter in his place and slowly raised my head to look outside. I could see nothing but the dark waltz of the pines. Gingerly I worked the screen off the window and handed it to Tabitha.

"I'll go out first. Then Luke, then you."

Standing up, I started winching myself outside, headfirst, holding on to the windowsill to keep from falling facedown on the ground. Then I heard a voice off toward the front of the house, talking low. I stopped.

"Done it. Them cars ain't going nowhere."

I hung there, frozen. Someone had disabled both

Tabitha's car and mine. And worse than that, the someone was talking about it out loud. That meant there were two of them. At least.

The voice, closer now, said, "There's a bike in the garage. What's a cripple need a bike for?"

"Shut up." A hiss.

I pulled myself back inside and squatted down. Footsteps passed by outside, crackling on pine needles. Slowly I raised my head again. Whoever it was had gone around the corner. And then we heard wood creaking as feet stepped onto the deck outside the bedroom plate-glass windows, fifteen feet away.

Tabitha was shuddering so hard I thought she might fall over. She said, "We'll never make it."

I forced myself to think. Could we barricade ourselves in here until the police came? No. "We can't stay. They'll shoot in through the window or the door. We'd be fish in a barrel."

She bit her lip and covered her mouth, stifling a cry. Luke watched her, his chin beginning to tremble.

"We can make it; we just have to be *fast*." I clasped Luke's arm. "When you get outside, run as hard as you can and don't stop no matter what. *Run*."

Standing up, I took one last look outside and wriggled through the window. I dropped to the ground with a thud. I heard Luke clambering onto the counter. His fingers wrapped around the windowsill.

From out of the night came a whistle. It was a signal. The bedroom window shattered. The front door banged open. In the bedroom a light flashed on. A man yelled, "This way!"

Tabitha started sobbing.

I heard her slam the bathroom door closed. She cried, "Go, Luke!" I heard heavy pounding on the door, someone trying to break in. Luke started crying. Tabitha screamed.

I shouted, "Luke, come on!"

His head appeared in the window, and his shoulders. The door broke open with a crash. Tabitha screamed again and again. Luke's eyes were wild with fear. I reached up and grabbed him under the armpits.

Somebody in the bathroom seized his legs and jerked him back.

He cried out, and his small hands scrabbled to hold on to me. I felt my grip slipping. To my horror he was pulled from my grasp and disappeared back inside. Noise rioted in the bathroom—Tabitha howling, Luke sobbing and shrieking. Then a man roared, "Stop it, you stinking brat!"

Luke was fighting back. It electrified me, filled me with terrifying inspiration. I ran toward the front of the house. Rounding the corner, I saw the front door splintered open.

A weapon, I needed a weapon. I rushed into the garage, looking for anything sharp or heavy. Inside the house Tabitha wailed. Underneath her keening I heard the skittering, squealing syncopation of the ferrets panicking in their carrier. My eyes fell on some cans of paint sitting on a shelf. Grabbing one, I ran outside.

Abruptly the air emptied with silence. Tabitha had stopped crying. My stomach cramping, I crept to the front door.

On the living room floor knelt Curt Smollek, his zitty face red with exertion. He was binding Luke hand and foot with duct tape. Luke's mouth was already covered, and his eyes were squeezed shut in terror. The tape made a wicked ripping sound as Smollek yanked it from the spool. On the floor near his foot lay a semiautomatic pistol.

Beyond Smollek, pinned down on the sofa, lay Tabitha. Her mouth and hands were taped, and she was crying noiselessly. Ice Paxton stood above her, his knee on her spine, the butt of a shotgun pressed against the back of her neck.

Smollek ripped off one last strip of tape and stood up, like a rodeo cowboy roping a calf. "Done."

"Sit him up." Paxton forced Tabitha's head around to face Luke. "Take a look at your boy, 'cause I'm gonna ask you a question," he said. "You betrayed the Remnant and fled from me like a wanton whore. By rights I should kill you."

Her eyes bulged. She rocked with a sob, and snot spewed from her nose.

"But I believe in second chances, so I'm giving you one. Your boy's going with us. You can come too, and live as my woman, and be with him. Your choice."

I had to move. But Paxton was facing the door, and would see me in an instant.

Tabitha squirmed, her eyes pinned on Luke. Paxton said, "What was that? I can't hear you."

Against the pressure of the gun she worked her head.

"Is that a yes?" He leaned on the shotgun, bending down close to her ear.

He was staring at her, and Smollek had his back to me. Telling myself, *Big windup, hard swing*, I ran inside. With all my might I swung the paint can and slammed Smollek in the back of the head. He went down like a stunned dog, and his foot kicked the pistol, sending it skittering under the sofa.

Paxton jerked up. He turned and came at me, leveling the shotgun on my midsection. Yelling wildly, I swung the paint can at his arm. Jesus, his finger was on the trigger; if I hit him wrong he could fire, but I couldn't stop the arc of the can. It pounded down on his wrist and the shotgun clattered to the floor. I swung at him again, the can thudding into his chest, the lid popping off, a gallon of Navajo White slurping loose onto his torso and face. Momentarily blinded, he staggered back, raking at his eyes, spitting and roaring. I dropped the can and dove for the shotgun, picked it up with paint-slick hands and kept running, around the sofa. Paxton shook his head and paint went flying. He blinked and saw me.

Pointing the shotgun at him with shaking hands. "Don't move."

He looked around at Tabitha, and Luke, and at Smollek, still down but moaning and starting to move. Back at me.

"You," he said, "are Satan's bitch whelp."

"The police are on the way."

"You'll die regretting this." He backed up a step.

"Don't move."

"You ain't gonna shoot me."

I pumped the slide on the shotgun. "I will."

"No, you won't." He stepped back again. "Take a look. You can't."

And *bam*, I saw my mistake. He had stepped behind Luke, putting him in the line of fire.

I edged around the sofa, trying to change the angle, and he swept Luke up into his arms. Holding him against his chest as a shield, he started backing toward the door. He pulled a palm-sized walkie-talkie from a pocket and spoke into it. "Bring the car." He kept backing toward the door. "Curt. Get up."

Smollek pulled himself to his knees. Outside, headlights rose and an engine droned up the driveway. Luke shot me a look over his shoulder, unalloyed terror.

"Coward," I said. "Hiding behind a child. You're no soldier."

Then Tabitha struggled to her feet. Though her hands were taped, she clenched her fists and charged at Paxton. She tried to catch him with an uppercut, but he sidestepped the blow and backhanded her across the face, sending her to her knees.

He said, "This ain't the time to be stupid. The boy's with me. You coming?"

The shotgun was heavy. Maybe I could batter him

with it, I thought, without him wrestling it away, without Smollek getting in on the act.

Like he'd read my thoughts, Paxton said, "Curt, get Delaney."

Smollek lurched to his feet. I knew that the second I took the gun off Paxton, he'd be out the door with Luke. I held my aim, but shouted at Smollek, "You'll die. Don't do it!"

Headlights blared through the splintered front door. Smollek was staring at the sloppy white floor in confusion. Searching, I realized, for his pistol.

Paxton said, "Take her, Curt!"

Not in nightmares could I have pictured myself helpless with a twelve-gauge in my hands. But as I stood there Paxton melted out the door into the headlight glare. Tabitha got to her feet. For an instant she looked at me. The light painted her starkly. Star-hot eyes, ghostly white skin. Then she followed Paxton out the door.

Smollek charged me. My heart hammering, I spun on him. Thinking, God forgive me; I'm going to do it, I pulled the trigger.

Nothing happened.

Smollek flew at me. Again I pulled the trigger and again nothing happened. He crashed against me, knocking me to the floor, and fell on me, all tangy BO and bony elbows and pained frenzy. The headlights arced away and the light in the room dimmed. And I heard, faint but insistent, a police siren.

We fought on the floor, grunting and sliding toward the kitchen. I was kicking, struggling under Smollek's weight, hearing the siren grow louder. We banged into the ferret carrier. Pip and Oliver jumped inside it, squealing and hissing. Smollek got a hand around my throat, and suddenly I couldn't get any air. His face was hideously intent. Though I clawed at his arm I couldn't shake him off. Desperate, I reached out and fumbled for the latch to the ferret carrier.

The little door sprang open. A gray blur zoomed past me, and Smollek shouted in distress.

He leaped off of me, screaming. Gasping for air, I scrambled to my feet and staggered toward the knife rack. But Smollek was spinning in circles, grabbing at the ferret. It was clawing at his head, its dark furry tail whipping wildly as they circled.

Shrieking, wearing the ferret like a hat, Smollek ran out the front door. I followed, stopping halfway up the drive, staring through tears into an empty night.

21

Detective Chris Ramseur came in through the French doors at my house and sat next to me on the sofa in my living room. His English teacher's face looked drawn, but he'd been up all night. Nikki Vincent paced back and forth in front of my fireplace, arms crossed on her enormous belly. The FBI agents had stepped outside to confer. I could see them, two men in blue suits standing on the lawn in the morning sunlight, earnest, sober, one now speaking on a cell phone. The press was at Jesse's house, standing outside the police tape, doubtless shooting photos of the smashed front door.

Ramseur said, "We've put together a lot of information in the last few hours." He had a small notebook in his hand. "The shotgun that Paxton was carrying. It didn't fire because there was sand in the action. These guys are sloppy."

I told him how I'd seen Smollek drop a gun in the sand out at Angels' Landing.

He nodded. "There's more. The pistol Smollek was carrying was military-issue. We checked the serial number, and it was stolen from China Lake."

I stared at him. "Is it the gun that killed Peter Wyoming?"

"No, but it's still valuable evidence. We've recovered fingerprints from it, and they match those on the liposuction cannula that killed Mel Kalajian."

Nikki stopped pacing. "Jesus, Ev, Smollek would have killed you. Thank God for that ferret. Light a candle for the little beast."

Ramseur said, "Disarming your attackers the way you did was amazing, Evan."

I didn't respond.

He flipped through his notebook. "Couple of hours ago we executed a search warrant on Smollek's place. It's a hovel out in Winchester Canyon." He ran a hand over his beard. He hadn't had time to shave, had a dark five-o'clock shadow. "He was keeping a menagerie, these stinking cages out back of the house. We found bats, sick ones, and a hutch full of dead rabbits. Also some dogs that had to be destroyed." A strange look entered his eyes. "Big things, like nothing I've seen."

I said, "Coydogs. A dog-coyote cross."

He nodded again, slowly. He was being almost ceremonious in acknowledging that everything I had alleged was proving true, but his contrition was belated and irrelevant.

Smollek was gone, along with Paxton, Tabitha, and Luke. Worse, the Remnant had gone to ground. Their church was abandoned, their homes empty. Angels' Landing was deserted. The only person the police could find was the woman who owned the retreat, Mildred Hopp Antley. She was Chenille Wyoming's mother, and she was in a nursing home with Alzheimer's. I sat staring into my cold fireplace, feeling as though a void had yawned open and I was falling into it.

"And one other thing." Ramseur was scratching his head. "Public Health can't find Peter Wyoming's body."

"What?"

"There's no record of its being interred anywhere in the Tri-Counties."

Nikki and I both gaped at him.

"Ms. Delaney."

The FBI agents had come back inside. The older of the two was addressing me, a man with thinning hair and brown button eyes named DeKalb.

"You say that last night your sister-in-law followed Paxton out the door. But by your account, at that point he was unarmed. She could have remained behind." He tilted his head. "Are you positive that she was acting under duress?"

"She went with him to protect Luke."

DeKalb looked briefly at his partner.

I said, "This isn't a domestic dispute. Tabitha didn't set it up."

"Why else would the Remnant take the boy?"

"I don't know. Tabitha said that Chenille Wyoming has . . ." The skin on my neck was creeping. "She has some kind of fascination with him."

DeKalb remained expressionless. I balled my fists and pressed them against my eyes to keep from crying. A moment later Nikki sat down next to me and slipped her arm around my shoulder.

She said, "It might have to do with Halloween."

"What about it?" said DeKalb.

Ramseur said, "Miss Delaney's been told that's when the Remnant plans to launch some kind of attack."

DeKalb shifted his weight and said, "You know a tremendous amount about this group's activities, ma'am." His tone set off my inner alarms. "In fact, your family is seriously entwined with the Remnant, and has been involved in a number of violent acts, up to and including murder. Do you want to tell us what's really going on?"

I stood up. "What's going on is that the Remnant

is dangerous, and if just once any of you had stopped laughing at me or blaming me when I warned the authorities about them, Luke would be home safe right now."

His button eyes didn't even blink. "The Bureau is involved now. Your best chance of getting him home safely is letting us handle it."

Ramseur nodded gravely. "We'll find him, Miss Delaney."

Nikki said, "Damn straight you will."

I said, "You'd better get it in gear. Halloween's five days away."

DeKalb buttoned his suit jacket, as though getting ready to leave. "There's something else."

His partner gave me a heavy look. "It's about your lawyer."

I felt my vision contracting around the edges.

Jesse had not come home the night before. He hadn't stayed late at the office, or stopped to see friends after work. His family hadn't heard from him. He wasn't answering his cell phone. When I called, it just kept ringing.

DeKalb said, "That call I got was from the Highway Patrol. They found Mr. Blackburn's car wrecked in a gully two miles from his house."

My vision started to tunnel, and lights danced in front of DeKalb's face. I asked a big, dumb question. "Is Jesse okay?"

"There was no sign of him at the crash site."

"He didn't just walk away. He uses a wheelchair—"

"It was in the backseat," the partner said.

DeKalb said, "There's evidence that his car had been in a collision. It was forced off the road."

I felt Nikki's hand taking hold of my arm. I said, "The Remnant took him."

"We have to presume so."

I barely heard the knock at the door. But I sensed the agents' abrupt alertness, DeKalb going to the

door, escorting the messenger inside, taking an envelope from him. DeKalb examined the envelope, held
it up, asked me if I recognized the sender. My eyes
were swimming. It was from Jesse's law firm. They all
circled around me, waiting for me to open it, to see
if it was a ransom note.

I pulled out a sheaf of court papers. Squeezed my
eyes shut, shook my head, let them drop to the floor.

I said, "It's the restraining order. It was issued
this morning."

The guard opened the door and led Brian into the
visitors' room at the jail. When he saw me his eyes
brightened for just a moment, before he saw that
something was terribly wrong. I felt sick again.

I'd had to wait a whole day to get up to China
Lake. By the time the FBI had finished with me it
was late afternoon, too late to see Brian. I had phoned
his criminal lawyer with the news about the kidnapping, but had told him that Brian had to hear it from
me. Already, heading to the visitors' room, I'd had to
stop at the toilet to vomit.

He sat down behind the Plexiglas barrier. Alarm
was tightening his face. He said, "Luke . . ."

"They've got him."

His face drained of blood. He looked at the bruises
on my arms and around my throat. "Brief me."

I tried to speak in a level voice, couldn't. "They
broke into Jesse's house."

"Jesse swore that they didn't know where he lived."

"They didn't."

"They fucking well did."

"Brian—"

"What did he do, draw them a map?" His fingers
pressed down on the countertop, white as bone.

"No. Jesse's missing, Bri. The police think the Remnant ran him off the road. They got his wallet; his
driver's license has his address on it, and . . ." My

voice broke. I couldn't manage to tell him the rest: The police had found blood in the car. They thought Jesse was dead.

He stared at me. His jaw muscles flexed. "Continue."

I ran the back of my hand across my eyes. Breathed out. "You want to yell at me? Go ahead, do it. I love you, Brian, and I'll die for Luke. So go on and give it to me with both barrels, and then let me go try to find him."

I could see his pulse jumping in his neck. He said, "Just tell me."

"Tabitha's left the church. She came to me for help." I told him her story, told him she believed in his innocence, told him how the Remnant had attacked the house. Told him that we almost made it out. My voice cracked again. "Tabitha did a brave thing, Bri. She went with them, and she didn't have to."

"She was trying to protect Luke?"

"Yes."

He looked down at the frayed cuff of his orange jail coveralls. His hand, still pressed tightly against the countertop, was twitching. "Maybe she can find an opportunity to escape with him."

"Maybe she can."

Quiet hung over us, a comment on long odds.

I told him about the FBI, and that the authorities had issued a statewide BOLO—Be on the Lookout. He said, "And what do you plan to do?"

"I'm going out to Angels' Landing. The police say it's deserted, but maybe I can spot something they've overlooked."

"Don't go alone. Take Marc Dupree with you." His flying comrade.

Behind him, the door rattled open and the guard stepped in. Said, "Time's up."

Brian drew his twitching hand into a fist. He stood up, but didn't turn to leave. Slowly he leaned close to the Plexiglas, close enough that I could hear him when he whispered.

He said, "You should have taken the gun when I offered it to you."

The Explorer roared through the dazzling afternoon sunlight as I sped away from the jail. The road stretched ahead of me like an arrow through the heat. I was exhausted, fried, and trying to outrun the overwhelming sense of shame I felt for failing to protect Luke. But it hit me again, right in the chest: despair. I thought about Luke and my throat constricted. Where was he? What must he be feeling? Terror, abandonment?

And Jesse. In my mind I saw his blue eyes and wicked grin, felt his arms encircling me. Jesus. God. Merciful One, Immanence, Ancient of Days, Still Small Voice in the Wind. Don't play dice. Be there. Be true. Mea culpa, mea maxima culpa, forgive me for the last words I spoke to Jesse, and let him be alive.

Looking down at the speedometer, I saw that I was going seventy on city streets. I pulled to the side of the road, stopped, and let my hands drop from the wheel. After a minute I turned off the engine. The wind buffeted the car, raising sand, hazing the distant mountains with a Sahara sheen. Above, an F/A-18 ripped the sky.

I got out my cell phone and called Marc Dupree, but he wasn't home. His wife said he was at the base, and would be back around dinnertime.

I couldn't wait that long. I had to check out Angels' Landing, and Brian was right: I shouldn't go alone. The memory of Ice Paxton aiming the shotgun spread through me like a stain. But the police weren't about to accompany me. I opened the glove compartment and scrounged around for the scrap of paper that Garrett Holt, U.S. Navy, at your service, had given me with his phone number.

If he thought it was a first date, he was in for a rude awakening.

About half an hour later, the guard at the jail surprised Brian by unlocking his cell and saying, "Visitor, Delaney." Brian wondered why I had come back so soon.

But it wasn't me. Brian stepped into the visitors' area and saw two people sitting beyond the Plexiglas, a woman and a man. He stopped in the doorway. The guard looked at him.

On the visitors' side, her lips pinched white, sat Tabitha. Next to her, his face shaded under the brim of a cap logoed with ED'S FEED & AMMO, was Ice Paxton.

He tipped his head and said, "Afternoon, Commander."

22

Garrett Holt met me at a gas station on a fringe of empty highway south of China Lake. He climbed out of his Jeep as calm as a windless day, cocksure and concerned. He wore civvies—jeans and a polo shirt—and was chewing gum, his square jaw flexing. His green eyes and terrier demeanor struck me as alert, almost apprehensive.

He said, "We have to stop meeting like this."

"This won't be fun, Garrett."

"I'll be the judge of that."

"A few nights ago one of these people aimed a shotgun at me from three feet away."

He tipped his head toward the Jeep. "I have a deer rifle. A Winchester."

"You're sure?"

He was evaluating me, trying, perhaps, to assess my nerve. "These people have your nephew, right? The child of a fellow officer. Let's go."

My heart started pounding again. I unrolled a USGS map across the Explorer's hood, showed him how we were going into Angels' Landing the back way, off-road, up an arroyo. We'd walk the last part.

He examined the map, and me again, and couldn't resist. "I don't see a boyfriend here today, so . . . I presume that's good news for me."

I rolled up the map. "The Remnant ambushed my boyfriend. The police think they killed him."

He took it quietly. Put on a pair of sunglasses. "Then let's light 'em up."

Brian stood in the doorway to the visitors' area, feeling coiled, senses pinging. He knew I hadn't seen Paxton come into the jail, hadn't been able to warn anyone. Paxton was too shrewd to let that happen. Behind him the guard coughed. Brian realized he could turn around, tell him, and bring down an immediate armed response. He could rescue Tabitha. She was staring at him, her pupils pinprick-tight with fear. He could get her back right then. He knew it might be his only chance. And he knew what would happen if he did. He told me afterward, countless times. He would never see Luke again.

Brian sat down. The guard said fifteen minutes, and the door clanged shut.

Paxton said, "Wise choice."

"Where's my son?"

"Time's short, so listen up."

Brian turned to Tabitha. "Is Luke okay?"

Paxton said, "Tell him to shut that mouth of his, Tabitha."

Only her lips moved. *Do it.*

Brian saw live-wire intensity in her eyes, but fragility on the rest of her face. Her lip was split, and a bruise colored one cheek.

He said, "Did he hurt you?"

She started to nod but Paxton reached up and wound his fingers into her hair, holding her head still.

He said, "Discipline is for our good, that we may share God's holiness."

Brian looked at him. "You're a dead man."

"Zip your pecker back inside that dirty orange jumpsuit. 'Without chastisement, then are ye bastards.' " He let go of Tabitha's hair. "Hebrews twelve."

Brian closed his mouth and slowed his breathing, letting Paxton take his silence for compliance. In his peripheral vision he saw the closed-circuit TV camera in the corner. The China Lake Police Department had received the BOLO. He wondered if they had given it to the jail. Did they have photos of Paxton or Tabitha? Were they even monitoring the camera?

Paxton spoke quietly. "Tabitha's having trouble cleansing herself of the pollution called *you*. That's a shame, 'cause if I can disinfect her of this . . . *fungus*, she'll make me a fine wife. Look at her, strong legs and a young womb—put some meat on them bones and she could nurse up a storm. I figure she could bear me eight, nine babies." He leaned forward. "There's even hope for the one you got her with if I give him the right guidance."

"Shove it up your ass."

Paxton adjusted his hat. "What an arrogant attitude. But pride does go before a fall, and you are definitely fallen. Look around. Them's bars on the door, Top Gun."

Brian thought, Never let 'em see you sweat. No matter what.

"Bait me all you want," Brian said. "You're a tin soldier who terrorizes women and children to make himself feel powerful. I can take it all day from a creep like you. So you can insult me, or you can tell me why you're here."

Paxton sucked his teeth. He slowly twisted his head. Several vertebrae popped.

"You want your boy back? Here it is," he said. "You're gonna get us a jet."

Twenty miles down the highway I turned onto an unpaved track and headed into the desert. I kept the pedal depressed, clattering over the terrain. Garrett asked what we were going to be looking for, and I told him, "Anything the police missed. Something I recognize that they didn't know was important." Low hills rose ahead, and I turned up the arroyo that led close to Angels' Landing. The dry riverbed was narrow, sandy, and rock-strewn. I urged the Explorer forward until the gully steepened too precipitously to go on.

When I got out the silence was powerful. We were in the lee of the hill, and not even the wind reached our ears. I looked over at Garrett. He was standing beside the car, loading his Winchester, deadly serious. The cartridges slid into the rifle with a soft metallic click.

I said, "Over this hill."

He slung a backpack across his shoulders. "I'm on your six."

We climbed quickly. He was surefooted over the sandy ground, quiet and intent behind me, carrying the rifle at his side. After fifteen minutes we approached a saddle between two hills. The wind kicked through the gap. We crept forward until we could see down the slope. Below on the flat lay the dusty cabin and trailers of Angels' Landing.

We crouched behind a large rock. Garrett scanned the compound.

He said, "Nothing. No vehicles, no activity, no movement inside the cabin."

Still, we watched for five more minutes before leaving cover and starting downhill toward the camp. The wind twisted and teased, and the sun hit us from all angles. If anyone was watching us, we were easy targets.

The first structure we came to was the ramshackle barn. It was empty except for a guano-spattered red pickup that looked as if it hadn't been driven in years. Anxiously I peered up into the rafters. There hung the bats, sound asleep. I touched Garrett's arm, urging him back quietly.

Outside, he said, "They were out of here before the kidnapping."

"They have another bolt-hole. Maybe we can find a clue to where it is."

We checked the trailers, looking for a message, a footprint, any sign that Luke had been here, anything that might indicate where he had been taken, but found nothing. Finally we came to the cabin. Its grimy windows were covered from the inside with aluminum foil. The front door was locked. Tacked to it was a notice that the police had searched inside under authority of warrant.

I said, "Let's try the window."

The rusty screen squeaked loose, and to my surprise the window slid open. Pushing aside the venetian blinds, I climbed in.

Immediately I bumped into a cold metal object. The blinds clanged out of my way and I saw that it was a large freezer, the kind with a glass lid to display the contents. Inside it, mottled with freezer burn, were packages of Lean Cuisine, haunches of meat, Reddi-Wip canisters, and the body of Peter Wyoming.

He lay pale beneath a blanket of frozen lilies. His lips were blue, his brush-cut hair white with frost. Shock zipped through my gut and I jumped backward into the blinds, just as Garrett came through the window.

He said, "Holy shit."

I clung to his arm, steadying myself.

He said, "Didn't you say the Remnant expects him to be resurrected?"

"Yeah. This is what I call hedging your bets."

"How the hell did the cops miss this?"

I kept staring at Pastor Pete. "They didn't. They would have taken this away."

He tightened his grip on the rifle. "The Remnant's been here since the search. Recently."

My pulse crackled. I edged around the freezer. The rest of the room, crazily, looked exactly as it had the first time I had been here—black Naugahyde furniture, dust motes riding the stale air. The heat was oppressive. The wooden floor creaked under my feet.

I went into the kitchen. Dishes were drying in a rack, and the sink was wet. A side door had a key in the latch, and it was unlocked. Outside, a tumbleweed scratched at the window, emaciated gray branches raking the screen. I opened the refrigerator: boxes of Entenmann's low-fat brownies and more canisters of Reddi-Wip.

From the living room Garrett called, "Evan, take a look."

He was bending over the freezer, pointing to a note card taped in a corner.

WHAT TO DO IF PASTOR PETE ARISES

1. *Let him out.*
2. *Get blankets, put on coffeepot.*
3. *Open doors and windows to get ready for ascension.*

He said, "Check the bedrooms and let's get the hell out of here. This is too freakin' weird."

I had gone ten feet when I heard a scraping noise. I froze. Slowly I turned. So help me, I stared at Pastor Pete, and the pounding of my heart made it look as if he were shivering in the freezer.

"Garrett."

He looked around. Then we both heard it: the sound of something scraping against wood.

"It's under the floor," I said.

He backed away from the freezer, rifle now pointed at the floorboards, finger on the trigger. The heat squeezed me.

Scrape.

I pointed at the center of the room. He swung the Winchester. All I could think of was the scene in *Aliens* where they burst through the floor and grab Bill Paxton from below. I backed against the wall and gestured for him to do the same.

"Angle of fire, Garrett."

If somebody under the floor had a gun, they'd probably fire straight up. He stepped back. Jinked the rifle up snug against his shoulder. Looked at me, eyes questioning. Then he shouted, "Come out. You're surrounded."

The blinds clanged against the windowsill in the wind.

He said, "We're armed. Come out with your hands up."

Nothing.

"I am not a patient man." Raising the rifle toward the ceiling, he fired.

The noise jolted me. Plaster showered on the floor. He brought the weapon down again. The scraping started, consistently now.

"It's moving," I said. "Toward the window."

He shouted at the floor. "We're tracking you. Come out or I'll shoot."

In front of the freezer the floor rose up.

I said, "Jesus God."

A figure emerged from beneath the floor. Garrett rushed forward, rifle aimed.

He was pumped, juiced. "Down on your knees! Do it! Do it!"

"Don't shoot!" It was Glory, climbing out from a crawl space beneath the cabin's floor, hands in the air.

Brian squinted at Paxton. He said afterward that he could barely find his voice, not believing what the man had just said. "A jet?"

"You're gonna get us one F/A-eighteen, fully loaded," Paxton said. "We want Sidewinders, Shrikes, CBW warheads, fuel-air bombs."

"This is a joke."

"I don't joke."

Brian sat back, incredulous. "This is your ransom demand?"

Tabitha said, "He's serious, Bri. The Remnant wants to kick ass for Jesus."

Seeing how scared she was, he thought that she had guts saying that.

"Woman, watch your mouth," said Paxton, still looking at Brian. "You're gonna get me a jet armed with every weapon the navy tests at China Lake. I'm talking biological warheads, nukes if you got 'em."

Brian said, "You're crazy."

"You're gonna get me a jet, and you're gonna fly into the Sierras and drop it down low, under the radar. Disappear off the screen, and it's gonna look like you crashed into a mountain, way that air force pilot done a couple years back."

Brian was dumbstruck. The Craig Button incident: Every pilot remembered it. The air force captain had broken away from his formation on a training mission and vanished. For weeks his A-10 ground attack jet remained missing, and speculation ran wild that he had stolen the jet and landed at a secret airstrip, with plans to commit a terrorist bombing. In the end the truth proved equally bizarre. Wreckage was found high up a peak in the Colorado Rockies—the plane and Button's remains, but not the bombs he'd been carrying. The air force concluded that he had committed suicide.

And Paxton wanted to use Button's self-destruction as a blueprint for action. He was saying, "What you do, you hug the terrain, keep it under the radar till you get to a landing site in the high country. We'll have your boy waiting there." He pushed up the brim of his cap with his thumb. "And I know you wouldn't fire on any landing site where your boy was waiting for you."

Brian said, "You're out of your mind."

"No, I ain't. It's easy as pie."

"You want me to steal an F/A-eighteen? Just stroll into the weapons shed and load up on warheads like I'm shopping at Costco? Fix you a picnic hamper of assorted missiles, tell my CO, 'Hey, gotta give this jet to some psychos, be back after lunch'? You're fucking nuts. Besides, if you haven't noticed," he said, leaning close to the Plexiglas, "I'm in jail for *murder*."

Paxton sucked on his teeth. "I'll fix that."

Brian's mouth slowly dropped open.

"I'll get you out, and I don't mean no jailbreak. I'll get you released free and clear, get the charges dropped. If you get the F/A-eighteen."

Brian held still, thinking this guy had set him up. Paxton killed Peter Wyoming and framed him just to get him to this point.

Paxton said, "I'm leaving this room in three minutes. Decide."

The man was crazy, Brian thought. Crazy enough to kill Luke if he didn't stop him.

Paxton turned to Tabitha. "Show him."

She raised her hands from her lap, where they had lain out of sight under the counter. Brian drew back. A series of tiny cuts notched her wrists and palms.

She said, "He marked the spots where the tendons are easiest to sever. If I disobey him he's going to cut me until my hands are paralyzed."

Paxton leaned toward Brian. "I'm talking discipline, fungus. You don't do it, the lady gets cut." He reached out and lifted Tabitha's chin with his index finger. "She thinks she's all tore up right now. She has a lot to learn."

Brian looked at Tabitha, appalled. She was pegging him with her eyes, hanging on to him through open

terror. He spoke later about that look, said it hit him
like a blow. But he also said that looking at her, he
felt himself focus, felt himself assess the threat and
the tactics needed to repel it. He felt himself enter
the zone.

He said, "You can actually get me out of here?"

Paxton nodded.

And perhaps, Brian thought, he could. This was
liar's poker. The Remnant would not readily give
Luke back. And he would never supply the church
with weapons. So which of them could pull off the
bigger bluff?

Tabitha mouthed the word, *Luke*.

He slowly nodded.

Paxton said, "Ninety seconds."

"I can't get nukes," Brian said. "And air-to-air missiles will be useless to a ground-based combat unit."

"You leave us to decide what's useless and what's
not," Paxton said.

That was when Brian felt himself putting on his
game face. "A biological warhead—that's tricky, but
manageable. I'll have to take the warhead from its
secure storage facility at China Lake."

Paxton stilled.

"But I'd never be able to load a missile with a live
BW warhead on a Hornet. The weapons techs would
see it and take me down at gunpoint."

"Don't you lie to me."

"You want a warhead? I can get you something
with the power to wipe out the West Coast. Is that
good enough for you?"

Paxton's chilly blue eyes crackled to life. "Might
do."

"Forget the F/A-eighteen. If a Hornet disappeared—"

"I want the jet."

"If I go missing in an F/A-eighteen they'll launch an
immediate search-and-rescue effort, multiagency, high-

profile—navy, air force, coast guard. The Sierras will be crawling with feds."

"What are you, yellow?"

"Tabitha, tell him what a brass-balled son of a bitch I am."

She said, "He has a heart of death, Isaiah. He'd kill you as soon as look at you."

Paxton snorted.

"Listen to me," Brian said. "The Hornets at China Lake are an advanced prototype, constructed from an alloy that embeds a unique tracking signature in the airframe. The Pentagon can trace them via satellite and pinpoint their location anywhere on the globe. Even if they've been painted over or stashed in a hangar. You go near one of these jets, you send the FBI a greeting card. Get it?"

Come on, he was thinking, *buy it*. Paxton merely looked at him.

"The jet isn't the weapon you want. It's big and loud and obvious. But a warhead's portable and stealthy. It won't hinder your ability to hit and run. And if I do it right, it'll take days before China Lake notices it's missing. That, you asshole, is the weapon you want."

Paxton considered it. "Days?"

"Yeah." Brian watched him. "If I do it, Luke and Tabitha go home with me."

"And I go home with the warhead."

"Yes."

"Deal."

Paxton stood up. "Don't let nobody follow us outta here. If they follow, Tabitha's hands turn to meat."

Then they were gone, and Brian was pounding on the door. He wanted to talk to Detective McCracken, and the Naval Criminal Investigative Service. But before the guard could come he heard a girl's voice saying, "Don't do that." A new visitor was sitting down across from him, a teenager with elaborate blond hair, wearing a blouse with the name Candi stitched above the pocket. "Ice told you, don't let anybody follow. Just sit tight for a while." Then she smiled at him and said, "Are you saved?"

"I was keeping vigil."

Glory was sitting on the cabin's black Naugahyde sofa, hands pressed between her knees, rocking back and forth. I was pacing the floor. Beneath us, Garrett scuffled around the crawl space. After a minute he pulled himself up through the opening.

"Nothing down there but canned hams and a hundred boxes of potato flakes. And a tunnel, looks like it leads to the barn."

Glory pushed her hair out of her eyes and wiped her nose with the back of her hand. Sweat trickled down her chest. With the dust streaking her face and arms, she looked more like Lara Croft than ever. *Tomb Raider Millennium Edition: The Quest for SPAM.*

I squatted down in front of her, getting to eye level. I had to handle this right. I couldn't just slap her. She kept rocking, looking away from me.

"Just keeping vigil, taking my turn." She glanced at the freezer. "We have to be ready."

Garrett snorted. She glared at him from under her lashes.

I said, "Glory, where's Luke?"

"I don't know."

I set a hand on her knee. "Please. He's like my own son."

Garrett crossed the room in two strides. "For chrissake. We don't have all day." He jammed the muzzle of the rifle under her chin. "Tell us where the kid is, right now, or you can join Pastor Pete in that freezer."

I jumped up. "Garrett, no."

"You'll get nowhere by sweet-talking her, Evan. She's a terrorist, fucking revival-tent Hamas."

"Not this way. Put it down!"

He stood rock still. "You want your nephew back? Trust me on this."

Glory spoke through clenched teeth. "Go ahead. I'm not scared of dying. But I don't know where Luke is. Our cells operate independently, and I'm not in the unit that handled the retrieval of the boy."

I swore. "Garrett, lower your weapon. She doesn't know."

He looked at me.

I said, "Leaderless resistance. That's their strategy."

Slowly he withdrew the rifle. "Shit."

He stood breathing hard. I watched him, shaken, trying to gauge what had just happened, alarmed by the ferocity of his eruption.

I said, "Give me ten minutes."

Glory said, "Better make it five. The others will be here to relieve me soon."

"What?"

"Shiloh and the Brueghels. They all plan to keep the next watch over Pastor Pete. They'll be here anytime."

Garrett said, "Goddammit. Where are they now?"

"Patrolling the perimeter."

"You have two minutes," he said, "while I check outside to see if they're coming." Shoulders bunching, he strode through the kitchen and out the door.

I sat down next to Glory. She was hunched and skittish, and a feral intensity fizzed in her eyes. Amid the streaks of dirt on her face I could see the scar left where Mel Kalajian had removed her tattoo. The sympathy I'd once felt for her had faded.

Still, I said, "You can come with me. Get out of here."

"No. They find you, wherever you go. You know that now."

She had a point. I said, "Stay, then. I won't offer to help again."

She wiped her nose and started rocking once more. "That guy with you."

"Garrett. He's a soldier. I brought him to protect me."

"Yeah, I know. He's part of the puppet government. But you're okay." She glanced toward the kitchen. Garrett was gone outside. "What I'm going to say, don't tell him. Promise me."

"Fine."

"Promise me." The volume of her voice punched up a notch.

"All right. I promise."

"You can still be saved. But it has to happen before you die." She leaned toward me. "So don't leave China Lake. Not yet, not till after Halloween."

A jolt ran from my groin up to the center of my skull. I put my hand on her arm. "Glory, what are they going to do?"

"I told you, Halloween is an aperture. The wall between this world and hell gets thin and lets Satan attack more easily."

I remembered.

"Chenille plans to turn it around. She's going to go for it on Halloween, because she can deliver a deep blow. The attack will strike right down into hell itself. She can give the beast a fatal injury."

"What's the battle plan?"

"Cripple the government. You incapacitate Satan's puppet, you strike the beast right in the heart," she said. "She plans to destroy as many federal agents as possible."

"Washington?" I said. "The Remnant is attacking D.C.?"

She shook her head. "Washington is a vortex of evil. The Remnant isn't big enough to counteract its sucking power. Chenille's going to draw a whole bunch of federal agents to one place, as far from the D.C. funnel as possible."

"How?"

"Her crew's going to cause a disaster that'll get the FBI, National Guard, CDC, all kinds of feds together."

I was picturing western vortices of sucking evil. "Los Angeles, Las Vegas?"

"She's going to get them to Santa Barbara."

"Oh, Jesus. Glory, why?"

"L.A.'s too spread out. You couldn't get them in a small enough radius. Same with Vegas. Nothing but desert in all directions, with high winds probable."

That shock, a bone-deep pain, hit me again. I knew where this was going.

"But Santa Barbara's containable," she said. "It's a compact metropolitan area with mountains on one side and the ocean on the other, and no easy escape routes. There's just three roads for people to evacuate on, and you can cut them all off—the One-o-one Freeway on either end of town, and San Marcos Pass. So once she gets the federal agents into town, she's going to take them out."

She sniffed and wiped her nose. "Plus Chenille totally hates Santa Barbara, because that's where she became a whore. She wants to see it trashed."

I said, "She's going to release biological weapons."

She gaped at me. "How'd you know?"

"I know about the Botox, Glory. And about the robbery at Mel Kalajian's office the night he was murdered."

Her eyes jumped before her mouth tightened. "Now you know the real reason why I can't leave the church. I know too much."

I didn't say anything. I didn't care about her innocence or guilt anymore.

Hurt, and feisty slyness, heated her face. "All I've done is what Rowan would do." Talking about the heroine of my novel. "I've fought to stay alive. I've done whatever it takes."

"That's not Rowan."

"Yes, it is. She's an outcast who bucks the odds, just like me."

I stood up. "No, Glory. Rowan refused to become a collaborator, even to save herself. You've done exactly the opposite. You've submitted, and compromised yourself forever."

She drew in on herself, eyes widening, lips slowly parting.

I stood over her. "How does the Remnant plan to draw federal agents to Santa Barbara? What's the disaster they're going to cause?"

She looked away and started rocking again. "I don't know—and don't go ballistic like your man did the other night at the university. Shiloh's handling the trigger event, and she keeps her mouth shut tight."

"You must have some idea."

The kitchen door banged open. Garrett strode into the living room. "A vehicle's coming. It's far off, but won't be for long. Let's go."

I said, "Glory?"

"I can't tell you any more."

Garrett was wound so tight that he was practically ticking. "Evan, *now*."

I heard the rumble of a truck engine. I started to follow him, but stopped. He exhaled, aggravated.

I turned back to Glory. "I have to know. What happened to Jesse?"

She was looking out the door, nervous, hearing the truck approach.

"Just tell me," I said. "Is he . . . ?" The word *dead* simply would not form on my lips.

She kept staring out the door, now fidgeting.

"I'm not leaving until you tell me. Even if it means they catch you talking to us."

She grabbed her head with both hands. "All right! *Yes.*"

A buzzing started in my head, and the room seemed to swerve. The furniture, the walls, the freezer, all warped and started smearing together.

I stammered, "How?"

Glory's face seemed to swell like a balloon. "They ran him off the road and dragged him out of the car. He put up a fight, but they outnumbered him."

My throat constricted. "Why did they do it?"

"They wanted a guinea pig."

"I . . . What? I don't understand."

"They needed a person to test the biological weapons on, to make sure they work. Sorry, Evan, I know the guy's your lover but this is war."

I reached for something to grab hold of, but found only air. "Oh, God, they exposed him to Botox?"

"No, not to anything, not yet."

Tears were burning my eyes. "Then why the hell did they kill him?"

Her balloon face swam and tilted quizzically. "Nobody killed him."

I grabbed her by the shoulders. "What do you mean?"

"He's still alive. He's being held as a POW."

23

It felt as if lightning had flashed through me. I pulled Glory to her feet. "Where is he?"

"In an old fallout shelter out in the desert."

The blinds clacked and swayed. Outside, the engine rattled nearer, approaching the cabin.

Garrett hefted the rifle. "Evan, we either climb out the back window in the next ten seconds, or we shoot our way out the door. Come on."

But I had Glory by the shoulders. "How do I get there?"

"It's up Copper Creek, in the hills east of China Lake. But I don't know how to tell you—"

Garrett wrenched me away from her. "I know where that is. What defenses do you have on the place?"

"No defenses. In his condition, where's he gonna go?"

A truck pulled up and shut off its engine. Garrett towed me toward a back bedroom. We heard women's voices in the kitchen.

"Who left this door open? Glory? Glory Moffett, you do this?" It was Chenille.

"Sorry. It was so hot in here."

Garrett slowly slid the bedroom window open.

Heavy footsteps in the living room. "You're filthy. You go in the crawl space?"

"I heard noises. I didn't want rats to get the supplies, so—"

A new voice, higher-pitched, taut as wire. "What's this white stuff on the floor—plaster? Hey, the freezer lid looks frostier. Did you open it?"

"No, Shiloh."

Chenille said, "You better not have touched my Reddi-Wip."

"I didn't go near the freezer." Startled silence. "Maybe it was Pastor Pete."

Garrett leaped nimbly through the window and held out an arm for me.

Shiloh said, "You think—"

"Oh . . . !" Chenille moaned. "Peter! Open them eyes, baby—"

We ran.

Halfway up the hill I looked over my shoulder at the dried-biscuit landscape. The cabin's aluminum-foil windows glittered like eyes. No one was coming after us, but we still ran. Garrett paced me, weaving over the rocky ground, holding the rifle at the ready.

I said, "Glory won't be able to explain the bullet hole in the ceiling. Chenille's going to figure it out."

"You worried about us, or her?"

I pushed ahead. "Jesse."

He shot me a look. "Glory was in the crowd that kidnapped him, I'd give you even money." We reached the saddle in the crest of the hill and surged over it. He said, "I know I was rough with her. But she has no remorse, and the only way you get people like her to play ball is to threaten them with absolute, immediate pain." We accelerated, half sliding down the grade. He said, "What'd she mean, this guy can't go anywhere in his condition?"

"He's disabled. He can't walk."

He wobbled, almost losing his balance. "You're kidding."

"I wish I were."

When we reached my car I was blowing hard and drenched in sweat but exhilarated, in fact wild with relief and the urge to hurry, to get to Jesse before something intervened. As we drove back to Garrett's Jeep, he told me how to find Copper Creek. I listened, and he touched my arm.

"Here's the problem. I can't go with you. I'm on duty in half an hour. You'll have to call the police."

"I'll never get a signal for my phone out here."

"I'll call when I get back to town. Just wait for the cops."

"No, Jesse might be hurt. And Glory said there are no guards."

"You believe her?"

"I have to." That was adrenaline talking, or maybe faith; maybe they're the same.

We reached his Jeep. Garrett put his hand on my shoulder.

He said, "I can tell by your enthusiasm for finding this guy that we aren't going to have a second date."

His voice sounded winning. He looked intrepid, and gracious—the good loser. I felt a pang about rejecting him after he had put himself in danger for my family.

I touched his cheek and kissed him quickly. "Thank you."

Then I was racing away down the highway toward Copper Creek.

The men were waiting for Brian in an interrogation room at the jail. Detective McCracken he recognized, the redheaded cop with the Brahma bull chest. Two others had to be FBI, he thought. They looked the way he'd expect Bureau agents to look: intelligent, wearing blue suits and broomsticks up their butts. A fourth guy, casually dressed, sitting on a table by the window, was with the Naval Criminal Investigative Service, the NCIS. Brian was on his own. He hadn't called his criminal lawyer, hadn't wanted to wait for him. He should have.

The NCIS agent turned on a television set. It started playing the CCTV tape of Brian talking to Paxton and Tabitha.

The FBI agent, DeKalb, said, "Have a nice chat with your wife?"

It went downhill from there. The tape was low-quality video, so they couldn't discern the terror in Tabitha's eyes, and it had no sound, so they couldn't hear the conversation. But they could lip-read Tabitha mouthing, *Do it.*

DeKalb kept rewinding the tape to show it again and again. "Do what?"

Brian told them that Paxton wanted to ransom Luke in exchange for weapons. He told them he was willing to arrange it. They could set up a sting.

They didn't believe him. They didn't think Paxton was about to provide evidence that would lead to his release. He was a murderer. He wasn't going anywhere, and he certainly wasn't going to be permitted to handle navy weaponry. The FBI agents stalked around him, smelling of aftershave and suspicion. McCracken sat wheezing, his arms crossed on his gut. The NCIS agent loitered in the back of the room, a cop, he thought, who probably spent his days investigating procurement fraud, a pencil pusher. But he was the one who gave Brian a clue to what was going on.

"What did the Remnant want, the name of another contact on base?"

Thieves from the base were selling weapons to the Remnant; that was certain. But the feds apparently couldn't prove it and didn't know who the insiders were. So they were trying to stick him with the blame.

"Come on," said the NCIS agent. "Your wife is involved with these people."

The man put a piece of gum in his mouth, staring at him. He wore a look Brian recognized: the look of a drudge who resented pilots. The room suddenly smelled sour.

"I can understand," the agent said. "Here you are, a fighter god, but the government pays you dick, and every night you go home to a crappy little tract house. Meanwhile all those weapons are sitting on base, millions of dollars' worth of firearms and munitions. It has to be tempting."

"Maybe that's how it looks to a desk jockey like you."

DeKalb said, "The way I see it, Tabitha brought the Remnant to you, and you realized what excellent customers they'd be. They were flush with cash and eager to buy big. And you could deal with them directly, instead of selling the goods through a fence. You could keep all the profits."

Brian said nothing.

DeKalb said, "Rewind the tape. Show him again."

Brian said, "Why don't you pull your head out of your rectum? Let me bait a trap. You can spring it."

DeKalb handed him a business card. "When you're ready to come clean, give me a call."

And not one word from any of them about rescuing Luke. Any hopes he had, any vestiges of trust in these men, seeped steadily away.

It was up to him. He was going to have to get Luke back himself.

The road was dust, an aisle through gray-green sagebrush, twenty miles at sixty-five mph with my arms dog-weary on the steering wheel. Beneath an aching blue sky the landscape unfurled, heat weighing on it like a flatiron. This kind of heat could knock you face-down in the sand, hyperthermic and near death, before you knew what had hit you. Jesse, I feared, would be in bad shape.

Again I tried my cell phone. No signal. No civilization either, not a barbed-wire fence or a plume of dust from other vehicles. The Remnant had picked this hideout well. The sand whitened to gleaming gypsum, and I knew I was closing in. I saw rounded red rocks off to the left, a pair of them pointing at the sky. Looking like a pair of double-Ds, Garrett had said. I braked. And I found it: a rutted path leading up a gully toward rocky hills. This was Copper Creek. Rolling down the window, I leaned out and looked at the ground.

Tire tracks.

The edges were well defined, the tread pattern readable—they were recent. I turned up the path. The car strained and slid, climbing gradually into a canyon, lurching over rocks until finally, afraid that I might break an axle, I stopped. I got out, and the heat spanked me.

Ahead, the canyon narrowed to a crevasse. Its vaulting stone walls formed a corridor, a wind-sculpted passageway that ebbed into ochre shadow and curved out of sight. I approached the entrance and crouched down. In the sand were more tire tracks, with a narrower wheelbase and fat treads. An ATV: all-terrain vehicle.

The tracks ran both ways, into the crevasse and out. I couldn't tell which was newer. But it didn't matter; I had to risk it. Grabbing a water bottle and a first-aid kit from the car, I started off.

As soon as I entered the crevasse I was in shade. The cooler air was a reprieve, but only briefly. The trail ran uphill on soft grit, and after ten minutes my legs felt dead from fighting the sand. Things became basic: breath, sweat, muscle and bone; red and gold stone walls, a chicane of stark beauty. I was exhausted, and almost a mile from the car, and still hadn't found anything. The tire tracks were soft humps in the sand. Who knew? They'd probably been made by high school kids out boondocking.

Then the crevasse snaked and abruptly ended. The

rocks met in a solid wall rising fifty feet, and in the rock wall was a metal door. Rust speckled its rivets. Dead center on it was a bright yellow radiation-hazard symbol. I pushed it open.

I found myself in a cave, deep in darkness. Getting my flashlight from my backpack, I saw a second door five feet ahead. It was massive, thick, a blast door. Throwing my whole weight against it, I shouldered it open a few inches. Dim electric light piddled through the crack. I raised the flashlight like a truncheon, ready to crack it down on a hostile head, and I listened. I heard nothing from the other side.

Shoving again, straining, I forced the door farther open. I whispered, "Jesse?"

I slid through the doorway into a rock chamber dully lit with hanging lightbulbs. Against one wall stood a metal desk with a ham radio set on it. Against the other wall, stacks of canned food towered toward the ceiling. Beyond it . . .

"Ev."

I ran toward the sound of his voice, tears smudging my vision even before I pushed past the food stocks and saw the camp stove and the dented bunkbeds with the stained mattresses, and Jesse pushing himself up on one elbow, his face stunned, wearing the look of a child who's just seen his first magic trick.

He said, "You'd better not be a hallucination."

I fell on him, wrapping him in my arms, burying my face against his neck. His warmth, his voice, even the salty sweat on his skin, were miraculous.

He said, "See, you just can't stay mad at me."

Straightening up, I brushed his hair off his forehead. "Let me look at you."

His mahogany hair was lank, his face flushed, his cobalt eyes sharp with unruly light.

I put my hand to his forehead. "You're burning up."

"Yeah." He swallowed drily. "Feelin' kinda punk."

Alarm spiked in me. "What symptoms do you have? Coughing? Vomiting?" Jesus, what were the signs of botulism?

He shook his head. "They haven't dosed me with anything. I convinced them I have investments maturing next week; they think if they keep me alive I'll authorize a funds transfer to them. I gave them some shit about random revolving passwords and voice recognition. They believe it, but I don't know for how long."

"Thinking on your feet, there, kiddo."

"Not really." He fought to sit up. "My leg's broken."

He pulled up the cuff of his trousers. Beneath a crude splint fashioned from a magazine tied with strips of fabric, his left shin was purple, swollen, and bowed. I stretched my hand toward it. Even without touching it I felt the heat off his skin. My stomach coiled.

I said, "They splinted a fracture with a copy of *Life* magazine."

"No, I did. They don't know about it and I didn't tell them. Don't want them to think I'm more damaged than they already do." He scanned my face, tried to calm me. "Don't worry; it doesn't hurt."

But it made me dizzy. I was thinking blood clots, septicemia, gangrene. I checked his pulse. To my unpracticed hand it felt fast. I handed him the water bottle and gave him two aspirin from the first-aid kit.

He drank. "God, that tastes good."

"I'm going to get you out of here."

I looked around. Despite its obvious age the fallout shelter was well maintained. It had food, electricity, communications equipment, and even board games, honest to God, stacked on a shelf: Monopoly, Scrabble, Chutes and Ladders. The red scare had stopped being a family activity shortly after the Cuban Missile Crisis, yet here was a freeze-dried slice of Cold War dread. Someone still waited for the lithium sunset, and they must have stocked something I could use for a sled or travois to haul Jesse out of there. I started scrounging.

I said, "How did they get you?"

"Shiloh and those baton twirlers grabbed me. How insulting is that? Kidnapped by fucking pom-pom girls. I may kill myself."

Joking couldn't hide the rueful truth behind his words. I said, "I hear that you gave as good as you got."

"I rammed Shiloh in the eye with the Club steering wheel lock. She's a hurting puppy. But the twirlers Maced me, and one grabbed the Club, and she was like Jackie friggin' Chan with the thing. I think I have her to thank for the leg."

Nothing. I couldn't find anything big enough, and light enough, to turn into a travois. I went back to him and propped a greasy pillow under his shin.

"But there's payback." He pointed to the magazine wrapped around his leg. "July 1969. The moon-landing issue. I splinted it with a collector's item."

I actually laughed.

His face turned grave, and he said, "You have to see something. I found Jesus."

I stopped laughing. "Oh, my God, you have brain damage."

"He wrestles with Elvis. WWF-style. The King of Kings versus the King."

I felt his forehead again. "You're delirious."

Pushing my hand aside, he pointed at the door. "Close it; take a look."

Wary, I went to the door and muscled it shut. Gawked. A mural was painted on the back. Raw and heaving with color, it depicted hot cars, spaceflight, Christ grappling with Presley, and, looming gloriously above them all, Raquel Welch in her two-piece pelt from *One Million Years B.C.*

"Blast door art," I said.

It emulated an obscure air force tradition from the

bad old days: painting the doors of ICBM launch control centers buried in silos beneath the American prairie, truly an underground art form. Examining it, I saw that a length of rope was hanging from the wheel that locked the door. Then I noticed the rest, the desk chair pulled near the door, the rope burns around Jesse's wrists.

I said, "You tried to escape."

"They tied my hands, but not well enough. When I got loose I used the rope like a lasso, pulled the door wide enough to squeeze through into the air lock. Then got the front door open."

It must have taken him hours. I sat down next to him and took his hand.

He ran a hand through his hair. His voice was tiring out. "The thing is, they brought me up here blindfolded in a trailer behind an ATV. So, surprise, I get outside and find myself in Upper Shit Creek, with the thermostat set on shrivel. I came back in, shut the doors so they wouldn't know I can get out. Went with plan C."

"What happened to plan B?"

"Opening the doors was plan B. Calling the cops on the ham radio was plan A. But they'd yanked its guts out. So." He reached under the mattress and pulled out a length of pipe. "Plan C. I beat the crap out of whoever shows up, before they spray me with Botox."

Violence had never sounded so endearing. I lifted his hand and kissed it.

He said, "I was waiting until nightfall, gonna go when it cools off."

"You're thirty-five miles from town."

He sobered. "Good timing, then, you showing up." He looked dazed; he was unaccustomed to good luck. He said, "You have to see something on the mural. Give me a hand. Help me stand up."

"You can't put weight on that fracture."

"If I lean on your shoulder I can get to the chair just using my good leg." He swung his feet onto the floor, taking care with the splint.

Arguing would just waste time. "On three," I said, planting myself in front of him with my hands under his armpits. His arms were hardwood but I did the lifting, and when he balanced against me we hobbled to the door, three-legged. The fever thrummed from him.

Forget plan D, hiking down the canyon this way. With the sand and rocks he wouldn't make it fifty yards. I'd have to go back to the car and drive down to the bottom of Copper Creek, meet the police, get them up here to help. Garrett would have called them by now.

Jesse dropped onto the desk chair and touched the mural, brushing his fingers across a tiny, cobwebby space where the illustration was black-and-white.

"That's new."

On the door I saw drawings within a drawing. Sketched quickly but with a sure hand, they skeined across small white spaces in the mural.

"It's Tabitha's, isn't it?" he said.

I ran my fingers over it. "Yes." She had been here, and she had left behind drawings. Why? Because words would have been noticed? I looked closer.

It was a new iteration of "HELL-o-ween." Kids in costumes—ghoul, ballerina—on a playground . . . swing set, BigToy, school building in the background. It was the playground at Luke's school. The skin on the back of my neck rippled.

Next drawing, kids eating their Halloween candy. These children were in wheelchairs or on crutches, and I thought of Karina Eichner. Final drawing. Kids on the ground, clawing their throats or dead. Candy in their hands.

The air tasted bitter, and so dry that it excavated my head. "It's a warning."

"The Remnant's going to poison a bunch of kids."

"Yes."

"Why?" His voice was raspy. "As punishment? The Remnant's own final judgment?"

You know how Satanists kill kids every year with Halloween candy, Glory had said. *Chenille's going to turn it around. . . .*

"As bait."

That was how Chenille planned to get federal agents to swarm Santa Barbara. My head throbbed. I felt a warm trickle and touched my lip. My nose was bleeding.

I wiped it off. "I'm going to get help."

"We have to warn people, get police out to the schools, pull candy from store shelves."

I took his hand. "It'll take me a while. Maybe a couple of hours."

His eyes, jagged blue, pinned me. "I'll wait."

Anguish hit. I did not want to leave him. "I'll be back with the police and paramedics."

"If I get bored I'll read my splint." The heat in his eyes focused. He touched my cheek. "I love you. I get out of here, I want you to marry me."

Boom. Classic Blackburn: Swing a proposal like an ax. Tears swelled and ran hot down my cheeks.

"You get out of here," I said, "we get your fever down and make you lucid."

"I am lucid."

"What's my name?"

"Raquel Welch."

I couldn't stand the thought of letting go. I leaned down and kissed him hard. "I love you too."

I was halfway to the door when he said, "You can't let Luke go trick-or-treating, Ev."

I didn't look around. He didn't know and I couldn't bear to tell him. "No chance of that."

I headed through the door and didn't look back.

I flagged down a police car on Highway 395, halfway back to China Lake. The cop was flying down the road, lights flashing, and almost didn't stop. The car braked late, the cop finally deciding to stop for a lone woman waving and hollering from the roadside. Something, I knew, was wrong.

I ran toward the car as it stopped in a surge of dust. It was Laura Yeltow, the blond cop with the linebacker's thighs. She got out and walked toward me, her hand riding the nightstick in her belt.

"Evan Delaney. Why am I not surprised?"

I pretended I hadn't heard that. I told her I needed paramedics to rescue an injured man, and maybe a helicopter to medevac him out of Copper Creek. She pursed her lips. "He's disabled," I said, "and has a broken leg; he's in serious trouble."

She got on the radio. When she finished, she said, "We already got a call on this." Garrett had to have phoned it in. "Fire Department Rescue rolled on it, but can't pinpoint the location."

"I'll show them. Tell me where to meet them."

"Not so fast. You know a woman named Glory Moffet?"

"What about her?"

Her eyes were stones. She wanted to see my reaction. "She's dead."

My jaw fell and sweat broke onto my forehead. The wind blew through me.

24

Yeltow had been at the police station when Shiloh came in. "The girl was beaten and tearful, big black eye, looked like she'd been rammed in the face with a blunt object. I caught her before she collapsed to the floor in the lobby."

I leaned against the patrol car, feeling light-headed.

"She was shaking, real scared," Yeltow said. "She told me Glory was wigging out. That she had a gun and was holding it on some girls at their church retreat."

I pinched the bridge of my nose.

Yeltow kept talking, describing the scene in the police station. She had shouted at the desk sergeant to get Detective McCracken, and then helped Shiloh to a chair. The girl looked desperate, hair half-pulled from a ponytail, blouse ripped. She was stammering, saying that she and the triplets had walked into the cabin and caught Glory taking a pistol out of the freezer.

"She asked what Glory was doing hiding a weapon under the Lean Cuisine," Yeltow said. "And Glory freaked, started hitting her with the butt of the gun. Shiloh ran out the door, and the next thing she knew Glory was shooting at her. Her truck was parked outside, so she jumped in and just floored it. She was praying for the Lord to protect her when Glory put a bullet through the back window of the cab."

I started to shake my head. "This sounds wrong."

"Shiloh drove straight to the police station. She had bits of glass in her ponytail. And the bullet was lodged in the roof of the cab. I pried it out. Glory was definitely shooting at her."

Shiloh was lying, I thought. Then Yeltow told me the rest, and I knew I was right.

Two China Lake patrol cars had headed out to Angels' Landing, speeding through an afternoon suddenly as bright as an explosion. Detective McCracken rode with Yeltow. His bull's chest strained under his Kevlar vest. They'd barely pulled up to the cabin when the front door burst open and a teenage girl ran out screaming.

A gunshot cracked from the cabin, shattering the front window. Officers ducked and drew their weapons. The shrieking girl dove into the arms of a uniformed officer, who pulled her to the ground behind his patrol car. She sobbed, "Don't shoot. My sisters are in there."

The air twitched around the officers crouching behind their units. McCracken gestured for patience, showed them a calm face. But radioing for backup, crisis was in his voice.

The uniform who had grabbed the girl was a man three years out of high school, with a broad, shiny face. He asked her, "What's your name?"

"Brandi Brueghel." The girl had big blond hair and a tightly sprung cheerleader's body. She clutched at his blue shirt. "Don't let Glory kill my sisters." Throwing her head back, she shouted at the sky, "Smack down mine enemies, O Lord! Guard my sisters with thy fearsome might and take *down* the unrighteous one who has turned against thee!"

The uniform shushed her, uselessly. Yeltow scuttled over to them.

"*Fling* her down. Head-butt her into the depths of hell!"

"Miss," he said. "Brandi. Help me out here. Tell me what happened inside."

"We found Glory disturbing Pastor Pete's mortal remains," she said. "At first we thought she was stealing Miz Wyoming's Tribulation supplies. She had a bunch of Reddi-Wip canisters set out at her feet, and the maraschino cherries. But she was reaching under Pastor Pete, half turning him over—oh, man, she had him lifted by the buttocks!—and she was pulling out a pistol from underneath him. Shiloh says, 'What are you doing?' and Glory goes after her, whacking her on the face with the gun."

Yeltow nodded, hearing the girl confirm Shiloh's story.

"My sisters are in there trying to protect Pastor Pete, but they can't, not with Glory holding them at gunpoint. You have to get inside!"

"Calm down, Brandi."

She squeezed his arm. "You don't understand. *She unplugged the freezer.*"

The uniform was frowning, baffled, when they heard an engine racketing to life in the barn. After that, Yeltow told me, it happened very fast.

A red pickup skidded out of the barn, tires throwing up sand. Brandi popped to her feet, clawing her hair, yelling, "Candi! Randi!" The officers swung into firing position across the trunks and roofs of the patrol cars.

McCracken held his arm up, called out, "Hold your fire!" The officers were tracking the pickup with their weapons. Yeltow squinted at the vehicle, saw three people in the tight cab, two blondes and a brunette in the middle. Brunette the hostage taker, she thought, positioning the triplets as bulletproofing, making a run for it.

The passenger door swung open. The blond passenger jumped out, a quick, powerful leap, no hesitation, and hit the sand like a pancake. Shaking off the landing, she started crawling for the police cars.

"Randi!" Brandi called. "Hurry!"

The girl scrambled along the ground. The pickup swung around, did a one-eighty, and charged toward them. The brunette held her arms out. Yeltow saw her bracing against the dash—no, couldn't be . . . pointing where to ram them—

The driver's door flew open and now the blonde behind the wheel sprang free and fell hard, rolling, making lots of noise. A second later there was a loud *bang* from inside the truck, and a spray of white mist.

Grenade, Yeltow thought. Suicide bomber, strapped to blow, heading straight for them. The young uniform, standing next to her, must have had the same fear.

He pulled the trigger.

His shot dissolved the windshield, and then the others opened up. The truck kept coming, looking with its open doors like a great sick bird, and the brunette screamed, threw her arms up to shield her face. Bullets popped and cracked against the truck, until it hit a patrol car and stopped.

McCracken shouted, "Cease firing!" He heaved himself to his feet, both hands on his revolver, and inched around the patrol car toward the pickup. Brandi Brueghel raced past him to the girl who had jumped from the driver's seat, sobbing, "Candi!"

The triplet stood up, spitting sand. She said, "Did they get her?"

Yeltow stared into the pickup. They had most definitely gotten her. Glory drooped on the seat, her eyes wide, blood pouring from gunshot wounds in her face and chest. The blood running down her rib cage mixed with the white foam splattered inside the truck. It dripped onto the gun stuck in the waistband of her cargo pants, a nine-millimeter Beretta. Next to Yeltow, the young uniform looked nauseated. Death smelled sweet and creamy, he mumbled. What was that stuff?

Behind them Randi Brueghel was chattering to McCracken. "I heated it up on the stove," she said, "got it *so* hot. The can says 'Warning, contents under pressure,' so I thought, if I can make it burst it'll so totally distract Glory. . . ."

Yeltow saw the exploded canister, made out *-Wi* on the side. The uniform said it sounded like a bomb. It did. How could he have known it was a can of Reddi-Wip?

Yeltow continued staring me down. She said, "That girl Randi put the can in an oven mitt under her shirt. In the truck she shook the canister just to the bursting point, right before she jumped. Very gutsy."

My chest felt tight. "It makes no sense. Glory was scared of those girls, the triplets and Shiloh. Not the other way around."

Yeltow squinted at me. "I guess you're not part of this after all."

"What?"

"You're not hearing what I'm telling you. This Glory had a gun on her, a nine-millimeter Beretta. Same kind that killed Peter Wyoming. Considering that your brother is down for the murder beef, you should be taking this as good news."

I knew then what was going on. Glory had been found out. Chenille and Shiloh had discovered that she was my informant and had set her up. I rubbed my forehead. Had they seen me and Garrett running from the cabin? Had Glory told them what we had discussed? Had she told them that I knew Jesse was being held captive?

I straightened. "Oh, my God. Jesse. We have to hurry."

The Fire Department Rescue Squad met me at the turnoff to Copper Creek. We got to the fallout shelter fifteen minutes later, and we knew it had all gone bad. Both doors hung open. Smoke wafted out, and the mural on the blast door was scorched. A firefighter said, "Stay back." I stood in the sand, shuddering. He came out shaking his head. "Burned out. It's empty. Whoever was in there, he's gone now."

25

Two days later Brian walked out of the jail, staring straight at me but not seeing me at all, wholly engaged in putting distance between himself and confinement. Sky, sunlight, air—he consumed them without appreciation. He swept me under his arm and kept walking.

The murder charge against him had been dismissed. The Beretta pistol found on Glory's body was his missing service automatic, and ballistics tests had proved it to be the weapon that killed Peter Wyoming. Glory's fingerprints had been matched to those at the scene of Mel Kalajian's murder, and the police had decided that she was to blame for both those deaths. Brian was free, exonerated.

It was victory, and it was hollow. Glory was dead. Luke was somewhere in the thin, brittle air. Jesse had vanished again. I had let him down.

"Commander!"

Detective McCracken was lumbering toward us across the parking lot, his beefy chest humping up and down as he trotted, scratched eyeglasses bouncing on his nose. Brian grunted.

McCracken hitched up his trousers and wheezed in a breath. "I wanted to assure you this department is committed to finding your son."

Brian just stared at him.

"Committed a hundred and ten percent. We'll do everything in our power to bring your boy home."

Brian said, "The same way you brought Glory Moffett home?"

McCracken shoved his hands in his pockets. After a second he said, "You're a free man. There's no hard feelings on our part."

"Really? I'm suspended from duty, NCIS is trying to tie me to these thefts from the base, and the FBI is treating me like I'm dog shit on the bottom of a shoe."

McCracken said, "In time, I hope you'll get some more perspective. Everyone's just doing their job."

"Sure." Brian walked away, pulling me with him. McCracken watched us go.

Brian said, "Asshole. He didn't even apologize." He looked back at the detective. "Gung-ho idiots pumped a twenty-two-year-old girl full of bullets. You think I'll leave Luke's safety to them? No fucking way. If they bungle a rescue . . ."

He held out his hand. It was shaking. "Give me the keys. I'm driving."

We roared away, heading for his house. He said, "You think Glory really killed Peter Wyoming?"

"I have my doubts."

"Ice Paxton set her up to take the heat off of me."

He had told me about Paxton demanding a BW warhead, and claiming he could get him released from jail. He thought that Paxton set Glory up to accomplish that goal.

I said, "I wouldn't put it past him."

We hadn't shared this suspicion with the police. I had told them that Glory provided me with information, and about the warning drawn on the blast door mural. McCracken and the FBI agents had looked at me severely. With the mural scorched I had no proof. "Warn the Santa Barbara police," I'd said. "Tell them that crackpot Evan Delaney is threatening mayhem, but call them." McCracken did. Then I phoned the

superintendent of Santa Barbara schools, and Kevin
Eichner, and Sally Shimada. Told her, "Shut it down,
Sally—get the word out, Halloween is *off*."

There was a breathtaking silence on her end before
she said, "all right." Then she said what I knew: Publi-
cation wouldn't stop the Remnant from attacking a
schoolyard, or movie theater, or any public event.

"Do it anyway," I told her.

Brian said, "Paxton had my weapon all along, the
cocksucker. He sent Shiloh into town with this story
about Glory attacking her and holding the triplets hostage, and McCracken's boobs took it from there."

From what we could gather, the police never actually saw Glory pointing a gun at anyone. Everything
they heard, they heard from the triplets. What had
really happened inside the cabin? Had the triplets told
Glory it was a police raid, and scared her into crawling
through the tunnel to the truck in the barn, saying
they were going to escape?

Brian said, "These Remnant girls, their loyalty is
phenomenal. I mean, Shiloh took a beating just to set
up the scenario. That's intense."

"She didn't. Jesse gave her that black eye with the
Club."

He looked over. "No shit?"

"No shit."

"Good for him."

Low buildings flashed past, hunkering in the heat.

Brian said, "He'll hang tough, Ev."

Damn straight he would. Jesse's whole life was
about hanging tough. Had Brian just now seen that?
"Yeah, I know."

He was quiet for a moment. "One thing. Where'd
Chenille go?"

I had wondered that myself. "She lets other people
do the dirty work, so she won't be implicated. She's
cagey."

"Big Mama, pulling the strings offstage."

I watched the heat shimmering off the asphalt. "It's your strings she's pulling. She has been all along."

He raced along. Being in China Lake seemed to turn us both into adolescent drivers, lead-footed with the gas pedal.

I said, "Her animosity toward you apparently goes way back. What happened between you in high school? Did you insult her, cold-shoulder her, stand her up, what?"

"It's irrelevant. She's a hostile person. She hates everything."

"It's relevant if it helps predict her behavior."

"She's after me because she wants weapons. End of story."

I didn't think it was. Brian's eyes were black and colder than a snake's. But he wasn't going to say more about it.

"The wild card here is Paxton," he said. "He gets a hard-on just thinking about bloodshed."

"You don't think he's going to follow the script?"

"He'll write his own script." He ran through a red light. "What's the idea behind leaderless resistance? The power of a dedicated individual to carry out cataclysmic acts of violence. That's Paxton. He has his own ideas, and I don't think they involve following a woman into battle. Not after seeing how he treated Tabitha . . ."

He braked, swearing hotly. He had driven past his own street. He jammed the Explorer in reverse.

"By the way." He nodded toward my gold crucifix, shining in the sun. "I know that was Grandma's, but how can you wear that thing?"

"It's a cross. Don't confuse the Remnant with Christianity."

His stare was bitter. "There isn't any God, Evan. Up there beyond the atmosphere there's nothing but a howling vacuum."

I had never seen him openly afraid before. All his

supports were gone, his whole life hauled out from under him. He swung around onto his street, pulled into his driveway, slammed the door getting out. Halfway up the front walk I stopped him.

"Luke prays for you, Bri. Give him credit for knowing when something's worthwhile."

The skin around his eyes stretched tight. He stared at his boots, blinked, gathered it back. "Thanks. But Luke believes in Santa Claus, too."

Inside, Brian threw the car keys on the kitchen counter. The house smelled like paint and antiseptic floor cleanser. I'd had it cleaned by a company that specialized in mopping up bloody crime scenes, people I'd found in the Yellow Pages. Sign of the times.

It couldn't have been a minute later that the phone rang. We looked at each other, and I picked it up.

"Put your brother on."

It was Ice Paxton. Brian took the phone, leaning close to my ear to let me hear.

"Told you," Paxton said. "Free and clear."

"So you're a man of your word. Halle-fuckin'-lujah."

Paxton sucked his teeth, cleared his throat. "You wearing a watch?"

"Just tell me what you want."

"You better synchronize. By my clock it's one twenty-two p.m. You got twenty-four hours to get what you promised."

Brian's face was gun-barrel rigid. His line of sight focused beyond the walls.

"Did you hear me, Delaney?"

"Loud and clear."

"We'll call back and tell you where to make the delivery."

"No. I'll tell you."

"You don't got no say in this."

"I'm not dropping off cash, you jackass—it's a BW warhead, extremely volatile. I can't just toss it in a

Dumpster behind Wal-Mart. I'll tell you when I have a safe location secured."

"Don't mess with us."

"You bring Luke and Tabitha. Otherwise I abort."

Paxton hawked. "Officers. All of you the same—think you run the world. Twenty-four hours, clock's ticking."

Brian dropped the phone back in its cradle. He leaned against the counter. Veins stood out on his arms.

I said, "Are you going to call the police?"

"No." He turned to me. "There's only one person I trust with Luke's life, and that's you. So get yourself in gear."

I felt the boosters kicking in. I knew what he was offering me. Brian renounced the possibility of God, saw a barbarous and insensate universe, but by trusting Luke's life to me he was giving me a chance for redemption.

I said, "Now what?"

"Now we get ourselves a warhead."

I said, "Leave that to me."

When I pulled into her driveway Abbie Hankins had just walked her kids home from school. The front door was open, backpacks and small shoes and bunched socks clogging the entryway, air-conditioning rolling outside into the angled afternoon sun. I had three Happy Meals, a quart of Pralines 'n' Cream, and a six-pack of Coors, Abbie's beer. I knocked.

Abbie stuck her head into the hallway from the back of the house. "Here for the Weight Watchers meeting, are we?"

"I thought the kids could eat while we talk."

While the kids tore into the food, Abbie poured two glasses of iced tea, handed me one, and said, "Let's sit out on the patio." We settled onto rickety metal deck chairs and she said, "Okay. Shoot."

"I need a favor. A huge one that could get you in trouble."

"Something illegal?"

"Unquestionably. But it could save Luke's life."

In the sunlight her hair shone Valkyrie blond. She said, "I got you in big trouble once with something illegal. And you got me out of big trouble recently. I'm doing the arithmetic, and you're coming out on the 'greater-than' side of this equation."

"Want me to tell you?"

"Yes."

"Help me steal the Sidewinder missile from the China Lake Museum."

Back at the house, Brian met me at the door. "Results?"

"Tonight at eleven. Abbie will meet me at the museum with the key."

He clasped my shoulder. He looked, I thought, surprised. "Good girl."

"But once I get it you have to be ready to roll. I'm not parking my Explorer on the driveway with a big-ass rocket sticking out the back."

"We'll drive it out to the meeting site while it's still dark."

"All right." We headed into the kitchen. "And for your information, you get three chances to call me 'good girl,' and I mean in your lifetime."

Standing at the kitchen table was Marcus Dupree. "Better learn, man. You don't say 'good girl' unless the woman in question wears diapers, or she's a golden retriever. Good afternoon, Evan."

"Marc."

He was making amends, I thought. I hadn't seen him since the day I'd told him off, charged him with being no friend to Brian. He was in civvies, jeans and a Naval Academy T-shirt, but still looked martial.

"You've been shopping," I said.

On the table lay two slim fire extinguishers, several small aerosol canisters, and an assortment of bits and gadgets from Radio Shack—sensors, LEDs, and two electronic thermometers.

I said, "What's for lunch?"

"Anthrax," Brian said.

"Holy Christ."

"Or sarin gas. I haven't decided."

Marc said, "Maybe it's plutonium particulates. They'll mess their shorts; I guarantee it. You can't go wrong with radioactivity."

I said, "I love it when guys cook."

Brian said, "I promised these assholes a BW warhead, so that's what we're going to give them. We're kludging together 'detectors' to prove that we're delivering the goods."

Marc pointed at the Radio Shack gadgets, said in his jazz-deejay voice, "We could rig them to act like Geiger counters, add a clicking sound."

I picked up one of the little aerosol canisters. "What's this?"

"CS gas," Brian said.

"Pepper spray?"

"Just in case."

"In case what?"

"In case the Sidewinder doesn't sufficiently impress them. If things get squirrelly, I want to disable and confuse them quickly. The CS gas can do that."

"And the fire extinguishers?"

"I'm putting one in the 'winder. Know how fast people run when they see smoke shooting out the end of a missile?"

He saw my thoughtful look.

"I'm not taking firearms into the exchange. Luke's going to be there," he said. "The Remnant's a bunch of amateurs. I don't trust them to hold their fire in a tense situation, and my carrying a weapon would simply make them more trigger-happy. I'm not going to

take that risk. Marc will be outside, so he'll be armed.
But I have to do it another way."

I gazed over the items on the table.

"If things turn sour," I said, "you want to do more
than disable the Remnant. That will be difficult anyway, considering that they'll probably outnumber us."

"You're not coming."

"Bro. Don't be asinine. My point is, you're creating
the illusion that you've got a biological warhead, so
why not extend the illusion to scare the Remnant, and
control them if things go bad."

He crossed his arms. "Go on."

I pointed at the electronic gadgets. "You're engi-
neering detectors to convince them that the warhead
is lethal. Take it a step further. Engineer the warhead
to release the biological warfare agent if Paxton doesn't
behave."

"Doesn't behave. Doesn't set Luke free, you
mean."

"Yes. You should be ready to force his hand." I
was also thinking that we could force Paxton to tell
us what had happened to Jesse. I picked up a spray
canister. "If he double-crosses you, gas him."

He rubbed a hand across his chin and started pacing. "Wouldn't that mean exposing myself to the BW
agent as well?"

"You've been vaccinated against anthrax. Paxton
hasn't." I turned to Marc. "This nixes the plutonium
idea. Brian couldn't claim to be vaccinated against radioactivity. But if he makes them think he's exposed
them to germs—"

"You could offer them an antidote."

"Exactly."

They looked at each other. A scimitar smile trans-
formed Brian's face. "I like it."

Marc said, "This crowd knows about anthrax vacci-
nations for the military. They'll know you haven't
been immunized, Evan."

"Then I'll have to take the antidote. It can be part of the act."

He thought. "They may also know that antibiotics can cure anthrax."

"Not secret, bioengineered military anthrax they can't."

He nodded. "I can provide syringes. Sheree's diabetic." He explained, "My wife."

Brian said, "Getting sprayed with anthrax would be painless, though. Pepper spray leaves you screaming and coughing on the ground, half-blind for an hour."

"So dilute it, give them a tiny dose, something. You guys know how to handle fifty million dollars' worth of fighter jet; you can surely manage to fiddle with a spray can."

Brian was nodding, thinking. "It won't fool them for long, but maybe long enough." He glanced at me edgewise. "You certainly have a dishonest imagination."

"The venom of asps is under my lips. Let's get to work."

Abbie was waiting when I backed the Explorer up to the rear door of the China Lake Museum. The night sky unrolled above us, moonless, punched with stars. The wind keened like the dead. The Explorer's tailgate sat half-open, and protruding from it were lengths of PVC pipe. I planned to place the Sidewinder underneath them, slide a short pipe over its nose, stuff a towel in the end, and hang a flag off the back. That way, when I cruised down China Lake Boulevard it would appear that I was doing some midnight plumbing, not packing a heat seeker, maybe looking to dogfight Range Rovers.

Abbie unlocked the door. "What a way to spend Saturday night."

"It beats the Lobo."

We hauled a section of pipe from my car and carried it inside. Abbie closed the door and flipped on a light. The stuffed animals in the display cases jumped into eerie relief, synthetic eyes glaring blindly.

Abbie said, "You're going to bring the missile back, right?"

"On my honor."

She set the pipe down. "By Monday. Then, just maybe, I won't get fired."

"This should all be over by tomorrow afternoon."

"Cool." She pulled out a large screwdriver and started unscrewing the Sidewinder from its display mount.

I reacquainted myself with the missile: a ten-foot needle, six inches in diameter, with guidance fins near the nose and on the tail. Those tail fins, too big to fit inside a PVC pipe, would have to ride next to me, resting between the front seats of my car. I looked at the rest of the exhibit, Technicolor photos of fireballs and shrapnel.

Abbie spun the screwdriver. "Relax, it's unarmed, no warhead or propellant. I'm almost positive."

"Ha-ha. Remember that air show, where the navy let kids sit in a fighter cockpit but forgot to disconnect the ejection seat? Some little seven-year-old—"

"Stop." She held up a hand, looking stricken. "Don't talk about kids getting hurt. I can't stand it."

And that, I knew, was why she had agreed to help me—not to repay a debt to me, or because she had a residual wild streak, or even because the Remnant had set loose the coydog that attacked her. She couldn't stand by while these people threatened a child's life.

"You're aces, Abbie."

She tapped the missile. "Put your shoulder under here."

I braced myself under the missile. With a final twist of the screwdriver the Sidewinder came free. Its weight bore down, heavier than I'd expected.

"See?" she said. "It's fine. Good enough for government work. Now let's get this pig into your car, so you can put our tax dollars to work."

26

The barn sat on a rise overlooking the bowl of valley
to the east. Decrepit and grayed, long abandoned, it
rested among hunched boulders and Ponderosa pines.
Behind it the Sierras rose like a granite blade, ten
thousand feet up into the empty sky. Inside it, the
wind whistled and banged against the slats, a one-man
band, blowing hot. It was Sunday, October thirtieth.
It was showtime.

We'd been there since four a.m., Brian, Marc Dupree,
and I. We were ready by ten thirty. We had our Radio
Shack anthrax detectors. We had syringes preloaded
with saline solution, which cures Radio Shack–variety
anthrax. And we had the Sidewinder resting on two
sawhorses in the center of the barn, covered with a
canvas tarp. The only thing missing was the Remnant.

I paced, catching glimpses of the desert panorama
through the slats of the barn. Around me, blowing
sand tingled in shafts of sunlight. Brian stretched out
on the ground and laid his head on his backpack.

"Ev, sit down and rest. We have three hours."

"Right." But I couldn't settle down. Though I
hadn't slept all night, I was wired, nerves popping.

"There's no point in running down your reserves.
I'll call Paxton at noon."

Marc was squatting against the wall of the barn.
"Listen to your brother. Conserve yourself."

Brian closed his eyes and clasped his hands on his chest, as though he were a suburban husband napping in a hammock on a lazy Sunday afternoon. It astonished me. Beyond that, it comforted and frightened me: the warrior's tranquillity.

The wind gusted through the slats. Despite the heat, I shivered.

And I did sleep. At noon Brian's voice drew me back through the wool into wakefulness. He was on my cell phone, talking to Paxton.

". . . off Highway three ninety-five, westward, uphill about five miles," he said. "No, before the turnoff to Whitney Portal."

Sounding relaxed. He listened a moment.

"You don't have to remind me. I'm keeping my end of the bargain; you keep yours. Now let me speak to Luke."

Listening some more, he gave me a sharp look and waved me near. I put my ear to the phone.

I heard Paxton say, "Hold on," and my heart jumped. But then came a click, static, and the voice on the line was not Luke, but a tape recording.

"Daddy . . . ?" Hesitation, a tiny voice. "Here's what's in the paper today. USC twenty-eight, Cal seventeen. UCLA thirty-four, Wash thirty-one."

"Son of a bitch," Brian said.

"Or . . . Ore-gon fourteen . . ." Luke continued struggling to read out the football scores, but Brian wasn't listening anymore.

"Let me speak to my son."

Paxton came back on. "The boy's fine. But we ain't about to put him on the phone so the navy can triangulate our location and track him down. They trace this call and attack us, they won't find him. Not now, not ever."

Brian's breathing accelerated. Explaining the facts or the technology to Paxton was pointless. "Have Luke and Tabitha here. In one hour."

Before Paxton could respond, Brian shut off the phone. "They're coming. Saddle up."

We heard the engines from half a mile away. Marc peered between the slats of the barn and said, "Two trucks and two motorcycles."

Brian walked toward him. "Can you see Luke or Tabitha?"

Marc shook his head.

We all looked through the slats, down the tawny slope to the dust plumes rooster-tailing behind the Remnant's vehicles. The big green Dodge was in the lead, sunlight flashing off its windshield as it ate up the ground.

Marc said, "I'm going."

He planned to take a position in the scrub pine and boulders uphill behind the barn. He opened the backpack and took out two small walkie-talkies. He tossed one to me. They were the same make—cheap, bright blue and orange—Paxton had carried the night they kidnapped Luke. If they used them again, we wanted to monitor transmissions. Marc then took a pistol from the pack. He tucked it in the waistband of his jeans, in the small of his back. Giving Brian a nod, he shoved aside a loose plank and slipped out the back of the barn.

The trucks and cycles bucked along the road, louder. Brian touched my shoulder.

He said, "Now we bring him home."

"All the way."

He pushed open the barn door. The dry world poured out beyond him—rocky slope, corn-bread desert, distant mountains the color of blood, bruise, gunpowder, bone. Brian stood silhouetted in the entrance, a singularity, a hole in the light. I waited behind him, about to cross the event horizon.

The walkie-talkie spouted static, two clicks, Marc's signal that he was in position. I pressed the transmit button once in reply and slipped the walkie-talkie into the pocket of my shorts.

The Remnant's vehicles rolled up and stopped. For a moment they sat guttering. Then the men on the bikes crept forward. They were young, with clipped hair, grim eyes, muscled arms. They drove slowly around the barn, reconnoitering. Brian stood in the doorway. The trucks growled, heat shimmering off them, smoked windows blazing with sunlight. We couldn't see past the glare.

The bikes swung back around the barn and signaled thumbs-up. In tandem, the trucks shut off their engines. Doors opened. Isaiah Paxton stepped into the sun, cowboy hat shading his spare face, tanned arms loose at his sides, worn-down boots noiseless as he crossed the ground toward the barn. From the second truck came Curt Smollek. He had a gauze bandage on the end of his nose, and a shaved patch on his scalp, where iodine covered a cluster of scratches.

Paxton stopped outside the barn door. Behind him Smollek chafed and jammed his thumbs under his belt. He looked in the barn and his eyes narrowed. There I was, the woman who had bested him with a ferret. He fondled the bandage on his nose.

He said, "What's Miss Doggy-style doing here?"

Paxton didn't bother looking at me. "Delaney? Just supposed to be you."

Brian scoffed. "You can't transport an air-to-air missile singlehandedly, unless it's hanging under the wing of an F/A-eighteen. I needed Evan's help."

Smollek hitched up his jeans and hawked a spit wad onto the dirt.

Paxton said, "She wipe your nose when it runs? No wonder the beast had a cakewalk infiltrating the military. Pilots got to have little sis help 'em tote ordnance." He took a step. "Show it to me."

Brian nodded toward the green truck. "Let me see Luke and Tabitha."

"The way it works, you do what we say; then you get what we arranged."

Brian kept looking at the truck, trying to peer past the smoked glass and the glare. "Fine. But let me see them."

Paxton shifted his stance. "No. Time you learned you ain't running this show."

Brian's shoulders drew upward, just the slightest motion, but it tightened his whole posture. The hairs on the back of my neck prickled. I knew: Luke and Tabitha were not in Paxton's truck. This was a double cross. We were going with the Sidewinder.

Brian said, "Your way, then. It's in here."

He turned around, confirmation on his face, a look that absolutely chilled me. I stepped back behind the shrouded missile, getting into position.

The walkie-talkie crackled. "Brian. Heads-up—"

Paxton was sauntering in. I shut off the walkie-talkie, my heart drumming. Marc had seen something. What? I tried to look around without looking around. Smollek and the bikers scuttled in, kids eager to see what Santa had left under the Christmas tree. The wind cracked through the barn like a horsewhip. Sand flew, flashing and jinking in midair.

Brian grabbed the tarp with both hands and pulled it off. The Remnant's men gaped at the Sidewinder like it was the Ark of the Covenant, the missing link, ball lightning.

Brian said, "Delivered as promised, Paxton."

Slowly Paxton began circling the missile, surveying it. The bikers stood rooted to the sand. Smollek leaned forward tentatively, as though fearful to approach it, and read the specs printed on the fuselage. Lips moving, whispering.

" 'U.S. Navy. Naval Air Systems Command.' " Louder, coming to all caps: " 'WARHEAD, GUIDED MISSILE . . .' "

He leaned further, his mouth gradually hinging

open. Tentatively he poked a tail fin with his index finger.

I slapped his hand down. "For God's sake!"

He jerked back, hand shriveling against his chest.

Paxton said, "Open it up. I want to see the works."

"Not until you let me see my son and his mother," Brian said. "It's time for a quid pro quo."

At the Latin, all the Remnant's heads snapped up in sync. As though words, not rough handling, would detonate the missile's warhead. Spells. The old name for voice activation.

Paxton sucked his teeth. "Smollek, persuade him."

Outside the barn light and shadow sped across the background like ghosts. But the revolver in Smollek's fist was not imaginary.

"Show us the germs." He was red-faced, his acne a landscape of nodules capped with the nose gauze. He extended his arm toward Brian's chest. "And speak English."

"Fine."

Stepping up to the Sidewinder, Brian started spinning wing nuts, loosening the ring clamp around the warhead. Smollek's shoulder quivered.

He said, "Take it slow, man. You might jostle it, you know, upset things."

"I know what I'm doing."

He spun the nut one final time. With a whoosh and a hiss, the warhead began spraying a white mist into the air.

Brian stepped back. The CO_2 and pepper spray hit the Remnant face-on. Hit me too. The pepper spray had been vastly diluted, but in the cold fog its hot hint felt like death. The bikers ran for the door. Smollek started squealing.

I dove for Brian's backpack. "The syringe! Where is it?"

"Front pocket."

Paxton was backing away from the missile, looking

enraged. The CO_2 billowed, filling the barn. Smollek's shrieking intensified. He waved his arms as though fighting off an attacking flock of birds. I ripped open the backpack and grabbed the syringe. Paxton saw me and started around the Sidewinder, but I stabbed the needle into my arm and pressed the plunger.

Brian shouted, "Too late, Paxton. That was the only dose I had."

Paxton's head swiveled. "Then you're doomed, too."

"No. I've been vaccinated against anthrax. And now so has my sister."

Smollek said, "Anthrax? Anthrax?"

Brian said, "Hardened military anthrax. You have one chance here. You want the antidote? You return Luke to me *now*."

Paxton blinked and started coughing. The CO_2 fogged the barn.

"Right now!"

Smollek said, "Ice! Do what he says!"

Paxton said, "God damn you to hell, Delaney."

"Ice! You tell him, or I will!"

The fire extinguisher inside the missile reached its bottom. It shut off with a squeak. Smollek jumped, screamed, and fired at the Sidewinder.

I stood transfixed, hearing the revolver pop and metal *ching* as the bullet hit the missile and ricocheted. Smollek fired again and again. I threw myself to the dirt.

Then hell arrived.

Men charged in the door, figures in black solidifying out of the CO_2, armed, one yelling, "Freeze! Down on the ground!" Smollek spun, eyes wild, gun chest-high. The voice roared, "On the ground! Do it! Do it!" Smollek's gun blared, and then answering fire.

It's an electrifying experience, being in the middle of a gunfight. My senses flung themselves open. My skin seemed to turn inside out. Cordite stank in the air. I pressed my face down in the sand and covered my head with my arms. A second later I felt Brian land on my back, shielding me. The voice shouted, "Federal agents!" Above us came more shots, shouts, a man barking orders, wood splintering. Moaning. I squeezed my eyes shut, nerves on fire, waiting for a bullet to rip into me.

One of the intruders shouted, "Outside!"

And I knew what I had seen through the slats of the barn—not shadows, not clouds passing by on a cloudless desert afternoon, but men positioning themselves to raid the barn. That was what Marc had been trying to warn us about over the walkie-talkie.

One of the agents, face covered with a balaclava, approached me. "Evan, sit up."

Startled at hearing my name, I craned my neck to look at him. He pulled off the balaclava. It was Garrett Holt.

People were shouting and running outside the barn, men barking commands, radios crackling, engines gunning. The moaning continued, weaker. The fog was dissipating, but not my confusion. Garrett stood above me and Brian, an automatic in his hand. He looked down and said, "Don't move."

On the far side of the barn a form lay twisting on the ground. It was Curt Smollek, flat on his back, bleeding heavily.

Brian was facedown, hands laced behind his head. He peered sideways at Smollek, said, "Shit," and called out, "Smollek. Luke and Tabitha, where are they?"

Smollek's hand groped the sand. He stared at the roof, beyond persuasion.

Garrett snapped, "Quiet."

Brian hissed out a breath, said, "Fuck." Turned to me. "You know this guy?"

I said, "He's the pilot I told you about, except he's no pilot."

Garrett grabbed my elbow and hoisted me to my feet. "Outside." Pointed at Brian. "You, don't move."

He led me from the barn, holding my elbow as though I were a disobedient child, pulling me past my car, past Smollek's truck, past a new vehicle, a silver Suburban with a big whip antenna. Government agents were all over the barn and grounds, moving alertly, faces on guard. They wore bulletproof vests, and some had labels on their jackets. FBI. ATF, the Bureau of Alcohol, Tobacco and Firearms. On the ground one of the bikers lay handcuffed. He was shaking his head like a dog tearing at a bone, roaring, "The Lord revengeth! He reserveth *wrath* for his enemies!" My eyes and lungs burned.

Finally moving out of earshot, Garrett let go. He unzipped his jacket with a ripping motion. "Shut up and listen to me, if you want to stay out of jail. I'm NCIS."

"You're a cop."

"I'm a civilian investigator for the navy."

"Undercover as an officer."

"Yes. I'm investigating weapons thefts from the base."

Jacked on adrenaline, I angered instantly. "So you're a fraud."

He had duped me. And, of course, he had done it with my complicity, by pretending to be exactly who I wanted him to be: Action Man, My Hero. He had played me like a banjo.

"We've been after the Remnant for months, trying to get evidence that they're buying stolen weapons, enough to take down this theft ring at the base. We thought this was a break."

"What did you do, plant a homing device on my car?"

He shook me. "Listen. We *thought* this was a break. Instead it's bait and switch. And you cannot imagine how much the Bureau and ATF hate being made to look like idiots."

I rubbed my eyes. They only burned worse. Near the barn, two agents came into view, flanking Marc Dupree. One of the agents held Marc's pistol in his hand.

Garrett said, "This was dangerous and stupid. What was your brother trying to accomplish?"

"Trying to get his son back."

"By trading him for a stolen 'winder?"

"He didn't steal anything. The missile doesn't belong to the navy; it wasn't stolen from the base."

"Then where'd he get it?"

"I got it. From the China Lake Museum."

"You'll have to do better than that."

"If you insist."

I took a letter from my pocket. It was typed on museum letterhead and began, *Dear Ms. Delaney: Pursuant to your request, we will be pleased to loan the museum's decommissioned Sidewinder missile (Case assembly no. 30043-65251957) for your exhibition the weekend of October 30–31.* It was stapled to a shipping invoice and receipt, all stamped and signed by Abbie Hankins.

Garrett smiled sourly. "Well, aren't you the clever cookie. I think you've just saved your bacon."

At the sound of voices we looked up. Outside the barn Brian stood arguing with an ATF agent, jabbing his finger at the man's face. The agent shook his head, gestured in our direction, and Brian looked around at Garrett.

That was when I noticed that the Remnant's motorcycles were gone.

Brian charged toward us. "You." Pointing at Garrett. "You ran this operation?"

Garrett stood motionless, watching him come on.

"You idiot. They were about to tell me where Luke is, and now everything's blown. While you were storming in the barn door, Paxton kicked his way out through the back wall. He's gone."

My stomach dropped.

Garrett said, "If this op's blown it's your fault, Commander."

"Bullshit. You weren't here to rescue my son. Not one of you. You were here to catch the Remnant stealing weapons."

Another agent started toward us. Garrett waved him away. He said, "You had zero authority to act on your own."

"But you knew I'd do it, didn't you? That's why you blew me off at the jail. You *wanted* me to do it. This was all a setup."

I said, "Wait. Garrett came to see you at the jail?"

"That day you went out to Angels' Landing. He came with the FBI."

It felt like a steel cable snapping deep within me. That day at Angels' Landing—Garrett hadn't left me to rush back to the base. He had returned to town to interrogate Brian. He could have gone with me to the fallout shelter, and together we could have gotten Jesse out. I had told him Jesse needed help, that we had to hurry. . . .

"You absolute bastard."

He misunderstood. "Who, me? This plan of your brother's was reckless and totally unprofessional. Exactly what I'd expect from a couple of jet jockeys."

Brian muscled forward, looking ready to head-butt him. "Listen, you whiny-assed pilot wannabe—"

I pushed my way between them and grabbed Brian by the shoulders. "Stop it," I said, forcing myself to focus. "We have to do something. Fast."

They looked at me.

"Don't you see what's happened? Paxton thinks that you poisoned him with anthrax, Bri. He's going to think you were part of the raid—that you set him up to be attacked by federal agents."

"Shit."

"They'll think you set the beast on them, that the battle's starting. They're going to attack."

27

"Shit!"

Garrett Holt was losing his cool. He was pacing in a tight circle, rubbing his temples, and keeping one eye on Brian, who was ready to punch him. He held up both hands, saying, "Shut up, just shut up," even though we hadn't spoken.

He pointed at me. "Glory claimed that the Remnant plans to attack Santa Barbara. Correct?"

"That's the flashpoint."

"I'll contact the Santa Barbara police."

Brian turned and started toward my car.

"Delaney. Where do you think you're going?"

Brian said, "To find my son and his mother."

"No, you're not."

Brian ignored him. Garrett again said, "Shit," and started after him, his jaw clenched, his face red. I followed, hearing him mutter, "Freakin' fighter god." Brian's crack about him being a whiny-assed wannabe had, I realized, hit home.

I said, "Let him go."

He gave me an acidic look. "Go? I haven't even started with you two yet."

"I know you're furious. But you know you can't arrest us."

"Just watch me."

"You'll only end up releasing us. So do it now, when we can still make a difference—"

He turned and glared. "You think I'm that stupid? You're going to run off and get yourself even deeper into this mess."

"Come on, you're still way up on points here. You've gathered a wealth of information about the Remnant by tagging along with me."

"You don't call it even with the FBI or NCIS, Evan. That's not how it works."

"We're wasting time. Look, SBPD can't comb the entire city. Brian and I would be two extra pairs of feet on the ground. We aren't going to try to battle the Remnant. We don't even have weapons."

He looked toward the barn and the Sidewinder.

"Give me a break," I said. "Don't force us to sweat out an interrogation right now. We'll come in another time, I promise. Tomorrow."

The wind rasped over us. The mountains reared like a wave about to break.

"Luke is Brian's life, Garrett." I looked into his sea green eyes and swallowed it all—the anger, the resentment, my pride. "Please."

He stared at me for a long while. Finally, for the last time, he said, "Shit. Where would you go, Tabitha's house?"

"Probably."

"Make that 'definitely,' so I can tell SBPD you're there and they won't accidentally shoot you. And I want both you and your brother on base at NCIS tomorrow at oh nine hundred. No exceptions. Got it?"

"Got it."

"Now go. Quickly, before I change my mind."

A minute later we were booming down the highway toward China Lake. Brian said, "We don't have time to drive to Santa Barbara. Head for the airport."

He rented a twin-engine Piper and flew us across the Tehachapis, droning toward the brilliant glare of the ocean. The tailwind chucked us around like a pin-ball. I clawed the seat, holding on, but Brian was un-fazed, could have been flossing his teeth for all the strain the turbulence caused him, and came into the airport on a steep, sweeping approach. I looked down at the city. It lay breathless under scoured skies, crys-tal clear and exposed.

Nikki and Carl Vincent met us at the airport. Nikki hugged me and handed me the morning's paper. It snapped in the wind like a flag. The headline read, "Cult Threat to Schools," by Sally Shimada.

Carl pointed across the parking lot at his Jeep Grand Cherokee. "I can go with you. Four-wheel drive and a full tank."

He looked sturdy and stone-certain, standing there in his white button-down shirt, khakis, and owlish glasses. I felt gratitude welling up, an immense fond-ness for him.

"No. You should get out of town. Drive to L.A. for the day." He started to protest and I said, "The Rem-nant knows where you live. Go somewhere."

He glanced at Nikki and handed me his car keys. Then he put a hand on my shoulder and said with conviction, "Fear no evil."

The power in his voice rooted me there. Brian snatched the keys. Calling thanks over his shoulder, he pulled me toward the Jeep.

We roared toward Tabitha's house, up San Marcos Pass and along the switchbacks of West Camino Cielo. Breaking out of the foliage along a ridge, we caught a view down the mountains. I wondered where Paxton was, whether he had sent word to Chenille Wyoming to light the fuse.

Brian jerked the wheel and shot along Tabitha's rut-ted driveway. He gunned it right up to the house and skidded to a stop, definitely not coming in under the radar. Reaching into the backseat, he unzipped his backpack and pulled out a handgun.

"Where'd that come from?"

He racked the slide. "It's Marc's. He got it back from the feds. Now I have it." He opened the car door. "Stay behind me."

We strode to the front door. My heart was pounding. Taking a breath, Brian raised the pistol and turned the knob. Stillness greeted us, a thick silence that contrasted with the wailing wind outside. He waited for a moment, listening, and then charged into the living room.

He stopped. The walls were covered with hideous black-and-white drawings. Tabitha's eschatological art gallery had expanded to cover every inch of wall space, floor to ceiling. He stared at a picture of the Antichrist with an ax stuck in his head.

"Jesus Christ." His gun arm wavered.

I went past him, looking in the bedrooms, the bathroom, the kitchen. Found nothing. I checked the garage: empty. The supplies Jesse had seen were gone. The only thing left was a piece of paper thumbtacked to the wall, flickering in the wind. It was the Revelation checklist. Smoothing it out, I saw that all the boxes were checked off.

Armageddon, you are go for launch.

In the backyard I found Brian standing at the edge of the lawn, the gun hanging at his side. Beyond the grass, sandstone and manzanita took over, covering the mountainside in a thick tumble all the way down.

His voice barely disguised his frenzy. "You've been here more recently than I have. Had she built a toolshed, a garden hut, had the Remnant set up a firing range down past the lawn?"

"I don't know."

"Think, Ev."

I thought. She had left a message before, in the fallout shelter. Maybe she'd left one here. I ran back to the house. She would have put it on the living room

wall, among the screaming meemies. But there were
dozens of drawings. Even if there was a message, how
would I find it?

What had drawn Jesse's eye to the message on the
blast door mural? I thought: contrast. It had been
black-and-white amid boisterous color. Stepping back
mentally, I took in the sweep of the walls, looking for
disparity, a break in the pattern. Looked and looked,
until I saw, snaking through a sketch above the fireplace, a ribbon of red. It had been sketched quickly—
and recently. In the past few days. I looked closer. It
was a dragon, wild in the sky, its tail hurling stars
down to earth. Revelation twelve. The stars tumbled
in a long trail, falling toward a mountainside. This
mountainside. This house, and the landscape beyond
it.

I rushed outside. A few yards into the brush I found
some boulders and climbed up. Now I saw it: a rutted
dirt road, nearly obscured by vegetation, running
downhill parallel to Tabitha's driveway. Yelling at
Brian to get the Jeep and follow me, I jumped down
and started pushing through the bushes, finally emerging onto the road. When Brian caught up I hopped in
the Jeep and we jarred along, half a mile down into
the dry, overgrown chaparral, until we broke into a
clearing and found the decrepit clapboard cabin that
had been sketched on Tabitha's wall.

It had a warped wooden porch running along the
front, and a big picture window filmed with dust.
There was a detached garage with a heavy padlock
on the door. Live oaks framed both structures, heavy
branches growing over the roofs. Late-afternoon light
ice-picked through the leaves. Santa Barbara Realtors
would have pimped the place for $350,000, if not for
one other feature: the slavering dog chained to the
porch rail. It was yellow-eyed and dusty, a big, shabby
animal that lowered its head and began growling when
the Jeep drove up.

"It's a coydog," I said. "One of Curt Smollek's rabies incubators."

"Wait here."

Brian got out. The dog lunged at him, barking furiously. He walked toward it, raised the pistol, and fired. The dog went down. He kept walking, not breaking stride, not even looking at the animal, and stepped onto the porch. With sudden clarity I saw what Tabitha had seen in him, his heart of death.

The door resisted when he tried to open it, and he put his shoulder into it, shoving it open with a crack. He disappeared inside. I leaped from the car, ran to the doorway. The cabin's interior was dim, and with my eyes tight from the sun all I could see was shadow.

I heard Brian crying.

My eyes adjusted. Brian was kneeling on the floor, cradling Luke's small form. Luke was utterly silent in his arms. Beyond Brian lay Tabitha, her mouth gagged and her hands bound behind her back, tied to an old iron stove. Her dark eyes were wide, staring fixedly. My breathing failed me.

Abruptly she kicked and squirmed. She grimaced at me, the *don't just stand there* clear on her face. I saw that Brian was untying a cord around Luke's hands. Luke's little fingers flexed and then clutched Brian's sleeve. His eyes were as round as quarters. Brian pulled the duct tape off his mouth.

He said, "Daddy, you took a long time to get here."

Brian pulled him to his chest, his shoulders heaving.

Legs like water, I went to Tabitha and took off the gag. She said, "I can't believe you're here."

"I found your message." I started untying her.

"Thank God. I only had a few minutes to sketch it when they brought me to the house yesterday," she said. "They told me they were going to kill you. Sacrifice you once you gave them the missile."

Brian said, "That plan didn't work out."

Ropes off, she sat up and crawled over to Luke,

who was balled against Brian's chest. "Told you if you minded me it would work."

Luke nodded. She touched his cheek. She said, "I told him he couldn't do anything without my permission. Sit down, stand up, speak—he could only do it if I said he could."

Luke said, "Even pee."

"He had to eat off my plate, drink out of my glass." She looked at Brian. "I thought of it after Ice took me to see you at the jail. To get Luke to do anything they had to keep him with me; they couldn't separate us. I told him, that way if help came they'd be sure to find us both."

Brian gave her a look from the old days. "Very smart, Tabby. And very tough."

Hot patches rosed her cheeks, whether from the compliment, or because she thought he should have appreciated her long ago, I couldn't say.

Luke said, "Can we go home now?"

I said, "Absolutely. Let's get out of here."

Brian extended a hand to Tabitha. She hesitated a moment, then took it.

She looked at me. "Did you bring the chair?"

I tilted my head. "Chair?"

"The wheelchair."

Stupidly I checked out her legs, thinking she didn't look too shaky to walk to the Jeep, before I understood what she meant. I grabbed her arm. "Jesse . . . ?"

"He's in the garage."

The garage door was padlocked. Finding a jack handle in the Jeep, I jammed it under the hinges of the lock and heaved. The wood splintered and the lock broke free, rusty nails flying. I dragged the door scraping across the ground.

Inside, Jesse sat on the dirt, squinting against the sudden sunlight. He said, "Hey, Raquel. What happened to your fur bikini?"

His attempt at a grin sank beneath beard stubble and fever. His eyes were glazed, his hands tied around the support beam behind him. I stopped short in the doorway, my skin creeping.

"Welcome to the destructo-hut," he said. "Don't come in."

The garage was an armory. Stacked all around him, on the ground, on tilting shelves, were assault rifles, handguns, bayonets, boxes of ammunition, crates heaping with dull-green hand grenades.

"Ironically, they're trying to bore me to death. No TV, no radio, the only way to entertain myself is masturbation." He looked over his shoulder at his hands, cinched to the support post with nylon rope. "But they tied me up to keep me from going blind." He exhaled. "However, Chenille covered herself, just in case the tedium didn't kill me. She left me a companion in that crate over there. It's a bomb."

"Jesse . . ." I stepped toward him.

"Careful. They buried stuff under the floor, too. It might be booby-trapped."

I looked at the dirt floor. I could see the faint outline of a wooden trapdoor.

I said, "Did you see them laying mines or wiring down there?"

"No. But I haven't been totally with it. Things have been swimming in and out." He swallowed drily. "I know one thing. Chenille made a point of telling me the authorities aren't getting these weapons. The bomb's set to detonate unless she disarms it." He leaned his head back against the beam. "She's got this place set on autohavoc."

I looked around. Saw no wires stretched across the doorway, no electric eyes, no motion detectors. I ran inside.

Jesse ducked his head, a reflex, then started breathing again. "Shit, Delaney. You do throw the dice."

I untied his hands. He flexed his shoulders, rubbed his wrists.

I said, "Yeah. Guess that means I'm going to marry you."

"Really?"

"Really." I turned and ran over to the bomb.

Goddamn, it really looked like bombs do in the movies: two sticks of dynamite, wires, blasting caps. It was an ignition switch to the hereafter, Chenille's pilot light for the New Creation. Wired to it were a digital alarm clock and a keypad, the kind used to enter the disarm code on home burglar alarms. My own internal wiring sizzled. The alarm clock was counting down. The red LED display stood at 9:54 . . . 9:53 . . . 9:52.

I backed away from the device. In a voice sounding tinny and distant, I said, "If I get you to your feet, will your good leg hold you?"

He shook his head. At the best of times, *good leg* was a stretch. Now it was hopeless. The fever and exhaustion were plain on his face. "Got no good leg," he said. "Got no legs at all right now."

"Hang on." I got his arm over my shoulder and started pulling. He winced, dug his fingers into my arm, bit back a shout of pain. I stopped. I yelled out the door, "Brian!"

Jesse squeezed his eyes shut and clenched his teeth. Louder, I yelled Brian's name again, and kept saying, "Hang on, hang on."

He opened his eyes. "Ev. These weapons were stolen from China Lake."

"We'll worry about that later."

"Somebody delivered them. He was at the fallout shelter, somebody who knows you. I heard him talking about you—"

"Later, Jess."

"No, think about it. Who knows you're here?"

"The police." I stood up, turned to the door, bellowed, "Brian!"

I jumped. Standing in the doorway, side by side, were Ma and Pa Doomsday: Chenille Wyoming and Isaiah Paxton. Cradled in Paxton's arms was Doomsday Junior, his shotgun, pointed at my face.

28

Paxton leveled the shotgun at my stomach and said, "On your knees." His eyes were wintry, pale as sleet. I couldn't move. I knew if I knelt down he'd shoot me. He said, "Do it," and pumped the slide. The wind shook the trees.

Chenille grabbed his arm. "No. Isaiah, the cabin."

He said, "We got to take care of this situation. The device—you best disarm it."

She yanked on his arm. "Before Brian takes Luke. Bring her with you!"

Paxton looked at Jesse. She slapped him back and forth across his shoulder. "You can't shoot a twelve-gauge into the garage; you'll set the whole place off. Do it later."

"Guy's a waste of oxygen, Chenille."

"Look at him; he ain't going nowhere." Her olive T-shirt and camouflage pants adhered to her flesh under the force of the wind. She cried, "Quick!" and pushed Paxton toward the cabin. His face as hard as a shovel, he grabbed me by the hair, shoved the shotgun into my side, and followed her. We went around the corner and saw Brian stepping into the doorway. Behind him was Tabitha, with Luke at her side.

Paxton saw the pistol in Brian's hand. "Throw it down. Out here."

Shock and resistance fled across Brian's face. He put himself across the doorway, forced Tabitha back into the cabin. Chenille said, "He'll blow a hole through your sister the size of Texas." Brian held on a second, wanting to fight, then threw Marc's Beretta onto the dirt. It landed beside the dead coydog.

Paxton pushed me onto the porch behind Chenille. She said, "Inside."

We went in, and Paxton herded me into a corner with the others. Brian nudged me back, putting himself in front of us. Tabitha was shaking so hard that I could hear her heels concussing the floorboards.

Chenille said, "Give Luke here."

Paxton widened his stance. "I got 'em covered. You go disarm the device."

"We got plenty of time."

"Don't dawdle. This ain't no manicure appointment, something you can miss."

Anger flashed in her dime-size eyes, quickly camouflaged, like sheet lightning in a thunderhead. "It's under control."

Jesus, Mary, and Joseph, they were going to scratch and sniff, play top dog with a bomb ticking down six feet from Jesse's head.

I said, "The timer's below ten minutes."

Tabitha gasped and put her hands over her mouth. Brian cut his eyes at me. Paxton worked his shoulder up and down, snugging the shotgun against his side. I could hear his breathing. I realized that he didn't know the code to disarm the bomb.

He said, "Chenille, at least get on outside and listen for helicopters."

"I'll let you know when it's time to go outside, Ice."

"Navy agents might be easing into position. These two managed to get here awful quick." He eyed us suspiciously, maybe thinking we had beaten him to the cabin by taking a shortcut through a doorway to evil.

Brian was focusing on him, looking, I knew, for the out. Something to counter the threat. Retreat, block, attack. Feint. Stall.

He said, "You let us go, I can still get you the antidote."

Paxton said, "Liar. That wasn't no biological warhead."

"You want to stake your life on that?"

"My life's in God's hands."

"You're just pissed off that you didn't get your anthrax. You killed Peter Wyoming and pinned it on me, to force me to get you a BW warhead. And just when you thought you had it, everything turned to shit."

Paxton jeered. "The military killed Pastor Pete."

"The United States military didn't give one fart about Peter Wyoming."

"They wanted him dead. A NATO Beretta killed him. Ain't no question about that."

Brian looked at Chenille. "That Beretta was found at your church retreat."

Paxton snorted and tipped his head at me. "She put it there."

Brian said, "Evan? That's stupid and you know it."

Paxton shook his head. "I laid Pastor Pete in the freezer unit myself. There wasn't no gun in there, not till she come to Angels' Landing. Course she done it."

Here came that sensation again, like wire snapping and twanging as it recoiled. The freezer. I remembered climbing out the bedroom window at Angels' Landing, hearing Shiloh ask Glory, *Did you open it?* But Glory hadn't gone near the freezer. I told myself no, but the dots connected. It wasn't me, and it wasn't Glory.

Garrett.

No, I thought, can't be. But it couldn't have been anyone else. Garrett put the gun in the freezer. He'd had it all along, from the moment of the murder, the moment he pulled the trigger. Too late, I saw him clearly: a liar, quick to threaten people who crossed him with absolute, immediate pain. And the rest of the tumblers clicked. Garrett giving me perfect directions to the fallout shelter in Copper Creek, a place not even the Fire Department could find. Jesse telling me the weapons thief had been to the shelter, that I knew him from China Lake. Oh, shit.

Garrett Holt—who always happened upon me just after I'd seen the Remnant. Who knew where and when the Remnant was meeting with Brian to exchange the Sidewinder. He had been colluding with them all along. He was the insider at China Lake. He hadn't just been investigating the weapons theft ring; he'd been running it—and suppressing evidence, protecting himself, deflecting suspicion onto Brian. I didn't know why he'd done it, or why he'd killed Pastor Pete, but I did know one thing, a bad thing: He had told me I should go to Tabitha's, *definitely*. And I had listened.

He had sent Brian and me into this trap. He had pulled me aside, away from the other agents. Nobody else had heard him promise to call the Santa Barbara police. He had never phoned them. Help wasn't coming.

Paxton said, "Enough of this. We got to lock and load. We can't afford to lose the munitions in the garage."

Chenille ignored him. She was lifting her leg on the hydrant, showing her superiority by waiting till the last second.

All I could think was to set them on each other. I pointed at her. "Holt planted the gun in the freezer, and you've known it all along."

Her pebble eyes regarded me.

Paxton said, "Who?"

Garrett Holt, I realized, probably wasn't his real

name. I said, "The NCIS agent, the one who ran the raid. The guy who's been selling weapons to you."

Paxton's head clocked around at Chenille. "He run the raid?"

She said, "He couldn't stop it. FBI and ATF wanted in."

Anger rippled in his eyes. "They shot Curt."

"You lie down with dogs, you wake up with fleas, Isaiah. It's the price we paid to arm ourselves for what's coming."

My pulse raced along. I said, "He planted the murder weapon. He's the one who shot Pastor Pete. And you knew it all along, Chenille."

Paxton said, "That true?"

Her smooth indifference turned his face dark.

He said, "You knew, and didn't tell me?"

She hitched up her fatigues. "Wasn't no point. Pete was prophesied to die. You accept destiny; you don't fuss about the mechanism that brings it to pass."

Beside me, Tabitha started crying.

Chenille made a disgusted sound. "You feeble little girl. You don't got the strength to deal with destiny. You're every bit as weak as Pete was."

Paxton now looked at her with frank consternation. "Woman, what are you talking about?"

"Destiny. Pete's and mine. They're connected, but he couldn't see it, even though it's right there in Revelation, plain as day. The witnesses prophesy and are killed; then the woman appears, Chapter twelve, it follows straight on, 'And there appeared a great wonder in heaven, a woman clothed with the sun.' Isaiah, stop giving me that black stare; the two passages are on the same page!"

Paxton stood shocked. "Chenille, you are not the woman with the moon under her feet, and upon her head a crown of twelve stars. Judas Priest, she was expecting. 'And she being with child cried, travailing in birth.'"

"Different paragraph."

"Connected by a colon. Same sentence."

"My Bible has a semicolon."

"Not my King James—"

"Isaiah, it's poetry!"

"You ain't never had a kid and never will. Anybody's the woman, it's Tabitha."

Chenille's face heated. "That scrawny thing? You see the two wings of the great eagle on her, given so that she might fly from the serpent into the wilderness? Wings'd bust them dainty shoulder blades. I swear, Isaiah, you're as bad as Pete." She glared at Tabitha. "What is it about you? You're a thankless crybaby, and men still drag their tongues on the ground over you. Brian had you bear his child, and Pete couldn't walk straight with you in the room. And now Ice—"

Paxton said, "Chenille, we're done with this. Trot yourself out to the garage and punch in the code!"

She turned to him. "Did I hit a sore spot, Mr. Man?"

Brian flexed, drawing down, looking for his moment. Tabitha, crying behind me, murmured something. I cocked my head, heard her whisper, "Chenille told him where to get the gun." I glanced at her. Her face looked as if it were collapsing. "She asked me where Brian kept his sidearm. And I told her." She looked desperate to make me understand. "She has to be the one who told Holt where Brian kept his gun."

I held her gaze for a moment, then looked at Chenille. I said, "You got Holt to kill your husband."

Paxton's face furrowed. I went with it.

"She says Pete couldn't face his destiny. She means he didn't want her to take control of the Remnant, so she had him killed."

He looked at her.

I said, "Ask her!"

Paxton's face was an anvil. "That so? I'm figuring—

did Pastor Pete prophesy a thousand two hundred and three score days? Did you cut it short?"

I said, "What did he do, Chenille, taunt you once too often about your past?"

She spoke to Paxton. "What did you expect me to do? He stabbed me in the back. Threatened to expel me from the church. Me!"

And that would have ruined all her plans. It would have cut her off from her power base and the weapons she had accumulated.

She looked at Paxton with total exasperation. "Pete went blind," she said, "and you know it. Fame and fear put his eyes out. All he could see was his picture on TV, and the germs he thought was all around him. He turned into a cripple; he couldn't never have led the Remnant against the beast."

Paxton said, "You shouldn't have cut his time short. It's unscriptural."

"He brought it on himself. It could have been a gentle destiny. He could have gone out doing what he loved, fighting germs. It just took a lick from the dog on his face where he cut himself shaving." She put her hands on her hips. "But rabies was *slooow*. What a dud bioweapon. Curt Smollek ain't the biggest bean in the brain field, Isaiah. I blame you for convincing me he could run the program."

Paxton said, "You ain't laying this on me."

"Well, Pete figured it out, what was wrong. In China Lake, when he couldn't swallow, couldn't feel his arms. He panicked. Ran into town to tell Brian; he would of gave the whole thing away. We would of all got arrested, us and Holt. I had to take the active hand."

Paxton said, "You should have told me. I could of done it without the government getting on us."

My God, was there nothing I could accuse her of that would get Paxton to take the shotgun off us?

Chenille said, "Then how would I have got Luke?"

He said, "How come this is all about you and what you want?"

"Like it's about you? Tell me where in scripture it talks about angels warring in heaven to save a peckerwood in a cowboy hat. They battle for the woman and her man child."

Paxton shook his head. "You ain't his mother."

It hit Brian and Tabitha simultaneously. Chenille hadn't wanted Luke kidnapped just for ransom, but for keeps. Brian inched back, and Tabitha drew Luke against her.

Chenille said, "Tabitha was just the womb. He's Brian's seed, and I've had that too. Don't get stuck on details. Look to the message."

Tabitha was staring at Brian, blinking hard, thunderstruck. I felt a slow, melting sensation, the sinking feeling you get when something you fear is confirmed.

Chenille looked at Tabitha. "You don't deserve this child. You know he ain't really yours. That's why you abandoned him." She started for them, hand out. "Now give him here."

Brian smacked her hand down and shoved her away.

She rounded on him. Her face was like a furnace. She cried, "Shoot him!"

Brian sprang. He lunged for the gun, trying to knock it aside, knowing that the spread from a twelve-gauge would hit all of us. Got his hand on the barrel.

Paxton fired.

The clamor was deafening. Brian spun, blown sideways by the blast, and hit the floor in a heap. I screamed. Tabitha grabbed Luke and curled into a ball, shielding him. I dropped to Brian's side. The shot hadn't hit him full-on, but blood was surging from his side near his hip, a red, rhythmic flow. Then Tabitha was there, shoving her hands against the wound, trying to stanch the bleeding. Under her arm, Luke shook and sobbed. Brian's eyes were unfocused, his mouth wide.

Chenille grabbed the collar of Tabitha's shirt and flung her backward. Luke tumbled with her, away from Brian. Chenille pointed at me, shouted to Paxton, "Her next!"

Paxton raised the shotgun. I saw his face, the polished barrel, and the gaping darkness inside the muzzle—an aperture, the wall between worlds that he intended to open with a roar.

I said, "Christ, have mercy—"

The house shuddered, shook; a new bellow erupted. The walls flexed. A back window shattered, glass spraying onto the floor. From outside came a rapid-fire *pop-pop-pop*, like a string of firecrackers going off. The bomb in the garage had exploded.

Through the cabin door I saw the corner of the garage. Orange fire cracked and leaped from it, smoke boiling, wood blackening, shrieking under the wind, boxes of ammunition firing off.

"Jesse!" I spun and crawled toward the door. "Oh, God!"

Chenille's pointing finger followed me. "Shoot her. Shoot her!"

I threw a glance over my shoulder and saw Paxton tracking me with the shotgun, lining up the shot. No chance, none at all. He had me, straight to hell.

Then the front window exploded. So did Paxton's throat, disappearing in a pink mist. He jerked and fell to the floor.

For a moment I couldn't think, couldn't feel, couldn't understand. Luke was screaming. Tabitha was sobbing. Paxton was on his back with a hole gaping in his neck, dead. I looked toward the big front window, where the glass was still chiming down from the frame.

Sprawled outside on the wooden porch, pistol gripped in both hands, sat Jesse.

He looked at me, eyes blue-hot, and said, "Get the shotgun."

The twelve-gauge lay beneath Paxton. Stumbling to my feet, I grabbed the barrel, heated and blood-slick, and pulled it out from under him. Heard Jesse cough. Black smoke was wheeling over him. He was breathing hard, pale with pain.

He took in my look. "You didn't think I'd leave all those weapons just lying there." Then he lowered the pistol and slumped sideways against the porch rail.

I turned to Brian. He was breathing raggedly. Blood was spreading beneath him into a thick, smooth pool, his heart emptying his life onto the wooden floor. His eyes stared skyward, toward the void. His hand clutched Tabitha's arm.

Luke yelled, "Mommy!"

I looked up. Chenille had him by the arm, dragging him toward a back room. Before I could react she slammed the door. We heard a lock turn.

Tabitha jumped up and ran to the door, shook the knob, kicked the wood. I said, "Move back," and rammed the butt of the shotgun against the knob. It bent but didn't break.

She beat on the door. "Chenille. No!"

We could hear Luke wailing in the bedroom. Outside came the popcorn chatter of ammunition firing, a grenade's baritone echo, unmanned guerrilla combat going full-tilt in the garage. And below that, the staccato crackle of flame. The fire had blown out into the live oaks. Embers showered outside the windows, the leaves reflected red, and smoke billowed, starting to infiltrate the cabin. The house was bound to go up, and soon.

Tabitha's eyes were wild. "She's going to burn them both to death."

Pushing her back, I swung the shotgun up and fired

at the doorknob. It exploded in splintering wood. The gun rammed against my shoulder. Tabitha kicked the door open.

The heat hit us like a wall. Flames were eating one side of the room, and smoke was crawling along the ceiling. Tabitha screamed, "No!" But the room was empty, the window open. Luke's distant voice rode above the growl of the fire, frightened and defiant.

I said, "She took him out the back."

Tabitha said, "The truck."

We ran for the front door. I pumped the slide on the shotgun but no shells ejected. The weapon was empty. I dropped it, ran past Brian, outside past Jesse, picked up Marc's Beretta from the dirt.

Chenille was not at the pickup. Tabitha said, "Where'd they go?" The wind was pounding us, the flames gathering strength, great ribbons of fire consuming the trees and streaking along the roof of the house.

Then we heard a high-pitched sound, maybe a voice, from beyond the cabin. We looked at each other and ran toward it. We rounded the house and saw Chenille dragging Luke down a trail into the chaparral.

Tabitha said, "You get Brian," and turned to go after Luke. Grabbing her arm, I put the gun in her hand. She closed it in her fist, wet with Brian's blood, and bolted into the brush.

The cabin was ablaze. Fire was spurting out the windows, smoke roiling through the roof. The trees and overgrown brush around it were immolating in a ruby dance, writhing inside flames that keeled under the wind. That wind was blowing downhill, in the direction that Chenille had run with Luke.

I ran to the cabin door. The heat was shocking. The noise was terrifying. Even more stunning, Jesse was inside, dragging himself across the floor, trying to reach Brian.

I yelled, "No, I'll get him!"

Thick smoke descended toward the floor, acrid, choking. Crouching down, I hurried toward Brian. Paxton's corpse stared impassively at the flames. Car keys were protruding from his jeans pocket. Chenille couldn't have taken the pickup if she'd wanted.

Brian was barely conscious. He didn't react when I grabbed him by the armpits and started dragging him toward the door, painting the floor with his blood. He felt, already, like deadweight, and I pulled harder, straining, thinking, *No*, not here, no way, I won't let him cross that border. I got him through the door, felt cooler air on my back, grunted, kept backing up, stumbling off the porch, into the dirt, breathing again. I saw Jesse off to my left, pulling with his arms, clearing the porch. His head was hanging low, his face streaked with soot. Just then the cabin's roof caved in. Flame ballooned through the door and front window. Feeling the strain in my legs, I hauled Brian along the ground toward the Jeep.

His head lolled to one side, eyes rolling, trying to focus on me. Just beyond the cabin a blazing eucalyptus tree exploded. At the sound, his eyes widened.

"Ev—"

"We're getting you out of here." I could barely speak for the effort of dragging him. He weighed about one seventy-five and most of it felt like meat. My eyes were tearing from the smoke. Reaching the Jeep, I opened the passenger door. "Brian. You have to get in the car."

He didn't seem to hear.

"Brian!" I couldn't lift him in singlehandedly, no way. "You have to do this; you have to help me."

His head swung. Halfheartedly, he swiped a hand toward the car.

I put my face in front of his. "On your feet, Commander! Get up! Now!"

He blinked and focused, some part of him coming

back. He grabbed my arms and struggled to stand. The moment he bent forward the pain hit him like a detonation.

I said, "Come on!"

He was beyond sound, working to get his legs underneath him and push up. He had no balance, no control, but he did have enough willpower to get off the ground, enough that I could lever him the rest of the way. He fell toward the car, through the door, onto the seat. I took his hand, pressed it against his side, and buckled the seat belt over it to keep pressure on the wound. Slamming the door, I ran back to help Jesse.

He was halfway across the ground between the cabin and the Jeep, pulling himself onward with diminishing strength. Above him the trees crackled, flames roaring through them in sheets, burning fifty feet up, fanned by the wind. I saw no sign of Tabitha returning.

I slung his arm around my shoulder. "Come on."

I got him up and we started hobbling toward the car. He looked back, saw that the fire was through the gate and gone, out of control. The mountainside was tinder and the wind was setting the flames free to eat, and eat, and eat. I pulled him toward the Jeep, taking his weight.

He said, "I dropped the gun on the porch; it's toast."

"Forget it."

He looked at me. "I killed Paxton."

"Yes, you did."

He said, "Is Brian dead?"

"No. But we have to hurry."

And the fear grabbed me, deep down, balls to bone, as they say. Brian was bleeding to death and Luke was on the mountain with a maniac. I couldn't help them both. I couldn't bear to leave either one. I didn't know what to do.

Tears blurred my vision. "Come on—we have to get out of here. . . ."

He was leaning against me, his face close to my ear. "Give me the car keys."

"What?"

"Give me the keys," he said, stronger. "I'll get Brian to the hospital. You go after Luke."

The wind was whipping his hair across his face, half obscuring his eyes, but I knew he meant it. It tore my heart to speak the plain facts. "Jesse, you can't. It's not your car; it doesn't have hand controls."

"I know. The keys, Evan."

Jesse Blackburn, patron saint of the unpredictable, strikes again. With the heat and flames billowing up, he intended to do it.

I said, "How do you plan to drive? You can't work the pedals."

"We don't have time to argue. Open the goddamn door."

I did. He lurched against the driver's seat and I helped him pull himself in.

He held out a hand. "Keys."

I gave them to him, and he fired up the engine. He looked over at Brian. My brother was slumped against the car door, breathing like a fish on the dock.

Jesse said, "Get me a stick. Something big."

I found him an oak branch about three feet long. When I handed it to him, he said, "We're going to make it. Go find Luke."

Then he jammed the branch down on the gas pedal, shoved the car into low gear, and lurched away. I watched him go, heart hammering.

Alone in the heat and the roar, I turned and plunged down the ravine.

29

I crashed down the trail, punching my way through tinder-dry brush that scratched and pulled on my shirt like skeletal hands. Smoke barreled overhead. Flames towered behind me in the wind.

In 1990, just up the road, an arsonist had stepped out into a windy afternoon, stared down the mountains at brush so dry and overgrown it might as well have been gasoline, and lit a single match. He ignited the Painted Cave Fire. The wind sent the flames downhill like a blowtorch, advancing a mile every five minutes. Five hundred homes burned. People evacuated, whole neighborhoods throwing the kids and pets and wedding photos into their cars and hauling for the beach, or fleeing on foot. Not all of them made it.

With a single match. And Chenille had primed the pyre with a garageful of explosives.

I ran, smoke stinging my eyes and lungs, through thick brush now glowing red under the lurid sky. I didn't see anybody ahead, couldn't hear Luke anymore in the hiss of the wind. Then I saw a child's shoe lying on the narrow trail, Luke's shoe. I kept going, saw Tabitha ahead, fighting her way through the chaparral. She was panting, nearly staggering with exhaustion, but not conceding anything.

When I caught up, she pointed down the trail. "I

saw them. She must be heading for a road down there."

"Come on." I pulled her along, knowing that roads were scarce up here. It was miles down the mountain. Miles. I looked back over my shoulder. To my shock and horror, the flames had spread into a phalanx wider than a football field. The fire was probably three hundred meters behind us, but it was gathering strength and starting to roll down the hill.

I said, "Run. We can catch them."

She looked anguished. But she ran, wheezing, sweating, arms grabbing at the air. I thought about how little she had eaten during this ordeal, which worried and impressed me.

Then she said, "There they are!"

Below us on the trail, Luke's bright blue shirt flashed through the bushes. Chenille's camouflage gear was barely visible. I sprinted, closing on them, glad that Chenille outweighed me, because I was faster and more agile than she was. Luke's shirt streaked in and out of the brush, slowed, and jinked onto a new heading, up the far side of the ravine.

Closer. Uphill now, my legs and lungs screaming. Luke saw me and cried out. Chenille half turned. Her face contorted, and then I was on her, tackling her with everything I had, crashing into her midsection.

I barely budged her. She grunted, kept her grip on Luke's arm, and punched me in the shoulder. It hurt, but the pain turned to rage and I planted my feet, grabbed her around the thighs, and lifted, toppling her off balance. We fell to the trail. Punches rained on my back.

Then, like a banshee, a revenant, Tabitha's thin form appeared above us and started kicking Chenille. She bashed her ribs, her buttocks, her legs with a steel and force I could not believe she possessed. The look on her face was unhinged. She kept kicking, com-

pletely forgetting the pistol in her hand. Chenille gut-
tered and groaned and let go of Luke.

I dove on Chenille and punched her in the face.
Her head banged back with a thud.

I yelled, "Go, Tabitha. Get him out of here!"

But Tabitha staggered above us, teeth out like a
feral animal. "Kill her!"

I knew I couldn't hold Chenille. Even battered, she
had a meaty strength and was trying to bunch herself
under me. I said, "Go!"

Tabitha suddenly remembered the pistol. Shouting
at me to move, she brought it around with a shaking
hand and pointed it at Chenille. That was when Chenille whipped into a wrestling move, flipping me,
knocking us both into Tabitha. She cried out, fell
backward, and the gun went flying into the bushes.

It was absurd, three women wrestling in the dirt
while a fire was booming in our direction. I looked up
at Luke and said, "Run!" Then I grabbed Chenille by
the hair and pulled. She yelled and windmilled her
arms at me, a huge, rage-knotted human who smelled
like smoke and sweat. I pulled harder, keeping her
focused on me, and Tabitha managed to squirm out
from under the dogpile. She gripped Luke's hand and
together they ran up the trail, climbing away from us.

I watched them grow hazy in the thickening smoke.
Beneath me, Chenille squirmed. I punched her, kneed
her, bounced on her chest, appalled at my enthusiastic
barbarity, keeping it up until I felt her weaken. Then
I scrambled off her to follow Tabitha and Luke.

She grabbed my leg.

I looked down and saw her hanging on to me, her
face gnarled. Her lips drew back and she said,
"Demon!" She clawed her way up my leg. "You're
defying scripture. Give him back!"

I grunted and cried, trying to break free. Her hold
was terrific.

"He should be mine!" Her voice was half scream, half sob. "Brian used me, him and all the rest, used me up. He owes me!"

She sank her teeth into my calf.

Screaming, I fell to the ground. She spun and pounced on top of me. Lowered her face close enough to kiss me. She looked catastrophic. She pulled something shiny from her pocket and waved it in front of my eyes. It was a vial.

"Well, sister, screw you," she said. "Welcome to the Apocalypse."

She brought the vial down on a rock next to my head, smashing it. Started to cry, then to laugh, then to scream.

Holding my breath, I shoved her off me. She didn't resist. I crawled away, started to run, trying not to breathe, but gasped, wondering if I was about to drop dead. Kept going, climbing uphill. I shot a glance back over my shoulder to see if she was coming after me. She wasn't. She was standing on the trail with her fists raised, like a boxer celebrating a victory, as the fire swept toward her down the mountainside.

I ran up the trail, climbing the far side of the ravine. Thinking, It doesn't matter whether Chenille just poisoned me, because I can't do a thing about it. All I can do is run. I'll live, or I won't. *Inshallah*, whatever God wills.

Thinking, Will me out of here. Come on, God, get behind me, dammit. The trail was steep, the brush clinging, the smoke choking. I felt desperately thirsty. Uphill I saw Tabitha struggling beyond exhaustion, out of fuel if not out of grit, carrying Luke on her back. Then I looked back downhill and felt an emotional blast. Digging in, I climbed toward Tabitha with everything I had, knowing how much *everything* was going to have to be.

The flames had jumped the bottom of the ravine

and started ascending the hill behind me, only a hundred yards back. And fire, unlike human beings, accelerates when running uphill.

Beyond Tabitha rose the crest of the ravine. If we could reach the crest, we could make it. When the fire hit the top the wind might catch it, might shift it to run along the ridgeline. We could get the downhill slide, get a breather, get out. But the ravine was steep and we were slowing, fighting every step.

I looked back again. The flames were closer.

I drew in a hot, hard breath. Throw the dice, Delaney. Bet you can outrun the bitch, the beast coming behind you. Screw fire as purifier, renewer, ecological balancer. I didn't want to be purified, renewed, recycled, turned into potting ash, carbon, fossil fuel. Forget all that circle-of-life crap, and run.

I yelled aloud and pumped my arms and legs, hard, harder than I thought I could, knowing I had to find the strength or there wouldn't be anything left to hold back for. At the sound of my cry Tabitha accelerated, only to slip on the trail. She fell to her knees. Jolted, Luke slid off her back to the ground.

I reached her, pulled her to her feet. Behind us the flames swallowed chaparral and jumped from treetop to treetop, leapfrogging toward us, roaring like a freight train. Smoke and terrible heat pressed down on us. Hot ash and sparks stung our skin. Luke sat on the trail like a zombie, staring at it.

I crouched down. "Get on, piggyback."

His face looked numb with terror. But he climbed on my back, and I ran with him clinging to me like a second skin, a second heart. Behind me Tabitha fought to keep pace, wheezing, saying, "Hold on, sweet pea." Any scrap of hostility I still felt toward her dropped away. I simply couldn't carry it.

Upward, upward, freight train running at us, thirst deepening, smoke lowering, heat. *The crest,* I prayed. *The crest.* It was hidden in the smoke, but I knew it was there, pushed on, tears streaming from my eyes, coughing. Then, for a moment the wind cut, shifted, cleared the smoke. I stumbled to a halt, feeling as if I'd been stabbed. We were almost at the top, but the trail petered out into a line of boulders that ran along the crest like battlements, blocking our path.

A sob escaped Tabitha's mouth.

The flames were fifty yards behind us now, a howling maw. I saw no alternative. Over the roar I yelled, "We have to climb them. It's our only chance."

Her chest was heaving. She nodded.

We scrambled up to the boulders. They were sandstone, ten feet high, rough, chunky, normally easy to climb. But not with Luke on my back. I got three feet and a loose hunk of rock broke under my foot. Off balance, I said, "Hold on!" and jumped back down.

I grabbed Tabitha's arm. "I'll climb up and you hand him to me."

She nodded. Her face no longer looked delicate, but jewel-hard. She took him in her arms and I started climbing again, awkwardly, feeling a shudder in my arms and legs, desperate to get up without knocking loose more rock, hearing Tabitha's voice like a snare drum below me, rolling in cut time. "Hurry, Evan. Hurry, hurry, hurry."

Then my hand topped the boulder. I winched up, and through the smoke I could see the downhill slope—the air clear, the land untouched. I stretched myself flat on top of the rock and reached down for Luke.

My arms weren't long enough. He reached up but was three feet short.

Tabitha spoke to him and he started a rickety monkey climb onto her shoulders, balancing precariously, fingers digging into her hair for balance, small chest gulping in and out. She took a step onto the first boulder. I kept stretching down, still too far away, and she strained another step. The flames surfed ever higher, swaying, roaring, leaping into the trees just behind her. Luke stretched his hand. His eyes were empty, as though looking at me through a wall beyond time and space.

Still out of reach. Tabitha stepped up onto a loose rock. It tilted. She yelled, threw herself forward against the boulder, and caught herself. Her legs were shuddering wildly, doing an Elvis. Her tank was running on fumes. She met my gaze. In her eyes should have been desperation, but instead I saw brilliance, lightning: faith.

"Reach down for him, Ev." Her voice was shaking. "Luke, climb." But Luke was frozen, clinging to her, starting to cry. She shouted, "Come on! Hold on to the rock. Reach for Aunt Evvie, and go! Now!" Slowly his hand came up toward me. I stretched and grasped his wrist. She said, "Climb, climb!"

His feet started windmilling against the boulder, and he grabbed me with both hands. I pulled him up.

He scrambled into my arms. For a second I clutched him, then said, "Keep going; scoot down the far side of the rocks. It'll be safer there." He clambered away. I turned back, knowing I'd have to help Tabitha to the top.

I lay flat again and stretched down. The flames were almost on us. Twenty feet behind Tabitha a tall tree had ignited, backlighting her with an insane bloom of fire, a monstrous red stripe switching and thrashing at the sky. She reached for my hand. Her fingers, warm with my brother's blood, touched mine. Above her came a cracking sound, the noise of a heavy limb about to break off the flaming tree. She looked up, saw it twist and swing toward her. I said, "Look out!" and she jumped down, just getting clear before the limb crashed against the rock where she'd been standing.

She landed on all fours but got up again, checking the line of boulders for somewhere else to climb, wiping her sweaty curls off her face with one hand. Spotting a route, she started to the right. The burning tree gave way and swept down like a great red tail, embers arcing out behind it. It crashed on top of her.

I scrambled to my knees but she was gone, swallowed up. My voice mixed with the howl of the fire, screaming.

I slid down the far side of the rocks. Luke was standing at the bottom. I grabbed his hand and ran, downhill now.

"Where's my mom?"

"We have to run; we have to keep going."

I said nothing else, but ran until grief overtook me and I had to look back. The flames were cresting the lip of the ravine, ready to barrel down, having taken one game woman and getting a taste for it. This was it, the truth. It was the instant when the universe shrugs. It's the moment when you're running on desire and a belief in free will, and you feel a tap on the shoulder, and turn to find inevitability standing there.

We staggered out of the brush and onto a road, into the path of a firefighting crew pulling up the hill.

30

The firefighters bundled us into the cab of their truck. They put an oxygen mask on Luke. He kept looking up the mountainside, waiting for Tabitha. The crew chief, a rugged man with a white handlebar mustache, got on the radio and called the sheriffs to evacuate us.

I touched the sleeve of his khaki turnout coat. "My boyfriend's trying to get down the pass to get my brother to a hospital. He's been shot."

He stared at me, incredulous and hard-eyed. Then he said, "The pass? The highway, or the old road?" A Highway Patrol car had been cut off by flames on Old San Marcos Pass Road.

I was numb and exhausted, but when I heard that, the panic began crawling through me all over again. I said, "The highway."

He grabbed the radio, put out the call.

Luke pulled down the oxygen mask. "Aren't they going to get my mom?"

The firefighter hung in the doorway of the truck, poised, tense. "Somebody else is out there on the mountain? A woman?"

Luke said, "My mom."

I looked the man in the eye and shook my head. Gathering Luke in my arms, I told him the truth.

* * *

Luke walked by my side, small hand in mine. He wouldn't let it loose. That was what kept me going. Nikki had an arm around my shoulder, pacing me through the big double doors into the emergency room at St. Francis Medical Center.

This was our last stop. End of the line. I had phoned hospitals and the Highway Patrol, had searched the frantic ER at Cottage Hospital, and no one had seen Jesse or Brian. They had gone into the smoke and hadn't come out.

St. Francis was bright and sterile. A television in the waiting room showed the mountains raging red, hysterical reporters, houses burning, girls fleeing down main roads on horseback. My head buzzed. I walked toward the desk, where a nurse in pink scrubs was speaking briskly over the phone.

"Excuse me," I said.

She raised a finger, indicating *just a minute*.

Nikki's arm held me up. "Excuse me," she said to the nurse. "We need to know if you have a gunshot wound here, Lieutenant Commander Brian Delaney."

Her voice could have driven fence posts into the ground. The woman looked up. Nikki said, "And we need to know right now, because otherwise we have to get a rescue crew to go into the fire and find him."

The nurse took a good look at me and Luke: grimy, reeking of smoke, coughing and ragged. She hung up the phone.

"I'll check," she said.

She disappeared back into the ER, through another set of double doors. I leaned my head against Nikki's shoulder. Luke stood mute, his fingers warm in my palm. How, I thought, how would I tell him if Brian was gone? I blinked, staring vacantly past Nikki, looking through the open double doors down a long hallway. I heard myself say, "Oh."

Straightening, I headed through the doors and down the corridor. My eyes were welling. Luke trotted to keep up with me, fingers squeezing mine. The grief, the pain, all I'd been straining to suppress, rose and spilled out. A sob broke from me and echoed off the walls.

At the end of the corridor an orderly was pushing a gurney. A nurse walked alongside it adjusting an IV bag, and a doctor in blue scrubs, talking to the man stretched out on it. It was Jesse.

I started running. "Wait."

Jesse turned his head and saw me. He told the orderly to stop. I rushed to him, threw myself across him, weeping.

The orderly said, "Ma'am, we got to get this man to X-ray."

"Hold on," Jesse said. His voice was a hoarse whisper. He lifted my face to his and kissed me like nothing before. Everything was in that kiss: need, distress, relief, love, all at once, overwhelming. He pulled back, still holding my face. His eyes were bloodshot and filling with tears. I had never seen him cry before.

He said, "I wrecked the Jeep. Coming down the pass."

"Brian?" I looked from him to the doctor, helpless.

The doctor said, "The gunshot victim?"

"My brother."

"He's in surgery."

My jackhammer heart drowned out the rest, the cautions, the *we'll have to wait and see* and *they're doing everything possible*. Brian was alive. Jesse had driven through miles of rough terrain and reached the highway. He'd gotten Brian out; he'd gotten help.

"Too fast," he was saying, "missed the curve—"

He kept talking in that hoarse, ragged voice, as

though words would seal off his tears, and I knew he wasn't upset that he'd crashed Carl's Jeep. He had thought I was dead. I stroked his hair.

"—on this empty stretch of road, grille's smashed, radiator blowing steam, and your cell phone rings."

"What?"

"Your phone. I didn't even know it was in the car. I thought, with my luck, it was an insurance agent cold-calling to offer me cheap collision coverage, but you will not believe this. It was that reporter, Sally Shimada. She was looking for a quote from you, and ends up calling the paramedics instead."

Words weren't working. The tears kept coming. I wiped them off his face.

He said, "Brian's in bad shape, Ev."

I took his hand. He squeezed my fingers, wanting to say something else.

"But he'll make it—I'd bet my life on it. He's a tough son of a bitch." He looked at me and at Luke. "Like all you Delaneys."

31

The fire burned for days. The sky hung red and the air-attack planes thundered. It leveled homes and businesses, laid a charred shroud across the mountainside. They called it the Camino Cielo Fire, a name insufficient to describe what I had experienced, and what it had done.

Tabitha's body was found under the tree that had crushed her. She was lying faceup, the coroner told me. Reaching for the mountaintop, I thought.

Chenille Wyoming was not found. Though Isaiah Paxton's scorched bones were recovered from the ashes of the cabin, no other body was found on the hillside. She had disappeared.

With her, so went the Remnant. The church dissolved into chaos. Shiloh and the Brueghel triplets were arrested near Reno and charged with kidnapping. Curt Smollek survived his wounds and was booked for the murder of Mel Kalajian, as well as for various assault, weapons, and animal-cruelty charges. No one rose up to liberate them or to strike out at new targets. Leaderless resistance flopped. The Remnant needed the whip; without Chenille they were like a sack of headless snakes. Dawn came; that was their problem. The lithium sunset did not ignite.

However, their cry—"Justice for Pastor Pete!"— was answered. Garrett Holt was arrested for killing

Peter Wyoming. Charged with capital murder, plus theft of government property and national security violations, he confessed under a deal that spared him the death penalty.

Holt was not a religious fanatic, but a man driven by greed and resentment against the navy. He had joined NCIS after washing out of navy flight school, and nurtured a grudge about failing to make the cut as a pilot. It bred the loathing that Brian had recognized in him, and the envy. When he posed as an aviator, he wasn't just lulling me into trusting him; he was indulging his ego, bringing a ruined fantasy to life.

But beyond spite and jealousy, Holt was also corrupt. Bribery was his middle name. At China Lake he had uncovered a ring of petty thieves, enlisted men who were selling equipment through a fence in town. Instead of arresting them, Holt took money to look the other way. Then, when the Remnant started nosing around, shopping for military hardware, he grabbed the chance to enrich himself at the navy's expense. He took control of the theft ring. Getting the enlisted men to do the heavy lifting, he started selling firearms and munitions to the cult.

Inevitably the navy realized how much ordnance and ammunition were going missing, however, and Holt's game turned dicey. Then came an event he hadn't counted on: the rift between Chenille and Pastor Pete. Their battle to control the Remnant ultimately destroyed his scheme.

The night of the killing Chenille phoned him in a panic, saying that Pete had gone over the edge. He knew he was infected with rabies, and that she was behind it. Betrayed, and fearing that the Remnant's zealots would rally behind Chenille, Pete had phoned Brian.

Why Brian? Holt gave the only plausible explanation: Peter Wyoming knew that Chenille wanted Luke for herself, and that once she got him she would not hesitate to destroy Tabitha. Facing death with a strange burst of nobility, he had tried to protect Tabitha by seeking help from her husband. He had decided to sell his wife to the enemy.

But Chenille reached Holt in China Lake, telling him to stop Pete from talking or they'd all end up in federal prison. Holt was alarmed, and furious that Chenille had lost control of the situation. But above all, he was enraged that Peter Wyoming planned to tell everything to a fighter pilot. Holt was about to go down, and a fighter puke would get the credit for blowing the theft ring.

Stop Pete, Chenille said. There was a gun in Brian's closet. *Make it look like Brian did it, like it was a crime of passion, of frenzy.*

And he did. Pinning the crime on a naval aviator, screwing the fighter jock who would have turned him in, that was just the poisoned icing on the cake.

It was an old story. Avarice, fear, ambition, and jealousy have always made a murderous combination. Read the Bible; it's full of the stuff.

Brian was in the hospital for a month. His wounds were severe. He faced a long recovery and extensive rehabilitation. The doctors did not predict permanent physical damage, although the damage to his flying career was another matter. The navy had informed him that they intended to convene an inquiry about the scam involving the Sidewinder. His future as an officer, and an aviator, was clouded.

But he said it was worth it, every bit of what he'd done, even if he never flew an F/A-18 again. Luke was safe. No regrets. And I believed him. Still, he looked diminished when I saw him, and not just from the wastage brought on by injury.

Grief had decimated him. Despite Tabitha's disloyalty, confusion, and disastrous actions, he mourned her passion, her beauty, her heroism. Knowing that in her final moments she had lifted Luke to safety, he now tormented himself for failing to prevent her death. He lay there reliving those minutes in the cabin, over and over, eyes lost to sight, locking on outcomes forever out of reach. If I had gone for Paxton sooner. A second earlier. A finger snap faster, I could have grabbed the shotgun from him. Could have stopped the whole thing right there. If only.

I couldn't pull him out of it. Our parents arrived and couldn't either. Finally Jesse talked to him, nobody he would have listened to a month earlier but the only man who could speak to him with authority. Not because he'd driven him down the mountain, but because he knew about chance and the irrevocable pain it inflicts. He talked about the Fucking Facts of Life. About death taking the person beside you, and leaving you breathing but damaged so badly that you fight against believing it. About the futility of reminiscence, which was a way of talking about acceptance. Perhaps someday Brian will hear it.

Jesse had to have surgery on his fractured leg, more pins going into bones that had already set off airport metal detectors, and he was treated for a severe kidney infection and dehydration. He checked himself out after two days, saying he hated hospitals worse than being held captive, and that the food had been better in the fallout shelter.

He came to stay with me. He's the one who told me that I had to stop running so hard every day, that I'd lost too much weight. And he's beside me when I wake up shaking. In the nightmare I reach for Tabitha's hand, feel her fingers touch mine as she stretches up the face of the rock. Her skin feels like electric silk. Her eyes are bottomless and black, full of calm freedom, certain of me. The tree slashes down and it's a dragon's tail, embers flying from it like stars, and it sweeps her away. When I sit up shouting, Jesse pulls me against his side. Sometimes we make love, a hungry brand of sex that convinces us we're still alive. Sometimes he lies staring out the window. He has his own incubus. It feels like a trigger and sounds like gunfire, looks like a throat ripped open, and it says, *Your decision.*

The last time I had the dream, he told me, "Take this nightmare to a priest. You should." He ran his fingers through his hair. He didn't have a priest.

I said, "And maybe you should talk to Brian."

He took a bottle with him when he went.

Luke was also staying with me while Brian recovered. He had a long way to go, but at least he hadn't reverted to hiding in his closet. He had returned to school, and was seeing a child psychiatrist to help him deal with Tabitha's death and the traumas he had endured at the hands of the Remnant.

Acceptance isn't easy. Uncertainty is a devil. But that's what I'm living with, because the vial Chenille smashed near my face, the substance she called the Apocalypse, could not be found. Toxicological tests on me couldn't identify anything. No one knows what it was. I have to wait, and wonder.

The weather stayed hot straight through November. Thanksgiving afternoon, after dinner, Jesse and I took Luke to Shoreline Park. The wind was brisk, the sky endless, the grass emerald in the late sun. The ocean rolled cold against the cliff below. We brought kites, and they snapped in the air, dogfighting, neon bright. Luke raced up and down the lawn until his cheeks were flushed.

I spread a blanket on the grass and stretched out with Jesse. His leg was still in a cast. The sun shone on his face and reflected from his eyes. We watched Luke circle around the lawn, running with that smooth Olympian stride of his.

"How about Eastertime?" he said. "Right here."

It was the first time since that day on the mountain that either of us had spoken about getting married. I said, "Could rain. How about the Old Mission?"

"A Catholic church? Sugar, treat me gently. That's full-bore."

I lay back and gazed at the sky. "Your house, and a Gospel reading?"

"I get to choose the music."

"No Hendrix." He opened his mouth. I said, "Nope, no Clapton either."

"Then you can forget Patsy Cline."

"Motown?"

"Agreed."

Luke ran up to us, wrestling with the kite as he tried to sit down. He stared up at it. "What's the longest string you can put on a kite?"

"I don't know," I said, "maybe a hundred meters? What do you think, Jess?"

"I guess. You want to send it way out there?"

Luke was thoughtful. "If a kite flies high enough, can Mommy see it in heaven?"

It was one of those moments when knowledge and emotion snap together with unexpected consequences. Feeling my heart ache, looking at his solemn face, what brimmed in my ears was a long-ago strip of Latin prayer, rising unbidden from memory.

In paradisum deducant te angeli. . . .

It was the burial prayer of the Catholic funeral rite. *May the angels lead you into paradise. . . .*

Luke looked at me calmly.

"Yes," I said to him. Something told me to try to believe it. "I'm sure she can."

He said, "That's what I thought."

He gazed back up at the kite. My eyes went with his.

May the choir of angels receive you . . . may you have eternal rest.

May it be true. I watched the kite spin red, blue, red, the tail whipping silver. In its dance against the sky it was, perhaps, one of those bright beckoning spirits, soaring, bearing her home.

Read on for an exciting preview
of Meg Gardiner's brand-new thriller,

THE DIRTY SECRETS CLUB

Available wherever books
are sold or at penguin.com

Fire alarms sang through the skyscraper, piercing and relentless. Under the din people poured across the marble lobby toward the doors, dodging fallen ceiling plaster and broken glass. Outside, Montgomery Street crackled with the lights of emergency vehicles. A police officer fought upstream to get inside. The blonde was ten feet behind, struggling through the crowd.

The man in the corner paced, head down, needing her to hurry.

People rushed by him, jumpy. "Everything crashed off the bookshelves. I thought for sure it was the Big One."

The man turned, shoulders shifting. The Big One? Hardly. This earthquake had just been San Francisco's regular kick in the butt. But it was bad enough. On the street, steam geysered from manholes. And he could smell gas. Pipes had ruptured under the building. The quake was Hell saying, *Don't forget I'm down here—you fall, I'm waiting for you.*

He checked his watch. Come on, girl, faster. They had ten minutes before this building shut down.

A fire captain glanced at him. He was tall and young and moved like the athlete he was, but nothing clicked in the fire captain's eyes, no suspicion, no *Is that who I think it is?* Out of uniform he looked ordinary, a plain vanilla all-American.

The blonde neared the doors. She stood out from the crowd, platinum sleek, hair cinched into a tight French twist, body cinched into a tighter black suit. A cop stuck out an arm like he was going to clothesline her. She flashed an ID and slid around him.

He smiled. Right under their noses.

She pushed through the doors and walked up, giving him a hard blue stare. "Here? Now?"

"It's the ultimate test. Secrets are hardest to keep in broad daylight."

"I smell gas, and that steam pipe sounds like a volcano erupting. If a valve blows and causes a spark—"

"You dared me. Do it in public, and get proof." He wiped his palms on his jeans. "This is as public as it gets. You'll supply my proof."

Her hands clenched, but her eyes shone. "Where?"

His heart beat faster. "Top floor. My lawyer's office."

Upstairs, they strode out of the express elevator to find the law firm abandoned. The fire alarm was shrieking. At the receptionist's desk, a computer was streaming a television news feed.

". . . minor damage, but we're getting reports of a ruptured gas line in the financial district . . ."

The blonde looked around. "Security cameras?"

"Only in the stairwells. It's bad business for a law firm to videotape its clients."

She nodded at a wall of windows. The October sunset was fading to dusk, downtown ablaze with light. "You plan to do this stunt against the glass?"

He crossed the lobby. "This way. The building's going to shut down in"—he looked at a red digital clock on the wall—"six minutes."

"What?"

"Emergency procedure. If there's a gas leak the

building evacuates; they shut down the elevators and seal the fire doors. We have to be out by then."

"You're joking."

The wall clock counted down to 5:59. He started a timer on his watch.

"Yeah. I was meeting with my lawyers when the quake hit. It limits damage from any gas explosion." He pulled her toward a hallway. "I can't believe you're scared of getting caught with me. Not Hard-girl."

"What part of 'secret' do you not understand?"

"If we're caught, they'll ask what we're doing here, not what we're hiding in our pasts."

"Fair point." She hurried alongside him, eyes bright. "Were you waiting for an earthquake before you did this?"

Good guess—this was the third minor quake in the last month. "I got lucky. I've been looking for the perfect opportunity for weeks. Chaos, downtown—it was karma. I figured, seize the day."

He rounded a corner. A glass-fronted display case along the wall had cracked, spilling sports memorabilia onto the floor.

She rushed past. "Is that a Joe Montana jersey?"

His stopwatch beeped. "Five minutes."

He opened a mahogany door. Across a conference room the red embers of sunset caught them in the eyes. The hills of San Francisco rose in front of them, electric with light and packed to the rafters like a stadium.

He shrugged off his coat, took a camera from the pocket and handed it to her. "When I tell you, point and click."

He crossed the room and opened the doors to a rooftop terrace. Kicking off his shoes, he strode outside.

"You complained I was using the club as a confessional. You told me I was seeking expiation for my sins, but said you couldn't give me absolution," he said.

Deep below them, the building groaned. She walked outside, breathing hard.

"Damn, Scott, this is dangerous—"

"Your dare was—and I quote—for me 'to offer a public display of penitence, and for Christ's sake, get proof.'"

He pulled his polo shirt over his head. Her gaze seared its way down his chest.

Now, he thought. Before his courage and exhilaration evaporated. He unzipped and dropped his jeans.

She gaped.

He backed toward the waist-high brick railing at the edge of the terrace. "Turn on the camera."

"You came commando-style to a meeting with your lawyers?"

Naked, he climbed onto the brick ledge and stood up, facing her. Her lips parted. Thrilled to his fingertips, he turned to face Montgomery Street.

A salt breeze licked his bare skin. Two hundred feet below, fire and police lights flickered through steam boiling from the ruptured pipe, turning the scene an eerie red.

He spread his arms. "Shoot."

'You have got to be kidding me."

'Take the photo. Hurry."

"That's not penitent."

He glanced over his shoulder. She was shaking her head.

"*Bad?* You tattooed *Bad* on your tailbone?"

His watch beeped. "Four minutes. Do it."

"You're a badass?" She put her fists on her hips. "You get all torn up about a nasty thing you did in college, and want to unload it on us—fine. But you can't tattoo some preening jock statement on your butt and call it repentance. That's not remorse. Hell, it's not even close to being dirty."

Frowning, she stormed inside.

He turned around. "Hey!"

Was she leaving? No, everything depended on her getting the photo. . . .

She ran back out, holding a piece of sports memorabilia from the display case. It was a jockey's riding crop. He swallowed.

She whipped it against a potted plant with a wicked crack. "Somebody needs to take you down a notch."

He nearly whimpered. She wanted points, too. This was even better.

Snapping the crop against her thigh, she crossed the terrace. Evaluating the ledge, she unzipped her ass-hugging skirt, wriggled it down, and stepped out of it.

"It's time to make your act of contrition," she said.

In the tight-fitting black jacket, she looked martial. The stilettos could have put out his eyes. The black stockings ran all the way to the tops of her thighs. All the way to—

"What's that garter belt made from?"

"Iguana hide."

"Jesus, help me."

"I have a drawerful. I got them in the divorce." She held out her hand. "Don't let me fall."

"I won't. I have perfect balance." He felt crazed and desperate and *God*, he needed to get her up here, now. "I get paid four million dollars a year to catch things and never let them drop."

A wisp of her blond hair had escaped the perfect do. It softened her. He wanted her to put it back in place. He wanted her to put on leather gloves and maybe an eye patch. He pulled her up on the ledge beside him.

She gripped his hand. Her smooth stocking brushed his leg.

He could barely speak. "This is penance?"

"Pain is just one step from paradise."

She looked down. Her voice dropped. "Christ. This is asking for a heart attack."

"Don't joke."

She looked up. "No—I didn't mean it as a crack about David."

But if David hadn't dropped facedown with a coronary, they wouldn't be here. The doctor's death had created an opening, and Scott wanted to fill it. This was his chance to prove himself and gain admission to the top level of the club.

The breeze kicked up. In the lighted windows of the skyscraper across the street, people gazed down at the fire trucks. Nobody was looking at them.

"Right under their noses," he said. "Bonus points for both of us."

"Not yet." She handed him the camera. "Set it so we're both in the frame."

He set the autotimer to take a five-shot series and set the camera on the ledge. His stopwatch beeped. Three minutes.

She planted her feet wide for balance. "What happens to guilty people?"

Blinking, he turned around and carefully knelt down on all fours. "I've been bad. Spank me."

She slapped the crop against her palm. "What's the magic word?"

Relief and desire rushed through him. "Hard."

The camera flashed. She brought the crop down.

The pain was a stripe of fire along his backside. He gasped and grabbed the ledge.

"Harder," he said.

She whipped the crop down. The camera flashed.

He clawed the bricks. "*Mea culpa.* I've been very, very bad. *More.*"

She didn't hit him. He looked up. Her chest was heaving, her hair spilling from the French twist.

"My God, you actually want to be punished, don't you?" she said.

"Do it."

She swung the crop. It slashed him so hard, he shouted in pain. She wanted to dish out punishment, all right, but not to him. She would use this to send a message to somebody else. The watch beeped.

"Christ, two minutes," she said. "Let's get the hell out of here."

His eyes were watering. "Not yet. Nobody's looking."

"*Looking?* You're nuts. If there's an aftershock I'll lose my balance. We—"

A thumping sound echoed off skyscraper walls. A helicopter swooped over the top of the building above them.

It turned and hovered above Montgomery Street, rotors blaring. Everything on the terrace blew about in the air. Dust, leaves, their clothes. The camera tipped over. Scott grabbed for it but it fell off the ledge.

She yelled, "No, the evidence—"

The camera dropped, hit the building and sprang apart. He let out a cry. His penance, his memories—

The terrace lit with a blinding white searchlight.

"Oh, no—it's a news chopper," she said.

She leapt from the ledge to the terrace. Landed like a gazelle on her stilettos. He scrambled after her, buttocks stinging. They grabbed their clothes and ran for the door. The chopper rotated in the air, searchlight sweeping after them.

She looked back, her eyes brimming with joy and fury. The searchlight lit her hair like a halo.

"Turn around," he shouted. "You want them to get a close-up?"

'The city knows your face, not mine."

"But it's about to know your glorious ass."

He ran into the conference room, stopped and wriggled his left leg into his jeans. The spotlight caught them. He bumbled for the door.

Fumbling her way into her skirt, she sprinted into the hallway. "It's chasing us like those things from the damned *War of the Worlds.*"

He urged her forward. "Take the service elevator. The lobby downstairs is full of cops."

She ran beside him, agile in the heels. His watch beeped.

"Oh, crap. No time."

In the lobby, the fire alarm wailed a high-pitched tone. The digital clock flashed red: :58, :57. The TV news was showing pictures from the chopper's camera.

"Two people are trapped on the roof," shouted the reporter. "A woman was signaling for help. If we swing around . . ."

The alarm rose in pitch.

"How long to get down?" she said.

They ran to the service elevator and she pounded on the button. The searchlight panned along the windows. Like a white flare, it caught them in the eyes.

"I see them. They're attempting to escape from this deadly tower. . . ."

She whacked the elevator button with the riding crop. *"Open."*

With a *ping*, the elevator arrived. They lunged inside.

On the ground floor they burst out a back exit into an alley. The asphalt was wet and steaming. Scott clicked his stopwatch.

"Seven seconds. Time to spare."

"Maniac," she said.

They dashed through puddles toward the end of the alley. On the street a police car blew past, lights flashing. The helicopter thumped overhead, searchlight pinned on the roof.

Scott nodded at it. "They got it on tape. You have evidence."

"You're reckless. I think you actually want to get caught."

"I carried out the dare. Did I make the cut?"

She fought with her zipper. "We'll put it to a vote. No promises."

They rushed out of the alley. The street, lined with banks and swanky stores, was being cleared by the police. They slowed to a walk, trying to look normal. He buttoned his jacket. She smoothed down her hair.

Elation flooded him.

"Admit it—that was awesome."

"It was outrageous." She pointed at him. "And do not tell me it ended with a flourish."

"Really?" He reached into his coat pocket and withdrew a baseball.

"What's that?"

He tossed it to her. She caught it.

"A Willie Mays autographed ball?" She looked up, surprised. "From the law firm's memorabilia collection? You stole it?"

"On our way out. And it's not just any baseball. It's *the* ball—from the 1954 World Series. The greatest catch of all time."

She gawked. "It's got to be worth—"

"Hundred thousand." He smiled, broadly. "Right under *your* nose."

Anger flashed across her face. She shoved the ball back into his hands. "Okay, bonus points for chutzpah."

He laughed and tossed the baseball into his other hand. "Fear not—it'll be returned. That's the next challenge."

"How? The building's locked down. And your fingerprints are all over it."

"So? I'm a star client. My lawyer let me hold it. It doesn't matter that my fingerprints are on it." He glanced at the police car down the block, then back at her. "How will you explain that yours are?"

She stopped dead on the sidewalk.

He held up the ball. "Return it without getting prosecuted. I dare you."

He turned, faced the jewelry store they were passing and hurled the ball straight through its front window. Glass crashed. An alarm shrieked. He spun back around.

"Have fun, Hardgirl."

He took off running down the street.

FIRST-RATE THRILLERS
FROM THE MASTERS

PRINCE OF FIRE
DANIEL SILVA

In this stunning, *New York Times* bestselling thriller
from "the world-class practitioner of spy fiction"
(*The Washington Post*), art restorer and sometime
spy Gabriel Allon is pulled from his cover to
face his most determined enemy yet in an
exhilarating plot of astonishing intricacy.

A CERTAIN JUSTICE
JOHN LESCROART

In what *Publishers Weekly* hailed as "an unusually
thoughtful, exciting thriller," the *New York Times*
bestselling author of *The Motive* takes us back to
San Francisco, where an angry white mob attacks
an innocent black man, and the only man who
tried to save him becomes the next target.